CROSSFIRE

THE ARBITORS ROUNDED THE plinth and raced forward. The space in front of them was empty, the crowd shoving away to the sides.

'Nothing here!' Calpurnia was whirling on the spot, trying to–

Was that movement?

She ducked to one side instead of standing to shoot and it saved her life. The bullet gouged the side of her helmet and knocked it askew – a second earlier and it would have punched through her top lip. She wrenched off the helmet and scampered crabwise away from the others. Whatever it was, a moving target seemed to give it a little trouble.

A WARHAMMER 40,000 NOVEL

CROSSFIRE

Matthew Farrer

For B&B

A BLACK LIBRARY PUBLICATION

First published in Great Britain in 2003
by BL Publishing,
Games Workshop Ltd.,
Willow Road, Nottingham,
NG7 2WS, UK

10 9 8 7 6 5 4 3 2 1

Cover illustration by Clint Langley

A CIP record for this book
is available from the British Library

ISBN 1 84416 020 3

Set in ITC Giovanni

Printed and bound in Great Britain by
Cox & Wyman Ltd, Reading, Berkshire.

See the Black Library on the Internet at
www.blacklibrary.com

Find out more about Games Workshop
and the world of Warhammer 40,000 at
www.games-workshop.com

IT IS THE 41st millennium. For more than a hundred centuries the Emperor has sat immobile on the Golden Throne of Earth. He is the master of mankind by the will of the gods, and master of a million worlds by the might of his inexhaustible armies. He is a rotting carcass writhing invisibly with power from the Dark Age of Technology. He is the Carrion Lord of the Imperium for whom a thousand souls are sacrificed every day, so that he may never truly die.

YET EVEN IN his deathless state, the Emperor continues his eternal vigilance. Mighty battlefleets cross the daemon-infested miasma of the warp, the only route between distant stars, their way lit by the Astronomican, the psychic manifestation of the Emperor's will. Vast armies give battle in his name on uncounted worlds. Greatest amongst his soldiers are the Adeptus Astartes, the Space Marines, bio-engineered super-warriors. Their comrades in arms are legion: the Imperial Guard and countless planetary defence forces, the ever-vigilant Inquisition and the tech-priests of the Adeptus Mechanicus to name only a few. But for all their multitudes, they are barely enough to hold off the ever-present threat from aliens, heretics, mutants – and worse.

TO BE A man in such times is to be one amongst untold billions. It is to live in the cruellest and most bloody regime imaginable. These are the tales of those times. Forget the power of technology and science, for so much has been forgotten, never to be re-learned. Forget the promise of progress and understanding, for in the grim dark future there is only war. There is no peace amongst the stars, only an eternity of carnage and slaughter, and the laughter of thirsting gods.

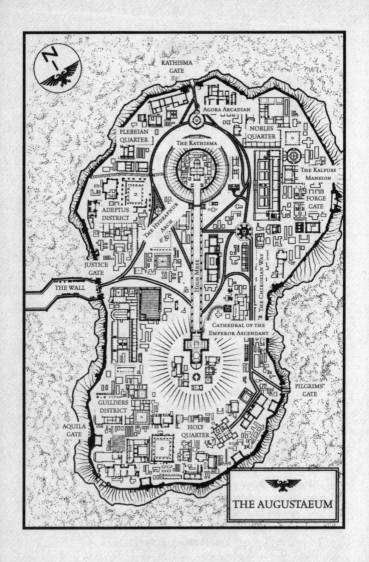

THE AUGUSTAEUM

Sixth Day of Septista

Twelve days to the Mass of Saint Balronas.
The Festival of the Sevenmark. The Day of Shuttered
Tithing (Administratum).

WITH SEVEN DAYS *until the beginning of the Vigil of Saint Bal-*
ronas, all those with duties, debts, obligations, or any other
Imperial or personal business, should be looking to discharge
them. The disgrace, both before one's Church and one's peers, of
having unfinished business by the beginning of the Vigil should
always be borne in mind.

Tradition tells us that this is the day on which masters announce
to their servants and workers both the fact and the particulars of
the holidays they are to be granted for the period of the Vigil –
both generosity by the master and gratitude from the servant are
appropriate on this day. Masters should lead their workers, and the
heads of households their families, in modest celebrations; the
exchange of small gifts and tokens is appropriate. A traditional
token is a roll of blank parchment or an empty data-slate to sym-
bolise the clearing of debts.

On this day the halls of the Administratum will be sealed as
that order conducts certain devotions of its own. Any tithing or
Administratum business must be completed before the halls are
closed at dawn.

Celebrations should still be conducted with an air of temperance
and deference, and the working day should end with a service or
prayer meeting in garb and circumstances traditional to one's
duties and station. The evening should be a time to take stock and

ensure that the correct devotional items and clothes are ready for the period ahead, and that one's person and home are clean and orderly.

CHAPTER ONE

THE MACHINE-CULTISTS OF the Adeptus Mechanicus are not prone to strong emotions – the beautiful coldness of the Machine is held up as a model for admiration and emulation, even for those orders of the Mechanicus not directly concerned with physical mechanics and the gradual transfiguration of their own bodies into cybernetics. Genetor-Magos Cynez Sanja was of the Order Biologis, with a greater understanding of the emotions of the flesh than most, but this evening the ability to catalogue the exact neurotransmitters that flared inside his skull and how they reacted to and reinforced his thoughts and stimuli, let alone the Cult of the Machine's scriptures and psalms in praise of pure reason, were small consolation. Here in his own domain, in the very shrine of the Adeptus Mechanicus in the Adeptus district in what was supposed to be the safest enclave of the capital hive of the fortress world of Hydraphur, Cynez Sanja had found himself under siege. He was displeased, he was frustrated and he was – to his own dismay – angry.

Noises from the turmoil outside were seeping through the walls as Sanja stood in the forechamber behind the shrine's great adamantite doors, listening with his head bowed and his eyes closed. He had severed his link with the external opticons half an hour before, refusing to watch what was going on outside any longer, but now came a four-second burst of ultrasonic machine-code from the throat-mounted vocoder of his assistant, Brother-Postulant Chaim. Sanja reluctantly decompressed and scanned it; the reports and message transcripts unfolding neatly in his brain.

They were not pleasant. The avenues to the Administratum towers were blocked and the tally-house and the Ordinates' dormitory were ringed in. The bridge over the water-gardens to the Scriptoria was cut off and a brave group of adepts from the procurator-general's tower who had tried to force their way down the hopelessly-overrun Street of Quills had not been heard from again. The Adeptus Quarter, it seemed, belonged to the Adeptus no longer.

As if to underscore the point, there was a ringing thud that seemed to come through the walls and floor at once. Sanja glowered and cycled the tiny augmetic layers in his skull through a precise series of adjustments, but the walls still muffled the sounds to the point where he couldn't pick out much more than a rhythmic, concussive hammering and the faintest traces of hoarse shouts. He wondered again why nobody had thought it necessary to raise the void shields.

He opened his eyes and looked around him, drawing what serenity he could from his surroundings. The forechamber was a shortened rectangle, its measurements calculated to within a millionth of a millimetre to mimic the proportions, if not the size, of the forechamber of the high genetor's own shrine on the Mechanicus heartworld of Mars. The black steel of the floor was inlaid in gold and ruby with illuminated circuit patterns and alchemical forms. The friezes on the walls were burnished brass arrays of pistons and valves, their constant, silent hydraulic motion carrying binary-language catechisms of praise to the Machine God back and forth. Setting his veiled hood back on his shoulders and tilting his head back, the genetor-magos contemplated the works above him: layers of interlocking cog wheels, the simplest but most sacred icons of the Mechanicus priesthood, hung weightless, slowly rotating in the air, obscuring the roof.

Sanja murmured a prayer and felt the circuits tattooed around his eye-sockets tingle as he merged his sight with the opticon in the steel gargoyle on the wall ahead and examined himself through the machine-spirit's eyes.

His own scarlet tech-priest's finery seemed to shine even in the dim light of the forechamber. Behind him, framed by the second set of giant doors that led into the shrine's central cloister, was his retinue, standing with dignity in ceremonial formation and waiting upon his order. Chaim stood two paces behind Sanja's right shoulder. Behind them were four skitarii, the dedicated templar-soldiers of the Machine cult, their burnished carapace armour pierced with cybernetic cables and leads and their power-axes held at arms. Flanking each skitarius, two guardian servitors, mindless vat-grown automata hung about with mechanised implants of their own, weapon-muzzles pointed demurely down. His two luminant skulls, each half-plated with gold leaf and trailing clusters of perceptor vanes and mecha-dendrites, hung in the air over Sanja's shoulders.

The forechamber was not wide, but its high-vaulted roof was lost in the shadows above the layers of free-hanging cogs. The retinue formation, small though it was, stretched almost the width of the room.

The genetor-magos made a small sound of approval, feeling stronger for his moment of contemplation. He would not be cowed here, in his own temple. Whatever was going on out there, they would meet it as befitted their station.

'It is time, magos.' Chaim routed his speech through his own larynx this time, not the vocoder-plate. 'You asked to be notified.'

Sanja did not respond, as was only proper with a functionary, but simply disengaged himself from the gargoyle, took a quick moment to readjust to his own eyes, then made a single pace forward and, through the transmitter above his right temple, commanded the doors to open.

An avalanche of noise was the first thing to pour in, and Sanja almost flinched before he had the time to cycle down his senses and put up filters. What had been soft thuds with the gates closed was now a bellow of drumming that felt like physical impacts, as though someone were tapping him rapidly in the chest and tugging at his clothes. Underneath that came shouts, screams, squeals, and every so often the sound of breaking glass or splintering plastic. The air was full of smoke and vapour, the swarms of figures milling around the foot of the steps indistinct at fifty metres and an invisible source of yells at a hundred.

How many were packed into the plaza Sanja did not try and guess, but he had seen it hold thousands when Adeptus processions had mustered on the half-kilometre circle of engraved flagstones. That was an inspiring sight, rank upon rank of the Emperor's chosen servants in the rich golden Hydraphur sunlight, but this…

In fact, this almost seemed a deliberate mockery of those processions. Sanja could just make out the row of gaudy trucks and floats that they had apparently all followed here on their damned parade, covered in gaudy foil-and-plastic props to turn them into half-hearted versions of Astartes Land Raiders, Leviathan command juggernauts, Ecclesiarchal reliquary carts, whatever else, their cabs and beds decked with dancers and clowns scattering baubles and sweets. Sanja had no desire at all to recalibrate his cortical implants to see them more clearly: as he and his attendants moved forward in stately ceremonial gait, half-pace and all in step, he was seeing more than enough.

Two diamond-glass pillars stood at the foot of the ramp up to the shrine doors, and each pillar stood on a waist-high metal plinth. On the left plinth stood a pudgy young man with a blond ponytail, dressed in an imitation Imperial Commissar's uniform with the cap sliding down over one ear. He was digging candied nuggets or some kind of stimulant chew out of his pockets and tossing them into the cheering crowd around him. Another equally corpulent boy in a poor attempt at an Ecclesiarchal prayer shawl was trying to scrabble onto the plinth and grab his ankles, but was too drunk to lift himself up. The right plinth was swarming with bodies in varying shades of green: mockeries of Navy uniforms or Scholastia Psykana robes. A woman wearing what she probably thought was an Imperial Legate's uniform brandished a bottle, popped the top with her thumb, and scattered the contents all over her happily shrieking and now sticky companions as a burly man in an Administratum scribe's robe grabbed her around the waist and clamped his mouth over hers.

Nothing in the sea of bodies was any more edifying: everywhere were hideous over-ornamented attempts at Sororitas surplices, arbitor helmets, military and Administratum uniforms of every design. Despite his determination to remain calm Sanja bristled at a brief glimpse of a sequinned, dandified version of his own scarlet Adeptus Mechanicus kimono, the seals and badges placed grotesquely at all the wrong points, before the crowd closed and hid it.

There was no sight of his visitor. It was time, was it? Chaim had miscalculated, and Sanja was not appreciative of having to stand out here watching over this display for a moment longer than he had to.

One or two people below them had noticed the doors opening. They weren't yet drunk enough to think about coming up the ramp, but the whoops and cheers were starting. Sanja was about to march back inside when he caught sight of what had to be the person he was to meet: a wedge of a dozen black Adeptus Arbites uniforms, too stark to be props, forcing their way through the press of glitter and noise. At the bottom step, with only a few more paces to go, they ground to a halt – it took a moment for Sanja to focus his hearing on them and realise what the problem was.

'Stand aside.' It was the voice of the lead Arbitrator, a head shorter than her squad and with honour icons on her armour that Sanja had no doubt were real.

'Ooh! Yes, madam! Stand aside for the lady justice!' Giggles. Another woman, much younger and considerably drunker. Sanja guessed it was the one with her back to him, with her hair fluffed and glow-dyed, wearing a lurid attempt at an Administratum Praefecta's formal tunic that was a size too tight for her.

'I'm not joking, and I'm not in the mood. Stand the hell aside!'

Sanja tensed reflexively as his sensors picked up the hum of a power weapon charging.

'Oh, is that real? Wherever did you get it? A real one of those arbitor things, what is it, a power-thing, I don't know.

I'm one of these Administr... Administratum thingies... Pref... perf... It's a good touch, though.' More giggles. Someone else was slurring, 'Arrest her! Arrest her!' over and over. The girl grabbed a vial.

'Let's drink to that Arbites thing, and to, to my new friend here, with a very dull costume, I have to say, you know... no, let me finish, you lot, you're really doing the part.'

'I am playing no "part", woman. This is the seal of an arbitor senioris of Hydraphur. You will stand asi–'

'See, now, arbitor seni-whatever, you're starting to just get tiresome. You need to have a drink and–'

Crack. Sanja winced, despite himself.

Ignoring the wails of the partygoers behind her, the arbitor stamped up the ramp to where Sanja was waiting, her squad behind her, power-maul hissing in her hand. On the top step she thumbed its field off and relaxed with a visible effort before they stepped forward to greet each other. Sanja stretched one hand out of his sleeve and made the sign of the Great Engine while his guest clicked her heels and touched the maul to her forehead, then shuffled her right foot a half-pace back and made a slight bow: the short-form salute of the senior Adeptus.

'In the name of the masterful and enduring Machine God I welcome you to his temple and his benediction. May the miracle of the Machine watch over you.' Sanja had to raise his voice over the din around them. 'I welcome you also in my name, Cynez Sanja, magos and genetor of the great Mechanicus, and pledge my goodwill in the name of the Emperor Omnissiah.'

'I receive and return your greeting and make my humble respects to the Mechanicus,' his guest replied. 'Shira Calpurnia Lucina, arbitor senioris of the Adeptus Arbites, extends her greeting in the service of the *Lex Imperia* and the God-Emperor of Earth. The Emperor protects.'

'Thank you. I think we can agree that this is not the place for high ceremony. Will you accompany me?'

Sanja was itching to get the temple doors between himself and the crowd. The arbitor must have felt the same way: Sanja drew back politely as she gave some curt instructions to her squad, who fanned out into a half-circle with their backs to the door. They remained there in sentry positions as the Mechanicus retinue moved back into the shrine. The arbitor senioris herself fell in beside him as he swept back through the doors.

As the adamantite slabs began to swing shut Sanja risked his dignity long enough to glance over his shoulder: a dozen or so of the revellers were clustered around the glow-haired girl's prone body, most of them gawping up at the temple or wringing their hands. Sanja haughtily turned his back on them and let the doors boom closed.

THE MECHANICUS ZIGGURAT rose above them in precise geometrical ratios and burrowed into the side of the Bosporian Hive underneath them, but everything that Sanja would need to deal with his visitor was here in the chambers ahead. As they walked across the forechamber, the servitor-sentries built into the lintels of the inner doors singing a benediction in binary, Sanja saw that his guest had taken her helmet off and was looking wide-eyed at the tech-arcana around her. Sanja nodded with approval: she was impressed, and was paying him the compliment of letting it show. As the song finished and they moved up the steps into brighter light, he studied her a little more closely.

She was a head shorter than he, with an easy, confident way of moving. Her features were even and her green eyes chilly but bright with intelligence. Dark blond hair fell to just below her ears, tousled from the helmet, and there were the first suggestions of lines around her mouth and eyes. Her expression was stern – when those lines came, Sanja thought, they would not be kind ones. Three parallel scars, long healed and barely more than pink lines, started in her left eyebrow and ran straight and neat up into her hair.

They passed through the inner doors into the broad cloister that ran to the heart of the tower and branched into stairs at each side. Here the walls and floor were stark grey rockcrete and the contrast with to the richly ornamented forechamber seemed to unsettle the woman somewhat; she fell a pace back as they walked up a long slope of stairs and turned into the passage to the genetors' devotory. Her face was composed and dutiful and he realised she was unsure of whether she was allowed to speak. Deciding to be a courteous host, Sanja dropped back also and walked alongside her.

'We have prepared the fundamentals of the ceremony while you were on your way to us, my lady justice, so we will be ready to begin at your word. However, your trip here was… somewhat less serene than this quarter normally is. If you wish to clear your mind and prepare yourself before we begin, my junior will show you to our chapel. It is small, but quiet.'

'My thanks, master genetor, but I am prepared. That affair outside was irritating, but not fatal to the equilibrium, I think.'

'Dignity and composure are admirable qualities. I commend you on them, Arbitor Lucina. This way.'

'Calpurnia.'

'Your pardon?'

'Arbitor Calpurnia. My apologies, Master Sanja. An act of carelessness on my part. In formal greeting I use Ultramar protocol. The family name is second, the private third. Here I am Shira Calpurnia as you are Cynez Sanja.' She gave a small, contrite smile. 'Once again, I apologise. I intended no slight.'

'No slight is taken, Arbitor Calpurnia.' He saw her relax and then, to his private amusement, tense again as she followed him through the lacquered double doors of the Devotory. The narrow little chamber, its walls red-panelled and ceiling dancing with holo-sculptures of amino-acid molecules, had been prepared just as Sanja had said: two rows of servitors carrying medicae flasks formed an aisle to the little kneeler cushion before the shrine. The relics on the crimson altar-cloth – centrifuge, injector-glove, inscriptions of the gene-codes of Mechanicus saints etched into scrolls of paper-thin steel – reflected the mellow golden lamplight.

Calpurnia saluted the altar from the doorway and then walked to the kneeler without further hesitation, unclipping her half-carapace as Sanja faced her from the far side of the altar. Chaim took and held her armour as she unfastened the top of the uniform bodyglove, holding it against her chest but shrugging it down to leave her shoulders and back bare. Her composure was still good, but Sanja was looking at her now through the eyes of the luminants as well as his own, and in the mosaic of images being fed into his augmented cortex her apprehension showed in her breathing, her body temperature, the acidity of her skin, her brainwaves. The luminants moved down the row of servitors, dendrites clicking as they took and loaded the vials of biotic fluid and extended their injectors, then glided silently to station themselves behind Calpurnia's shoulders, dendrites extending a glittering fan of needles.

Sanja murmured a brief High Gothic blessing, then switched to machine-code and guided the luminants down. Calpurnia's breath caught for a moment as the hypodermics went home, and then the luminants rose into the air again and it was done.

'Walk with me.' Sanja was already stepping down from the altar-dais by the time Calpurnia had stood and fastened her bodyglove back into place. Chaim came forward with her carapace and she turned, shrugged into it and clipped it closed with barely a wince, then fell into step again as Sanja led the way back out through the antechamber, to the gallery that ran around the temple's central hall.

'We shall pace a while.' he told her. 'The movement will help the anointments to integrate faster. Chaim will have given you the tokens–' She held them up. 'Good. The Iron Wheel and the Caducal Helix are strong talismans of the Mechanicus. Grip them well and they will make your blessing a powerful one.'

They walked in silence for several minutes: out of the Devotory, past the stairs they had come up, around a circular chamber full of doors where the half-skull-half-cog crest of the Mechanicus gazed inscrutably down from one wall, back past the stairs to the Devotory doors and so through the circuit again. The skitarii and servitors followed them for the first circuit, then Sanja ordered them away. Calpurnia gave an occasional surreptitious half-shrug, trying to get the armour comfortable on her needle-tender shoulders; Chaim silently trailed them with her helmet. They were halfway through their third circuit before Sanja spoke.

'I would venture to suggest, Arbitor Calpurnia, that this was not the first time that you have had a rite of vaccination performed. You seemed to know your part in it as well as I did.' She smiled.

'My career has taken me through postings across the Ultima Segmentum and now to here, magos. Most of those moves have been across sufficient distances for me to need fortifying for my new position, although the ceremonies were never this involved. They were usually done on board the Arbites ship by one of our own Medicae staff, with a junior genetor overseeing, and they did not involve these...' she gestured behind them with her head.

'The luminants? They are relics as well as servants, perhaps not common on smaller worlds with less distinguished Mechanicus traditions. The honour of continued service to the Machine God after one's organic death is not earned every day.' He gestured behind him. 'That one is the skull of Clayd Menkis, the chief adept of this shrine just after the overthrow of the Apostate Cardinal. The other is Bahon Sulleya, my immediate predecessor and mentor. I had the great honour of preparing her skull for its mechanisation myself.' Calpurnia shot the luminants another, slightly uneasier look.

'They can act by themselves?'

'I am appointed as their instructor as I am the instructor of my servitors. That privilege accompanies my rank here. The luminants assist me with my work and my studies. Their precision and senses are all that one would expect of idols of the Machine God. Normally such a rite as yours would not require more than one, but for you to have come so far and to a world like Hydraphur, to which viral and bacterial strains from all across the segmentum are brought, you needed a far more rigorous treatment and I called both of my luminants accordingly.'

'And they are also monitoring my chemical spoor and behaviour to make sure I am who I say I am and that I carry no psychic or hypnotic taint to cast doubt upon your safety in admitting me.'

Sanja snapped his head around to stare at her and she laughed aloud.

'I said that the practices here were different, magos, not that I had never had dealings with your priesthood before.

Admission to your shrine is a great honour, and humbling – but when I passed into this shrine with no searches, no weapon-checks or security vigils, I started to wonder how it was that you were making sure I was no danger to you. I'm Adeptus Arbites, remember. We enforce the Emperor's law, pass the Emperor's judgement and enforce the Emperor's peace. We get into the habit of thinking about things like this. You don't need to confirm it if you'd rather not.'

'You are as sharp as my own luminants' needles, lady justice,' Sanja told her, not sure whether to be angry or amused. 'I am sure the arbitor majore will not regret sending for you all the way from, Ultramar, was it? A long journey. It's a compliment to you.'

'I grew up on Ultramar. Iax. But my last post was at Ephaeda, north-west of there. But still across a lot of space. I'm a long way from home.' A sombre note had crept into her voice and they walked in silence for a few minutes more. Every so often the bio-augurs on one of the luminants would buzz or click, recording some detail of how the arbitor's metabolism was responding. It did not take long for Sanja to be satisfied, and he led the way to the doors back into the forechamber.

'Am I done, then? Have the luminants given the word?'

'They have, and I have confirmed it through their eyes and spirits. You have not reacted adversely to our anointments, and their eyes show that your body is accepting the inoculations. The preliminary rites and treatments you had before your arrival here laid the groundwork well. My arts are more sophisticated than those of the medicae, and the process will have completed itself within a day or two more. An envoy of mine will visit you tonight and instruct you in the correct prayers and readings to close the day and open the morning tomorrow to ensure this. There should be little problem, arbitor, in your taking your place at the Mass of Balronas and the Sanguinala.'

'Good. I'm looking forward to them. I read Galimet's *Pilgrim's Letters* during my journey here and he describes the mass in spectacular terms. I'm certainly expecting it to be a little more edifying than *that*.' She nodded toward the outer doors as they reached the forechamber again. 'Galimet gave the impression that the period leading up to the mass was one of self-denial and penitence. The dossier I was sent said the same thing.' As if on cue a quick syncopated bass thump came through the walls. 'But I have to say, magos, that if that display outside is Hydraphur's idea of penitent reflection, I'm further from home than I thought.'

Sanja smiled without humour.

'Your first lesson in Hydraphurn behaviour, lady arbitor. Part of the ritual of the season nowadays is the Ministorum's plaintive attempts to have the aristocracy conform to the more general ideal of pious behaviour, but when the nobility assemble and reach a certain critical mass, as they've done here, they obey rules of conduct all of their own. I am given to understand that among less rarefied circles the Ecclesiarchal dictates on behaviour are more strictly followed, if that brings you any consolation. This should blow itself out in another couple of hours.'

'I'd like to have it cleared out before then,' said Calpurnia with a scowl. 'I got caught in the middle of the damn thing when they all started pouring into the area and it was too late to double back to fetch a transport, but I'm sure riot squads will have mobilised from the Wall by now… What?' Sanja was regarding her. 'I mean, apologies, magos. Did I speak out of turn?' He shook his head.

'To speak candidly, Arbitor Calpurnia, although I am part of an order known for its detachment from the day-to-day affairs of the Imperium, I can't help the thought that the workings of Hydraphur are just a little less straightforward than you perhaps perceive them to be.' Before she had the chance to ask him what he meant, the doors swung wide and once again the din of the party piled in.

The fog was thicker now. The still, warm evening air filled with a soup of coloured ornamental smokes and perfumes and some kind of refractor mist that made lights and colours sparkle unnaturally; Calpurnia hastily took her helmet back as Sanja lifted a filter-veil over his face. There was no sign of the girl Calpurnia had struck, and the other revellers were only visible now as a boil of movement through the mist. By the sounds, the party's momentum had not been dented.

'Any further trouble, Bannon?'

'None.' Calpurnia and her deputy had to shout over the noise. Somewhere out beyond the ramp, pyrotechnics were starting to flash through the fog: showers of glowing confetti and miniature starshells flashed and cracked over the heads of the crowd, leaving hazy trails and puffs of hot smoke. Calpurnia fell in with her squad, then turned to salute Sanja in farewell.

The first bullet hit her shoulder at a bad angle, whirred off her carapace and struck a spark off the temple wall, a single tiny chip of black ceramite stinging the chin of the arbitor next to her.

Her reflexes had taken charge before she realised what was happening, sending her darting down the ramp and to one side. The second bullet struck her helmet over the right eye, not penetrating but cracking the armour and staggering her backward in a daze. The third whipped past her ear as her squad pelted down the steps after her, unlimbering shotguns and shields and firing loud bursts over the heads of the crowd.

The movement began like a ripple in grass as a strong wind springs up. The nearest partiers shrieked and ploughed into those further away, until the crowd thickened too much for anyone to force their way through. The mob rebounded off itself, swayed and broke in three directions at once as the Arbites split into two squads and closed around Calpurnia. As she lurched to her feet, groggy and shaking her head, their shields juddered under two more shots and one pitched over backward as a third shattered the cheek-guard of his helmet against his jaw.

Calpurnia tried to will the ringing in her ears away as things seemed to swim around her. It took an age for her to goad her legs into action and another to get into formation behind her guards' shields. They held the foot of the ramp in a textbook Arbites firing line: one row kneeling, shotguns locked through the gunports in their shields to pump out a steady, suppressing fire; the second line standing behind them firing more carefully, aiming shots over their heads. They were aiming high for the moment, trying just to drive the crowd back, but the answering bullets kept coming.

'Bannon! What can you see? Place the shots!' The beat
over the vox-horns had fallen silent, and the tumult of the
crowd was something the Arbites were more used to shouting over.

'Nothing! We can't spot any shooters, no weapons, no
sounds, no flashes!' Bannon's voice had an edge of fear in
it. A party-goer, leering with terror, stumbled toward them
and two of the squad sent him sprawling with expert shoves
of their shields. As that movement parted them for a split-
second a third bullet whipped between their shields and
scraped Calpurnia's carapace with an impact she felt all
down her ribs. She swore and back-pedalled. The shots were
coming in flat, somewhere at ground level, not a sniper up
high. No one she could see had been anywhere near the
angle to make that shot. They–

There was a crash from off to her left, a perfume-brazier
going over. She glanced at it, registered only a couple of
frightened partiers running away, no guns with them. She
hung low and kept moving, sideways across the ramp to the
left-hand pillar-plinth. The Arbitrators broke their shield-
wall into a more fluid line for a mobile firefight, some
covering Calpurnia and two on guard over the man who'd
fallen. A bullet cracked into the armour on her shoulder and
she staggered and cursed; the bastards were all around her.
She ran the last couple of paces to the plinth and–

But there was nobody in that direction. This was small-
calibre ammo, handgun slugs. And there was no one
remotely in handgun range.

The plaza roared with the riot the party had become as
they surged back and forth trying to find a safe way away
from the shooting. But there was nobody to her left, nobody
around where the brazier had been knock–

Bannon leaned out from the plinth for a quick glance
beyond it and a bullet smacked into the edge of his shield
and ricocheted past Calpurnia's ear so that even through her
helmet's padded earpiece she could hear the whine. She
grabbed Bannon's shoulder and yanked him back in as a second bullet clipped the rim of his shield.

No. Not possible. Nobody could plan a ricochet shot like
that. Could they?

She had to move.

'Go. Fan out towards that overturned brazier. Cover every single side. Assume concealment by the enemy. Now!'

They rounded the plinth and raced forward. The space in front of them was empty, the crowd shoving away to the sides.

'Nothing here!' She was whirling on the spot, trying to–

Was that movement?

She ducked to one side instead of standing to shoot and it saved her life. The bullet gouged the side of her helmet and knocked it askew – a second earlier and it would have punched through her top lip. She wrenched off the helmet and scampered crabwise away from the others. Whatever it was, a moving target seemed to give it a little trouble.

With no polarising filters over her eyes the refractor-fog set every light to glittering and sparkling. She narrowed her eyes and almost saw–

She sprinted two steps to the side and vaulted an upended table as two more shots skewered the air behind her. A third smacked into the heavy wood and she put three booming stub-shots through the space where she thought she might have heard firing. She had been careless about placing her feet and the recoils slammed her through almost a quarter-turn; as she turned it into a backward jog to regain her balance there was a roar as three shotguns opened up to support her.

Nothing. Mist and light, echoes and sobs from partiers sprawled on the ground. Her head was throbbing – one of those head shots had hurt, even through the helmet, and it was catching up with her. She willed herself to stay on her feet.

An eddy in the mists. She put a bullet through it as her squad caught up with her, kept her gun high and moving back and forth in front of her face, wanting a shotgun but painfully aware of the momentary lapse in her guard that a weapon-swap with one of the arbitrators would mean. The giant-bore stub pistol she had been issued with was a commander's weapon, a shock-and-terror weapon, something for a senior arbitor to use for great, ruinous shots at high-profile targets to terrify a crowd of rioters, showing Imperial authority in brutal terms while other Arbitrators and sharp-shooters did the actual combat shooting. Calpurnia was becoming bitterly aware of its limitations in a straight fire-fight. She kept moving, dodging, reversing her direction. The lack of a helmet made her almost nauseous with nerves.

A woman lying on her back nearby gasped and twitched, and Calpurnia came within a hairsbreadth of shooting her on reflex. It took her a moment to realise that it had been not panic but physical shock, as though someone had stepped on her. She tucked her body down towards her boots, crouching into a foetal ball and sending two shots over the prone woman, aiming high in a last-moment hope that the rounds would pass over any bystanders beyond and letting the recoil roll her over and put her back on her feet. Bannon sent a shot-burst through the same space a split-second later and the little dark-haired party-girl seemed to decide her time was up. She shrieked and scrambled to her feet, frightening the people around her into doing the same, and suddenly a score of people were rising up out of the smoke and running for their lives. The mist between them roiled as if…

As if there were another person there, a shape pushing its way through the crowd, displacing air and bodies.

Calpurnia skittered to one side. The ringing in her ears was turning into a yammering that fought against the screams of the crowd. There was a distant crash as one of the parade-floats went over. She hunted for signs, half-saw them. Smoke moving the wrong way here, there a tremor and backflow in the mob as the moving crowd snagged on nothing she could see. It was moving around the edge of the retreating mob, and she could almost feel its gunsights crawling over her.

Her squad was frantic, desperate for a target. There was no time to instruct them – by the time she explained she'd be dead. She'd have to rely on them to follow her fire when she spotted something. It could be moving into position now, or…

She knew what she was looking for now, and had her pistol ready to bear. The stampede in front of her was wavering, the crowd parted and one man stumbled against something unseen. *Now*. Running on nerves and reflex alone, with barely a conscious moment to aim, Shira Calpurnia put a slug through the clear space and straight through the assassin's heart.

Seventh Day of Septista

Eleven days to the Mass of Saint Balronas.
Feast of Saint Rapanna and Saint Skey. Commemoration
of the Second Sacrifice of the Colchans. The First
Congregation of Intercessors.

IN THESE DAYS *before the vigil the Imperial shrines will station
preachers at every street pulpit, with sermons delivered at sunup
and sundown. On no account should any be absent from these
except in direst straits or by dispensation, for these sermons will
have been passed down from the Eparch of Hydraphur himself to
strengthen mind, body and soul for the physical and spiritual
labour ahead.*

*It is at this time that the Ecclesiarchy hears certain special pleas
and petitions. All those with indulgences to beg should have discussed the matter already with their local preachers and be ready
to present themselves either at their appointed shrine, at one of the
Imperial chapels on the slopes of the Bosporian Hive or on the
High Mesé, or at the gates of the Cathedral.*

*This is also the first day on which pilgrims hostelling below the
Cathedral move through the Augustaeum at the hive peak, and
proper respect should be shown to all in the brown pilgrims' mantle. Those travelling to the Augustaeum through the Pilgrims' or
Aquila Gates may wish to take a small offering of simple food or
distilled water to offer to the pilgrims as they walk past on the
paths to the Artisans Quarters or along the Chirosian Way – it is
a traditional mark of favour and good fortune to have the food one
has set down by the side of the path collected by a pilgrim. The*

*small tokens and devotional items set out in the Artisans Quarter
are there for the same purpose, and to interfere with them is a
matter of some shame and should not be countenanced.*

*Those participating in services commemorating the Second Sac-
rifice should wear a small stone on a thong about their neck or
waist. The likeness of Saint Rapanna may be worn by any making
devotions to her, but the likeness of Saint Skey is sacred on this
day and must only be touched or worn by officers of the Adeptus
Ministorum.*

CHAPTER TWO

THERE WAS A series of overlapping clacks as the pile of data-slates finally tumbled off the hassock and scattered over the floor, then a thump as the pile of faxcopy collapsed, and then the little suite of rooms, Calpurnia's new home on her new world as of three days ago, was quiet again. She didn't bother to take her hands from over her eyes. Just half an hour more, she promised herself then she'd sleep – better to tackle this fresh tomorrow morning than cudgel herself any more over it tonight.

She opened an eye long enough to pluck the wine-glass from the hassock and drink the last sip of the mellow red. She stayed sprawled on the recliner as she let the taste fill her mouth and then shade to aftertaste, then reluctantly got up and put the glass aside for the stewards to remove. The idea of having servants still bothered her, but just for tonight she was glad to have things taken off her hands. She was wrung out: formal duties, the injuries from the previous afternoon – she had spent that morning being fussed over by the arbitor majore's personal physicians – and lingering nausea from Sanja's vaccines. It occurred to her now that she hadn't

cleared the drinking of wine with the genetor, and wondered
if it might interfere with the inoculations. That rankled – she
wasn't used to forgetting things like that. She finally did sigh
as she glanced out of the great window at the last of the daylight draining out of the sky, then dropped back onto the
recliner and reached for the next slate.

It was her notes from the first full, formal, working meeting with her new colleagues as the freshly appointed and
ordained arbitor senioris of Hydraphur. They had met in the
ornate chambers of the arbitor majore, high in the topmost
tower of the great Arbites fortress known as the Wall. Sitting
around a table with the three most senior Arbites of arguably
the most famous system of an entire Imperial Segmentum
had been pressure enough, but one thing she hadn't imagined was that the meeting would be exclusively focused on
her. Or to be accurate, she thought as she flicked through her
notes yet another time, exclusively focused on the man who
had tried, very hard and very nearly successfully, to kill her
the previous evening.

'Let's eliminate the most obvious possibility first,' Dvorov
had begun, tilting his chair back and stretching his booted
feet in front of him. Arbitor Majore Krieg Dvorov, Grand
Marshal and Grand Praetor Judicial of Hydraphur, had a
long, seamed face and a dry, distracted way of talking.
Somehow, he wasn't what Calpurnia had been expecting.
'The first thought into my head, as I'm sure it was yours, was
that it was a simple revenge attack for our colleague decking
that young lady who wouldn't get out of her way. What was
her name again?'

'Keta Merkoli-Ballyne,' put in the man opposite Calpurnia
at the little round table. 'Or, as I'm sure she would have me
put it, the Distinguished Lady Keta of the Noble Ballyne's
most respected Merkoli. Assuming she didn't stand on ceremony and used the short form. But then her behaviour
before even such a civilising influence as our own newly-
welcomed colleague does not suggest to me that this
particular darling of young society enjoys a particularly formal mindset.' Calpurnia gave him a sharp look at his last
sentence, but as far as she could tell she wasn't being got at.
She sometimes found it a little hard to tell: Arbitor Senioris

Nestor Leandro, foremost of Dvorov's three deputies, had a courtly manner and an ornate way of speaking that she sometimes found a little overdone. His theatrical manner went well with his rolling, resonant voice and handsome swirl of silver hair – Calpurnia had not been surprised to find out that Leandro was a patron of dramas and operas, and kept a library of famous Imperial oratory.

'As for what all of that means,' Leandro went on, 'there is no reason you should have heard of the Merkoli, or of the Lady Keta in particular. The Mass and its associated festivities has come at a time when Ballyne would really rather its households be agitating to try and reverse their recent sidelining for close-traffic contracts at Contoscalion, but there has been considerable anguish within Ballyne about whether a good presence here for the Mass will sap their efforts in that direction or reassure their allies that they are strong and in control and build their stock that way. None of this has been more than a background whisper, you understand, it's what I uncovered after peeling back a few layers of disinterest and indifference.

'The upshot, though, is that even if Merkoli-Ballyne had the resources to organise such an expert attempt, and even if they were stupid enough to expose themselves by staging it, and even if they were supremely stupid enough to select an agent of the Imperial Adeptus as a target, there would be no logic behind them doing any of that for a disposable, peripheral flibbertigibbet like the Lady Keta, who as far as I can tell only earned the privilege of a trip here for the Mass because the family didn't know what else to do with her apart from trying to pair her off with some moderately reputable local boy in the hopes of a marginally useful political marriage. All things considered, I suspect a smack across the nose with a power-maul is about the most interesting thing that will happen to anyone in her family all season.'

'I wish you'd pause for breath occasionally, Nestor. By the time you end of some of your sentences I feel dizzy on your behalf.' Dvorov turned to the fourth at the table. 'We have a good idea of somewhere he didn't come from, then. Any ideas about where he did?'

'No.' Arbitor Senioris Ryo Nakayama could hardly have been better calculated to be Leandro's opposite. Squat where Leandro was tall, gruff and raspy-voiced where Leandro was poised and mellifluous. 'Nestor's right, this is something that took a stack of resources. Not just money. Clout, access to rare equipment and highly illegal personnel.' He looked at Calpurnia. 'You remember handing the corpse over to the genetor after you killed it?'

Calpurnia nodded. Her memories of the afternoon were a little fragmented, courtesy of the light concussion that the bullets had managed to give her through her helmet, but she remembered that much. The space in between the partgoers, nothing but smoke and sparkle, became a pale blur which became a brown-grey silhouette which became a tottering, hazy outline which became a collapsing body. She dimly remembered staggering forward and putting two more slugs into its back, and her next memory was of half-lying on the inlaid floor of the Mechanicus shrine while Sanja and Chaim shouted at servitors.

'The Mechanicus have helped us with these kinds of problems before,' Nakayama went on, 'although not often. Their genetor-magi have the finest tools and arts for stripping knowledge out of evidence, bar none, better than our own verispex laboratoria. This time Master Sanja took the remains and set his adepts to work on them without waiting to be asked, or even before we could ask him to hand the body over to us. I think he takes it happening right in front of his shrine as some kind of personal slight that he wanted to redeem. I've read his report – he asked for you, Shira, but you were at the Kalfus-Medell meeting.'

Calpurnia allowed herself a moment's hope before Nakayama doused it.

'They came up blank, of course. They were furious, apparently, or as close as they ever get to it. Sanja was sure they'd missed something at first, but they've cast their best augurs and instruments over our friend and there's still next to nothing they can tell us. Was he a mutant? Yes. A trained psyker. That was how he blocked himself from sight. Was he augmented? Of course. His eyes and the motor parts of his brain were massively enhanced, specialised trick-shooter

stuff. Is he traceable? Not a chance. His death triggered a
toxin implant in the small of his back which caused massive
damage right through his tissues. Sanja invoked his secrecy
prerogative pretty quickly when I wanted to get to details,
but it's clear we'll never get a usable gene-print. Anti-tracing
measures like that need a lot of skill and resources, and
they're illegal to boot. On an assassin whose psyker nature
put him under an automatic death warrant in any event,
they add up to a hell of an investment on a single agent and
a single attack.'

'Surprise me, Ryo,' said Dvorov, looking at the ceiling. 'Tell
me we're going to be able to trace the weapons.'

'We're going to try, but they don't seem to correspond to
any established Mechanicus archprint. So far, anyway. Magos
Sanja has a fairly sophisticated medicae chamber there but
that shrine isn't much more than a diplomatic outpost when
it's said and done. They wanted to send the stuff to one of
their bigger Constanta Hive foundries, but I didn't want
them trotting out prerogatives again and keeping them. I
don't think we're going to get the bionics back as it is.'

'We probably shouldn't push it. Give them an easy time on
that, Ryo, just thank them for their help and express the
hope that they find the bionics of interest. Frame it so that
we're doing them a favour in return for the quick action in
going over the body. Level Four delegation.' Dvorov
drummed his fingers on the table. 'Ryo's right. Just thinking
of the care that went into preparing this man for his mission,
and into keeping us from tracking him, makes me queasy.
Shira, if it had been any of the three of us we could have
gone straight away to dossiers of enemies and with some
ideas on what might have pushed someone to that much
trouble. But you have been in the system for, what, two
weeks? And Hydraphur itself for a matter of days.'

'Which I've spent here in the Wall,' Calpurnia said. 'Yesterday was almost literally my first taste of Hydraphur air. I've
been over my movements time and again in my mind and I
can't come up with a single thing that might have prompted
something like this.'

'Then I trust your judgement,' Dvorov told her. 'We can't
rule anything out, but for the present the idea of an

opportunistic strike against our order in general should be our primary take. We can't treat this as purely a hive or a planetary matter, either. The Mass of Saint Balronas pulls in visitors from all over the system and a dozen I can think of from across the subsector. For all we know it could be some minerals baron from Stahl-Theta who's avenging an estate impoundment ordered by one of our colleagues four systems away. Just speculating, Shira, that's all.' He had spotted Calpurnia making a note. 'Word of this is already out. I've had a dozen requests for audiences from all kinds of parties wanting to know what's going on, or to put together some case or other to do with this. Kalfus-Medell is probably the most important of them so far but he's certainly not the only one.'

'We'll need to be inventive with this one, my colleagues.' Dvorov had finished the meeting by saying: 'I think we're all agreed that it's Shira's prerogative to command the investigations into her own attempted assassination. I don't need to tell you that you'll need to work closely with these two, Shira. I have the confidence in you that your reputation commands, but this won't exactly be a routine investigation.'

'Local knowledge, sir. I understand.' That was what she had said to him.

And she did understand. She was beginning to suspect that one of the truths of a career like hers was that you never did get used to the wandering from one world to another. From one place to another on the one planet was easy, and within a small realm was easy too: her parents had both had senior duties to the governance of Ultramar and she had travelled more than most before her induction into the Arbites. The training station at Machiun had been bearable because she had been there with seven hundred and ninety-nine other frightened inductees, but her first garrison post at Drade-73 had been much worse. She hadn't been able to get used to the smell, or the constant noise from the pumice floes that came washing down the canals, or the coarse local manners, or the continual grime of ash.

MG-Dyel, Hazhim, Don-Croix, Ephaeda. She was sure she had exhausted the court libraries in each one by the time she had been reposted, but she couldn't remember any treatises about that wrench that came from being dropped into an unfamiliar world where you couldn't take your most fundamental assumptions about things for granted. Perhaps one day she would write one herself.

And one thing she would be damned sure to put in a whole chapter on, she promised herself as she reached for the next slate, was culture shock. *It is a fact to which I would commend my reader's attention*, she wrote in her head, *that although the faith and dedication of the Adeptus Arbites is as steadfast as the Emperor's light itself, as you travel across all the Imperium's worlds you will find our order addressing its duties in ways unfamiliar to you and for this you must be prepared. I shall recite my own experiences in passing from Ephaeda to the world of Hydraphur...*

She made a face, tapped the new slate and watched the text swirl onto it, notes from her other two meetings of the day. Two names, of the double-barrelled sort the Hydraphur bluebloods seemed to like: Tymon-Per, Kalfus-Medell. One in charge of the disaster in the Adeptus plaza, the other the master of the great religious festival that was one of the major pivots for Hydraphur's year.

She tapped the entry for Tymon-Per and made a wry face when she saw she had left a blank area at the top of the note space to record the cell the interrogations would be conducted in.

'Culture shock,' she muttered again to herself. The 'interrogations' hadn't used a cell at all. She had followed Leandro to a gracious audience chamber where the young man she had expected to find in chains was sitting on a chaise and inhaling from a herbal steamer. Her first impulse had been to knock the cur's teeth out, then outrage had turned to bewilderment as Leandro had greeted the boy and she realised that this was not going to be like any interrogation she was used to.

Athian Tymon-Per had been the one behind the 'Adeptus' party-parade and it had been quickly obvious to both Arbites he had nothing much to tell them – every one of Calpurnia's notes was a negative. No, nobody had put him up to annexing the Adeptus plazas for his party. ('It was my idea, you see, the Adeptus theme hadn't been done for *years*, and I thought, well, it would be original, and daring, but festive, too, and it would be, well, you know, pleasingly, you know, *audacious*… don't you…' and he had wilted as they both simply stared at him.) No, nobody had approached him about the parade's timing or its route. No, nobody had told him there would be a senior arbitor moving through the Adeptus Quarter. No, he hadn't checked credentials; the partygoers hadn't been vetted except for someone's half-hearted attempt to make a list for a best-costume contest. No, he didn't know this was the very Arbitor Calpurnia at whom the attack had been directed. No, no, all no.

'No guilt, no help and no clue,' had been her whispered opinion after they had retired to confer.

'I agree, but the hour has not been wasted. The whole hive is always in a ferment at this time of the year, and there's usually a point where we have to put a stamp of authority on it. Word of this will be all over by the end of the day, and whatever its value to the investigation, the account of our giving a young noble such a sharp questioning will show people we mean what we say when we're enforcing the vigil curfew.' Calpurnia looked past him to where Athian was nervously picking his nose and wiping his finger clean on the underside of the chaise.

'Such a – with respect, Arbitor Leandro, I can't help thinking that the message this will send out is that we're treating the matter like a parlour game! If these people have forgotten that the reach of the Emperor's own Adeptus is absolute, then I believe that a roundup of all of those party attendees by Chastener squads would send the message much more effectively. How could it hurt to have so many potential troublemakers penned up for a few days? It would be the lesson that some of these people seem to need.' She was proud of the way she had kept her voice as low as Leandro's.

'The principle of your advice is perfectly sound, Arbitor Calpurnia,' he had replied mildly. 'As to its exact application, well, the affairs of Hydraphur are perhaps more complex and rarefied than that of your previous postings, the position of the Arbites more fraught and delicate. We calibrate our actions to our circumstances.' Seeing her expression, he added, 'And our actions here are quite sufficient. We already signalled our intentions when Arbitrators broke up the last of that morass of unruliness that this young man thought he presided over, and we signal them afresh now. The elite of Hydraphur are accustomed to being invited to a diplomatic audience by an Arbites herald, with plenty of notice and due regard for their rank and with any questions we have couched in a dozen layers of protocol. This boy brought here and openly questioned, with none of their own retainers on hand, will have exactly the psychological impact of the roundup you proposed, without the side-effect of stirring up so much hostility to us among the nobility and other Adeptus that any traces of the attack upon you become impossibly kicked over.'

With that Leandro had given the signal for the doors to be opened. Three more young nobles hurried in to form a twittering clump around Athian, who shook in theatrical distress and whispered back at them until Leandro broke in.

'Your presence is no longer required by our investigation, my esteemed young man of Per. It is always hard to know, though, how the twists and turns of our duties may take us. You are to consider yourself available to us, in exactly the manner of today, until we advise you otherwise. For now, a respectful farewell.' The words seemed uncommonly mild to her, but it prompted a fresh wave of hissed conversation that only stopped when Calpurnia, unable to restrain herself, rapped on the side of the chaise with her maul.

'And before you leave, Tymon-Per, I will thank you to clean your snot out from under our furniture.'

All four stared at her, dumbstruck, until Athian finally realised she wasn't joking and bent down, kerchief in hand and white faced with outrage and humiliation. That, at least, had made her feel a little better.

Time and timing, she thought now as she reached for another file. It was supposed to have been slower than this. Dvorov's initial brief to her had been for a clean and orderly appointment period. Time to settle into her surroundings, completion of her medical fitout courtesy of Sanja, a week or so of familiarisation time until her formal appearance at the Mass marked her official commencement of duty, time to learn about Hydraphur and her new position. She snorted and flicked the new slate into life. Learn that suspects here were welcomed to courteous formal audiences and have their hands held while they are questioned. Hydraphur was going to take some getting used to.

Her notes from the second hearing of the day were cross-linked to one of the dossiers she had been issued when she had first arrived. The opening screen was taken up with titles and honorifics that would be meaningless to her until she had the chance to look them up – she suspected they wouldn't mean much even then. The name at the top of the page: Lord Hallyan Kalfus-Medell, ordained Master of the Vigil by the Eparch of Hydraphur.

She and Dvorov had met the lord in one of the formal galleries over the Justice Gate, two hours after Tymon-Per had been shooed away. He was no tenth-rate like Tymon-Per or Lady Keta, but as powerful a man as a civilian could be in the Navy-dominated Hydraphur system, and that was still powerful enough. That called for a different message and a little more ceremony: Dvorov was dressed in the antique, formal robe and high headdress of a Judge; he sat on a dais surrounded by a guard of junior praetors and heralds whose staves carried steel plaques engraved with teachings from the Commandments of Justice. Protocol allowed Calpurnia to stay with her simple black-and-grey Arbitrator uniform, but she felt rather self-conscious in it now as she made her way to the side of the dais and saluted. Dvorov gave her a nod in return, and then two of the attendants swung the doors wide.

Hallyan Kalfus-Medell had come striding in straight away, a big man in the prime of middle age, only the first traces of fat about his waist and jaw and a profile like the prow-ram of one of the Battlefleet Pacificus cruisers orbiting high over their heads. He bore straight down on the dais, all blue and purple silks and piercing voice.

'My Arbites! The earliest messages I received told me that the officer who had been the target of this atrocity had survived. Magnificent news, news to take the edge off the terrible reports that such an attack had even been made. I was en route from Constanta Hive when I heard and I came for an audience with you as soon as I was able. I am sorry it has taken so long for me to be able to meet you.'

We were the ones who granted audience to *you,* Calpurnia wanted to say. Kalfus-Medell had stopped with one foot actually up on the edge of their dais, but Dvorov seemed minded to let that slide.

'The attack was unsuccessful, my most respected Kalfus of Medell. Arbitor Senioris Calpurnia was slightly injured but is already recovered and has assumed her active duties, as you see.' Calpurnia nodded. She noticed a look of surprise in the noble's expression: she realised he had seen her duty uniform and taken her for one of Dvorov's guards. The look turned into one of appraisal. Hallyan's eyes were deep-set and sharp, and as they sized her up they confirmed the impression Calpurnia had already brought away from his file. Kalfus-Medell might be pompous, but he wasn't stupid.

'Arbitor senioris.' He bowed. 'Allow me to express my relief. I was not associated with that… disturbance that coincided with the attack, but as the Master of the Vigil for all of Bosporian Hive I felt responsible for the injury you suffered.'

'I appreciate your concern, sir, but the injuries were minor and fleeting. The would-be assassin is dead by my hand and we are following his trail. Whoever is behind the attack will be brought down, I assure you, and the Arbites will not stand for any further "disturbances".'

'I had noticed the change as I made my way here,' Hallyan said as Dvorov stepped down off the dais. Somewhat surprised, Calpurnia followed a step behind as they strolled back toward the doors. There was an Arbites checkpoint at every entrance to the Augustaeum and squads on every street. I trust that this has not damaged your ability to control the rest of the hive and around the Cathedral itself?'

'The specifics of our operations must of necessity remain an Arbites matter, my trusted ambassador of Medell,' Dvorov replied as the two men made a slight turn away from the doors. Calpurnia spun and quickstepped to catch up. 'But I would take no action that would threaten our ability to defend the Emperor's order and the holy Mass. Arbitor Senioris Nakayama is personally overseeing the locking down of controls over Bosporian and his skills at that kind of operation are superb. Delegations have been issued for heightened vigilance in all parts of the system under Arbites jurisdiction. And far from being slowed by her injuries, Arbitor Calpurnia has taken up active duty a week early to command the hunt for those who orchestrated the attack. She is new to our system and its ways, but her record and reputation are of the first order and she will have the support of myself and Arbitor Leandro. I do not expect the hunt to take long, respected Kalfus of Medell.'

They had slowed to a quarter-pace. Hallyan gave her another sharp stare.

'Good news builds on good news, then. You are alive, my admired arbitor, and not only that but you are healthy, and not only that but you are pursuing your enemy with a dedication I can only commend.' He and Dvorov turned to stroll at another angle and Calpurnia, disoriented, turned once more to keep step with them.

'It is a point I hesitate to bring up, esteemed young arbitor,' said Hallyan, 'but my current responsibilities weigh my shoulders and require it.' He paused to allow Calpurnia to answer, and when she simply looked at him he frowned and went on. 'Despite the impression you may quite understandably have gained during your short time here, the time approaching the Mass of Saint Balronas and the Sanguinala is a time of sacred significance. Now, it is my understanding that the Judges of the Adeptus may pursue their quarry in ways that, how shall I say it…'

'I think I understand where you're taking this, Lord Kalfus-Medell. I know that I'm brand-new to the system, and that I'm ignorant of a lot of local protocol. I'm sure I've made a dozen minor gaffes simply in the time I've spoken to you.' She noticed a flicker of placated smugness in his expression before he caught it and erased it. 'But I know that you will overlook them just as I will do my best to track down the assassins without disorder profaning the festival. We have the same objective, sir. The celebration of our devotion to the Emperor and the destruction of any threat to His orderly and united domains. Where is there room to disagree?' He smiled at that, and Calpurnia relaxed a little.

'I am almost ashamed to admit I had concerns, my much-distinguished arbitor,' he said. 'But I am delighted at the chance to enjoy your most eminent company, even for so brief a time as the pressure of both our duties allows us. You have set me at ease that nothing will further trouble us – should unrest and disquiet be kept down I guarantee the Sanguinala will welcome you to your new home with the most glorious ceremony you will have seen!'

He was turning to exit the room; Dvorov remained where he was and gave a miniscule tip of his head for Calpurnia to follow. The etiquette was familiar to her, an important guest being escorted away to blunt any feelings of dismissal, and she walked beside Lord Hallyan out past the double-file of uniformed guards, saw what was waiting for them in the hall and stopped dead, her hand darting toward her gun. She only stopped the move when Hallyan calmly walked over to the monstrosity that towered among shafts of thick yellow daylight from the high windows.

The bodyguard servitor stood a head taller than Hallyan; Calpurnia, helmet and all, would barely have come up to the family crest embossed on its chest-plate. Between the augmetic plates and cables its flesh had the sickly, slablike cast of muscles grown in a vat and maintained by gene and hormone commands rather than exercise and use. Clone-grown skin and filigreed armour shone slick with ornamental perfume-oil, but as Calpurnia reluctantly drew closer she realised that underneath the spicy scent it had the same smell that almost all servitors had, the smell of a fresh-cleaned hospital corridor, antiseptic but somehow still faintly sickening. The vision slot in its extravagantly-worked gold visor was shadowed and there was no way to tell where it was looking.

Hallyan was watching her staring at it, again with that faintly smug expression. No more words passed between them: he spoke a short, stuttering phrase and the servitor pivoted and shuffled after him. Its feet were padded in soft synthetic wads, and the only sound as it fell in behind its master, blotting him from her sight, was a soft soughing sound like the brush of robes against a floor.

Calpurnia barely realised the effect the sight of the thing had had on her until she realised minutes later that her jaw ached from clenching.

Looks like mainly hitter not shooter, read her notes now. *Multiple combat adaptations, heavy duty augmetic claw, bladed dendrite bundles in carapace? Some shooting ability, probably masked/disabled for access to us to be allowed. Voice-only trigger odd – weakness – follow up.*

'Follow up,' she said aloud, dropped the slate onto the carpet and stood up with a groan. The rough knot of scar tissue that twisted the skin of her right hip was stiff and twinging, the way it always got when she was tired, or cold, or had sat still for too long. She worked her leg to loosen it as she paced to the chillplate by the door and poured water from the decanter sitting on it.

As she stood there she could feel the faint prickle at the back of her neck from the energy shields on the other side of the window. Having all Bosporian see an arbitor senioris driven into hiding would be disastrous, so armoured shutters had been out of the question, despite Armourer Thekir's pleas. In truth, she was still a little overwhelmed by having an energy curtain brought to her chambers – before Hydraphur she had seen a void shield exactly once, during a putsch on Don-Croix when elite enforcer squads had come out with the pick of their arsenal to seal the streets to the Capitol Mount. But she still wouldn't feel entirely comfortable turning her back on the window until the initiator of the attacks had been caught.

The initiator. She hated that. The initiator, the organiser, the mastermind. Clumsy to say and frustrating to think about, but Dvorov had been right. They weren't close to being able to put a name to the corpse lying in Sanja's shrine. She still hadn't been able to pick out anything she had done that might spark such an assault and Leandro, their expert in politics and diplomacy, couldn't map out any current power-plays that might benefit from her death. Not that the current state of hive society was easy to read, the time of year being what it was. In the pile of printout next to her were sheaves of report summaries from precinct houses all through the hive and the great city-sprawl that spread out from it to the coast, and fuller reports from the Augustaeum, the enclosed and luxurious city-within-a-city at the peak of Bosporian Hive. The picture they added up to had made her dizzy and despairing of carrying out any kind of orderly investigation. She picked up a handful at random, glancing occasionally at the maps she had draped over the far arm of the couch.

The precinct commander at the Vastener's Spur over in the Nobles Quarter reported a spat between two cartel families from the mill-hives on the far coast over accommodation precedence in the tower they had co-rented for their stay. The dispute had mainly been in the form of intricate snubs that none of the Arbites on-site pretended to understand, but the previous afternoon two young bloods had convinced themselves each had been offended by the other and insisted on holding a formal duel, arriving outside the precinct house with supporters from each family in tow and clamouring for a judge to give the whole thing legal sanction. When the Arbites had refused, both families had taken insult and now had the idea that they could appeal to have the precinct commander's authority revoked.

The family Rhyos-Kauteer had kicked off the social season with a betrothal ceremony of one of its sons to a popular daughter of a highly-thought-of naval dynasty. The young man had taken his new fiancée on a tour of their fyceline foundry at the base of the hive, and when someone impressionable had seen her uniform word had started that a navy press-gang sweep was about to come down. The resulting stampede out of the sector had triggered riots along two major arterial roads, and suppression squads of Arbites arriving to restore order had only reinforced the rumour. The local commanders were counting themselves lucky to have had the area under control within the day, and the hunt for the last of the rioters and looters in the maze of underground freightways and canals was only just gearing up.

There had even been a disturbance involving the Cathedral of the Emperor Ascendant itself. A granddaughter of the Rogue Trader Rannyer Kvan had apparently had a religious awakening and taken vows as a novice in the Order of the Sacred Rose. The first that Kvan had heard of it was when he arrived back in the system for the Mass after a four-year absence, and he had shown up at the Cathedral insisting that the girl was being held against her will and demanding that

the Sisters give his child back. Now Kvan kept trying to park
an air-sled over the Cathedral in defiance of airspace laws
and Canoness Theoctista was adamant that they would not,
as a matter of principle, let Kvan disrupt the girl's religious
duties with even a visit.

Those were just three that had been thought worth bringing to an arbitor senioris. There would be more mundane
plots and feuds, petty violence or sedition that the Judges at
each fortified precinct courthouse would handle themselves,
and the cases that would not even reach the courthouses, the
lowest of crimes: defacement of Imperial property, malin-
gering, drunkenness, public affray, killings or injuries among
the giant hab-stacks where Arbitrator patrols rarely ventured
and used the simplest summary street punishments when
they did. Conspirators here simply wouldn't stand out as
they would on prosperous, pious Ephaeda.

She was starting to understand how hard this was going to
be. In his treatise, Galimet had concentrated on the ecclesiastical proceedings and touched on their history: how the
people of Hydraphur had lived with years of shame at their
system's surrender to the Apostate Cardinal, how Chye Balronas, returning to his home system as Pontifex Mundi after
twenty years on Earth, had instituted an annual vigil of fasting and penitence to bring the whole system together in
atonement and spiritual cleansing, and how the Vigil culmi-
nated in a mass on the eve of the great festivities of the
Sanguinala, when the citizens cast off their long fast and
ended their penance in joyful celebration of the Lord Angel.

Galimet had recorded in his treatise that it was the custom
for the greatest and wealthiest of Hydraphur to assemble for
the Mass at the capital hive's great cathedral, and she remembered thinking that this was only as it should be and moving
on. As an arbitor, she decided, she should have known
enough to deduce what that would actually mean. The
month before the Mass saw the place packed with dignitaries: every branch of the Adeptus, Rogue Traders and
powerful merchants, officers from the powerful naval dynasties with their spaceborne estates and fief-fleets.

And so naturally, the religious gathering had found other
purposes. She had already had an instructive example of

how the month leading up to the mass had become a frenzy
– a courtly, mannered and impeccably-choreographed
frenzy, a frenzy cloaked in so many layers of protocol it was
impenetrable even to half of the natives, but frenzy nonetheless as the system's elite packed a year's worth of high-octane
intrigues into three or four weeks. Families controlling
wealth equivalent to a whole planet's production would hag-
gle and trade favours for the tiniest change in positions at
one of the Kathisma's banquets; the right turn of conversation on a morning's stroll might mean an alliance that could
make or destroy lives. At the other end of the scale there was
the sort of half-spontaneous drunken free-for-all that she
had found herself caught up in the previous day. Someone
who might want to take advantage of all the confusion to
murder an arbitor? Calpurnia gulped water and sighed
again. Who knew how many strangers were out there, or
what they were thinking or hiding? Guilliman's blood, how
would you narrow it down to even a thousand?

She prowled to the window again, ignored the buzzing that
the power field made at the base of her skull as she looked
out. Her chambers faced away from the Cathedral and out
over the slope of the hive as it dropped to the great flat city-
plain. She was not new to the great artificial hives that
Imperial worlds sprouted when their cities grew too big and
concentrated for a simple conurbation to contain. There were
no hives on Ultramar, but two had grown up around the
orbital freight-launcher silos on Hazhim, and Don-Croix's
position astride three well-travelled warp currents had given
it a population that had cultivated a respectable twelve hives,
jutting up from its ravine-cut surface like tumours.

Bosporian was a modest little affair against the mind-
numbing scale of hives on Necromunda or Vanaheim. In fact,
technically, it was barely a hive at all, more a place where the
sprawl that had paved over the entire alluvial plain below
had reached a spur of the mountain range edging it and
crawled up its slopes. Bosporian was on bedrock, not artificial, hollow and packed with people as a true hive was. But
the view was still impressive enough – a great jungle of spires
and towers curved away down the mountain-slope and out
into the murkier, more humble city below.

Dropping away directly below Calpurnia's window was the Wall, tall and wide and with enough room in its towers and bastions to house a city and hold off an army on its own. It joined the Augustaeum wall at the towering Justice Gate, swelled into the imposing fortifications that housed the commanders' homes and chambers and the supreme courthouses, then ran down into the thirty-floor-high ridge of rockcrete and adamantium, sprouting towers that were entire precinct fortresses unto themselves, running all the way down to the foot of the hive to one last monolithic keep and gate.

The Wall held trial chambers, interrogation rooms, execution and penance cells, armouries, barracks, training halls, chapels, transmitter towers, generatoria, hangars full of Rhino APCs and Repressor riot-tanks, libraries of paper books and data-arks so vast that searching for a single old record might be a life's work. Around each gate glimmered the camp-lights where supplicants waited weeks or months or years, however long it took for the wheels of the Adeptus Arbites to grind out a judgement or pass on word of the fate of a loved one held in their walls. Breaking up queue wars was a regular feature of gate duties in any precinct house of this size. Calpurnia had even known Arbites who had been born and lived the first few years of their lives outside the gates of the courthouses they grew up to serve in. In most garrisons they were considered good luck to have on a squad.

Just learning her way around the Justice Gate and the upper towers would take Calpurnia a month or more. But learn it she would, she thought, some of her gloom lifting. She had been through this before. However alien Hydraphur felt now, soon place-names would take on meaning. People would stop being faces she passed and names she had to be reminded of. She would start to know who was meticulous and who was slapdash, who could take a broad perspective and who would get lost in details. She would know who backslid in upholding the sacred *Lex Imperia*, and at the other extreme who hid their own deficient judgement behind paralysing dependence on the letter of scripture. She would know the ones who were devout and truly understood the doctrines they practised, and the ones for whom 'for the Emperor' was nothing more than an empty phrase to shout before they swung a power-maul down on some random innocent's skull. She had worked with all those kinds and more and she had done well. The Provost's Wreath and three commendation seals hung on the wall behind her to prove it. She would do well here too.

She turned around and leaned against her chamber wall, rubbed the scars on her forehead as she looked around. The Master of Households and his stewards had thought the plainness of her quarters inappropriate for one of her station, but she had wanted at least something about her surroundings to be familiar and chosen small, spare rooms instead of the richly-appointed fortified tower that her predecessor had lived in. Three rooms, her bed, her books, a small shrine to the Emperor and an icon to Guilliman, a bust of Judge Traggat in a niche over the writing-desk, a clothes-chest and a small personal armoury. The walls were unadorned dark stone, and she relished the coolness and solidity of it through her tunic as she leaned against it – it reminded her of her room in the Ephaeda court barracks.

She had scandalised people there, too, by keeping that little room even after she had been given the garrison command. She had often held command meetings there, sitting on the bed or crosslegged on the stone floor, trying to drive home a lesson by example: their duty was to the Emperor's law and the Emperor's peace, not the worship of their own importance for its own sake. Although, she noted now with a rueful smile, there she hadn't been in the habit of leaving piles of slates and printouts scattered across half the floor. For a moment she thought about leaving that for the stewards too, and then gave herself a mental kick for her laziness. It took another half hour to get them gathered up and filed in order in the racks on her desk, and by that time her eyes were aching with tiredness and the old wound on her hip was throbbing again. Her single short prayer at the shrine was for rest and calm – she already had an idea that tomorrow was going to be exhausting.

Eighth Day of Septista

Ten days to the Mass of Saint Balronas.
The Second Congregation of Intercessors.
Vigil of the Icons Illuminate. First hearing of the
Assembly Encarmine (Navy).

THIS DAY MIRRORS the previous one, for it is traditional, after prayers and petitions to the Ministorum are completed, to devote this day to pleading favour with peers and fellows. On this day masters, friends and the officers in the Monocrat's service and that of the blessed Adeptus are expected to look kindly on pleas for favour or intercession in return for prayers and gratitude. Those seeking such favour will usually signal this by blowing a small brass horn at the gate or door of the one from whom they wish it, but to arrange audience in advance is also acceptable. However, no part of the proceedings of the Minor Intercessors must be allowed to interfere with any penance or devotions instructed by the officers of the Adeptus Ministorum the previous day. Those assigned particular duties of worship will be undertaking them at Ecclesiarchal temples and pulpits and it is appropriate for passersby to stop and pray aloud for them.

During this day portraits, icons and statues for the Procession of Further Saints are carried from the Artisans Quarter and arrayed for viewing along the road beneath the south-west face of the Cathedral. When considering whether to travel to see them it should be remembered that the Further Saints are those who spent their lives not only outside Hydraphur but beyond the Segmentum Pacificus, and that this is an opportunity to pay respect and devotion to hallowed servants of the Emperor that may not present themselves at other times. On the road itself anyone holding a certain personage as their patron is free to tend that likeness, keeping lanterns and candles lit through the night, praying and reading aloud the relevant scriptures. It is also customary and appropriate to hand out prayer cards and tracts; the practice of handing out confectionery, sweetmeats and baubles and not to be encouraged.

On this day dignitaries of all the Navy squadrons currently at dock in the system assemble at the space-station known as the Boucoleon Gate to conduct a ceremonial settling of debts, traditionally with the conferring and exchange of honours and the fighting of ceremonial duels. Dealings with Naval officers on Hydraphur itself on this day should be conducted with tact and an awareness of any special circumstances that these ceremonies might create.

Those selected to perform devotions at the Sainted Way the following day should fast from the fifteenth hour, and perform the Maklopin's Second Prayer before leaving their home to travel to the Sepulchre.

CHAPTER THREE

'I JUST WANT you to run me through this walking thing again,' Calpurnia said.

The Augustaeum, nestled within its walls at the peak of the Bosporian Hive, was not flat – its sides kept sloping up to the High Mesé, the avenue that ran along the hive's very peak. The formation of Arbites making their way through the steep, tangled streets of the Artisans Quarter were already high enough up to be able to look over the Augustaeum wall and down at the upper floors of the towers on the lower slopes of the hive. Above them on the left the Cathedral of the Emperor Ascendant speared the coppery Hydraphur sky. Its spire was twenty minutes' walk away and already Calpurnia had to crane her head up to look at it; they were getting close enough for her to be able to see the great statues of the Imperial saints that formed the columns for its upper tiers. Each statue was fifty metres high and carved from pure white marble that shone like gold in the thick butter-yellow Hydraphur sunlight.

Calpurnia and Leandro moved through the narrow byways between the flat-roofed workshop blocks, clustered between

the gracious Adeptus Quarter behind them and the pilgrims'
barracks ahead. Men and women bustled around them in
sober grey and brown garb, many with the aquamarine trim
of guild-sponsored artisans, nearly all sporting polished
brass augmetics for their chosen trade over eyes or hands.
Calpurnia had been looking about for any trace of the religious tokens that were supposed to be set out throughout
the quarter but the pilgrims had apparently taken the last of
them, leaving only the occasional empty shelf or trestle in
the street or against a workshop front. The tinny blare of a
ceremonial horn made her jump.

'A custom among the aristocracy,' Leandro told her, saun-
tering along with his crested judicial helm under one arm
and the staff in his other hand swinging and rapping against
the cobbles. 'The evolution of a lot of the elites' etiquette
and social codes has been documented by Dervick and
Ponn, three volumes between them which, despite their last
revision being over fifteen years ago, have not dated signifi-
cantly. It seems the custom evolves from a period when...'
He caught Calpurnia's look. 'Ah, well then. To summarise.
Less than crucial business on Hydraphur is often conducted
strolling through the hall, or gardens, or wheresoever, and
subtle changes in direction and pace send certain messages.
Moving toward an exit shows the matter is unimportant, the
caller inferior. Moving toward seats shows the matter is difficult and intricate, or possibly an advance of friendship, it
depends on the context and certain other actions. Pausing
before or moving towards a work of art means that a trusted
working relationship – not necessarily friendship, you
understand – is assumed by the speaking party, although
again that can draw all kinds of nuances from the kind of
decoration, what is being said, and touches of intonation
and body language, all of which make up another layer by
which the signals from movement can be reinterpreted.'

'I'm "less than crucial business", am I?' The words had
come out sharper than Calpurnia had intended them to.

'Not for a moment, arbitor, you know that. But think like
a Hydraphur noble. You rush to talk with Arbites who have
just been targeted by assassins, at a sensitive time of great
importance to your future. How will they soothe the fears

crowding your heated imagination if, for all their airy words that the matter is being attended to, they sit you at a conference table as though discussing a matter of gravest import? As well, try to convince your good self, my arbitor, that an action alarm in the Wall is of no real consequence even while you watch Arbitrator squads in full combat gear arming and singing a battle-psalm. The arbitor majore simply underlined his assurances.'

'I take it local etiquette is something I'm going to take a while in picking up,' said Calpurnia. Leandro's answering smile had a hint of pity in it.

'My arbitor senioris, "a while" is exactly what it will take you. I spent nearly all of my serving life on Hydraphur, and you will have noticed that the lord marshal tends to bring me to the fore when a situation calls for diplomacy rather than force. And nonetheless I know that I am considered comically flawed and flatfooted on matters of etiquette and manners. I assure you that I have to use the force of my rank to compensate for my social clumsiness in more circumstances than you might credit.'

'My own feelings, Arbitor Leandro, are that the force of our Emperor-given rank is all we should ever need and all the reason to respect us that these people should require. I'm not some thug who looks on cracking bones as her first recourse. I do, though, wonder at the effort we seem to expend courting the favour of people whose deference should be a matter of law. But,' she held up a hand as Leandro started to speak, 'we've already had that conversation. Let's drop it.'

It had been Calpurnia's idea to travel on foot, for the same reason she had refused to have the window to her chambers sealed: to show that this new arbitor would not be chased into a bunker. But now she found herself trying to scan every angle of the crowd at once, looking for a movement that seemed out of place or the glint of weapons, trying to maintain a befitting dignity all the while. She had allowed Leandro to talk her into bringing a small escort – a file of five Arbitrators on each side and a proctor marching before them parting the crowds – but she was still tense.

The streets met at intersections that were almost ledges cut in and then built out from the face of the slope: this was one

of the steepest faces of the hive, and the traffic around them
was made up of pedestrians or little tracked pack-gurneys that
clattered along cleated rails in the middle of each road. They
stopped at an intersection and took stock: an Arbites checkpoint occupied the central rockcrete island, where a belt-fed
heavy stubber nosed the air and cyber-mastiff handlers
flanked it, ready to move under the stubber's support. Knots
of Arbitrators stood at each road surveying the traffic and
stopping random travellers for papers and questioning. The
setup was repeated at every junction they had passed since
leaving the Justice Gate, and on every thoroughfare and public space across the hive, and Calpurnia was pleased with
what she had seen so far. Arbitor Nakayama's lockdown had
been quick and expert. The duty squads saluted the two
seniores and went rather self-consciously back to their work
as Calpurnia and Leandro moved on.

'This might be an easier subject of conversation,' Calpurnia said eventually. 'Why is it so important for Lord
Hallyan's family that there not be any disturbances during
this mass? I won't pretend to have had time to read every
one of my dossiers thoroughly, but I couldn't find anything
in the man's history that explained why he's suddenly turned
up in association with it this year. Not that a concern for
proper order is not fitting in a subject of the Emperor,' she
added conscientiously.

'Ah, you must build the bridge from both sides of the river,
as they say in Constanta,' said Leandro with a smile. 'The key
to that is in the organisation of the mass itself rather than a
characteristic of the man. You shall need to broaden your
studies a little, I think. Were you provided with a briefing
slate on the mass itself? I'm sure we've discussed it in the
broad outline.'

'Let us just assume, Arbitor Leandro, that perhaps I still
have some gaps in my reading owing to recent attempts on
my life,' said Calpurnia, nettled. 'What would I be looking for
in my file on the mass should I have time to study it tonight?'

'The mass, then.' replied Leandro cheerfully, not ruffled in
the slightest. 'It was instituted by Saint Chye Balronas twelve
years after Hydraphur was reclaimed from the Plague of
Unbelief. It… ah, you know this part? Excellent. Well, as part

of its role in reuniting the system in faith to the Emperor, the Sainted Pontifex decreed that it would not belong to any one part of Hydraphur society. It was important that people not dismiss it as simply another piece of high-flown pageantry in a place few of them would ever visit. So he decreed that the Vigil would not be the sole property of the Ecclesiarchy, and that not a single part of Hydraphur's society would be without a share in it. While the Adeptus Ministorum will always officiate at the mass and all the formal rites, the Vigil itself and many of the Sanguinala festivities will be planned and overseen by the designated Master of the Vigil, who is outside the Ecclesiarchy completely. The orders of precedence by which the office is conferred from year to year is a matter of what I would understate to call some complexity, although we have a small office dedicated to tracking and monitoring it and reporting to myself – it is unusual but not unknown for criminal techniques to be used to attempt to push the revered Ministorum's choice in one direction or another.'

There was an abrupt burst of shouting at the top of the street they were walking up, and Calpurnia stiffened and put a hand on her pistol. A pair of heavyset greybeards with glossy aqua-dyed sashes were arguing with the Arbitrators, apparently over the street being blocked off while she and Leandro came up it. The Arbitrators around them shifted into a wedge formation, the better to keep the two commanders protected, but then one man at the top of the street took his arguments a step too far and the Arbites were onto him. Two of them bent his knees with deft taps of their mauls and slammed him to the ground, and two more kicked over the platform and began breaking the packages open. Calpurnia and Leandro paused where they were and Leandro continued talking.

'The designated Master of the Vigil has some latitude in the festivities, the chance to place their own stamp on them in certain ways. Accordingly, no two years' festivities are quite the same, since it's a point of some disgrace to present a bad one or one too like another year's. It's also the high point of the Hydraphur's year after Candlemas, so you can understand why competition for the honour is rather heated.'

'I'm starting to understand why Lord Medell is anxious that nothing goes wrong,' said Calpurnia. 'So, the Medell are presiding over the Vigil this year...'

'*Kalfus*-Medell. Kalfus is the family, Medell is the syndicate affiliation.'

'Kalfus-Medell, alright. Hallyan's dossier said he was in something of an awkward position in the family: late child, caught between generations with no natural peer base. Being appointed Master of the Vigil must be an enormous coup for him.'

'And for his family, not that they need it. Kalfus-Medell is one of the most powerful family syndicate combines in the system.'

They began walking again. Calpurnia felt vaguely uneasy as their escorts ranged ahead: she had not had the time to speak with any of them, and she was used to knowing the names of her squads. Up in the square the two men had already been locked into heavy strait-capes that covered their heads and pinned their arms to their waists, and were being dragged away. Four other arrestees, two men and two women, had been cuffed into a line and, silent and quaking, followed at shotgun point – they wore tunics and caps of a similar cut but without the sashes, and Calpurnia realised they must have been servants or retainers of the shouting pair.

She turned an eye to the baggage strewn across the cobbles. The bundles had been kicked open, and a young Arbitrator was marking them with green paint to show a poison-snooper had cleared them. Most of the plastic sacks had held glistening grey-brown lumps that reminded Calpurnia of melting candy-eggs. One or two held bright metal shavings or what looked like mineral salts. She swung around on the Arbitrator who had moved up behind her.

'Summarise the problem, please.'

'Those two men are from a fabricators' collective quartered down against the Augustaeum wall. I'm not sure of their exact line of work, but I think they were hurrying to–'

'Summarise the *problem*, please,' Calpurnia repeated. The man swallowed. She wondered if he'd addressed an arbitor senioris before, let alone two of them standing shoulder to shoulder.

'Yes, ma'am. These men protested our closure of the street and demanded passage. They would not stand away when ordered or move their possessions. Er, their baggage. Ma'am.'

'You saw us coming up the street. You realise that any number of assassination devices could be loaded onto one of these gurneys and rolled down to us.'

'Yes, ma'am.'

'Nonetheless, you allowed it to be brought to the head of the street in control of its owners, where we would have to walk past it, instead of halting it or ordering it diverted elsewhere.' There was a pause.

'Yes, ma'am.'

'You are?'

'Lead Arbitor Madulla, ma'am. Green-Four Echelon, Holdark Precinct House.'

'Thank you, Lead Arbitor. Tighten and improve your efforts, please. You may continue.'

Flushing, Madulla supervised as the two prisoners were stowed on the Rhino, the rings on the backs of the straitcapes clipped to the hooks on the tank's chassis, their feet dangling off the ground. It was a way of transporting and displaying prisoners Calpurnia had not seen before coming to Hydraphur. The servants sat in a miserable knot at gunpoint a few metres away, and what little foot traffic was left in the intersection scurried and shied away from the Arbites. Calpurnia nodded approvingly. It was always useful to drive a lesson home.

'And am I guessing that if anything disrupts the Vigil while Hallyan is charged with presiding, he will be badly disgraced and that will ripple on to his family and his syndicate?' she asked as they began walking again. 'And do I further suppose that the assassination of a senior Arbites officer might be a good way to stir up trouble which popular opinion might hold against him, however illogically?'

'Well done, my arbitor senioris! You're starting to think like a local.' Calpurnia growled and smacked a gloved palm against her forehead.

'Agh, I hope not. These people are insane! They celebrate a Vigil dedicated to penance by drowning themselves in parties and politics, they treat a sacred mass like just another carnival-spectacle and they interpret your whole conversation by whether you take a few steps while you talk! I don't think I was ready for this place, Nestor.' She regretted the last part the moment it had passed her lips.

'Lord Marshal Dvorov thinks you are, my senioris,' Leandro told her as they began to climb the next street. 'And believe me, the lord marshal knows what he's doing.'

Calpurnia threw a last glance at the junction behind her and followed him.

TWO MORE INTERSECTIONS, then a final stretch where the street got steep enough to become stairs. They ascended past etched slabs of iron between friezes of famous and long-dead Hydraphur artisans on their left; on the right, a six-metre gap between them and the walls of the craft-houses, then their roofs, then just empty air. Calpurnia spent the climb thinking of the target she made up here and kicking herself for thinking that the bravado of coming out on foot was a good idea. Amateurish, she told herself, a rookie's mistake, a child's mistake. She took her mind off it by concentrating on Leandro's talk of the Artisans Quarter, which had its privileged place in the Augustaeum through the patronage of the Cathedral and the devotional materials and religious art it made, which was bought by connoisseurs and the devout throughout the subsector. The cargo that the luckless arrestees somewhere below them had been carrying were phyo shells, resinous cocoons of a coastal amphibian whose caustic juices produced a prized burnished effect when applied properly to soft metals. The shavings and salts had probably been to refine the colour and exact tone of the polish and reflection, Leandro had explained as Calpurnia, nodding grimly, put one foot in front of the other and tried to keep her eyes away from the drop on her right.

The stairs switched back and climbed through a tiered series of landings to a broad stretch of paving beneath a thick obelisk, then suddenly they were among people again and on blessedly flat ground. Their escorts spread out as they walked past the obelisk and onto the High Mesé.

This was the high crest of Bosporian Hive, the paved avenue that ran from the gates of the Monocrat's palace at the eastern end across to the Cathedral at the west. It jutted up from the jungle of buildings around it like an axe-edge – or like a chainblade, Calpurnia corrected herself, looking at the pairs of obelisks that marked off the space along its edges. Up here she could look out over the whole sweep of the capital: the towers and roofs of Bosporian, the carpet of industrial city that covered the plain, the mountains behind the Cathedral and the vast ochre sweep of the sky. Even in the daylight, she could look up and see that sky sparkling with the crisscrossing lights of the ships and the great Ring of Hydraphur.

No more earnestly purposeful artisans or pack-carriers here. Up on the high walk Hydraphur's elite promenaded in the early afternoon sun, striking elegant poses, chattering quietly behind copper-lace fans, bowing and flirting, or gazing out to the smog-smudged horizon. There were fewer people here, less hurry and more room between the little groups, but the richness of their clothes and movements still made them seem kaleidoscopic. The dour troop of Arbites marched through them like a black beetle among butterflies.

It didn't take Calpurnia long to start noticing patterns. A common style of skirt and shawl here, a gesture repeated there. She noted and filed away a certain kind of deeper bow that seemed to go with greeting someone dressed in a certain cut of coat, and a particular pattern of jewellery that seemed unique to people accompanying the Navy officers in their elaborate green dress uniforms. (Those at least she had expected to draw comfort from, knowing Navy traditions from senior members of her own family, but Battlefleet Pacificus dress used far more lavish and complex insignia than Battlefleet Ultima and medals she didn't even recognise.) Some were more extravagant: she saw skins that had been inlaid with gems or shimmering electoos, and twice their paths were crossed by packs of young bloods who strutted on shoes soled in stilt-like curls of metal that gave them a springy, prancing, jaunty gait.

She could spot particular rituals in the way certain groups greeted others, or ignored them, or changed their positions to keep certain relative distances. She was sure it was all part of some eye-watering social clockwork which she decided she had no interest at all in learning – until she noticed the subtle little dance seemed to extend to the Arbites too. Every so often one of the strolling groups would turn and salute them, or allow themselves to linger in the way so they could make a show of bustling to make way. After the fourth such encounter, as a group of middle-aged men in particoloured cloaks made into swirling wings by implanted memory-wires extravagantly waved them past, Leandro confirmed her suspicion.

'Word, it seems, has spread outwards and upwards about you, my Arbitor Calpurnia.' Ahead of them, a young noble-man in a green bodyglove and white fur cape waved his entourage – three shrouded servitors and a maid carrying a blue candle in her cupped hands – to a halt and took a showy step out of their path.

'I was going to ask what you mean, but I have the unpleas-ant feeling that I already know.'

'Would it surprise you, my Calpurnia of Ultramar, to know that the blow you landed on a certain youthful scion – or is "scionette" a proper word? – has done something of a round in the more rarefied levels of the Bosporian Hive?' Calpurnia looked around her. Every pair of eyes she met seemed to have the same appraising look that Hallyan had given her the previous day. Or perhaps she was imagining it.

'Not particularly, I suppose. I'm mildly surprised at such consternation for such a whatever-you-called-her.'

'"Shallow, disposable flibbertigibbet", I believe my words were, for the benefit of any eavescopes that might be trained on us,' said Leandro, and Calpurnia stifled a smile. 'They're a contrary breed, my arbitor, ready to invest a sincerely stag-gering quantity of energy in undoing each other in the most unscrupulous of ways, but still ready to form a seamless front if they feel one of their own has been slighted.' He con-sidered for a moment. 'In point of fact, I may exaggerate. There is every possibility that the reaction to you is simple wariness. You are a senior officer of the Adeptus, arrived to a position of power and authority here. You agreed yesterday that you have been here barely any time and had no contact with Hydraphur society at all. Thus, many here will be set-ting eyes for the first time on an unknown and potentially important new player. They may simply wish to see what you're about.'

Calpurnia grimaced.

'A player. That's what I am to them, am I? She tapped the medal ribbons on her chest and the helmet over her scarred forehead. 'I got these at play, I suppose?'

'Their point of view, nothing more.' Leandro was as unfazed as before. 'Well?' he said then, pointing forward and upward with his staff, 'what do you think?'

They had arrived.

Before them was the great ramp to the Cathedral doors. It was the same grey stone as the paving they stood on, but carved into polished frescoes of the deeds of Ecclesiarchal heroes: Uriah Jacobus crushing the genestealers on Solstice, Master Reynard leading the Travian Fire-raising, others that Calpurnia didn't recognise. The carvings looked too precious to walk on and gave Calpurnia a moment or two of hesitation, but their proctor was leading the way up the ramp with barely a break and so she mentally shrugged and followed him, trying not to tread any saints underfoot. Slippery-polished as it looked, the footing was not hard. She peered up at the sheer face of the Cathedral front as it shot up into the clouds, and regretted it: the wall here began at the ramp and rose straight to the very peak of the spire, and looking up at all that carved stone looming over her gave Calpurnia a sort of inverted vertigo.

The arched Cathedral doors tapered to a point fifteen metres high rather than following the smoother curves that Ultramar builders favoured. Calpurnia supposed that there were blast-shutters and defence gates – the Adeptus Ministorum was a warrior church and its sacred buildings were supposed to be military strongpoints – but they seemed to be retracted and sealed and they stood before an open arch.

The Arbitrators around them stood to attention, and the proctor rapped his staff on the stone three times.

'The Honourable Nestor Leandro, Praetor and Arbitor Senioris of the High Precinct of Hydraphur, and the Honourable Shira Calpurnia, Arbitrator and Arbitor Senioris of the High Precinct of Hydraphur.'

He was speaking to the armoured forms that stood in a line to block off the arch. These were warriors of the Cathedral's guard, Adepta Sororitas, battle sisters of the Order of the Sacred Rose, stern and proud in sleek white power-armour and black surcoats, gold-embroidered with the fleur-de-lys of the Ecclesiarchy. Their bolters were trained on the Arbites, as unwavering as their gaze, until a hooded sister superior stepped through the line of her squad and gestured for them to put up their weapons. They came to attention with a crash that echoed through the Cathedral's outer vestibule and parted, ceramite boots stamping on the stone as they wheeled and came to attention again. The sister superior clasped the golden aquila at her throat and bowed, gestured behind her to the junior deacon who had appeared at the great doors, and stepped aside into formation with her sisters. Calpurnia and Leandro walked past the Sisters and into the Cathedral, the proctor and the other Arbitrators fell back to the door. Not a word had passed after the first introduction.

The deacon was young and stocky and ill at ease, rubbing his fingers nervously over his tonsure. He led them through long passages of carving-filled niches and past long lamp-lit walls engraved with the names of Imperial martyrs; another thing Calpurnia was noticing about Hydraphur was the layers of antechambers that official buildings liked to put between their entrances and their cores. The colours around the antechamber changed from the yellow-brown daylight outside to stone walls, forests of ornate pillars and cool grey dimness, statues watching them solemnly from plinths and high galleries. Somewhere deeper inside the building a choir practised phrases and notes, distant fragments of plainsong laying a soft texture to the air. Calpurnia realised she was trying to walk on the balls of her feet, to quiet the noise from her boots.

AFTER THE SUCCESSION of vestibules and anterooms Calpurnia only had a brief glimpse of the great, soaring spaces of the Cathedral proper, a moment for it to snatch her breath away before their nameless guide steered them down a long narrow hall walled in dark tapestries, parked them under a stained-glass mural of Saint Sabbat and bade them wait. Leandro sat on a wooden pew and admired the mural; Calpurnia paced up and down.

'All part of the learning experience, I'm sure,' she said after a while. 'I'm getting a valuable crash course in the front halls and audience rooms of Adeptus buildings all over the hive. I wonder if I'll get shot at coming out of this one?'

'Your first couple of weeks in office were always going to be like this, my arbitor. Such a hub of the Adeptus is not the sort of world where a handful of Arbites can do their job walled up in a precinct fortress that they only ever leave to break a riot. Wait until you get started on introductions to the Navy authorities. There are a great many more of them – Hydraphur is effectively their system, after all. If it eases your mind to any degree, assure yourself that the work we do with Curate Jenner today will most certainly be of value to the investigation of your own assassin.'

'He wasn't my assassin.'

Leandro waved the tart remark away and went on. 'There is, what, a week until the beginning of the Vigil of Balronas? Less, in fact. A matter of days before they ring in the Vigil and all of Hydraphur is bound by the restrictions of the Vigil itself. The goodwill of the Ecclesiarchy will be essential then if we are to continue our hunting, Arbitor Calpurnia. Their edicts regulate even other Adeptus, and their dispensation will allow us a freedom of operation that your conspirators, whoever they may be, might be expected to lack.

'And in any event,' he finished, getting to his feet as they heard footsteps on the other side of the door, 'Clah Jenner is a man whose acquaintance will benefit you. For all that he may strike you as untrustworthily young, his skills as a tutor are admirable. I feel called upon to comment, however,' he added as an afterthought, straightening his cloak, 'that imposing a wait such as this upon guests of what I may immodestly refer to as our calibre is uncharacteristic of him. It lacks diplomacy.'

Every time the subject of her 'tutoring' came up Calpurnia had to stamp down the usual flare of reaction: a first jerk of resentment, then thoughts of how complex the Hydraphur's religious customs actually were. Anything that helped stave off the feeling of being a child traipsing about behind a didactic grandparent was probably worth it, she decided.

Ecclesiarchal Curate Clah Jenner was a slight man, not much more than Calpurnia's height and looking a little weighed down by the heavy brocaded clerical gown he wore. He had little of the youth Leandro had described, nor the softness she had expected: his face was harshly angular, leathery and grizzle-skinned. His hair was tonsured as severely as the deacon's had been, but a thin iron-grey braid ran from each temple back past his ears. As he bowed, Calpurnia saw the braids were elaborately knotted at the back of his head.

'You are not Clah Jenner.' It was a sign of Leandro's surprise that he was stripped of his usual flowery speech. The man bowed again.

'You ARE CORRECT, Arbitor Senioris Leandro. And you will be Arbitor Senioris Calpurnia. Or is it Provost Marshal Calpurnia? Or Arbitor General? I'm told any of those can apply. Your most respected order has a particularly intricate system of ranking.'

'Any of those titles apply, but the High Gothic seems most common at Hydraphur,' Calpurnia told him, saluting. Leandro was still regarding their interlocutor in mild dismay.

'Arbitor Senioris it is, then. Good. And I am Mihon Baragry, Nuncio to the Eparch Hydraphur and Vicar General of the Hydraphur Curia. Come through, please.'

They stepped into a room so small and high-ceilinged it was almost an oubliette, the walls gnarled in scriptural carvings and a great steel sculpture of a warrior-angel leaning out from the wall to hold a chandelier over three small hassocks. Calpurnia didn't doubt that Ecclesiarchal servants would be concealed somewhere and listening in.

'I realise your meeting was to be with Curate Jenner,' Baragry said as he took a seat and motioned the Arbites to do the same, 'but certain circumstances to do with the approaching mass have meant that the curate will be unable to assist you. So I will open by presenting our apologies for such a precipitate change of plans.'

'Precipitate changes of plans do seem to be the order of the moment, Revered Baragry.' Calpurnia could feel herself relaxing. It was refreshing to deal with someone halfway direct. 'I'll apologise for one of my own. I'm aware that arrangements were made before I arrived in the system for detailed tutoring that extended beyond just the specifics of this mass. Jenner was going to go into the broader etiquette surrounding the smaller feasts and ceremonies that the Adeptus were involved in, some kind of vocal coaching, that kind of thing.'

'I haven't had the time to fully check the curate's notes, but that sounds right. The voice coaching would have been for the devotions of the mass. There are differences of melody and intonation required by the pentatonic scale, which we use here, whereas I understand that the galactic South prefers the full octave. It will probably take a few lessons for you to get comfortable with what you'll be required to sing. I might try and arrange a session with one of the choirmasters.'

'Your reverence, my point was that there will be little to no chance of that tutoring going as planned. If you haven't heard about the attempt on my life two days ago I can supply the details, but the lessons here are going to have to go by the board for as long as the investigation lasts. I'll try to make time for a session on the actual mass if I can but that may well be all.'

'We had indeed heard,' said Baragry, 'and your point brings us to mine. You are not the only one who wants to see whoever ran that attack dragged out into the daylight. I speak for the Eparch when I say that the use of a witch-psyker – hah, even the presence of a witch-psyker – practically in the shadow of the Cathedral spire, in the capital hive of a world such as Hydraphur, strikes at all of us. This is a time of great significance to the Ecclesiarchy and our interest in stopping it from being polluted is as great as yours. Possibly, if I can say this without being indelicate, greater.' Baragry was leaning forward on the hassock, elbows on knees and sharp black eyes on Calpurnia's face. 'I want to make it clear that the Arbites will have the full weight of the Adeptus Ministorum behind them in whatever measures they – well, you – take on the matter. Legal, diplomatic, force of arms, anything you require. Canoness Theoctista has stepped up the Cathedral

Guard and the Eparch has conferred with his witch hunters. Your work in keeping order within the hive has been excellent; now I think it is time to pick up the trail.' Calpurnia and Leandro exchanged a look.

'This has been an excellent meeting, then,' said Leandro, 'not the meeting we perhaps came here anticipating, but still. Your emphasis on the need for liaison between Imperial Law and Imperial Faith is well-placed, and I believe that such a relationship will move our investigation on at a most desirable pace. Might I inquire, Revered Baragry, if you are the one with whom we shall be maintaining contact to that end? My understanding is that Curate Kaleff of the Eparch's personal officio is–'

'I will be the one working with you.' Baragry held out a small plas-wax disc with the mark of a signet ring in its centre. 'My seal. Familiarise your staff with it. Your gate-guard will need to know that I will be calling on you tomorrow afternoon with a formal letter from the eparchal chambers and we can plan our next moves then. The Hydraphur Curia has delegated me as Ministorum representative and your personal aide on matters religious for the duration.'

'The graciousness of the curia humbles us, your reverence, and I am confident your delegation will be met with the utmost generosity of will by our admirable arbitor majore, to whom I shall present your name in due course.' Leandro and Baragry were looking steadily at one another. It was obvious sparring was going on at some level, so Calpurnia was a little surprised when after only a moment more Baragry suddenly stood and bowed to them.

'Then duty calls. We both have work to be about and will meet again soon. Go with faith in the Emperor and the blessing of the aquila.' Baragry walked with them as far as the chamber door where a deacon waited – not their earlier guide, but a sallow looking sub-vicar with an electoo on his scalp that projected holograms of religious maxims into the air over his head. 'The fifteenth hour tomorrow. You may expect me.' He singled Calpurnia out for a bow, and the door swung shut.

* * *

WALKING OUT OF the doors and down the ramp carried enough déjà vu to make Calpurnia shiver. The public symbolism of walking up to the front of the Cathedral had been all very well, but she told herself next time she would drive a Rhino. Leandro seemed to have thought on the same lines: he had instructed their proctor to call up three of the squat black tanks while they had been in the Cathedral and now led the way up the boarding ramp of the central one. The well-appointed interior told Calpurnia that this was probably Leandro's personal transport, and the shocked looks she noticed from the people who were hurrying out of their way told her too that armoured carriers were not common on the rarefied streets of the upper Bosporian. Well, that was fine.

'So,' said Leandro, 'what intelligence would you say we can glean from that little exchange of credentials?'

'We're going to have to work out how we're going to deal with active interference from the Ecclesiarchy. He as good as told us that they were powerful enough to do that, and I didn't like that reference to their own witch-hunters at all. And Baragry's no pious catechism tutor and singing coach, although he seemed to have done some homework to appear as one. Not much of the cloister about him. He's a man of action, I think, a field agent.'

'Controlled, businesslike and unafraid to use his authority,' Leandro agreed. 'The idea that the Curia has assigned him to us with their minds solely on our own wellbeing is not one upon which I shall waste a great deal of time.'

'You're right. He's there to monitor us and make sure the Ecclesiarchy knows exactly how our work is going. Notice that mention about keeping order within the hive? Lord Hallyan went on about the same thing.' The Rhino tilted slightly as they began their S-shaped route through the Mercantile Quarter, toward the Kathisma Gate and then back beneath the Adeptus Quarter all the way to where hundred-metre stone eagles flanked the triumphal arch of the Aquila Gate, before they swung back around to the Justice Gate and their own fortress doors. Their visit to the Cathedral had taken longer than she had realised, short as the audience itself had been, and with the relatively slow pace of the drive the afternoon was already dying: the light on the other side

of the vision slits was deepening steadily into orange twilight.

'I suspect,' said Leandro at length, 'that this thought may
gall you, my arbitor, as it galls me. The thought being that
while the desire of the eparchal agents to take their own
heads in this matter is something to take up with the arbitor
majore, the initial fact of Baragry's presence on our investigation is perhaps beyond our ability to change, at least
straight away.'

'I'd been afraid of that.' The Rhino slowed, shifted and
sped up again, the driver cocking his head to pick up
some piece of chatter from the Arbites vox-band. 'I mean,
it doesn't surprise me. I wish they'd let us just get on with
it, but alright, this is in a different league with Kalfus-
Medell wanting to plant a staffer on us. If we can't get
them to pull Baragry out without a confrontation let's
leave him. It's insane to be picking fights with one
another when somewhere out there is someone who
raised and controlled an unsanctioned psyker and used
him to attack an Adeptus.'

'Raised?'

'Apparently, by Sanja's and Nakayama's report. The kinds
of augmetics he was using were delicate, top-notch stuff. The
kind that have to tune themselves to their user over years of
training. He was part of a stable, not some alley-trash wyrd
who earned a favour from an outlaw medicae.'

Their driver leaned over the vox-grille again, and Calpurnia twisted around.

'What's the issue?'

'Some kind of disturbance at the Aquila Gate, ma'am. I
don't think it's serious, there's been no alert call. We're just
coming up on it now. Lead Rhino reports traffic backups and
some kind of dispute at the checkpoint.'

Calpurnia was already strapping her helmet into place and
checking her pistol loads; Leandro watched her from his
seat, one silvery eyebrow raised.

'Arbitor Leandro. Care to conduct a snap inspection? I
wouldn't mind seeing the main Augustaeum Gate procedures up close.' She steadied herself as the APC ground to a
halt and the ramp releases clanked.

'I will await your report, my arbitor. One of us should be enough, I think.' Calpurnia shrugged and stepped off the ramp as it finished lowering itself.

The Aquila Gate stood at the head of the Telepine Way, the great traffic artery for the south-western slope of the Bosporian Hive. Its arch was so deep it was almost a tunnel, bright with sodium lamps the same colour as Hydraphur daylight. Layers of galleries and catwalks ran along each wall, crowded with pedestrians who jostled along shoulder to shoulder with worn carvings of parading Adeptus a thousand years dead. At ground level the road to Bosporian proper was combed into lanes, the outer ones thin and filled with bemos and mechshaws, the inner lanes holding giant freight-drays rumbling treads or wheels so fat they were almost cylinders. Arbites were everywhere, blocking every pedestrian walkway and inspecting papers, rummaging through the mechshaw baggage racks, swarming over the drays like ants on a housebrick or prowling in squads the space beyond the gate where queues of vehicles backed up. Drivers hung out of their windows and shouted, or waved paperwork or identity seals, engines revved, Arbitrator boots tramped. The din was stupefying.

Calpurnia had thought to slip in quietly, but her habits had not yet caught up with her rank. The escort that had walked with her up to the Cathedral that afternoon were suddenly around her again, the proctor with an amplifier horn from the Rhino's equipment rack: 'Adeptus Arbites! Make way for the Adeptus! Part for the Arbitor Calpurnia!' They moved through the crowd like an icebreaker driving through a polar crust. There goes the surprise inspection, she thought ruefully.

The roil around them made it impossible to pick out any kind of order, but it was the central line of drays that had seemed to stop moving and Calpurnia steered her formation through the crowd until she was standing by the proctor who was supervising the dray searches. He was pink and sweating – whether from the close air and exertion or from seeing her rank badges she wasn't certain.

'The drays,' he shouted, having to hunch to reach her ear, 'are hard to search. Their superstructures are built with too many internal spaces. Some of the drivers are indentured servants and don't have the access to let us in.'

Calpurnia was looking down the line of drays. The driver of the one they were standing next to was halfway up a little flight of stairs built into the side of the giant cab, working the hatch on a crawlway that led into the engine space while two Arbites watched. Two drays down a driver and crewman were going through a sheaf of papers with a brown-armoured Arbites comptroller. The one in between, though...

'Why are those two still in their cab?'

The proctor had only heard half the question, and had to lean in again to hear it again. His sweat was sharp beneath the smell of armour polish. In their cab the two crewmen watched Calpurnia intently as she pointed them out with her maul.

'Everyone in the line is down on the ground dealing with you and your squads. Why aren't they? They're next through.'

The proctor was already nodding, and Calpurnia stepped aside as he started gesturing to a knot of Arbitrators nearby to fetch the two men down. A bemo drove by in one of the outer lanes, and the squeal of its engine distracted her for a moment, but when she looked back the cab of the next dray was already empty.

Something twanged against her instincts. Too quick. Something wrong.

Reflexively she was running, her escort suddenly pushing to keep up. The drayman was vaulting off the bottom of the ladder and sprinting back through the gate. His companion was nowhere to be seen.

A shake of her maul was all it took – her squad had seen them too. They took off, yelling for troops at the gatemouth. The confusion in the gate redoubled.

Calpurnia had let herself fall a pace back, watching the way the squads deployed, checking for weak points in their advance. She allowed herself a glance up at the side of the dray, and so was the only one to see the very first explosion.

It was a small one, just a *crump* that bent out the metal side of the dray and flared dirty yellow flames out of the gaps between the panels, but it was enough to send her into a skidding pirouette, jabbing her maul frantically at Arbitrator and civilian alike.

'Down! Down and away! *Now!*'

The second explosion was bigger, rocking the whole dray on its suspension and sending out a wave of heat that had Calpurnia cringing away, but it was the third that did it. The sides of the dray shimmied then collapsed, falling majestically away, a scorched metal seed-case giving birth to a gorgeous fire-flower that roared up and filled the Aquila Gate with screams and yellow-white wash.

Ninth Day of Septista

Nine days to the Mass of Saint Balronas.
Pilgrims' Devotions. The Stations of the Sainted Way.
The Procession of the Further Saints.
The Master's Pageant.

ON THIS DAY *the pilgrims receive blessings from the chapels on the western slopes of the Augustaeum, and in certain cases will be received into the outer chambers of the Cathedral itself. This day is set aside for those fulfilling their sacred office of pilgrim, and for a resident of Hydraphur to intrude on these rituals is inappropriate, offensive and impious. Those without a specific religious duty in the hive should remain in homes or barracks where possible. The Eparch Lydre's* Considerations on the Journey of Devotion *or the first and fifth chapters of* Starfarer's Psalms *are appropriate readings for this day.*

Those favoured with the blessings of the Eparch will have the right to perform the Stations of the Sainted Way. The roads to the Sepulchre and the Way's entrance, and from the Cathedral gates and the Way's ending, will be guarded by the Ecclesiarchy and must be kept clear for the postulants and pilgrims. Remember that by Ecclesiarchal decree, the only sound audible on the Way should be the voices of the postulants as they read the verses inscribed into its surface, so speech and movement must be kept muffled and no engines run within one kilometre.

The trappings of the Further Saints will be taken from their places along the road no later than sunset, and carried in lantern-light procession up along the Chirosian Way to the Confessor's

Seat. They are accompanied by those who have been tending them during the night and it is appropriate for those who feel taken by pious sentiments to join the procession. Once the trappings are placed, the pageant commissioned by the Master of the Vigil will begin in the plaza – those unable to attend it in person should endeavour to see it retransmitted by pict-slate through local shrines and temples, and it is appropriate for the heads of households and workplaces to make arrangements for all those under their command to be able to view the pageant as it unfolds or as soon as possible afterwards.

CHAPTER FOUR

CALPURNIA AWOKE, TANGLED in the sheets from a short and restless sleep, blinking at the morning sunlight which shone in the privacy curtain drawn across the shielded window. She had slept less than five hours, the timepiece on her writing-desk told her, but she felt far more rested than that and in the best mood she had been in for days. Even the silence in her chambers was suddenly pleasant – for the first couple of days in her new quarters she had jolted awake, far too aware that the noise she was used to from living in a barrack-block was absent, fuzzily sure she had overslept.

She scrubbed a hand over her face and grimaced. Although she had let the Arbites medicae team irrigate her eyes after she had emerged from the inferno at the Aquila Gate her skin was still filth-smudged and her hair stank from the thick and oddly bitter-spicy smoke. There would be a lot for her to do this morning, so much to follow up on, their first new lead on whoever was launching these attacks. Two prisoners to catalogue and interrogate, and then the prosecutions would have to be started, and she would need to oversee them. The verispex forensic teams would almost certainly have findings to report to her since she had spoken to them last night, or at least they had better have after five hours. And she definitely owed the other three arbites generals a report, but first she had to bring herself up to speed on–

She stopped herself. If there had been urgent developments, she would have been woken. Consideration number one: an arbitor general did not step out to greet the duties of a new day filthy and stinking like a slum-cat.

Ten minutes later she stepped out of the ablutory cubicle in the rearmost chamber, gasping from the water-jet but feeling newborn. She did a double-take to find a fresh uniform laid out on the bed and a stack of message chits on the desk. The stewards must have come in as soon as they realised she was awake. Another thing to get used to, she thought, laying the chits out and reading them while she dressed.

> *ARBITOR CALPURNIA – Lord Marshal Dvorov is in receipt of your initial summary report and requests another such from you at such time as is practicable during the morning and as developments continue. In the interim I am authorised to confirm your Level Four delegation to continue with this matter. – Pavlos Calapek, Adjutant to the Lord Marshal*

She narrowed her eyes as she buckled her belt. Sleeping in while the others waited on her was exactly what she hadn't wanted to do, but a second reading reassured her. A Level Four delegation meant she could proceed in her own time.

> *Shira. Most admirable work last night, for 'last night' is what it shall be by the time you set eyes on this, I'm sure. As for myself, diplomatic concerns over the assassin's remains are coming to the fore again. The Ministorum feels it has our approval to attempt a demand upon the Mechanicus for the body. I shall smooth the troubled waters and hold off on a position until I have conferred with you. LEANDRO.*

His signature was as flowery as his speech. Calpurnia glowered at it. Politics, politics. The damned psyker-bastard was still making trouble for her even when he was more than two days dead.

Arbitor senioris, we have received a message from the epar-
chal chambers. The Reverend Baragry wishes to
communicate his pleasure at the news that you were
unharmed in the explosions during the night and his expec-
tation that your meeting this afternoon will not be affected.
Arbitor Intendant Raf Draeger, Clerk of the Watch, Justice
Gate.

Security had been raised another notch, then – it read as if
the messenger from the Cathedral had been heard at the
gates and then turned away.

Well, she was pleased that Baragry was pleased. She was
pleased about being unharmed herself. In the chaos after the
dray had exploded she had been busy dragging herself out of
the way of the sluice of burning fuel: after the initial flare it
had burned with a low, smoky flame rather than the white-
hot fireball she had been expecting, but that had been bad
enough. By the time she got clear the vehicles on either side
were splashed and burning, and by the time she had regained
her feet the flaming oil had been washing across the gate's
rockcrete floor in a shin-high carpet of thick yellow fire.

The barely-controlled bedlam at the gate was suddenly
without any control at all. Terrified pedestrians clogged the
catwalks overhead and sent one another screaming over the
railings into the flames. Drivers tried to bulldoze their way
through other vehicles, destroying any hope of orderly
escape. The Arbites had been caught as much by surprise as
the rest of them, but Calpurnia was proud of the gate teams.
With no orders from her, the hivespeople had been driven or
dragged through the outer doors by respirator-masked Arbitrators while the squads at the inner end of the gate had
instantly formed a double line of shields and tanks through
which not a single civilian, no matter how frenzied, had
escaped into the Augustaeum. If the explosion had been the
cover for some kind of mob invasion to defeat the tough-
ened checkpoints then it had failed.

She picked up her rank badges. Someone had polished
away the soot and street-grit of the previous night, and she
winced a little – that was something she should have done
herself, exhaustion or no. And she still didn't even know her
chamber-attendant's name.

For the Attention of the Arbitor Senioris Calpurnia. Respected arbitor, I now have five prisoners catalogued against your name and assigned to preliminary holding pens – initial cataloguing details are attached. Special measures for the incarceration of the two prisoners early this morning are now in place as dictated by yourself last night. All prisoners are now ready for your judgement or decree as to their handling and I await your instructions. Nomine Imperator. Tranio du Toit, Lead Chastener, Augustaeum Cadre.

She considered this as she clipped on her holster and weapon-harness. The two men that the message made special mention of were the draymen that had bailed out of their vehicle a few moments before it exploded. Her most vivid memory was of their backs: both powerful and hulk-shouldered, one with his scalp shaved and tattooed and the other with a skinny blond braid bouncing against his tan bondsman's shirt as he ducked and leapt through the crowds.

Her nostrils were clogged with smoke and an indefinable sweet scent; that and shoving her way through the mob had taken her unpleasantly back to the Mechanicus shrine. There had been no time to look back to see if any other Arbites were following her: she had already lost ground to them having to circle and dance around the edges of the spreading pool of fire and she was desperate not to lose either man in the crowd. She had tried yelling for the crowd to part, but the ones who could hear her over the racket were too frightened to pay attention and after a dozen steps she was using her maul on a low-medium charge to bash people aside as though she were beating her way through jungle growth.

Another message from Draeger, the time-stamp less than twenty minutes old.

Arbitor senioris, we have word from Lead Verispex Barck at the Aquila Gate. She confirms that the initial inspection of the Aquila Gate event is complete and waits upon your arrival. She has asked that I communicate the fact that others are in attendance. Nomine Imperator.

And clipped to it:

Arbitor Calpurnia, I understand that you will be wishing to attend the Aquila Gate in person this morning. I have taken the liberty of notifying Arbitor Bannon and having a small escort assembled at the Centre Dock. It should be ready to leave by the time of your arrival there. – Hrass. Steward.

So that was his name, or hers, or at least one of their names. Before the end of the day, she decided, she was going to meet them and speak with them. They deserved at least that.

Her pistol and maul were in a rack in front of the shrine. She touched each of them to the silver aquila with a murmured blessing, then bowed to the icon of Guilliman, tucked her helmet under her arm and was gone.

THE VEHICLE HANGAR in the Justice Gate reassured Calpurnia. Its bright arclights strung from the roof gantries and the barrage of noise, the shouts of squad leaders, the tramp of boots, the roar of engines and the squeak-grind of tank treads. Cranes rumbled and clattered on the rails that crisscrossed the ceiling high overhead, swinging crates of ammunition, canisters of fuel or chained-together bundles of whimpering prisoners through the high space. Before her was a fifty-metre-high adamantite slab that stood just inside the gate entrance itself, forcing incoming traffic to weave around it and blunting any rush assault.

Although the scale was greater, it was like most other gatehouses she had worked in, and as always the balance of opposites pleased her. Outside, facing into the Augustaeum, the silent dignity of the gate-pillars, the carved aquilae and inscriptions and the statues of great Arbites past, presenting the stern face of Imperial Law. Inside, the comforting clangour of the Law's servants at their work. She breathed the smell of engine-oil like perfume.

The long rockcrete spine of the Central Dock ran from the main entrance to the Wall barracks out through the middle of the space, splitting it into two half-kilometre hangar floors. Along each side dozens of Rhino and Repressor tanks were lined up like suckling piglets, anchored to the dirty grey walls by fuel lines and maintenance booms. From the walkway on top of the dock, Calpurnia could look down on their roofs as men, women and the occasional servitor scrambled in and out, stopping to peer upwards and salute her as she passed. Finally she saw Dvorov leaning on the rail of the overseers' turret at the end of the Dock, waving her over.

'And a good morning, Shira, pleased to see you none the worse for wear. I thought I'd probably catch you down here. Always leading from the front. Have you eaten yet?'

'Lord marshal. Uh, yes, thank you, I collected some bread and grain-cakes from a commissary I passed back past the, er…' She motioned over her shoulder to the doors that opened onto the Dock. 'My apologies for not appearing before you sooner with a report, sir. I–'

'Not a concern, but thank you for your apology anyway. I trust you to report to me as and when you need to. It'd be quite an indictment of your fitness to be an arbitor senioris if I couldn't.' Calpurnia couldn't quite help the disloyal thought that this hadn't stopped him from checking on copies of the messages that were coming to her, but then she dismissed it, nodded and walked across the turret platform to look down at the Rhinos waiting on the hangar floor. Lead Arbitor Bannon, standing in the top hatch of the lead one, tipped her a salute.

'Of course, now I'm going to go and contradict myself by giving you a direct instruction. Well, not an order as such, but I wanted to drive home to you personally a general matter of procedure I've ordered.'

'Tighter security,' she said.

'Correct. I think I understand the point you made going up on foot through the Artisans Quarter yesterday, and I see the sense behind it. But this new attack starts to make it look like the opening of a campaign, not a single attempted murder. So, no more of it. I won't pretend that you can do your job in a bunker wrapped in void-shields, but no more gadding off on foot with another arbitor general and only a foot squad for security.' He gestured down at the Rhinocade below them. 'Senior Arbites go with full escort and transport. What you have there is a minimum. Junior officers and patrols will be operating in strength. I'm formalising that directive this morning, but I wanted to make sure that you in particular knew it and understood it.'

'Because I'm an unknown quantity.'

'Not entirely unknown, but alright, that might be part of it. In addition, you were the target of the first attack and will be very visible in running the Arbites response. You're going to be a prime target, Shira.'

'I understand, lord marshal.' She saluted him carefully, and then when he seemed to have finished she turned and climbed down to the Rhino hatch.

AFTER A STILL night the smoke from the fire had been trapped between the Augustaeum wall and the steep upward slope of the land, and around the Aquila Gate the brown haze made the yellow sunlight even muddier, thick with that peculiar bittersweet stink. Just stepping out into the grimy air made Calpurnia edgy again.

'It's from inside the gate,' Bannon told her when he noticed her sniffing. 'The fuel that was coming out of that dray turned out to be scented lamp-oil, for some of the early festivities before the congregation.' Calpurnia nodded and tried to dredge the term out of her bruised memory. The Twilight Congregation, when the Cathedral bell rang in the beginning of the Vigil and lanterns were lit to mark the night.

The Aquila Gate was still blocked. Calpurnia was mildly surprised that there seemed to be no physical shutters for the gigantic tunnel-arch; instead the gate was cordoned at each end by a string of Rhinos parked in a semicircle out into the concourses, with chain-nets strung between them and watchful Arbitrators shoving back a constant flow of onlookers. On the other side of the gate the scene was being repeated on a larger scale – from there she could hear engines and klaxons.

'Why hasn't the traffic through this gate been routed away to the others?' she asked. 'Sounds like there's a hell of a congestion on the other side there.'

'I'm not aware of any reports on it.' Bannon said. 'We would have people doing that, certainly, but there may have been problems.'

'May have been?' The Arbitrators on the barricade were unshackling the chain-guard to let them through, and she took the moment's delay to stare over her shoulder at him.

'With your permission, ma'am, I'll head through and see. My initial thought is that there's no ready access to the other gates. The hive has not been allowed to extend around the south-west slopes of the mountain to the Pilgrims' Gate, and the Wall runs right the way down the slope of the hive, so a truck of any size would have to reverse down the Telepine Way and right around the bottom of the Wall, then join the queue up the next face. I'd guess that it's jammed up right the way down to the plain.'

'Would you care, then, to head over and see if your initial thought and your guess are correct, and if there is anything more I need to know?' Calpurnia had spotted a lanky middle-aged woman whose insignia marked her as the leader of the verispex team, and changed course toward her as the chastened Bannon hurried away.

The verispex was standing inside the shadow of the arch. A riot of paint-marks and winking marker-pegs stretched away through the wheels of the burned-out tractors and drays. Despite the commotion outside the gate, it still seemed tomb-like compared to the previous night. Calpurnia grimaced at the word as soon as she'd thought it, and wondered what the eventual death toll had been. Another thing to find out.

Barck was standing between two of the hulks with a tall man in a thick blue bodyglove, a servitor with vox-recorder wands jutting from its face swaying back and forth to capture the conversation. The man wore no Arbites insignia, and Calpurnia would have felt no compunction about interrupting in any case.

'Lead Verispex Barck. Thank you for your message.' The tall man had not stopped talking. His voice was quiet and throaty, and his back was still to her. Calpurnia gritted her teeth and was about to give the man a sharp rap with her maul when she saw Barck's expression, the face of someone yanked between two points of authority. She took a step around him to glare up into his face, and saw the scarlet rosette pinned below his double chin.

'...must be brought back to me before the trail is cold.' He held Barck's gaze for a moment until the woman had taken a step back. The pause before he turned to Calpurnia was just long enough to emphasise that he was the one deciding

it was time to talk to her. He had a high, bony forehead
and nose but soft jowls about his jaw and throat. The contrast with his lean body was strange. His brown hair was
cut military-short and his eyes were pale and cool.

'You are Arbitor Senioris Shira Calpurnia.' Telling them
their name and withholding yours. If there was an older,
more basic trick she couldn't recall it.

'Stefanos Zhow,' he added after a pause.

'Of the Imperial Inquisition.'

'Of, as you say, the Imperial Inquisition.'

The recorder servitor would have to be the inquisitor's
property – it was not made to any pattern Calpurnia had
seen before. The stumps of its arms ended in bundles of
shrouded data connectors and data-arks hung at its waist,
enough to make it a walking library. Behind it, she saw now,
stood another retainer, a chubby man in identical blue, his
shaved scalp a mass of augmetic wires and cables. A pin jutted up above each socket in his skull, each pin holding aloft
a scrap of parchment, giving him a bizarre paper halo.

Calpurnia took all this in, then turned back to Inquisitor
Zhow. 'Greetings and compliments, inquisitor. I trust that
the Adeptus Arbites have been helpful in providing you with
whatever you may need from us?'

'So far, yes. My staff and I are examining the site.' Zhow
made a brief gesture at his coverall, explaining his work-
man's attire. 'Meanwhile you will probably want to see to the
problems the backflow along the Telepine Way is causing.'

Calpurnia bristled.

'You can be assured that that has my attention, inquisitor,
but give me credit for being able to walk and chew at the
same time. I am investigating attempts to disrupt the Vigil
and Mass of Balronas, beginning with an attack on me and
continuing with the explosion last night.' From the corner of
her eye Calpurnia could see Barck anxiously lacing and
unlacing her fingers. Zhow's fat retainer seemed to be looking right through her. 'I am here to confer with my
colleagues about last night's attack. If you are doing the
same, then I believe we can be of help to one another.'

'Oh, I am fully aware of your situation, arbitor.' Zhow's
gaze had hardened. 'And I will be wanting to speak to you

directly about just that matter before too long – rest assured I would have done so already had this not come up.' He gestured to the hulks and smoke filling the gate. 'But by all means, confer. We will need to be somewhere more private for me to talk to you anyway.'

They parted, Calpurnia and Barck walking toward the wreck of the exploded dray, Zhow towards yet another blue-garbed assistant who was deep in conversation with two proctors. Calpurnia waited until they were out of earshot before she growled at Barck out of the corner of her mouth.

'It would have helped to know he was here. Did no one try to get a vox-link to my vehicle, or did he only just arrive?' That seemed unlikely: looking around for more dark blue garments she was able to count four more bustling about the hulks without turning her head. They looked like they had been there a while.

'Ma'am, I did notify you.'

'No, lead verispex, you didn't. And stop wringing your hands like that. Let's get this underway, please.'

The fumes were still noticeable, and they both slipped on filter-masks. The wrecked dray loomed over them, gutted by the explosion and slimy from anti-incendiary sprays. Barck hopped up onto a trestleboard that had been set up along its side and motioned for Calpurnia to join her; Calpurnia had to stand on tiptoe on the board to look through the rent in the dray's side that Barck was peering into.

'It was carrying a consignment of oil, but it's not just a bulk fluid tank. Look.' The dray's carrier was packed with metal drums, a gap in the stacks next to the hole they were looking through. 'The nearest barrels weren't obliterated, we just took them away. But the ones nearest the hole were pretty badly wrecked. From what we've been able to piece together the flames started outside the barrels. There was a spark of some kind within the hopper that got to a leak, going by the burn patterns we found. The actual oil itself burns quite cool and with a low flame.' Calpurnia nodded, remembering the expanding pool of shallow fire. It had been enough, though, enough to cook the legs out from under the hivefolk who'd tried to run and to set the other trucks and drays burning when it reached them.

'So it's the fumes that flared and created the explosion, and from the different characters of the residues I think some extra element may have been introduced along with the induced leak to make them even more volatile.'

'Induced leak?' Calpurnia asked.

Barck stopped and shook her head. 'Apologies, ma'am, I'm getting ahead of myself. There's damage to several barrels that the explosion itself doesn't explain. Weaknesses in the seals and thinning of the metal.' Her voice was getting quicker and more confident as she spoke. 'I sent my message to you because Lacan and his metallurgists confirmed that the damage predated the explosion but was relatively fresh. There were even particles of the barrel-metal in the burnt residues around the barrels themselves, and when we checked with a microvisor it looks like they were scraped, not burned.'

'So someone deliberately weakened the barrels so they would leak flammable oil, then somehow arranged a spark in there.' Calpurnia eased herself down off the trestle onto the residue-slick pavement.

'Correct.' Barck climbed down after her and motioned another verispex officer forward. 'Luxom, did you find what you thought you would?' He nodded and bobbed nervously, holding out a circular ceramic bung.

'The sealant around this got baked hard rather than melted, ma'am, uh, ma'ams. It made it easier to clean away the ash and gunk, which is what we were, uh, doing, uh, finishing while you were talking just now.'

'Thank you, Luxom,' said Calpurnia, taking it from his hand. 'Am I looking for similar tampering here?'

'Those, uh, lines directly across the edges there. Through the sealant residue. That's right, that's one. We may need a microvisor check to be absolutely sure, I, uh, haven't had the time to do one yet. But it looks like someone pushed a needle or something like it through the sealant while it was still soft, not long after the barrels had been filled and sealed, to allow very slow seepage.'

'Can either of you tell me where the spark came from?' The two looked at each other.

'We can find no signs of damage to the dray,' said Barck, 'or at least no damage that seems to predate the explosion. Only the Mechanicus can tell us these things for sure, but we've arrived at a reasonable idea of what kind of decay to a machine causes its spirit to spit and spark. At this stage I think we're looking at some kind of caller-amulet, some kind of machine hidden in the barrels that caused the explosion and either was consumed or blew itself apart to the point that we haven't been able to find any noticeable pieces of it yet.'

Calpurnia nodded, brooded and paced through the wrecks again. Barck and Luxom followed her as she began asking more questions, questions on the pattern of explosions and fires, the crowd movements, how many had died and how they had died. It took over an hour before she decided she had heard enough for the moment and began picking her way back through the wrecks and markers.

'Lead Verispex Barck,' she said, 'I realise you will make your judgement on the matter formally when you place your written report back at the Wall. However, at this point, with what you've seen here over the last few hours, is there any doubt in your mind that this was a case of deliberate sabotage?'

'With what I have seen here... none whatsoever, arbitor senioris.'

'Thank you. When will your full report be ready?'

'By the end of next shift, ma'am. I'll have a runner bring it straight to you.'

'Once again, thank you.'

Bannon fell in behind her as she strode back toward the Rhinos.

'Arbitor senioris, the feeder roads into the Telepine Way are all closed off. Urban Mobility Command reported the last barricade was in place an hour ago.'

'As recently as that? I see.'

'Word seems to be a little slow getting out to the other routes. The drays that are trying to reverse down the Way are probably there for the next day at least. There's already been some violence along the Way's base and Hakaro down at Eight-West is mobilising half an extra watch to patrol. He says there have been a couple of reports of gangs hitting the stranded trucks.'

'Are schematics of the roadways around the bottom of the Wall available?'

'Ma'am? Er, of the major ones, certainly. Do you need me to obtain…'

'When we get back, yes. I'll work out exactly what I need. This inquisitor changes things a little, too. I wish to hell that Barck had notified me that he was here.'

'She didn't?'

'She says she did. The only hint was her original message about "others in attendance".'

'Ah.'

She stopped and glared at Bannon. Arbites got good at reading one another's body language through armour and helmets and he took an involuntary step back.

'Something else I should know, Bannon?'

'Ah. It's local vox shorthand. A reference to "others in attendance" means people from outside the Arbites impinging on our work. Usually in the Augustaeum it's the Monocrat's agents, and up in the docks it's usually the Navy. Sometimes it's someone unusual like the Administratum or…'

'Or the Inquisition.' She looked over to where Zhow was talking to his rotund assistant. As she watched, the inquisitor held up a hand and both men waited while the servitor switched some connections around among its bandolier of data-arks. 'Since I've once again been forcibly reminded of how new I am to this whole quarter of the Imperium, can you tell me whether this is usual behaviour for an inquisitor here? What little interaction I had with the Pacificus Ordos tended toward rumours and cryptic orders and odd little directives from our high command. I don't remember any of them simply bowling up and flashing his rosette.'

'Perhaps it's because you are high command now, arbitor.' Calpurnia snorted, but it was a pleased snort.

'Perhaps it is. Alright, they're coming over, let's not be talking about them. Have the escort squad ready to re-board the Rhinos, please.' Zhow was closing on her now. Calpurnia suppressed a sigh and studied the marks on the ground. The arrows and lines showed where the Arbites had formed their containment line and charted the ebb and flow of the fire and the crowd; the pegs marked where bodies had lain after the stampede ebbed and the fire was out. There were a lot of them. Many had been on fire by the time they had crashed into the shield-wall and by the end the Arbites had been firing into the mob to try to fend it off.

Her left hand crept up towards her head, to rub her scars with her fingertips, before she caught the movement. She hated the way the mannerism persisted even when she had her helmet on – to her it spoke of lack of focus, lack of control. She looked at the pegs again, but each one was topped only by a light-cell and a number, nothing more to tell her who it was that had died on the ground she stood on now.

'Planning your next move?' Zhow managed to make it seem like an order.

'I know my next move, inquisitor. By now the two crewmen of the dray that exploded have spent quite a few hours in pre-interrogation cells. This visit has given me exactly what I need to begin questioning them.' She had to grit her teeth for the next part, but there was nothing for it but to extend the invitation. 'Inquisitor Zhow, if you would like to accom–' but he was already striding away to her Rhino.

'You are right, best that I be present for the questioning. Reassign your escort squad to the other vehicles in the convoy, please,' he told her, 'but make sure there is space for my own staff. Your assistant may ride with us if you insist but that is all.' He marched out from under the gate and into a flurry of murmurs from the crowd.

'I think I'm your assistant, arbitor senioris,' said Bannon helpfully. The rest of the Arbites had already overheard the inquisitor's orders and were distributing themselves among the other carriers in the Rhinocade. All three tanks were revving their engines and lowering their boarding ramps. 'He is an inquisitor, ma'am, after all. I know the name, although I've never met him. I believe Inquisitor Zhow resides somewhere in the Hydraphur system. They're supposed to have turned old Admiral Invisticone's estates into their own outpost. I've heard Zhow's had dealings with the lord marshal and the Eparch before. He, well, he is allowed...'

'*Allowed* I can deal with, I know what the rosette means. But there's such a thing as basic bloody manners, Bannon. All right then, come on.'

* * *

RHINOS WERE NOT made for chat, and Inquisitor Zhow did not appear to be pleased that he had to lean forward off his bench to be able to speak over the engine. The audio vanes on the recording-servitor were constantly clicking and flexing as they tried to sort out the words from the noise.

'This is rather unsatisfactory,' he declared. Calpurnia shrugged.

'It suits my needs, respected Inquisitor.'

'Does it now? Most arbite generals of my acquaintance have requisitioned a vehicle for their personal use and have had certain improvements applied. Sound dampening for one, so that the officer in question might conduct briefings and operational discussions on the move. Something I suggest for your consideration.' And he sat back, half-turned towards the vision slot in the hull, and would say nothing more. Calpurnia wished she had kept her helmet on: that slapped expression wanted to creep onto her face again. This time her hand did find the three seams on her forehead and her fingers were still running up and down the scars by the time they rolled back through the Justice Gate.

Bannon must have been right about Zhow working with the Arbites before. There was not even the most perfunctory glance about at the Justice Gate hangar: he simply walked to the base of the stepladder and motioned his tubby servant up it, the man climbing the gritty metal steps with agonising care and frequent stops. The servitor clambered up more quickly and deftly than Calpurnia had expected given its lack of hands, then Zhow himself. Once Calpurnia had climbed up to join him they set off at a stroll down the walkway. As they passed through the doors and turned toward the Chasteners' Tower Calpurnia fell in beside the inquisitor, who had finally condescended to shorten his stride a little.

'Do you think that the sabotage of the oil-carrier was aimed at you?' he asked her. Calpurnia thought for a moment before she answered.

'No. I did at first, because after the shooter this just seemed too pat a coincidence. Too close to me and too soon. It seemed–'

'Do you think the same parties are involved?' he interrupted. She took a breath.

'We still have little to no idea about who was behind the original attack, so it's hard to say. But that's the point, that's what's giving me doubts.'

'Explain.' They rounded a corner into a double column of marching Arbitrators. Calpurnia slowed and went to side-step; Zhow marched down the middle of the formation, the troopers breaking step and shuffling aside when they saw his rosette. The servitor, trying to keep them both in sensor range, shuffled hesitantly in between them until Calpurnia, swearing silently to herself, caught up again.

'The attack on me at the Mechanicus shrine was scrupu-lously prepared. The assassin had been carefully schooled and his equipment was some of the finest machine-craft that the Adepts at that shrine had seen. And there was enormous effort to make sure that the effort would be untraceable.'

'The gene-prints destroyed, his spoor damped and burnt-out beyond the ability of even my own augur to track,' (Zhow jerked his head toward his assistant) 'and his identity a mystery. I have availed myself of copies of the relevant reports, although I was unable to be present at the meeting where you first discussed all this.' He shot her an amused look. 'Does it surprise you? An assassin operating against an Adeptus officer in a hive in the heart of the premier Naval stronghold of an entire segmentum? What should surprise you is that it took me this long to speak with you directly.'

'I'm sure you had your reasons, respected Inquisitor.'

'And you see the contrasts with the incident in the Aquila Gate, do you?' he asked, ignoring the remark.

'The Aquila Gate effort was shoddy and slapdash, haphaz-ard at best. The sabotage to the barrels worked well enough, but it was nowhere near as sophisticated as the preparation behind the shooter. How could they know I would stop at the Aquila Gate? How could they count on my walking to that particular dray?'

'You responded, so I'm told, to the two crewmen running. You seem to have a style of plunging into things that an assassin could exploit quite easily.'

'And they would know this how? They would know that I would be passing at exactly the right moment, how? Traf-fic was heavy and slow because of the tightening of the checkpoint regimes, it simply wouldn't have been possible to count on the dray being in the right place to catch me. Even assuming that the sabotage got past the inspection point once it reached them. And if the two draymen were supposed to be assassins their conduct was so incompetent it verged on the bizarre.'

'Excellent! Your conclusions match my own.'

And with that Zhow stopped talking again. They were passing down the length of the Wall itself, through the internal checkpoints that marked each boundary. Calpurnia conscientiously stopped for the full identity scan at each point while Zhow, who tapped his rosette and breezed through each one, stood on the far side of it and glared at her while his chubby retainer puffed for breath. They passed through the interior gate checkpoint, the main junction where great stairs climbed away to the high concourse that ran through the upper floors all the length of the Wall, then through the smaller portals into the antechamber of the Chasteners' Tower.

Chastener du Toit was waiting for them. His eyes widened a little when he saw Zhow's rosette but Calpurnia was gratified that he spoke to her first.

'The two arrested in the Artisans Quarter are in the mass cells pending processing. The two in from last night are in individual softening cells, which seem to have worked. One is still quiet but he's had no sleep and is in some pain, the other broke quite early. He fears for his soul – he's been weeping and asking for a confessor for the last two hours or so.' Calpurnia nodded with approval.

'Do you see any reason for us not to start with that one, inquisitor?'

'I do not. I trust you also have copies of the full papers for both prisoners and their vehicle?'

'We will shortly,' said du Toit. 'They were used to track down the shipper to whom the dray belongs. Lead Chastener Klee will be delivering them shortly. As for the prisoner, well, it's a full Ministorum confession he wants to make, so...'

'Do you have a scourging rack?' asked Calpurnia. 'Not one of the standard ones, I mean the kind the confessors set up in public squares when they're raising a purge.'

'Yes ma'am. There's one in the second rotunda, up above us and on the southern wall, for *capita secundus* executions.'

'Good. Have – what's the name of this confessing prisoner?'

'Hiel Jakusch.'

'Have Jakusch brought there along with those papers. And you can show the inquisitor and myself there now.'

Zhow cocked an eyebrow as she finished speaking, but, mercifully, said nothing more.

You ARE A prisoner, arrested at the righteous hand of the Adeptus Arbites. A terrifying, stifling journey in a strait-cape, cocooned blind within tight canvas and crammed into an Abductor-pattern Rhino or simply slung from the carry-hooks on its sides. The cape is taken off in a cell in the giant honeycombed sub-levels of the Chastener's Tower, where the corridors and rooms are deliberately narrow and cramped but of darker stone, high-ceilinged, ill-lit so there's always the sense of being watched from above. How long you live like this, how much food you get, how much water or sleep, will be based on careful Arbites dogma about the breaking of prisoners.

Finally, at some point, bent and weak and exhausted and surrounded by stern brown-sashed Chasteners and their voices and lights, something gives. You beg a confession – and up out of the cramped dimness you come, staggering in shackles, and you stand in a beautiful vaulted glass room full of air and sunlight, looking out over the city and the mountains. The preacher speaks kindly to you and you know that once you have unburdened yourself, the scourging-rack in the centre of that marble floor awaits, and there as the Ministorum has taught you since childhood the pain will cleanse your soul before it leaves your body to stand before the Emperor. How could you not feel joy? How could you not burst out with all those secrets you have locked inside you?

Calpurnia understood the psychology of the chamber and appreciated it. Often the key to the most guarded secrets was the prospect of one final shred of dignity and redemption after the long grind of the cells. If she stood at the window with her back to the rack the room was almost peaceful, even if the sunlight was wrong. Even after several days on Hydraphur, she kept instinctively checking for the smoke-pall or sandstorm that was turning the light that colour.

But anything that got Zhow talking constructively was a blessing, she decided, and taking in the view while they waited seemed to have done that.

'My prediction is that we're going to confirm from this man that that explosion was artificial, but wasn't aimed at you. I doubt he'll know who you are.'

'Agreed. So if it's not an attack on me, are we agreed that it's an attack on the Vigil and the mass? That oil was lamp-oil, and there's a big lamplit parade this evening. The, what is it, further saints?' He nodded.

'Their statues and icons have been displayed in the Pilgrims Quarter for the last day, and tonight they get to the Seat around the other side of the Augustaeum before the Master's Pageant.'

'But the source of the explosion was in the dray, in the cargo hoppers it was carrying. Not the oil itself. If the objective was to sabotage that parade somehow... but I'm getting ahead of myself. Let me think aloud for a moment. The attack didn't need to be on the parade. In fact, it would probably be better if it weren't. From talking to Leandro, to undermine the Vigil is a balancing act. Any sabotage has to cause some kind of disruption to disgrace the Master but too much damage and it backfires. So wrecking that parade would be disastrous, but causing monstrous traffic problems all down one side of the hive is just enough to taint Kalfus-Medell by association. Hell, we probably even helped out by closing the Aquila Gate. It wasn't an assassination, and it wasn't about breaching the Arbites lines to try and get a mob into the Augustaeum, which was the other idea I was playing with. I think the disruptions were an end in themselves. Inquisitor, you understand this place better than I do. What are your thoughts?'

'You're clearly having fun with this, Calpurnia, but it's more your concern than mine.' That slapped feeling again. 'Any attack on the Emperor's peace on Hydraphur is the province of your authority, not mine, as any direct attack on

the Ecclesiarchy will be a matter for the Church officers and
the Adepta Sororitas. My charter is simply to trace the assassin and destroy his controller and all who had dealing with
him, my interest goes no further.'

'I would have thought, with respect, inquisitor, that–'

'Well, yes, you would, but at present the Ordos Hydraphur
are keeping our involvement in Ecclesiarchal affairs to an
absolute minimum, if you must know. I'm a little surprised
that you've chosen to dive in so deep yourself.'

'I'm not sure what you mean, inquisitor.'

'Has Leandro briefed you yet on the conflict between the
eparchal chamber and the so-called "flag curates"?' Calpurnia felt her heart sink. Not *again*.

'No, my respected inquisitor, the reference is new to me.'

'Well, perhaps you'd best not be briefed by me, and–'

'And that would be the appropriate course, certainly.'
Arbitor and inquisitor spun about at the interruption; neither had heard soft footsteps come through the door.

Mihon Baragry was standing about ten paces behind
them, arms folded, flanked by two Arbites Garrison preachers in red sashes and uncertain expressions.

'It is always prudent, Arbitor Calpurnia, to obtain your
information at the source,' the Curia emissary went on. 'I
would not dream of soliciting information about the affairs
of the Adeptus Arbites from a third party, for example. Simply make the request, and I'll acquaint you with as much of
the matter as I can.'

'Mind how you go, Baragry,' growled Zhow. 'Insolence to
the God-Emperor's Inquisition has a way of coming back
around to you. Ecclesiarchal harassment of the Arbites over
the body of that assassin is already on our records.'

'Harassment?' Baragry asked, walking calmly over to the
rack. 'Hardly. I've just come from a very civil audience with
Arbitor Senioris Leandro to explain the charter that the
Eparch's witch-hunters operate under. We have a perfectly
legitimate authority to be the ones to carry out the destruction of the body according to Ministorum law, of which I
know you have a good grasp, inquisitor.'

'That charter originates from the Eparch and has no weight
in–' Zhow got out before Calpurnia stepped between them.

The effect was slightly spoiled when they simply continued to glare at one another over her head.

'As constructive as I'm sure all of this will turn out to be, gentlemen, can we concentrate on something different for just a moment? Reverered Baragry, we have a prisoner due to arrive here shortly to make his confession.'

'Indeed, and I am here as his confessor. He is waiting outside in the company of your Chasteners.'

'You?' boomed Zhow. 'What are you brewing up now, Baragry? Calpurnia, what did you know of this?'

'Exactly as much as I just heard from the Reverend Baragry just now. Reverend, maybe it's just my inexperience of Hydraphur, but is it usual for an eparchal envoy to turn up unannounced and take such a role in an Arbites investigation onto himself?'

'As I said, I came here earlier today for an audience with Arbitor Leandro.' Baragry had finally moved his eyes from Zhow to Calpurnia. 'With that concluded, I took the opportunity to visit, pray and confer with my colleagues in the Justice Gate chapel, with the arbiter senioris's permission, naturally. During our conversation the message arrived that a prisoner required an Ecclesiarchal confessor and the Garrison chaplains paid me the honour of inviting me to take up the duty. Since the prisoner is catalogued against your name, Arbiter Calpurnia, and since you and I are working together in any event, it seemed like a happy arrangement. I assure you no breach of process occurred.'

'You are co-operating with Baragry on the disruptions to the mass, Calpurnia?' Zhow asked accusingly from right behind her.

'We have met on the issue. You indicated that that investigation was not an interest of yours,' Calpurnia told him with a certain amount of relish.

'Reverend Baragry, in order to earn his penance Jakusch will be telling us everything about his part in the conspiracy. Only when we are satisfied that we have every piece of information will he be allowed his scourging and whatever might come after.'

'Understood perfectly,' said Baragry. 'He spoke with me on the way up. I believe he will co-operate.' Zhow snorted.

Calpurnia gave a signal and the Chasteners at the double
doors swung them back. Hiel Jakusch turned out to be the
tattoo-scalped one, built like a slab but with a soft sheath of
fat around his waist and hips. There were generous tear-
stains on his face and he looked longingly at the rack and
then at Baragry.

'Confessor?' His voice was hoarse and high with emotion,
and the attentions of the Chasteners had put a lurch in his
walk. Zhow's retainer waddled over and leaned close enough
to the man to be almost breathing on him, before he turned,
went back to the inquisitor's side and whispered something.

'No obvious psyker-taint,' Zhow declared, and the word
made Jakusch look around wildly.

Two junior persecutors had brought in stools and a scroll-
tube; Calpurnia sat on one and took the papers to look
through. Jakusch plopped onto the other one, trembling and
staring at the rack. Calpurnia looked at him until he met her
eyes and whimpered – she had put a little Macragge per-
mafrost into her gaze.

'The rack is waiting, Hiel,' said Baragry softly. 'The cleansing you crave and the punishment you have earned. But
before that you must speak. Tell it all.'

Jakusch seemed to think about this for several moments.
Then, holding his quaking hands in the sign of the aquila,
he began to speak.

'...*Sanctus*. Went... wrong... we did it wrong.'

'Talk sense. Now.' That was Zhow.

'It was supposed... it should have happened when it was
gone. Gone, out of... gone from orbit. Left the world.'

'A ship,' said Baragry.

'Have him start at the beginning, Calpurnia,' said Zhow.

'He will,' she answered, 'we're going to hear everything in
order. First just tell me, though, Jakusch. The ship, the one
whose departure you said you had to wait on. The name of
the ship, Jakusch.'

'*Sanctus*, ma'am. *Sanctus*.'

'*Aurum Sanctus*.'

Tenth Day of Septista

Eight days to the Mass of Saint Balronas. The Festival of
Leave-Taking and the Shuttleman's Vigil. The Devotions
of the Mariners and the Commemoration of Chilaste the
Demi-Sainted. The Declaration of the Precepts.

ON THIS DAY pilgrims moving on to the sacred stations at Chiros
and elsewhere traditionally depart the Bosporian Hive and travel
to orbit to take ship. While there are customarily many who are
unable to have departed until after this day, pilgrims' business is
deemed to finish in the Augustaeum by sunset and after that time
pilgrims should not be acknowledged. The Devotions of the
Mariners are traditionally recited at the Arch of the Scarii and the
Chapels of Konnemahle and of the Revered Vinaphii along the
High Mesé. Many preachers outside the Bosporian Hive also make
these the centre of their services, so that those wishing to pray for
the outgoing ships should determine ahead of time where they will
be able to do so.

All pious folk should be in their homes or at their nearest place
of worship at the moment of sunset when the Cathedral bell is
rung. The roads to each temple, shrine or chapel must be clear for
the heralds appointed by the Master to travel out to them – there
will be a herald for every place of worship in and around the
Bosporian so there will be no need to travel far and those abroad
too far without cause may be stopped by the Adeptus Arbites, the
Adepta Sororitas or by order squads posted by the Master of the
Vigil. Those waiting at home should be alert for the bell or horn
of their nearest place of worship, which will signal the arrival of

97

the herald to announce the particular precepts and scriptures that the Master of the Vigil has chosen as the keystone for the obser-vances of the next few days.

The pict-cast of the Master making this Declaration in person at the Cathedral doors is for the benefit of the rest of the planet and the system and should on no account excuse non-attendance at one's own church for the announcement.

CHAPTER FIVE

THEY CAME IN on the *Aurum Sanctus* fast and silent, Calpurnia and Nakayama and Zhow. They rode in the Arbites Indictor-class fast cruiser *Judgement's Clarion*, a squat, blunt-prowed slab of armour and drives around a fat-bellied enginarium, her decks home to a dedicated garrison whose precinct house was their ship and whose specialty was the boarding and sacking of outlaw spacecraft. Nakayama and his personal command team had quickly and easily taken command; Calpurnia had brought no one with her and she had spent most of the trip trying to rest, attacking her first real meal in nearly twenty-one hours and avoiding Inquisitor Zhow.

Calpurnia had never fought in a boarding action before. She had trained for them, and she had led squads through the cramped industrial stacks on Don-Croix in conditions that she had thought were as near to shipboard as made no odds. But an actual ship-to-ship action, storming another vessel outside an atmosphere with life-suits, assault boats, decompression drills, the constant, agonising split of your thoughts between fighting the enemy and keeping the precious, fragile boarding seals intact from stray shots or even blows until the hull breach was secure… No.

So she understood why Nakayama was in charge, why he and Phae, the lantern-jawed Aedile Senioris who seconded him, would lead the storming of the *Aurum Sanctus*. Nakayama had spent nearly his whole career aboard the Arbites fleets that roamed their light-years long patrol beats back and forth across the Imperium, ready to reinforce a beleaguered planetary precinct. It was an Arbitrator's life at its most simple, the paramilitary side of their calling stripped bare, and Nakayama had excelled at every aspect of it. It made sense for him to be up here now.

Except that it meant that she had been sidelined, and as much as she tried not to, she hated it. She hated stepping aside from her own investigation, hated the way everything was obviously running so cleanly and efficiently under Nakayama and without needing her, hating most of all the fact that she could understand exactly why things needed to be done like this, but not being able to help hating it anyway.

Her spirits, revived by the overdue meal, had sunk again when Zhow had declared that he and his staff would participate in the boarding. She kept remembering a conversation with Heyd Maliqa, the old marshal of court on Hazhim, years before. 'Though it breaks my heart to host an impious thought about such famously heroic servants of the Emperor, I had four experiences with them when I was posted further to the Southern Fringe and, Shira, nothing plays merry hell with an Arbites investigation like an inquisitor. Emperor forgive me for saying so, but it's true. I hope you never have to put up with it, I hope you never have cause to. But as soon as they set foot beside you the field will belong to them and you'll wind up dumped back on traffic control, regardless of what you know or what you can do. And, Emperor help you, there is just nothing you can do about it.' Calpurnia had listened uneasily to the woman's throaty Hazhim accent shape the words (*Emp'rror hhelp you, thher's yust nodding…*) and had wondered if she should be reporting this to someone. She had never imagined that it would turn out to be so literally true.

And here came Zhow now, marching into the briefing room late and ostentatiously making his way through the assembled team leaders to the front rank of benches and sitting carefully down in the spot that two Arbites hastily made for him. When Zhow was seated Nakayama gestured to the holographic globe by his shoulder.

'The *Aurum Sanctus*.' He indicated a malignant-yellow fixator icon. 'A bonded trader craft operating under direct charter from the Adeptus Ministorum, captained by Vardos del Biel, formerly an officer of the Munitorum bonded-merchant fleet until he was disgraced in some kind of disciplinary matter. Three years after that he showed up on the passenger roster of the *Aurum Sanctus* at the Ecclesiarchal docks at Avignor and was listed as captain for its recent voyages to Hydraphur.

'However, records provided to Arbitor Calpurnia by the Navy system controllers as we passed through the Ring show at least three captains for this ship over the past eight years and crew turnover seems even faster. We know of at least a dozen different brokers and mercantile and legal staff who have conducted business on behalf of this ship just within the Hydraphur system in the past half-dozen or so trading quarters. The major constant seems to be the Navigator, one Peshto Vask Zemlya, who has been confirmed by Adeptus Astra Telepathica records as having been that ship's Navigator for at least the last hundred and twelve years.'

Nakayama glanced down at the faxcopy resting along the rim of the pulpit.

'For the last decade the ship's trading charter has been underwritten by the Adeptus Ministorum. Four times over the last two and a half years the *Sanctus* has invoked special Ecclesiarchal charters to avoid or greatly reduce inspection protocols. The ship has also had more than its share of clashes with the Navy, repeatedly invoking Church sanction for things like course-plan approvals, quarantine audits and access to docks. We have reports of actual armed conflict between the crew of the *Sanctus* and Naval Security, but we don't know much about those – both sides have been keen to keep it between themselves. We know enough to know the *Sanctus* has armed defences that it will use if it feels it has to.'

Nakayama gave a short pause before he made his last point.

'We don't know much about Navigator Zemlya, but both our own data stacks and Inquisitor Zhow's sources confirmed the family's background. From 874.M41 to 912.M41 three other members of the Zemlya family were implicated in a well-established contraband ring within and between the Obscura, Pacifica and Solar Segmentae. They worked through puppet captains and contractual trickery that made them seem innocent dupes, but the craft themselves were traced back to Zemlya holdings in nearly every case. They transported physical contraband through the barriers imposed by quarantine and warzone interdictions, and letters of credit and transaction that allowed them to siphon resources from one system and sector to another and bypass most Adeptus monitoring protocols. A great deal of wealth ended up with some very wrong people. Backtracking datatrails and interrogations of informers suggested that it may have been going on for as much as a century.

'The ring was broken by the Adeptus Arbites, Battlefleet Pacificus and the League of Blackships in 915.M41 and the captains and crews were ceremonially executed by Arbitor Majore Dayn Finegall the following year, but the Zemlya themselves were Navis Nobilite and untouchable. Peshto Zemlya was not in active service with the family then, but who knows what we'll find in another Zemlya-navigated ship? Which brings us to the now.'

He pointed at the string of bright emerald dots strung out around the *Sanctus*.

'For the last two days a carrier battlegroup attached to the Battlefleet Pacificus has been conducting fighter-bomber formation drills in the asteroid fields around the Psamathian Gate. Six hours ago the *Sanctus* appealed against an Arbites directive to change course for interception by the *Praetor Katerina*, citing the usual raft of Ecclesiarchal immunities by proxy. At this point Captain-Commodore Esmerian approached us through the Naval envoy's offices in the Augustaeum and volunteered to redirect his squadrons to blockade the *Sanctus* until we could catch up. Captain del Biel has been trying to bully his way through that blockade for the past hour, but he was forced to shed just about all of his velocity when Esmerian threatened to have his bomber wings start an attack run. At this point it's over to us.'

'What authorities or immunities the captain of this craft thinks he might have are nothing you need concern yourself with, Arbites.' Heads turned to Zhow as he spoke. He had exchanged the battered blue bodyglove for an elegant green full-carapace and cloak, his rosette displayed under a little armourglass box fastened to the centre of his chest. Calpurnia had to admit he had a certain presence. 'The mission to intercept this ship now has my own authority, that of the sacred Imperial Inquisition. My stamp is upon this venture.'

There was a brief wave of muttering until Nakayama started speaking again.

'I've distributed all the information we have about the ship's armaments and internal defences – we don't have much to go on, but pay attention to it nevertheless, please. We're hoping for a surrender but we should prepare for the opposite. It's hard to read their intentions: they haven't stopped us from closing but they've made no move to acknowledge or admit us. Remember also that command of the storming operation rests with me, but the investigation that's led to it belongs to Arbitor Senioris Calpurnia and Inquisitor Zhow.' This time it was Calpurnia that the heads turned to. Zhow was frowning, displeased over sharing mention with an arbitor or perhaps just at being named second.

'Take your stations, then,' Nakayama finished. 'There will be a klaxon at thirty minutes to interception, and you have until then to finish muster and weapon checks. Ship's chaplains will be at their posts; prayers and blessings will be by detachment rather than in a single service. *Nomine Imperator, Nomine Legis.*'

As Calpurnia repeated the words after him she was surprised to feel a thrill running through her, then surprised at her surprise. Throne of Earth, but it felt good to be doing something totally on the Arbites' terms for once.

THEY WERE GOING in with the second wave: Aedile Senioris Phae, Calpurnia, Zhow, eight Arbites from the *Clarion's* garrison, two augurs from Zhow's personal staff and six of his troopers, bulky in fully-pressurised carapaces and toting shotcannon and man-high flak-slabs that they used to box in Zhow and his armour-swaddled assistants in a way that would have been comical if it hadn't slowed the team down so much. 'These men are veterans in the service of the Inquisition and myself,' Zhow had told Calpurnia when he saw her staring, 'and experts at keeping myself and my staff from harm.' There didn't seem to be much to say to that.

The main passageway to the front ventral storming-lock branched off in every direction so that the storming-teams could form up in assault files and head straight out in whatever sequence they had to without getting in each other's way. Calpurnia, second from the front of her own file after Phae, braced herself against the juddering as the storm-locks clamped themselves to the locks of the *Aurum Sanctus*, then with the help of the vacc-armoured engineers who had launched themselves across the closing gap between the two ships they ground and pressed themselves in until they found the right combination of grapples and seals to form a passageway. Like a forced kiss on an unwilling maid, she told herself, and then shook her head and wondered where the hell that thought had come from.

The hatches blew with a *crump-WHAMM*, then a roar of air and popping of ears as pressures equalised. Turbulence from the seam between the two ships' artificial gravity fields sent strange breezes and eddies up and down the corridor as the first detachment stampeded down the passage and into the *Sanctus*.

"Second, *go*!'

At the cry over the vox band another double file stormed down the passageway past their own branch, then another. Calpurnia murmured 'Emperor protect' to each and realised that Phae was doing the same.

'Fourth, *go*!' If they had their planning right there would be a single long deck beneath this lock, two initial storm-detachments moving down it in each direction.

The communication torc built into the collar of her armour carried no talk, no red Engagement runes. So far, so good.

'First. At our initial waypoint. Layout conforms to briefing so far. Clear.'

'Second. In and at waypoint. Clear so far.'

The third detachment called in, then the fourth. The first wave was through. The command teams would lead the second bigger wave, then verispex and cyber-mastiffs would form the third.

'Clear for the second wave. Command one, *go!*' Nakayama's voice coming out of the torc, and Calpurnia and Phae launched themselves out of the side corridor and into the passageway. It was a pleasure to lose all thoughts and broodings in the simple rhythm of her feet on the decking and the weight of her shotgun and shield. The semicircular lock sucked them in with a burnt smell and a *whoosh* of air, and then there was the leap, the moment of free-floating and the wrenching ninety-degree turn as they passed from the *Clarion's* gravity into the *Sanctus's*. She landed, stumbled and scuttled aside, out of the way of the Arbites dropping through what was now, with the change of orientation, a chute opening into the ceiling of a long, high corridor. She had expected Zhow and his complicated little squad to plummet through in a tangle but inquisitor, guards and even the chubby augur and his companion made the drop neatly and were in formation a moment later.

Phae had an inertial auspex out and Calpurnia, who hadn't seen the need for one, now understood how damaging to the sense of direction that wrench between gravities could be. As they set off down the passageway Calpurnia heard, 'Command two, *go!*' and the sound of Nakayama's squad dropping through the hatch. They had broken in two-thirds of the way down the *Sanctus's* two-kilometre crenellated hull, between the engines and the bridge; Nakayama would oversee the move to the stern, the holds and engineering sector while Calpurnia, Phae and Zhow pushed in the other direction to the squat ziggurat that housed the bridge.

The lights in here were almost non-existent, but by the torches clipped to their shields and shoulders Calpurnia could see that the walls of even this outer passage were elaborately crafted, a non-stop frieze of holy symbols and carvings of grim faces surrounded by High Gothic inscriptions. The outer wall, the one that faced the hull and space,

was covered in scriptural banners and purity seals to ward off
the dangers of the warp, and gave off the smell of old parchment and stale incense. It was like being in the catacombs of
some deserted monastery, she thought as they began to
advance, and her mind snagged on that word: *deserted*. No
one to meet them? Whether to fight them or anything else?
She noticed dust was heavy at the foot of each carved and
decorated bulkhead, but thinned and disappeared in the
corridor's centre.

'These corridors are patrolled,' she muttered to Phae. 'The
devotional scripts on the walls haven't been attended to for
some time, but look at that dust. Just the advance teams
wouldn't disturb it like that. Somebody moves through here
regularly.'

'I see it,' Phae replied. 'Command one to all teams, 'ware
possible patrols,' and the string of acknowledgements had
still not died away when the team in front of them met the
arco-flagellant.

It came first as a burst of exclamations over the vox-band:
'Contact! Single contact, First! Shield and cover!' and then a
burst of shotgun-booms in the dimness ahead and a weird,
unearthly howl of anger. Then wordless yells and the clash of
metal, and the fizzing cracks over the vox band that meant
that power-weapons were discharging too near a transmitter.
The cadre team moved into a slow jog, advancing and covering and trying to stamp on the urge to race ahead.

'Fire-call is *hellbreak*,' came the voice of one of Zhow's
guards from behind her. 'If you hear it, get flat. At *hellbreak*
plus three seconds we open fire.'

'We appreciate the warning,' Phae answered as they came
through an arch where the passage broadened to double its
previous width and became a succession of archways that
stretched away into darkness. Now they could hear the
shouts without vox: 'Box it! Box it! Get it int–' and see the
intermittent gun-flares as well as two dancing, circling blue
lights that sparked and whipped back and forth.

Calpurnia had loaded her stubber with the special low-
velocity frangible rounds that the *Clarion* carried for
shipboard operations, but she had checked a shotgun and
shield out of the ship's armoury as well – in their haste to get

spaceborne she had not had the chance to load up on her own kit. Now as she got in formation beside Phae she felt the satisfying chunk of the shotgun locking home into her shield's gunport and watched the red spark, designating an Executioner shell, appear in the corner of the vision slot.

But the advance teams had beaten her to it. Half the squad had formed a rough line facing the thing as it had waded through the other half and now they caught it in a loose semi-circle of shields. This was a shock-team, suppressor charges built into their shields, and their strobing discharges knocked the creature forward into the staggering Arbites it had been tearing at, then the spark-burst of a maul sent it back the other way. By this time the cadre were close enough to see it, a lumbering pale shape whose sickle-tipped arms swung and scissored about it with inhuman quickness, until three point-blank shotgun bursts tore it open and sprawled it, limbs and innards, across the deck and wall. The Arbites put another volley into it as Calpurnia's team closed with them and took up support positions, but now the thing was definitely dead.

'Take stock and regroup,' snapped Phae, but the order was unnecessary: already the uninjured Arbites were reordering themselves into smaller squads while the medicae staff bent over groaning figures on the deck. In the middle of the mess their guns had left was a silver plaque that gleamed in the torchlight. Calpurnia turned it over with her toe: DEFILER OF SCRIPTURE. It was still riveted to a scrap of what looked like the flagellant's breastbone. It fitted. Arco-flagellants were not vat-grown but made, made from condemned heretics who had their bodies engineered with drugs and augmetics into pain-proofed murder machines and their conscious minds ripped away, leaving only a predatory animal's instincts and utter loyalty to the Ministorum.

Calpurnia spoke into her vox-torc.

'Calpurnia, Command one. One arco-flagellant encountered and destroyed on the fore approach. Casualties,' she shot a look at them, 'are three fatalities, three more injured and unable to continue. We need a buttressing team up behind us.'

'*Clarion*. Buttressing team on its way. Five go, Six stand by.'

'Command,' came Nakayama's voice. 'No resistance, but we've found two discarded cassocks, freshly ripped, covered in maxims and seals. Flagellant garb. There will be at least one more here somewhere. Push forward. Move it before the resistance can get more organised.'

The second arco-flagellant appeared two hundred metres on, where the broadened gallery split into an upramp and downramp to the other decks. They had begun to climb the upramp in a careful square when it appeared, running in great silent strides up the downramp and making an incredible arcing leap to crash into the outer line of Arbites. One of them managed to get a shot off that turned it in mid-air, and it was off-balance when it hit the shields. The Arbites were ready and shouldered their shields into it to knock it back out of the air even as the electrowhip bundles sprouting from the stumps of its forearms scored tracks over the rims of the shields and across their helmets and armoured backs. The thing twisted catlike in the air and landed on the balls of its feet, and Calpurnia saw it tense its legs ready for another spring before there was a cry of 'Hellbreak!' from Zhow's team, the flak-slabs swung wide and the shotcannon boomed. It twisted and leapt as they opened up and was actually in time to evade the first two bursts before a four-second volley shredded it. Calpurnia glanced over the edge of the ramp for a moment, but if this one had a plaque on it she couldn't see it from here. They climbed on.

Nakayama found his flagellant as Calpurnia's party found the first portal deeper into the ship. The door had been welded shut, but the welds were old, cold and plastered over with Ecclesiarchal seals. Calpurnia was running her hand over the seams when the burst of chatter came over the vox. The flagellant had crashed through two shield-lines and made for the command squad before a concerted salvo of Executioner shells brought it down. One fatality and three more who wouldn't be going any further. The third wave of storming teams was through the hatch and following up behind them, a fourth was mustering.

'I wonder if this is why there's so little resistance?' Phae wondered aloud. 'They welded these shut to have a complete layer of passages and corridors between the spaces they use and the hull. Then they leave the arco-flagellants roaming in those spaces as a permanent hunt-and-destroy patrol. But it wouldn't stand a chance against any kind of full-strength boarding action, we've taken them apart…'

'It wouldn't need to,' said Calpurnia, 'not if they were so confident about the protection of the Ecclesiarchy. They're not a warship, the most they'd have to worry about is piracy and most pirates don't mount military-scale boarding actions.'

'But they'd still need to come out to see to the flagellants – reconsecrate their machine-parts, make sure their human bodies are fed and properly maintained. There needs to be a way into this layer somewhere. One of these doors won't be sealed.'

'It's still a bizarre response to an official boarding. They let us dock with no signals and no resistance but they don't rein in these things. What the hell?'

'The inquisitor wishes to know why the advance has halted,' came a vox-call from inside the flak-slabs behind them. Calpurnia grimaced and they moved on.

There seemed to be no pattern to the movements of the flagellants, no attempt to organise. Nakayama's teams picked off two more over the next twenty minutes; and another came up the ramp behind Zhow, ran into the buttressing team that had moved up to provide a rearguard and killed two Arbites with a melta torch grafted into its shoulder before it was brought down. But by the time they had passed two more great sealed archways and found a still-functioning one, free of welds or dust, there had still been no other opposition, just these shambling once-human berserkers appearing out of the dark.

Breaking through to the inhabited decks of the *Sanctus* was an anticlimax. Zhow stepped from inside the portable bunker his guards were carrying around him and touched his Inquisitorial signet to a truth-plate by the hatch and there was the immediate rumble of motors in the bulkhead and deck. White-golden light washed out as the thick metal rolled down into the floor: fire-teams from first vaulted the shutter before it was fully descended and Calpurnia followed while Phae voxed for another wave to leave the *Clarion* in support.

The cloisters they were running through, veering left and right by the directions Phae shouted out from her locator, were elaborately vaulted and carved to mimic the design of the Ecclesiarchal buildings in and around the Cathedral complex in the Augustaeum, with a constant smell of incense that must have been deliberately circulated in the ship's internal air. There were even windows, set into the top of each niche and backed by glow-panels providing golden mock-sunlight.

The resistance here was still haphazard. Calpurnia had feared an Adepta Sororitas ship's guard but there were only gaggles of junior armsmen, desperately but incompetently trying to hold the odd set of steps or cargo-crane shaft. The Arbites took each blockade apart almost without slowing down: the shock-teams advanced with lasfire sizzling on their shields, fired a brief suppressing volley through ported guns or tossed a grenade while the second rank got their aim in, then the defenders were broken by quick, precise bursts of shot and any survivors picked off with Executioner shells. Calpurnia could already hear Phae on the vox channel, organising the cyber-mastiff handlers in the waves behind them to begin hunting down what few survivors had fled and scattered.

It was beneath the bridge-ziggurat that they met their only real fight. Two dozen armsmen, some bloodied from the earlier skirmishes, dug themselves in amongst serried rows of devotory cases and penance racks, joined by five gantrylike hauler-servitors whose fleshy quasi-human heads and torsos hung incongruously in the middle of their stilt-legs and clanking grapple-arms. They had flanked the door with servitors and flamer-crews, but when the Arbites assault came their organisation began no better than before and quickly dropped to non-existent.

Calpurnia led them through the doors and was knocked sprawling by a servitor's grapple-claw that warped her shield and numbed her arm. Cursing, she kicked out with her heels, pushed herself behind a heavy steel reliquary stand and tried to wrestle the cracked and distorted shield off her arm. Phae, running through the doors a moment later, dived down beside her and pumped three bursts of shot at the armsmen who were clustering behind the servitor and firing spindly laspistols. The servitor reeled forward, one leg-motor already chewed and smoking from gunfire, and tried to grab Phae out from behind her cover. Calpurnia popped up beside her and rapped the grapple-claw with her maul to short the mechanism, leaving the machine waggling its paralysed claw as if giving idiot benediction.

A moment later it tottered and crashed down as Phae shot its organic body apart, and the armsmen fled, yelping. Across the aisle a second servitor was smashed apart by krak grenades and a third began spinning in a mad circle and gouging great strips out of the walls as some minor injury to its organics threw its blank vat-grown brain into confusion.

Calpurnia switched her maul to her left and drew her stubber with her right, she and Phae falling in wordlessly with the fan of Arbites now spreading through the smoke and the maze of cases. The crew had not fled far, but their ambushes were half-hearted and their aim appalling: a lasbeam or an autopistol burst would ring off a shield in the front rank, then there would be a quick shotgun boom and sometimes a single cry.

Calpurnia, shieldless, found herself in the second rank now with little to do: every order she went to say was anticipated by the Arbites around her. They quartered, crisscrossed and flushed the last of them out into a vicious crossfire on the steps at the far end – the fourth servitor was felled by a methodical rain of krak grenades from two Arbites who had come in with the wave behind them, and the fifth simply stopped moving and stood slumped as the last of the armsmen fell and the control amulet he was carrying went rattling across the floor.

It had barely come to rest before the shot-pocked double doors at the top of the steps began to swing open. Instantly they were covered by the guns of more than thirty Arbites and Calpurnia, walking toward the front of the formation, dropped to a crouch and brought her stub pistol up.

But even before they could make out the figure on the other side of the door a voice came through the vox-horns in the ceiling, a soft, tired old man's voice:

'Put up your weapons, men and women of the Adeptus Arbites. I will not fight you, and you cannot fight me. Let this waste and destruction stop awhile.'

Calpurnia stood and with some effort of will lowered her pistol. The cowled figure was grotesquely tall, the shoulders beneath its purple and gold cloak too slumped and narrow, the fingers of the hand it raised too long and thick. A man in the uniform of a petty officer knelt on each side of it, hands stretched out before them with the weapons in their laps bound in white cloth to symbolise surrender, but it was to the cloaked man that Calpurnia's eyes returned. A long, stubbled chin and a quivering old man's mouth, but the cowl hid the rest and that was when she guessed it.

'Navigator Peshto Zemlya.'

'I am he, and I will have no more of… of this, on my behalf.' Heavy fingers gestured out at the room. 'You need not assault me to learn what you need. Come, woman of the Arbites, and I will tell you what you seem to desire to know.'

THEY RODE UP to the bridge in silence, in a glorious jewelled howdah that coasted silently up through a grav-shaft bathed in white light. At every level of the ziggurat the shaft was enclosed by a cage of gold filigree, fanciful wire-work gargoyles forever chasing one another in circles, and beyond it each of the floors, although lit, seemed quiet and empty.

Nakayama had remained down among the decks to take charge of a full-ship sweep, but Phae came with her. Although the two of them stood in front of Zemlya as a mark of trust, two proctors held their weapons on the hulking Navigator from behind where the warp eye in his forehead could not affect them if he should suddenly unmask it. Around them were Arbites that Phae had singled out at Calpurnia's request, cross-trained in space flight, ready to commandeer the ship if they had to. Zhow, who had left his guards behind, and looked as though he were regretting it, stared at Zemlya and gripped a bolt pistol plated in mirror-polished silver.

The ride was uneasy – the beautifully artificed and quiet structure around them was eerie enough, but the Navigator was simply wrong. There was no natural proportion about him: it was as if each measurement had been randomly twisted for longer or shorter. His chin tapered too much but the bulge of forehead under the low cowl was too blunt. His fingers were thick but his hands and wrists slenderer than Calpurnia's. But even over and above his physique, his swaying stance, his wheezing breath and his odd, acrid, smoky smell, there was just a presence about him, something that rankled their thoughts and senses. Calpurnia thought that even if she turned away she would still know which side of her faced him because that was where her skin would be crawling. She wondered if this was how the inquisitor's augurs felt in the presence of warpcraft. Was this how they sniffed it out?

The bridge itself was equally disorienting, in its own way. It was not the forbidding, harshly-lit bunker of an Arbites ship but a stately marble belvedere with armourglass windows framed in graceful arches of precious metals and wirework. Perfume-bowls were set on stands on either side of the captain's throne, warmed by gentle candles beneath them, and silver chains crisscrossed overhead holding lanterns, the filaments in hollow glass figures of cherubs and extravagant heraldic animals. The control plinths were fashioned like musical instruments, miniature buildings or tree stumps and the panels beneath the windows were worked into the shapes of trees and vines with coppery leaves that waved in gentle programmed motions to simulate wind. For a few moments after they reached the bridge she could hear mechanical songbirds chirruping in the metal branches. Calpurnia shook her head. Pampering like this was bad enough in a private home, but what would this place be like in an emergency alert?

Zemlya was stepping down out onto the floor in a rickety, top heavy gait that had her catching her breath waiting for him to fall. Beyond him servitors continued to nod and drone in the control pits but the human bridge crew, in splendid red and gold half-gowns, were assembled in a half-circle around a richly-uniformed corpse that sprawled face down on the deck. Calpurnia took in the dead man's epaulettes and chain of rank and decided she had found the unfortunate Vardos del Biel before she looked again at the officers. None wore pistols or sabres, and all were oddly hollow-eyed and gaunt, with a hunted look to their eyes. All had mechanical pads covering their ears, and looking closer Calpurnia could see filter wads in their nostrils.

Technically the bridge crew had the Arbites outnumbered and trapped, but as Calpurnia looked around them no instinctive alarm bells rang despite the fighting they had done. The officers stood in identical poses like chastised children, hands folded and eyes downcast.

She followed Zemlya down with Phae and Zhow behind her and motioned the other Arbites to fan out among the command plinths. There was a little stirring and muttering among the crew, which ended when someone spotted Zhow's rosette and a low moan ran through them. Zemlya swept his arms out for silence, arms that Calpurnia uneasily noticed were of different lengths and set too low on his torso.

'Well?' demanded the inquisitor, trying to take the initiative back from Zemlya's showmanship, beating Calpurnia to it by a moment. Zemlya nodded and pointed to one of the crew, a pallid yellow-eyed man with a drooping moustache.

'I am Jassala Kruthe, the *Aurum Sanctus's* Master of Auspex. My mother and uncle conspired to give shelter and succour to corrupt men who cheated the Sub-Eparch of the Beishi system of part of her triennial tithes. When the plot was righteously purged, my mother was executed. I live in shame for my tainted blood, in thrall to the Emperor aboard the *Sanctus* for my family's betrayal.'

'I am Schacht Eramo, the *Aurum Sanctus's* Lead Astrographer,' said a heavyset woman with hollow cheeks and lank blonde hair. 'I was trained by the Imperial Missionaria on Asherkin and honoured with the gift of a pilgrimage to Chiros, Macharia, Gathalamor and most holy Earth. I vowed that should I finish the pilgrimage in my lifetime I would return and preach of what I had seen. I was seduced by laziness and backsliding, and showed my unworthiness of such a sacred trust. When the Emperor's servants hunted me out in the rookeries of Iata I repented and begged for execution, but to earn that grace I serve the *Aurum Sanctus* on her travels.'

The words had a certain sing-song quality, more recitation than confession. Looking more closely at the crew, Calpurnia could see the edges of penitential chafe-cloths just visible at collars and cuffs.

Zhow was snapping his fingers at the first officer, who answered him in a halting voice. There was a light sweat on his forehead and even in the heavy uniform coat his posture almost shuddered with tension.

'I am Ammon Ginzane, first officer and, uh,' he glanced down at the corpse at his feet – looking at it again Calpurnia noticed blood seeping from its ears and pooling under its eye-sockets – 'Captain-nominate of the *Aurum Sanctus*. I captained the *Voice of Deacis* out of Avignor and Lodesha. My brother was anointed curate in the Eparchy of Crado and required me to speak as a witness at the investiture. For my sins, the Emperor chastised me with poor passage through the warp and I missed the service. My ship was forfeit and my command pledged to the Ecclesiarchy for three years, but in the second year of my service we were gutted by xenos corsairs. For my twofold failures I renounced my claim on full captaincy and boarded the *Sanctus* as First Officer under Captain del Biel and the direction of Curate Majjiah.'

The religious trappings in the outer halls, the relic cases they had fought their way through. A bridge crew of disgraced officers, surrounding themselves with beauty that they cut themselves off from. Perfumed air stopped with nose plugs, beautiful, luxurious uniforms but chafe-cloth scoring their skins underneath...

'It's a penance ship.' Calpurnia had said the words out loud before she thought about it, but Zhow nodded approvingly and spoke as if the rest of the crew weren't there.

'You know of the concept, then? It explains the turnover of officers and the arco-flagellants in the outer passageways. Presumably crew are assigned on and off as their expiations begin and end. What I don't understand–' and he wheeled around to Zemlya 'is your role, Master Zemlya. You are the Navigator on a ship of miscreants and sinners, whose yearning to shed their guilt assures their obedience. But the Navigator families are outside almost every law in the Imperium, sir, and can do what they will. You have no need to fear the Church, and the Church considers you a freak whose existence the Navis Nobilite charters barely make tolerable. The fact that you are putting yourself at risk to stand before me here, instead of sealed in the Navigator's tower indifferent to what we do, begs the question, does it not?'

'Then let me make my own confession and set that question to rest,' said Zemlya. 'I am Peshto Vask Zemlya, of the House of Zemlya, grand-nephew of Novator Eskol Zemlya. My misshapen form is simple testament to my legacy of sin. The family of Zemlya are prideful and ever-grasping. They thought to pull themselves to heights of power through a grip on the throats of their rivals. The wretched feud of Belisarius and Ferraci, your own brethrens' pogrom against the D'Kark, all created turmoil amongst our breed that the Zemlya thought opened the gate for them. My family were desperate for the means to fund their push and found it in wealthy and influential circles who needed secret mobility. My corrupted relatives were righteously destroyed, but their shame endures. That my family laugh at their perdition and spit on the concept of penance only builds upon the foundation that my outlaw forebears laid. I tell you of the disgrace that so few outside our breed know of to show you why I live with this legacy, and why I continue to scratch and deface the great edifice of my family's offences.'

'A Navigator with a conscience.' Zhow's voice was flat and disbelieving. 'A Navigator with a religious epiphany.'

'A Navigator disowned by his family and by all his breed and left with only the burden of expiation to console him.' Calpurnia realised that the hoarseness in Zemlya's voice was emotion. 'Is it so surprising, inquisitor? In my high seat I gaze into the immaterium and see the shadow that our own universe casts into depthlessness. This eye,' and he touched his hood over his high-domed forehead, 'this eye sees gentle flows of soul-stuff where the becalmed mind might starve to death, and tides and churns of genius and hate. The warp mocks the power of words to describe. But what I can never turn my back on is the power and the beauty of the Emperor. I see His soul shine out from Earth and His presence fill every corner of the immaterium. I am scorned for what I talk of seeing, scorned by my family – so be it. Some say that every one of us sees a face of the warp meant only for him, a warp that none other shall ever see, but it makes no matter. I have known from the first time I beheld it that I could do nothing but follow that light with my life.'

There was silence on the bridge for a long moment until Calpurnia spoke. 'If this is a penance ship, and if all your crew have forfeited themselves to serving out their penance as you say, why did you fight? And where are the priests who should have *stopped you*?' She hadn't felt the anger steal up on her but suddenly it was there, cramping her shoulders and fists. Zemlya's great head swung around to stare at her.

'Vardos del Biel is gone into the darkness.' He pointed to the lumpen shape on the deck. 'His orders can do you no more harm.'

'Enough riddles, Navigator,' said Zhow, half-raising his pistol. 'What did he do? What did *you* do?'

'We were to ride the warp tides out to the galactic north,' Zemlya said heavily, 'and then hold ourselves against them while we sent communiqués to Avignor and the diocesan citadels there. Then I was to spy out the countervailing current lower in the galactic plane to carry us southward to Rhanna, Colcha, dark Gathalamor, blessed Chiros. To each we carried an envoy from the eparchal chambers here at Hydraphur. They were sealed into their chambers and I was not told their business, but there was to be one and no more for each of our destinations and they came aboard in secret.'

'I think I can fill in the rest,' said Zhow. 'It's this stupid, damnable squabble between the Ecclesiarchy and the Navy. The senior clergy at Chiros and Ophelia managed to get Baszle into the eparchal throne here as a loyalist to the stricter Terran factions, but the Naval curates all hate him now because he was shoehorned in here instead of one of them. Any communication he wants to make out of the system would normally go through one of the Navy's Astropath stations or aboard a Navy craft. Even sending envoys out by civil traffic wouldn't escape the Navy's notice.'

'So if he wanted to send out reports and requests for help with his power base,' Calpurnia said, 'send them out to other powerful Church centres in surrounding sectors and do it without interference, then he would have to do it not just in an Ecclesiarchal ship but in one that had a chance of getting out of the system without any kind of search or surveillance.

A penance ship would have all its crew fanatically loyal to their curates and preachers.' She could follow the logic, even if she didn't like it. 'The run in to Hydraphur must have been a dummy, just an excuse to be in orbit to meet the shuttle.'

'No wonder the Navy was so keen to help,' put in Phae. 'They even came to us with the offer before we asked them to intercept. They must have suspected why the *Sanctus* was being so secretive but they didn't have any way to make a move. I wouldn't be surprised if the evidence we have about the *Sanctus* being involved in all that shit in Bosporian was planted to nudge us into doing exactly this.'

'Del Biel thought so,' said Zemlya. 'The place of the penitent is obedience and submission, but del Biel had grown hot-headed. I attempted to remind him of his duty and instructed him to submit, but finally he broke away from me and began giving orders to fight you. When I looked at him I saw a mind like a hot coal.' The Navigator shrugged his misshapen shoulders. 'Not every spirit has the strength to stand up to its penance. I gave him my unfettered gaze and struck the life from him. He has gone in among the dark tides now. I do not think the Emperor will be kind to him.'

So it was all still politics after all. Calpurnia was not the only one, the anger was in the air now. The Arbites clubbed the crew out of the way and they yielded with a spiritless shuffle; Phae's team stepped to the plinths and began to reverse the security protocols that had locked the ship down. A message went from Calpurnia to Nakayama and an order went from Nakayama to the Arbitrators who were still coming off the *Clarion* and onto the *Sanctus*.

'Curate Majjiah. Other shipboard Ministorum staff. Passengers, probably with the Curate, probably Ecclesiarchal officers.

Find them.'

AND OF COURSE they were found. The Arbites sweep was efficient and merciless. The tech-priests in the enginarium had their men muster up and surrender instantly, and the skeleton crews in the cargo levels were quickly rounded up. The *Sanctus* was travelling crew-light and lacked the mammoth manpower of a warship anyway, and the roundup took less

than an hour. It was after that that the cyber-mastiffs and
their controllers began to comb the decks, armed with gene-
traces from the preachers' dormitories and bundles of
high-gain snooper auspexes.

As each little group was rooted out of its hiding-place it
was marched to the bridge where the Arbites kept the *Sanctus* in the centre of the ring of Navy ships. The preachers were
scared but defiant, while the last few armsmen who were
guarding them were simply scared. There were three
shootouts, all small and panicked affairs. Four more armsmen were dead and two Arbites injured before the priests all
stood in an indignant mob on the bridge.

And as the last hours of the day ebbed away Calpurnia,
Nakayama and Zhow took ship for Hydraphur again, empty-
handed and all in filthy moods. Zhow's rotund augur had
been marched, panting, up and down the ship over and over
and swore he could find not the faintest trace of witch-taint:
the aura of the Navigator found and accounted for, the rest
of the ship was clean. The cyber-mastiffs combed the same
tunnels and tanks and holds with scent-signatures from
Hydraphur locked into their brains and found nothing
either. No trace of scented lamp-oil, explosive or othwise,
and no scent-print belonging to the invisible gunman or to
any of the prisoners in the Wall. Calpurnia had been so sure,
and now all she had were more questions.

Dead end.

CALPURNIA SAT WITH her chin in her hands in a window-
gallery on the inner face of the Ring, the great adamantine
girdle that hung above Hydraphur's equator. Its wall curved
away to either side of the window, studded with turrets and
docking towers, glittering like the city that the Ring effectively was. The crinkled face of Hydraphur spread out below
them, but the window ran high enough that she could also
look beyond it to Galata, Hydraphur's moon, a peach-
coloured ghost from the surface but stark and ice-silver from
space, studded with glittering clusters of defence stations.

Around them were dark iron walls inlaid with panels of
wood, and curling metalwork adorned the furniture, doors
and rails. All the chambers of the Ring that Calpurnia had

seen had an odd, antique look that didn't seem to match any other ship or building she had been in, but the disturbing atmosphere took her mind off that in short order. Keeping a construct the size of the Ring from being pulled to fragments by the tidal patterns of the sun, Galata and the rest of Hydraphur's bizarre double ecliptic was a challenge that had surpassed even the building of such a thing in the first place: sections of it tens of kilometres long were built to flex and slide, allowing the Ring to gently distort instead of remaining rigid and shattering. At intervals the band of the Ring passed through great square bastions, the most heavily fortified and protected parts of a construct that was itself one giant fortress, housing the gravitic field generators that helped smooth out the roughest of the stresses without interfering with the gravity on the Ring's decks. Someone had told Calpurnia on her way to Hydraphur that the Mechanicus adepts trained there were renowned through the Segmentum for their grasp of gravitic engineering, simply from the experiences of managing the Ring.

The constant flexing and moving of the station was what allowed it to survive, but it meant a constant undertow of noise, soft groans, rumbles, and the occasional high squeal. Veteran crews joked about the Ring's chatter or the lullabies she sang; there was apparently a whole range of superstitions about what certain noises meant to those who heard them. All Calpurnia knew was that it was ruining her nerves.

The locked-together shapes of *Aurum Sanctus* and *Judgement's Clarion* were still somewhere out in space, and would remain so until the legalities were over. Calpurnia refused to let herself think about how long that might take. Captain-Commodore Esmerian, on the other hand, had been in a fine humour once he had heard the reports of the *Sanctus* boarding and had immediately ordered a dromon runnership to carry them back to Hydraphur at top speed. The dromonae were in-system boats, cramped and stuffy and with none of the soaring spaces of the interstellar ships, but that had suited Calpurnia's mood just fine.

'We have eliminated an alternative, arbitor,' Zhow told her now, 'and that is valuable.' It sounded as though he were trying to convince himself. Calpurnia thought that he still wanted to believe the *Sanctus* was the culprit – he had left his augurs on board to keep sweeping decks they insisted they had sniffed over thoroughly already.

'I don't know that we have. The timing is still suspicious. That ship may not have brought the wyrd in, but there still might be links to the explosion.'

Zhow grunted. 'My province is the psyker exclusively,' he said. 'Ruling the ship out of involvement with him was my priority.'

'I see,' said Calpurnia. 'You don't think that the Navigator's involvement with the Ecclesiarchy is a little strange? And what about their terror of the Navy? Why would the eparchal envoys be so frightened? Come to think of it, why was the Navy so quick to take our side? I understood all that talk about secret envoys and power bases, but I didn't understand why.'

'That, at least, I can answer,' Zhow put his back to the window, his hands laced behind him. 'That ship was in service to the Cathedral, which is to say to the High Reverend Eparch Baszle, the highest clergyman on Hydraphur. Now, the Eparch in reality has authority only over the world of Hydraphur itself, and some of the outlying civilian-controlled dockings and gates. Which is to say, just a pocket in the middle of the system. That makes the priests attached to the Naval squadrons a powerful force: they are answerable to their own military-religious hierarchy and have their own chain of command up to the Pontifex Militas aboard the Admiral's ship. "Curates of the flag", they're known as, although the title is a vernacular one with no formal Ecclesiastical currency. A powerful faction in the system since their positions can cross the divide between Naval and civil zones better than most. And because they recruit and appoint their own successors, they're self-perpetuating.'

'Sounds like an excellent reason for the Ministorum and the Navy to work together, not undercut each other like this. But there's something I don't know, isn't there? Of course there is,' Calpurnia growled.

'When Lord Admiral Invisticone was assassinated,' Zhow told her with a reproving look, 'the Ministorum on Terra took very swift action. At that juncture the appointment of a new Eparch was about due and with no formally appointed Lord Admiral they saw the opportunity to get one of their own in, someone who had a hard-line view about traditional Ecclesiarchal authority and would be a wedge against the curates of the flag, who in the cardinals' view have taken on a little too much Navy culture to be entirely trustworthy.'

'Which is why you know about all this?' said Nakayama across the room.

'I know it as background. We—' Zhow cut off whatever he had been about to say and began lecturing Calpurnia again. 'Baszle is a relatively recent appointment; it took that long for the infighting over whose choice would be Eparch to finish and the appointment to take place. He's been aggressively trying to build up the authority of the Cathedral ever since. Which is why, I think, his agents feared foul play from Navy ships, and why the Navy were so helpful in assisting an operation they knew would humiliate the Eparch's office. You should probably know,' he went on as Calpurnia got to her feet, 'that Baragry, your designated shadow on Hydraphur, is of Baszle's inner circle. He's certainly been assigned to you to monitor our investigation and to steer it in convenient ways. He will have something to say about being left behind, I'm sure. If you'll excuse me now, I shall check on our flight back to the Bosporian.'

'Thank you for your briefing, inquisitor,' Calpurnia replied. 'If you need me, I'll be out in the hall hitting myself repeatedly in the head with a shock-maul.' Zhow gave her an odd look, but left without saying anything more.

'Don't let it get to you, Shira,' Nakayama said. 'You'll never have everyone in Hydraphur pulling in the same direction, no matter how hard you try.' She sighed, her hand stealing up to rub her scars again: up, down, up.

'The worst of it is that I keep forgetting that this is only the start of my duties,' she said. 'Bosporian Hive is already a challenge. I'm sure I could spend the next ten years of my life learning about half of what there is to know about how that one hive works, and there are how many more hives here?'

'Eight on Hydraphur, not counting the smaller conurbations and the fortified shrines and forges. About twice that through the rest of the system, again not counting fortification clusters, Navy complexes and spaceborne settlements.' She had got used to Leandro's flowery speech and Zhow's lectures, so that now she kept waiting after Nakayama's sparsely-worded replies for more. The stocky little Arbitrator sat down in the chair Zhow had vacated; at rest, he gave the impression of a powerful machine packed and stowed. 'Twenty-five hives, who knows how many other communities, sixteen planets, hundreds of space-docks and fortresses, more than forty billion people. That's the permanent population. The Naval and civilian shipping through the system can boost that by anywhere from one to ten per cent.'

'It's humbling,' she said. 'I knew this system's scale as I travelled here, but it's only just hitting home at gut level. How do you go about even starting to keep the law in a place this complex?' She inwardly cringed at the question as soon as she'd asked it: it was a rookie's question, and she straight away wondered how it would sound when it got back to Dvorov. But Nakayama didn't seem to take it that way.

'By not trying to do everything yourself,' he said simply. 'Look at the way you handled the Aquila Gate incident. Promptly, correctly and thoroughly. But you did it all in person. Perfect example: fretting over the traffic patterns and keeping order on the Telepine Way at the same time as you were trying to confer with the verispex teams, decide on the processing of your prisoners and co-ordinate your operations with Inquisitor Zhow. Right in line with your style. Oh, you've been studying this system,' he went on as she turned to stare at him, 'but we have studied you too. Are you surprised we studied up on who we were getting? Did you think we won you in a round of seven-deck? Your reputation is sterling, I haven't read of too many finer careers from one of your age. Hell, finer careers full stop. But your reputation is also of handling everything yourself. I bet there weren't even a dozen times in your entire command at Ephaeda when you gave a delegation below Level Three, and I bet you can remember each and every time you did it. That's fine in a precinct house, but not here. Here you won't even have a fixed command. The majore sends us wherever in the system he feels our particular strengths are warranted, to take charge of a particular hotspot for as long as we're needed. You'll have been all around Hydraphur within a year, I don't doubt – Krieg will be picking your assignments with that in mind.'

Calpurnia still couldn't quite stop herself from blinking at his casual use of the lord marshal's first name, but she let it by. Outside the port the sky was still crowded with hundreds upon hundreds of moving points of light, each one a giant, centuries-old warship or defence fortress. Beyond them more points, the nearer planets.

She didn't yet know the Hydraphurn sky well enough to recognise them, or even pick their ecliptic. She had seen maps and models of Hydraphur's system and had dutifully tried to follow the astrographers' treatises on it, but most of them were technical enough to swamp her knowledge of the subject: she had decided to accept that no one really knew how two intersecting planetary planes could form or remain stable, accept that they had and did and get on with her job of policing them.

Hold that thought, she told herself, and turned to look at Hydraphur again. Soon they would board a shuttle and cast off, then the curve of the horizon would barely be visible any more, the drab surface would focus into mountains, shallow seas, hives and forge-towns full of people and plots and enmities and rivalries. Suddenly the descent back to the planet felt to her more like a drop into a mire that was waiting to suck her down to her death.

Eleventh Day of Septista

Seven days to the Mass of Saint Balronas.
The Master's Devotions and the Rite of Common Lamentation.
The Anchorites' Penitence (Ecclesiarchy).

TODAY MARKS THE *final week of preparations for the great mass
and the beginning of the Sanguinala. The Master's Devotions are
the first of the day's fixed observances, and those who cannot
attend the service itself should consider one of the 'proxy' services
held elsewhere between Ecclesiarchy and Naval preachers even as
the Devotions are conducted by the Master of the Vigil and the
Naval curia. Although those with pressing business may be
excused from the Devotions, all pious folk should be ready for the
Rite of Common Lamentation at noon and dressed in at least one
item of green; ideally the hands should be shrouded in green cloth
or gauze. Green gloves or green chain or yarn wrapped about the
hands is an acceptable substitute.*

*By today the festive clothes for the Sanguinala should be fin-
ished and ready. It is inappropriate to wear these garments
between this day and the morning of the mass, so this afternoon
is the final opportunity to make sure they are clean and of good fit.
This should be done in private and alone where possible, and the
clothes packed carefully away afterward, while those caring for
children or the infirm should provide whatever assistance is
needed in this regard.*

CHAPTER SIX

THE WEAPONS RESTED on rich midnight blue plush, secured by tiny silver wires beneath diagrams and fabricator's charts, painted and embroidered onto silk of the same rich blue. The weapons themselves were a simple gunmetal grey, devoid of ornamentation, and the contrast gave shapes on the thick cloth a menace all their own.

The microwire cutter, mounted in a bracelet and designed to flick out of a sleeve and back in a microsecond. The toxin wand to detect poison-snoopers and auto-immunisers and select just the right cocktail to bypass them. The quarrel-launcher with its deadly flare-winged skewers which could glide along a target's pheromone-trail for an hour before they accelerated in for the kill. And the long-barrelled sub-sonic pistol, quiet, accurate, deadly. Calpurnia knew she tended to be too straight-backed on such matters, but she was surprised at the strength of unease and distaste that looking at the weapons gave her.

The armourers had set up their display in the chilly grey briefing chamber of the Cross-Four precinct fortress, far out across the city-plain from Bosporian Hive near the sea-cliffs.

The fortress-tower served a dedicated Arbites landing-pad, built high above the surrounding slums on great rockcrete piles garlanded with razor-wire and defence spikes, and studded with vox-horns that every few minutes would bellow one of the stern maxims from the Arbites *First Book of Hours* out over the roofs below them. While she approved of the thinking, Calpurnia couldn't help wondering whether anyone in those hab-stacks below them got much sleep.

Half an hour after casting off from the Ring Nakayama had produced a data-slate and told Calpurnia to close her eyes and point to it. Self-consciously she had stuck out a finger, opened her eyes and found she was pointing, more or less, to a map on the slate's display. 'Cross-Four', Nakayama had said, 'as good a place as any.' And they had swung out of their registered course to land at Cross-Four. Calpurnia had seen the sense of randomising their flight path, and anyway the airspace restrictions had been tightened to keep a great column of clear air over the hive and it was best to keep well clear. By coincidence it was also close to the fabricatories and residential towers of the Tudela family, considered some of the finest boutique weaponsmiths in the Imperium, and Nakayama had taken the opportunity to have them rousted out of bed and brought to the fortress.

Now the normally bare chamber looked like a trade fair. The Tudela had recovered from their befuddlement at having to muster their wares for a midnight ride, and set up their displays as though they were in a hive noble's audience-court. Calpurnia and Nakayama received them there – Zhow had commandeered a Rhino just after they landed and had disappeared towards the distant hive, telling neither of them his business and showing little interest in the Tudela audience. Calpurnia had gone along with it, but it wasn't until a full squad of Arbitrators marched in around a motor-gurney that she fully understood Nakayama's plan. She had been building up to another one of her brooding moods about the Hydraphur garrison's velvet-glove handling of suspects. The Tudela weren't suspects, they were experts.

Calpurnia was happy with calling on knowledge from other Adeptus – Mechanicus, Administratum, Telepathica – whoever else shared her oaths of loyalty to the Throne of

Earth. If anything, she knew that her picture of the Adeptus as unquestioning allies seemed starry-eyed to a lot of her colleagues. But the idea of going cap-in-hand to an ordinary Imperial subject (doubtless a worthy subject, she added to herself guiltily, a worthy and pious citizen, whose type held the Imperium together) was alien. What was bothering her, when she eventually managed to nail the thought down, was her conviction that anything worth knowing should already be known by the Adeptus. The idea that this might not be the case was bothering her.

The Arbitrators carried the pannier to the centre of the chamber and hinged the top back. The knot of Tudela, huddled into a clump of midnight-blue velvet gowns, slender silver jewellery and face-shrouding collars and hoods, began muttering and shuffling forward. Dvorov or Leandro must have persuaded the Adeptus Mechanicus to part with their evidence, at least for a time.

There in the unfolded display racks sat another set of killing tools: a heavy augmetic eyepiece, mounted on a steel plate with a skull-fitting curve, trailing the filaments that had joined it to the man's nerves; a coronet studded with perceptor spines and inward-pointing wires that had fed and sped the brain; and finally, sitting on a rack of its own, the pistol itself, skeletal and long-barrelled with a swept-back handguard like Navy sabres, studded as the other two were with feeds and interfaces that had embedded the thing into its wielder. It should have been next to impossible to miss with, and Calpurnia gave yet another silent thanks for the hot fogs and incendiary displays that had cruelled that augmetic eye's aim. Imperial dogma took it for granted that the spirits of previous wielders hung over all weapons, and on each component was a scarlet purity seal and a film of sacred balms to exorcise any lingering presence of the witch-gunman.

The weaponsmiths closed in, weaving in and out between Imperial Gothic and some kind of odd, croaking dialect that she assumed was a House language or tech-cant. Two of them, a journeywoman in a filigreed facemask and a man who had been introduced to her as House Elder Makriss Tudela, with a shock of white hair and a discreet dusting of tiny platinum nuggets across the shoulders and sleeves of his

tunic, bent over the weapons to caress them with tiny augmetic microbrushes in their fingertips, taking exact measures
and tasting the weapons' forging and composition. The other
Tudela looked on solemnly from the rich cloth hoods that
stood high above their heads. The augmetics they carried
were startlingly delicate and elegant, silver like Makriss's
rather than brass like those of the Artisans Quarter. She didn't
know if that symbolised anything or not. It probably did.

The analysis didn't take long. Makriss and his offsider
both pulled back from the weapons and the whole delegation withdrew to the other side of a display of subcutaneous
flick-blades to confer. Calpurnia stepped to Nakayama's side.

'Were you able to hear any more of that than I was?' she
asked him.

'Not that I understood,' he said with a slight shake of his
head. 'But I think I picked up enough to know that they're
stumped and they don't want to admit it.'

'I had the same conclusion,' Calpurnia said. 'Hah, they
might be proud of their secret cant but they need to work on
masking their body language. Is that significant?'

'If they can't recognise them? Very significant, yes.' Several
Tudela had now produced data-slates and Makriss and his
journeywoman were stroking their augmetised fingertips
over their surfaces. Makriss's eyes were closed, his lids quivering; the journeywoman had begun to sway slightly. 'One of
the first things that old Makriss told me was that if he and
his staff don't know a weapon design then there's no standard design to know.'

'Is he right?'

'I suspect he is,' Nakayama told her. 'Tudela are the cream,
the best boutique weaponsmiths in the system, which means
in the sector and maybe the segmentum. They're so
respected they've been able to maintain their position without affiliating to one of the mercantile syndicates.'

'Which is why they don't have one of those double sur-
names, then? I'd wondered.'

'That's right.' Nakayama tilted his head at the weaponry
around them. 'Battlefleet Pacificus command commissions
Tudela weapons to present to its officers as battle honours if
that gives you any idea. And yet he looks at that gunman's

kit and says that they're so foreign he can't even pick the archprint they used or what school the designer followed. I don't have quite his expertise, but I can see that these display pieces they've brought in are examples of most of the basic Hydraphur design schools, and that weapon doesn't have much in common with any of them.' He stopped as the delegation approached again and Makriss Tudela bowed.

'Arbitor Senioris Nakayama, Arbitor Senioris Calpurnia. On behalf of the family Tudela we confirm that the weapons and devices are of the kind that we construct – cousins to our own craftsmanship, as it were. But we have bent ourselves to a search lest they bear traces of the archprints bequeathed by the beneficent Mechanicus, or lest they even should reveal traces of our own smiths or even, should I not be too bold in making such a reference, those of our rivals.'

'Your rivals?' asked Calpurnia. 'You can vouch for those weapons not being made in this system? Or are you talking about a bigger or smaller area?' Tudela blinked at the question and gave Calpurnia what she was starting to think of as the 'oh, you're the one who's not from here' look.

'From our own weaponworkers? No,' he replied. Calpurnia could sense him turning the flowery language down a notch. 'Tudela has inherited certain design axioms and privileged archprints which I will not detail, but to which your weapons do not adhere to. As to those occupying our own line of craft? There are only a handful whom I would consider capable of handiwork of this quality. Of those, the Zaphraoi are bonded to Kraegen-Medell for metals and use steels provided by that cartel; there was none of their distinctive taste to the metals we inspected. Durska-Haggan can produce sighting augmetics as fine as this, but their expertise in actual firearms is shallow. To bond the pistol mechanism and the augmentation of its wearer requires a grasp of both mechanical and biometric mysteries that I know to be beyond them.' Makriss pondered for a moment, running a thumb over the fine silver filaments braided into his moustache.

'The weapon shops at the Bescalion Dock – these are operated directly under Navy control in the Gyre Marmarea, you understand. They would have the finesse to produce these, I think, being presided over directly by Mechanicus inductees.

But all the major fabricatories at Bescalion operate in zero-gravity. Their micro-engineering processes quite depend upon the fact. And all the components of your specimens here were crafted under gravity.'

'You can tell that?' Calpurnia asked him.

'Certain minute biases in density and balance correspond exactly to equivalent weapons made by ourselves – that means your specimens were made in Hydraphur-equivalent gravity. Those biases are what gravity-free forging is specifically intended to counteract.'

'It rules out the Navy almost totally,' put in Nakayama. 'They like to keep their ships and stations a fraction below standard Hydraphur gee. Nothing you'd notice, but it would show up on the sort of scales I imagine Master Tudela uses.'

'Just so,' said Makriss, looking pleased. 'I believe that my original conclusion stands. My own suspicion is that these pieces came from some considerable distance from Hydraphur. Of the most respected armourers in this system, none had a hand in their creation.' He finished his words with a chivalrous little bow, and the sudden change of manner made it Calpurnia's turn to blink.

'Then thank you for your time, Master Tudela, for your help, and for food for thought. The proctor here will arrange an orderly return to your home.'

'The service was entirely the pleasure of myself and my family,' Makriss replied with another bow. 'All I might beg from you, should I presume…?' Nakayama gave a slight tilt of his head. 'I dare say I should not even need to point out that although our skill and our works are our best envoys, a position such as ours must also on occasion be maintained with, how shall I put it… a knowledge of…'

'I think I understand,' Nakayama told him. 'If we do find out who made these weapons and where, I shall see about sharing that with you.' Satisfied, Makriss bowed again, his retinue imitating him and staying bowed over while the two arbites senioris turned away. As they left the chamber Calpurnia heard a sudden, muted burst of activity as the Tudela began taking their display to pieces.

'And once again, we're back where we started,' she growled as the doors swung shut behind them and they climbed the great spiral stairwell that made up the fortress's spine. In the quiet spell between the night-to-dawn shifts the stairs were empty enough for them to hear their footsteps echo.

'Not exactly,' Nakayama said. 'We're able to conclude some things. I don't believe that the killer was smuggled in from elsewhere, I think that was Tudela's way of reassuring them-selves that a weapon can't be made in this system without them knowing about it.'

'I wondered about that. Didn't he confirm the weapons had been made under gravity identical to Hydraphur's? How would someone counterfeit that so exactly?'

'Well said. So the enemy has access to a private weapon-smith so secret they can produce high-quality designs that Hydraphur's finest armourer can't identify.'

'And said weaponsmith is also so unscrupulous that they will build those designs into a proscribed witch-psyker,' Calpurnia added. 'The weapons married up too well with the assassin's own abilities for them not to have been deliberate.'

'And we know that they were prepared to risk having all this revealed in the course of taking a crack at you,' finished Nakayama. They had reached the uppermost landing, where galleries led away to the corners of the fortress. Calpurnia paused to look up at the great steel aquila which hung from chains in the dome overhead and was mortified to realise that she was breathing hard – on garrison duty she could have run up and down these stairs and barely notice the effort. She wondered when this investigation would let her get some physical training in. It was just another little thing that seemed to be sliding out of her control.

'So our enemy,' she said, 'is even more powerful than we thought and even more intent on seeing me dead than we had realised.'

'If that isn't progress, what is?' asked Nakayama. His face was still deadpan, and Calpurnia simply had to hope that he was joking.

BEFORE INQUISITOR ZHOW had disappeared he had harangued the Arbites at length about the lack of a skimmer-car to carry him back to Bosporian and demanded a secure voxmat room where he could debrief with his staff. It had seemed to

Calpurnia to be as much a fit of pique over not being told
about their change of landing place as anything else. Now
they were met on the landing by a garrison clerk with a message for Calpurnia that the voxmat link had been kept live: the
Master of the Vigil of Saint Balronas, Hallyan Kalfus-Medell,
had received word that she was at Cross-Four and requested
that she speak with him at her earliest convenience. Normally
she would have waited pointedly for a while befor answering,
but she needed something to take her mind off the disap-
pointment of the still-untraceable weapons.

The transmission chamber was set into the topmost rampart of the fortress, beneath the dome itself, one of a forest
of metal fingers that carried encrypted vox and pict transmissions, anchored the fortress's void shields when they
were raised, or were simply dummies to throw off attackers
and saboteurs. The chamber itself was meant for private
transmissions by senior Arbites, or as a bolt-hole for an
arbitor or two to seal themselves in and keep transmitting if
the rest of the fortress was somehow overrun.

Calpurnia found herself in a narrow stone cavity with a
simple vox-panel at head height (her head, anyway) on the
far wall, the space partly blocked by an incongruously soft
leather seat. Whether it was a fixture or something Zhow had
had brought in was not apparent.

Calpurnia noticed a slight hum from the panel as she
composed herself and thought about her opening words. It
was time to start dealing with these people in the right way,
courteous but not servile. She thought that she–

'Arbitor Calpurnia.' She jumped as Hallyan's voice cracked
from the panel. Only slightly, but enough to make her glad
the link only carried vox and not images.

'Lord Hallyan,' she replied. 'Your message said you
couldn't wait until I returned to Bosporian. If it has you waiting into the small hours to talk to me I assume it was urgent.'

'So you are there, arbitor. I thought I could hear you moving around. I must speak with you about this apparent
investigation into the attempts to wreck what is the most
pious and holy time of year for the entire Hydraphur system, Navy and civilian alike. This is not something you can
be ignorant of. You've been right at the centre of every

important disruption since the moment when things started to go wrong.'

Lord Hallyan was livid, it was clear. The niceties of language and the careful manner from their first meeting were dropping away and his voice was snapping with anger, the effect magnified by the slightly tinny tones of the vox-link.

'To repeat your words back to you, Lord Hallyan, I've had a quite personal involvement at every step of the way.' She knew he couldn't see her but she was still adopting a formal stance, feet apart and hands behind her back. 'Involvement with minor things like attempts on my life, things that stick in the memory. What else would you like to remind me of concerning my "apparent" investigation–'

'I would like to remind you of a simple matter.' Hallyan was talking before she had finished. 'This is a crucial time in our religious calendar, and the Adeptus Ministorum has charged me with overseeing it. I believe, arbitor, that myself and those members of the Ministorum who are assisting me deserve better treatment than you have seen fit to hand out. Reverend Baragry and I have both been informed of the treatment of the *Aurum Sanctus*, a ship operating under the direct auspices of the Ecclesiarchy which for some reason the Adeptus Arbites felt necessary to subject to a disgracefully heavy-handed interception! The–'

'Have a care, my lord,' Calpurnia interrupted. 'Remember who you're addressing. Your *temporary* office allows you a certain familiarity of manner, but you are no Adeptus and you are no arbitor.'

There was a pause, long enough for the link to begin crackling and fizzing again. Calpurnia could even make out the faint buzz and clink of the Mechanicus prayer-wheels among the vox gear.

'Very well,' came Hallyan's voice eventually. 'My... my apologies for my abruptness, my duties weigh on me at present. I made the declaration of the Precepts last sunset and will be sharing the conduct of the Common Lamentation today, as well as certain ceremonial responsibilities conferred uniquely on me.' He sounded tired but still pleased at being able to point his station out. 'But I would ask that you recall,' he went on, 'the Ecclesiarchy were generous enough to provide you Reverend Baragry as an advisor because the religious implications of even the smallest Arbites action during this period could be profound. I am at a loss to understand why you have sidelined Baragry in the way that you did. I understand that you deliberately left him here when you took ship to intercept the *Sanctus*. Is this true?'

Calpurnia wondered at the question. If Hallyan was dealing with the Ecclesiarchy he would have known it was. On the other hand, his temporary but quasi-religious office made her baulk at the idea of telling him outright that the last thing they had needed was an Ecclesiarchal agent underfoot while they chased down a vessel operating under Ecclesiarchal charter. Nakayama had made a point of sidelining Baragry as they prepared to launch the interception flight, and Calpurnia had left Bannon behind with him to try to make it look less suspicious.

She thought of the overdressed aristocrats she had seen around the High Mesé and wondered what one of them would come up with, and how she would phrase it.

'It seemed to us, Lord Hallyan, that it was the best thing we could do for the Ecclesiarchy in the circumstances. I understand that there is some friction between the Ecclesiarchy and the Navy over certain matters of religious jurisdiction. We were unsure of the link between the ship and the Aquila Gate – it now seems tenuous, but we had no way of telling that at first. Given the possibility that intercepting the *Sanctus* might embarrass the Ecclesiarchy, we excluded the Reverend Baragry – and yourself, for that matter – so that it would have been that much easier for the Ecclesiarchy to distance itself and denounce the *Sanctus* as a rogue.'

She was not proud of herself. The story, and the ease with which she had plucked it out of the air, left an unpleasant taste in her mouth. But from Hallyan's reaction she seemed to have played it about right.

'I remain somewhat displeased,' he said after a moment, 'but I appreciate the tactics of your decision. You might consider informing us of any future situation, however, my arbitor. I assure you that we can play the part should we need to and still dissociate in the way that you spoke of.' It took a moment for her to understand what he was saying, and when she did her distaste deepened.

'What we can also do,' Hallyan went on, 'is appraise you of the ramifications of any proposed actions the central duty of carrying out the sacred mass. I have overseen much of the preparations myself. At any given moment I will be well equipped to brief you on any proposed course of action you might wish to take in pursuing your own business, on its potential to disrupt the religious proceedings of the coming week and therefore on its advisability.'

'Are you talking about giving orders to the Adeptus Arbites, sir?'

'How you order your own activities and pursue your investigations is probably largely your own affair,' Hallyan told her airily. Either he hadn't noticed the edge in her voice or the vox-panel had dulled it out. 'And I acknowledge the good work you have done on the sabotage of the oil shipment and in pursuing the denounced assassin who attempted harm upon you personally. But as a man of experience in the society of Hydraphur I am in a position to bring your attention to consequences that you, madam arbitor senioris, might have overlooked.

'For example, the sabotage at the Aquila Gate, which I understand you were on hand to witness personally. Now, the destruction of the last shipment of oil was of no great consequence and replacement stocks were supplied to the Augustaeum by the time that the Procession of the Further Saints was due to begin. In the scheme of things the matter may not have been of great import – the damage was not significant, nor were the fatalities. But I believe you were aware, arbitor, of the considerable disruption – indeed the immobilisation – of the freight and traffic up one entire slope of the hive and the disturbances that bred.

'This is a sensitive time, Arbitor Calpurnia. Respectable citizens of the upper hive and Augustaeum are endeavouring to fulfil their pious duties and complete mundane business in time to begin their observances. I cannot find it in me to believe that you do not desire to help them, and to remove from their way any obstacle that you have power over?'

'We sealed off the Aquila Gate for a reason,' Calpurnia said. 'The destruction of that oil-dray was not just the irritating disruption to the mass preparations that you seem to want to treat it as. It was a *crime*, sir, an act of destruction and of loss of life and a gross breach of the Emperor's law and the Emperor's peace and therefore fully within our remit to investigate as we need to. I acknowledge the possible links between that act and your mass and we have told you that keeping order is a priority for us, but the Arbites are not a private security force for the mass. Understand that, please. We are Adeptus, just like the Ministorum who have granted you your *temporary* position, and our charter is Emperor-bestowed just as theirs is.'

So much for subtlety and diplomacy. There was no doubt that her feelings had registered with Hallyan this time.

'I was told, arbitor senioris, that you had familiarised yourself with life on Hydraphur.' The lord's voice was cold. 'In my next dealings with your colleagues and commander and with the Eparch of Hydraphur himself I believe that I shall convey that your familiarity is imperfect.'

'I have never pretended otherwise, but my grasp of my duty is crystal clear. Other than that, say about me what you will. I will be reporting my latest findings to the arbitor majore later this morning, I'll be certain to make your feelings known to him then, and I will happily comply with any directive he then chooses to give me.'

'Findings?' demanded Hallyan. 'What findings? The whole *Aurum Sanctus* affair was reported to me as a dead end.'

Was it now? Calpurnia thought. And by whom was that reported, then? But she held back the question.

'Are you familiar with the family Tudela? They maintain a fabricatory spike in the city plain and have a hereditary charter to use certain Mechanicus weapon archprints and lay machining techniques.'

'Give me a little credit. The Kalfus family were patrons in chief of the Tudela pavilion at the Martial Exposition at the Monocrat's summer palaces last year.' His tone changed. 'You have not been harassing the Tudela too? To think that they might be involved with something like this beggars belief. I could have told you–'

'Nothing like that, Lord Kalfus-Medell, calm yourself,' Calpurnia cut in. 'Arbitor Nakayama and I consulted them on the weaponry that the witch-assassin used in the first attempt on my life.'

'I thought that the Mechanicus had seized what remained of that.'

'No. We presented the weapons to a Tudela delegation tonight. A Makriss Tudela surveyed them, and says that they correspond to no known armourer operating in Hydraphur – the handful of machinesmiths in this system capable of producing them didn't. It's really only useful in negative terms – we can expand our list of people we *don't* believe were behind it. But it suggests one or two further steps.'

'Which are?' he asked.

'Still being decided on,' Calpurnia bluffed. 'I will ensure you are provided with any information that will be useful to you, Lord Hallyan. We must continue to co-operate in keeping the Emperor's peace through the time of the Vigil and I am sure we will be co-operating in the investigation also. Why don't we discuss the matter when I return to Bosporian? I expect to be back there during the day.'

There was a quick double-gunshot of static and another long pause. Calpurnia was wondering if the link had died by the time Hallyan answered. 'It seems we do still have certain things to discuss and set straight, Arbitor Calpurnia. Very well. You will hear from me.'

There was no click as the link broke, just silence for a minute, two, three, until Calpurnia decided the conversation must be over.

CROSS-FOUR'S VEHICLE hangar sat on a platform between the pilings under the main mass of the fortress, with a tangle of ramps and chain-hoists giving access to the streets and sky-ways of the city below. Calpurnia disapproved of this setup in the short time she had to think about it: the hangar and ramps seemed achingly vulnerable to sniper shots and missiles from the tower-blocks around them.

Her Rhino convoy rumbled down the ramps five hours into the new day, right at the heart of the patrol changeover. The Rhinos went out one at a time, spaced between the rest of the traffic, then in unison swung and sped away down a broad elevated highway. A squad in the lead vehicle, a squad in the hindmost one, and Calpurnia alone with the two crew drivers in the middle with the benches to herself.

Nakayama was staying on at Cross-Four to audit airspace security procedures; Calpurnia had agreed, but felt his absence now – she had wanted to talk with him again. Casting her mind back over the last few days was almost dizzying: the Cathedral to the Aquila Gate to the *Aurum Sanctus* and back. The dead end at the *Sanctus* meant that the trail was colder than she had thought, and getting colder by the moment. She was even starting to wonder if the attacks at the Gate were connected to the witch-gunman at all.

And there was still fallout she had barely considered. The second prisoner from the dray, the task of tracking down the vehicle's owners. A review of security at all the Augustaeum gates, to make sure the Arbites were better prepared in future. The paralysing traffic snarls up and down the southwest slope of the hive were only just starting to abate after two days. For all its status and odd quirks, Bosporian Hive and its skirt of sprawl were no different from any other high-density Imperial city and so the snarls had created tension, the tension had created unrest, and violence had sprung up along the major traffic roots like brushfires.

Blameless Imperial citizens had also died at the Aquila Gate, trampled in the stampedes or caught in the flames. Calpurnia knew that had she had the whole terrible incident to do again her commands would have been the same and those people would still have died. *Ut iusta esse, lex nobis severus necesse est*, they had taught early and often at the Schola Arbitorum, 'to be just, our law must be cruel,' and also *Lex Imperatoris, quia via vitarum nobis, obiesquat*, 'the Emperor's law be obeyed, even in the manner of our lives' ending'. It was a harsh thing to dwell on, alone on a juddering steel bench in a rumbling tank in a strange city in the pre-dawn dark, but every arbitor knew that the rule of Imperial Law came at a price.

But 'the right to command is bought with duty' was an Ultramar maxim that Calpurnia had internalised by the time she was ten: it was carved into the polished quartz lintel of the Calpurnii's hearth-house, and it had been inscribed below the seal on her father's brief letter of well-wishing when she had been brevetted to the Ephaeda garrison command. In many Ultima Segmentum garrisons, where civilian deaths were necessary in an Arbites action, garrison preachers would visit their families for special devotions to speed the unlucky souls' passage to the Emperor's side. She didn't know if that tradition had spread this far (a resigned little part of her mind clocked up one more thing about Hydraphur policing she didn't know), but if it didn't then that was one little bit of her home culture she wanted to plant here.

There was a brief wash of light through the vision ports and Calpurnia peered out. They had just passed under an arch of rockcrete, arclit in the urban dimness swarming with work-crews blasting away the accretion of pollutant grime. She remembered something in her mountain of briefings about the last-minute rush of building and beautifications that both Bosporian Hive and the plain city crammed into before the mass; around her now she could see other projects dotted about the city, all lit up, all still being feverishly worked on despite the saints-forsaken hour to be finished before the enforced days of rest began.

The little lit patches got more frequent as the bright bulk of Bosporian loomed in the middle distance over the smoke-wrapped city stacks. Within half an hour they passed a procession of statues of Imperial martyrs Calpurnia didn't recognise, but with appropriately gruesome sculpted injuries and saintly heavenward gazes, then a miniature city of temporary amphitheatre-chapels of scaffolding and reinforced sheetboards, standing side by side in an empty pedestrian concourse. After that a pair of triumphal obelisks commemorating long-dead admirals, which workers were shrouding in dark drapes and carefully fitting with auto-launchers that would shed the mourning-cloth and fill the air with scarlet fireworks the moment the Sanguinala was rung in. Further in where the streets narrowed great hoardings were being set up and banners strung between buildings; in the festivities after the mass they would be joyous and bright-coloured, but now they were all in the spirit of the Vigil, sombre and urging repentance. The giant images were simplistic to the point

of crudity, but still striking: agonised, wild-eyed heretics
stumbling in the dark that symbolised their souls, or stylised
pictures of the Emperor with His face turned away and the
saints and angels weeping around Him. The localised, lit-up
pockets of activity gave the city a strange, on-off aspect as
they passed through it. Calpurnia realised they were seeing
so many because they were speeding down one of the arterial highways to the base of the hive itself, and that put a
thought into her head.

'Randomise our course, please,' she called forward into the
driver's compartment. 'Pick a minor patrol route into the
base of the Wall and follow that, not this main road. Notify
the other two Rhinos in code, even if the vox-band is safe.'

Less than a minute later they swerved off the highway and
down into the canyon-maze between the stacks and spires.
The lower streets were as narrow as slots and overhung by the
towers that boarded them; the Hydraphur fashion seemed to
be for sheer walls for at least the first dozen floors and the
roads were shut-in and dark. Now they were off the highway
she could see more people: shifting, scurrying night-time
people who shied away from the lights of Arbites Rhinos,
fearful of a credentials stop or an outright curfew-cull.

But even down here preparation for the celebrations was
going on, to Calpurnia's uncharitable surprise. The crews
were smaller, and she noted with approval that some were
dressed in the barbed circlets and heavy sackcloth jerkins of
penal details, working under foremen in Arbites or Ecclesiarchal uniforms. The works were more modest, too, fewer
giant statues and hoardings, more basic repairs to the roads
and buildings and simple devotional pennants.

There was a crackle from the vox-grille in the drivers'
cockpit, and Calpurnia shuffled forward to find out what
had been said.

'Route up ahead is blocked, ma'am,' the co-driver told her.
She had a knotted scar jagging down one cheek and in under
her jaw that made her lip move oddly. 'The comptrollers at
Lowdock Tower just voxed it through. Pre-Vigil civic works
running past due. We didn't know about it until one of the
foot patrols for this sector called it in. It just got voxed out to
us once the comptrollers realised where we were.'

'How did they know we were here?'

'Convoys are tracked, and we reported in when we turned off the highway.'

'Pick an alternative route at random, then. Now.' The driver nodded and muttered into the short-range vox, and a moment later they veered into a narrower street still, between cliff-like rockcrete walls and sullen strings of lights. 'And no more long-range vox-chatter. I don't care if the dispatcher hails us or not. Short-range only, and only to keep us tight when we change routes and to pass on instructions.'

'Understood, ma'am.'

Calpurnia approved of rules and order, and in her junior Arbitrator positions had been very suspicious of the importance that her trainers and commanders put on intuition and the feel of situations. That was a judgement she had been forced to re-evaluate, and she had made an addition to her list of the chief weapons of the Arbites: awe and fear; the shock-maul and grapplehawk and Executioner shell; the Rhino and cyber-mastiff and the Book of Law… and the way that a seemingly innocuous fact weighed oddly in the mind, the way that things struck the senses as being just a little unsettled, like a picture hung crookedly in the corner of your vision, the little unquiet voice whispering, wait… something about this feels wrong.

The feeling got stronger on the second redirection. Their new street was completely blocked with a caterpillar-tracked streetcrawler, parked in the middle of the road and supporting a thick web of scaffolding braced against the walls. Their lead driver was alert enough to veer off while there was still a turnoff between them and the workers, but Calpurnia was peering down the street through a darkvisor as they turned. There were men in the gantry it carried, working at anchoring it to the walls. But there was no other equipment, no banners or murals, and they had all stopped working as the Rhinos approached and watched them as they turned aside.

They sped through an alley narrow enough that Calpurnia could have slipped her hand out of the vision slot and lost the skin off her fingertips on the building walls. Then they were into another thoroughfare and intersection, the way ahead blocked by grumbling orange-painted engines just starting to break the surface of the road, and downramps to each side brightly lit but empty. In the one on the left two men ducked out of sight as they passed. A quick, tooth-sharp burst of satisfaction punctured Calpurnia's unease. They had slipped up.

'Turn. Full reverse, now, before the intersection. Back the way we came, retrace our steps. Move. Now.' The knowledge that something was badly wrong had sprung into her head fully-formed and she didn't waste time doubting it. She steadied herself as the three APCs spun in almost their own length and accelerated away again. She was impressed as they shot back into the alleyway – Rhinos were built for toughness and reliability, not high-speed agility, but the crews were making them dance around the corners like pursuit buggies. They came out of the alley, powered away from the scaffold and Calpurnia let them make one more turn, then called a halt and was rocked hard against the driver's partition as the three APCs braked. They were in a silent, empty street, almost overhung enough to be a passageway of asphalt and rockcrete grimed almost black, graffiti and ragged tracts covering the walls. Calpurnia ordered the lights off, armed her pistol and reached for the hatch.

IT TOOK THREE silent minutes to decide that the men from the roadworks were not coming around the corner after them, and another two to firmly override the protests of the convoy's proctor that he should call in backup. Eight minutes after they had halted and powered down the Rhinos they moved out. The first and third carriers each carried ten combat-kitted Arbitrators, and with them came the three co-drivers, lighter-armoured and nervous about leaving their partner-drivers behind.

'You three won't come with us,' she said softly, looking at the scar-faced woman from her own Rhino. 'Open the top hatches on your Rhinos and get the pintle weapons up and loaded. What are you carrying? Shotcannon, stubbers...? Storm-bolters. Good. The Rhinos will be the second wave. The rest of you, listen. These work crews are false. They were mobilised to trap us when we left the highway, but we foxed them by switching paths. They've been having to keep moving, trying to keep in front of us. They're good enough to keep spying or guessing the routes we switch into and moving to block them, but they had to move too fast to be able to keep it looking like coincidence.'

'Are we assaulting them, ma'am?' asked one of the squad proctors.

'Not front-on. Whatever they have in mind, it'll be set up to deal with three Rhinos coming at them, because that's what they expected. Every door in this city should have an Arbites override on its seals. Yes? Good. We're getting inside this building and coming out, well, somewhere, wherever we can break out into or behind that scaffold. We'll need a decent number of shock-grenades, have you got–? Good. Once we've got the ambush disorganised, the Rhinos will come round and lend fire support from the street. Report it to the nearest precinct house at that point too and we'll get our own backup on the move.'

'Arbitor senioris, are you sure that we shouldn't get backed up now and make sure we hit them with overwhelming–'

'No. Even if they don't intercept the transmission or hear the backup coming, by the time it gets here they'll have run or tracked us down and attacked on their terms, not ours. This way is risky, but not taking that risk is not going to work. We're taking too long as it is.' She strapped on her helmet. 'The Law commands and the Emperor protects. Let's go.'

The main doors to the tower between them and the street-crawler were under a shadowy overhang at the far corner. Calpurnia did not yet have a key-signet, but the proctor's signet was enough to override the locks and send the security shackles clanking back into the walls. After a moment they had picked their way up a narrow staircase and into a gallery around over a great chamber that took up the first three floors of the tower and, it looked like, possibly a below-ground level as well. It was the office of some kind of courier-house: the torchlight showed racks of crates and pack-harnesses for humans and servitors down below them, and the gallery was packed with row upon row of narrow, tilted clerking-desks over which the despatchers and ledger-keepers would be hunched during the day.

They were halfway through the gallery when they met the watchman. He was middle-aged and squint-eyed, nervously clenching his hands over a long-barrelled laspistol. Calpurnia doubted that he recognised her rank badges, but he must have realised that she was far senior to the lead arbitors and proctors he was used to.

'I am so sorry, sir arb, er, madam arbitor. I can think of no reason why you would have been called out, I know of nothing that would require you. Not that you, not that you are unwelcome, of course, but I–'

'We're not here for anything in your building, we need passage through it. We need to get over to the…' she tried to get her bearings. The west wall, the south? '…the wall out over one of the narrow streets where a work crew is putting up some kind of scaffold.'

'Oh. I've been keeping an eye on them, ma'am, nothing suspicious to report. I don't believe the watch on this building were told whether they were going to be doing that work tonight, which is a little irregular, but I understand that the procedures for informing–'

'Fine. We need access to a window or a balcony or whatever you have that opens out to near that scaffold. Now.' Guilliman's blood, was everyone on Hydraphur such a windbag?

The watchman scuttled ahead of them through the gallery to a wide lift that buzzed its way up its shaft for an ascent whose distance it was impossible to properly judge. Then they threaded through a disorienting maze of passages and cubbyhole rooms crammed with dim stacks of data-slates and papers, the Arbitrators surreptitiously cursing behind her as they manoeuvred their shields through the cramped space. She was almost twitching with anxiety by the time he opened a security shutter and motioned them into an echoing cavity between the inner rooms and outer wall.

Calpurnia could hear nothing. If the men on the scaffold really had been doing anything to the building instead of just keeping up an illusion of it, they had stopped.

'This takes you out onto a ledge we use to maintain the external airwells,' said the watchman from a little metal step below the access hatch embedded in the wall. 'The locks are off now. The ledge runs the way around the building, but it is narrow, ma'am, and with no railing. You'll want to be careful.' He blinked as a thought hit him. 'Perhaps if I go out on the ledge first, spy things out and perhaps–'

'No,' Calpurnia cut him off. 'These people will be quite happy to shoot you off the ledge as soon as they see you on it.' She was amused to see the sneaking relief under his crestfallen expression, and relieved that he hadn't pressed the point. The others were already gathering around the hatch, blessing their weapons and exchanging aquila signs. Calpurnia walked between them to put a hand on the release handle, murmured a battle-blessing and swung it open.

They came out of the building ten floors up and on the far side of the scaffold. The streetcrawler far below them supported the extendable girders of the central gantry and arms had swung out to strut it against the walls, secured to the rockcrete with grapples. Some peripheral part of her saw the racks and pipes on the struts and supposed that this was some kind of cleaning rig, designed to detoxify and wash the pollutants from the building sides. But all her conscious mind was exulting in the knowledge that she had been right. The people perched motionless in the scaffold were no cleaning crew: they were braced in wary postures, hefting weapons, watching the other direction in case the Rhinos came back around the corner.

The ledge was actually a groove cut into the building side, head-high and a metre deep, but the dimness helped Calpurnia forget how high up they were and she was able to move along it easily. They were still at a level where all the other buildings were sheer-walled and windowless, shutting off any view. The others followed behind her as quietly as they could, but Arbites' boots allowed only so much stealth and they had been unable to help the clank of the hatch itself. Some of the ambushers were twisting around to see what was making the sound behind them. No more stealth, no more time to feel precarious and perched here. Time to be Arbites.

'Hailing,' she said, and torches snapped on from the file of men behind her, held up high and away from their bodies. Their would-be ambushers turned from silhouettes into people, stocky worker-types in nondescript khaki coveralls, startled and blinking.

'ADEPTUS ARBITES!' Calpurnia declared into the pickup on her vox-torc. In the small-hours quiet of the street her own lungs were adequate enough, but her voice was also picked up and fired out of the little voxcasters clipped to the shield-rims of the Arbites behind her. 'In the name of the *Lex Imperia*, throw down your arms and surrender yourselves to righteous judgement.'

And of course the men in the scaffold brought their weapons around. The first one to fire had his aim thrown by the lights in his eyes and the krak grenade took a chunk out of the wall over their heads. As she took aim, planted her back against the wall and shot him off his perch, Calpurnia decided none of this surprised her at all.

THE ARBITES KNEW their roles well. The rearmost, holding the lights, kept the torch-beams playing over the ambushers' faces. Those further up wedged their backs against the building and braced their shields in front of them, brought their shotguns to bear through the ports and began a steady suppressing fire. Rounds sizzled and yipped through the air as Calpurnia moved down the ledge with half a dozen Arbites behind her, slamming her pistol into its holster and plucking her maul from her belt.

The ambush crew had been caught by surprise, and they were handling it badly. Too committed to their plan of firing down on a Rhinocade in the street, some of them had actually strapped themselves into their positions for stability and were struggling to free themselves. Others had panicked and started swinging down through the gantry, dropping their weapons or leaving them hanging from struts and beams.

'Rhinos, move!' she barked into her torc pickup. 'Cover the bottom of the gantry!' They had been waiting on her command and now came around the corner, alarm klaxons nearly drowning out the gunfire. The storm-bolters at each pintle-hatch sent their deadly micro-rocket shells scudding through the base of the gantry, blasting away the top of the driver's cabin and hammering at the base girders.

The ambushers were trapped but they weren't surrendering. The return fire from the scaffold began to get more focused. A frag grenade went off above the ledge and shrapnel crackled against shields and helmets – two Arbitrators were dislodged by the blast and toppled, yelling, into space.

'Ware shocks!' came from behind Calpurnia and she hunched and jammed herself home as best she could as three grenade-tubes chugged behind her. There was a moment for the grenades to arc up and in, and she could clearly hear them ringing and bouncing into the gantry, and then there was the flat *ka-whapp* of shock-grenades that compressed her ears even through the muffles on her helmet and more rings and clanks as stunned bodies dropped down through the gantry to the street.

Forgetting the drop, Calpurnia ran to where the gantry reached the wall of the building, grabbed a rail and swung into it. The Arbitrators behind her were moving forward a little more slowly, keeping their shields up and firing around her. They had loaded clips of homing Executioner rounds, and now their shots passed Calpurnia with their distinctive buzz as they curved into the scaffold to seek out their targets.

A grenade whistled past, pinked off an Arbitrator's shield behind her and exploded in mid-air. Knocked forward by the blast, Calpurnia used the momentum to grab another railing and swing down onto a steel-mesh platform. A bandolier of grenades still hung from a utility hook there; the man with the launcher had retreated to the web of beams below it and was peering up at her as he worked the slide. She wouldn't be able to reach him in time so she grabbed the railing, lunged out and whacked a crossbar with her maul. The blue power-flare made him yelp and flinch and while the afterimages were still dancing in his eyes she scrambled down, got her balance as he brought the launcher up and smashed his knee with an unpowered low swing. A chopping return stroke broke his fingers as he shouted and scrabbled for a handhold, and then he was crashing down and away.

Beyond him another shape in the dimness, the sound of an autogun clip slammed home. Calpurnia grabbed the support by her side, kicked her feet out and dropped down to sit hard on the beam she had been balancing on as his burst rattled through the scaffolding. To the sound of swearing and shouts from the Arbites above her she danced forward two

steps, finding her footholds as much by reflex and faith as
anything, and caught the gunner in the gut with an extended
fencer's lunge. The power discharge sparked and thudded,
doubled the man up and toppled him down.

The Rhinos had pulled up below them and ignited their
searchlights. Suddenly the scaffold turned from a dim web-
work of shadows, torch-beams and scrambling shapes to a
harsh-lit web of yellow and black metal. That broke their
attackers completely. With the Arbites on the ledge still in
shadow and the Executioner shells homing in earnestly, the
firefight became a rout, the last of the ambushers leaping
and swinging downward like startled primates, shouting in
fear or anger, one or two still bothering to fire wildly until
cruelly accurate bursts from the Rhinos' storm bolters blew
them apart. Two more landed on the streetcrawler and made
to flee until a shock-grenade sent them reeling with blood
welling in their nostrils and ears. The handful of others
stopped where they were, braced themselves in place and
extended their hands to show their surrender. Below them
lay their fellows knocked out of position by the fighting,
those that could now moaning and calling for help.

Feeling the exertion of the last few minutes in her arms
and shoulders, Calpurnia watched as her scar-faced co-driver
levered herself out of her Rhino's top hatch, hefting an arm-
ful of prisoner shackles. She stepped from the roof of the
APC up onto the streetcrawler platform, and that was when
Calpurnia, still perched metres above the gunmen below,
heard gasps and a strangled cry that sounded like, 'Her!'

That nerve, that *this-is-wrong* feeling was screaming again.
Sudden urgency seemed to make her hands and feet heavy
and slippery on the beams as she shouted for the woman to
get back, get back inside the cover of the stormbolters. Too
late, and even as the Arbites above her opened fire for a
warning execution and two men propped in the scaffolding
twitched and fell, one of the injured ones on the ground
gripped the hellpistol that had been slung at his neck and
took the front of the woman's head off before three streams
of shrill white fireflies from the storm bolters hosed every
living thing off the streetcrawler deck.

Twelfth Day of Septista

Six days to the Mass of Saint Balronas.
Commemoration of the Innocents of Suelae.

THE PARTICULAR OBSERVANCES *for this day will have been laid out by the Master of the Vigil and passed to each place of worship by heralds; accordingly, the three services will be conducted according to each year's selected lessons and texts and few general instructions can be made about them. The service at the Pilgrims' Gate commemorating the Suelae should only be attended by those whose direct descent from the Innocents of the Suelae has been vouched for by the Ecclesiarchy.*

Remembering the following day's feast, meals today should be frugal.

CHAPTER SEVEN

THE SHOOTOUT ON the scaffold had cost the Arbites four lives: the Arbitrators that fell from the ledge and one more to a lucky round that had gone though the visor slot in the shield. The murdered co-driver from the Rhino – it had taken Calpurnia more than an hour to find out that her name had been Lead Arbitor Vassbin – rounded out the count.

The other roadblocks had been ambushes too, just as she had guessed. The three-way trap at the intersection, the one the Rhinocade had reversed out of, had been set up with machinery across the street and shooters ready to come up the ramps and close the box. The one that they had been voxed about and not gone near had started out as a genuine repaving project, but by the time six Arbitrator squads closed in on it the gunners who had hijacked it were long gone, leaving only the rough earth rampart they had thrown up, a box of stub shells and a grenade launcher, still on its bipod, pointing down the street in the direction they had expected the Rhinos to come.

The three-way blockade had not broken up anywhere near as cleanly, indecisive at the sounds of fighting from the next street. They had dithered and argued; some had fled as the last of the gunmen on the scaffold were mopped up and some had stayed at their posts to be cut to ribbons by the first of the backup squads.

They had caught eight of them, six men and two women, none of them in command or knowing anything about who was behind the plan. Some of them had been actual labourers, some even off the work crews whose equipment had been purloined for the impromptu barricades; their orders had come from their crew overseers and none of those had survived. By sunrise, every designated civic worksite was swarming with Arbites, lining confused workers up against the sides of Rhinos and ransacking tool carts and truck beds.

That order had come from somewhere in the city precinct command, not from Calpurnia herself. She could have told them that there was little point – the ambushers had been low-grade muscle, long on quick availability and short on scruples and respect for the Arbites. 'Hookbacks,' the term apparently was here, a reference to the stowing of criminals along the sides of Rhinos. But by that stage Calpurnia was back in the Chasteners' Tower, watching each prisoner being brought in, making sure they were dragged past her on their way down to the cells. She had made sure her helmet was off and that each prisoner had the chance to see her face clearly, and their reactions gave cast-iron confirmation to her suspicions.

She only found out about the second batch of prisoners when their papers were put in front of her and she demanded to know why she was signing for prisoners from something called the Tell-Kerligan raids. While she had been chasing down the *Sanctus*, it turned out, a taskforce had hit the Tell-Kerligan shipping houses where the exploding dray had been based, dragging in two dozen terrified freight-clerks and draymen. They came with a report from Barck that Calpurnia had no time to read and so tucked into a belt-pouch.

Calpurnia had managed to doze in the second half of her ride back to the Wall, despite the noise and the jolting, but she made a point of being in her own rooms before she let the tiredness catch up with her. Stretched out on her bed, carapace off and boots jutting over the edge, she closed her eyes for a moment to rest them and woke with a start two hours later to find fruit, caffeine syrup and chilled towels laid out on the table in the main room. She wondered if it would be appropriate to nominate staff she'd never met in person for medals as she wolfed the fruit and relished the sting as the towel scrubbed across her skin. That was when the door alert sounded.

It was Pavlos Calapek, Dvorov's solemn-faced chief adjutant, dressed in an impeccable dress uniform and official sash and with a message that the arbitor majore would receive her in his chambers. She started to frame a reply, something about preparing a report on the prisoner intake to bring along, but the adjutant stood back and made a polite after-you gesture and it became evident that this was no at-your-convenience level-four delegation. She resignedly clipped her carapace back over her bodyglove and then followed him away.

Calapek apparently didn't hold with tramping the corridors on foot, and Calpurnia stood patiently on the back of the little power-sled that carried them through the quarter's levels and into the high-arched chamber in the heart of the Justice Gate bastion, skimming what she could of Barck's report on the way. (True to the Hydraphur character, nobody in this place seemed to start their reports with a summary.) Under the stern gaze of Arbitrators and Judges in mosaic, glass and marble she stepped off the sled into the locked and guarded lift that took her into the first of the string of antechambers that led to the arbitor majore's audience room. Those didn't help her mood as she stalked through them – she found them gaudy and lacking in gravitas, typically for Hydraphur – and she was only mildly taken aback when Dvorov pulled the last pair of doors open himself.

'Come in, Shira. You need to get used to coming and seeing me here, I think. You aren't so junior any more, you don't need to stand to attention outside my doors like some novice waiting on a lecture from their schola commander.'

The little round meeting table she had sat at on her first trip to this room had been taken away and replaced with a white-shrouded serving bench on which Dvorov's breakfast had been laid out. Beyond it the sun was just lifting its lower rim off the horizon: the bright pinpoints of the lower, brighter orbitals and the silver stripe of the Ring pricked and slit the apricot-coloured dawn sky.

'You have a real knack for running into trouble at highly uncivilised hours, Shira,' Dvorov said from behind her as he caught her looking at the sunrise. 'I'm sure that's what Nestor will say the next time he sees you. Me, I'll just admit to some concern. You're not helping me or anyone else by flaying yourself trying to stay on your feet every hour of the day.' Two stools carved from some dark red-black wood were set by the trestle, and Dvorov motioned her to one as he hooked the other with a foot and dropped onto it.

'I'm doing my duty as well as I'm able, sir,' Calpurnia replied, a little stiffly. 'Apparently I do have a reputation for being bad at delegation, but I think I do have a good reason to want to be at the forefront. It's attempts on my own life that I'm dealing with here, arbitor majore. Although I'm sure that Hydraphur has all sorts of convoluted protocols for how one is supposed to go about dealing with such things in a socially acceptable manner.' Events had left Calpurnia not feeling quite herself – she couldn't remember the last time she had spoken to a superior officer like that. To her rather confused relief Dvorov only smiled and pointed to the table.

'Well riposted,' he said as he skewered a syrupy fragment of pastry on a silver needle. 'But give me a little credit. I know that if I hadn't ordered you up here you'd be digging in for an unbroken day of interrogating the people you've just brought in and overseeing the roundup of the construction crews. And you'd be dead on your feet by the time that sun set again. And believe me, I'm worrying about your being dead almost as much as you are.'

'I see, sir,' she said, eyeing the food. She was suddenly aware, as she had been on the trip out to the *Sanctus*, of being ravenous as well as exhausted, but she couldn't spot anything on the table that she could easily identify and was already feeling too self-conscious to start eating an arbitor majore's breakfast for him.

'For the first part, Shira, I'd hate to lose such an estimable and promising young arbitor as yourself, particularly after bringing you all this way. Even leaving you personally out of it, I also hate the idea of anyone carrying out such an organised assault on the Adeptus Arbites and the order it stands for. I particularly hate it coming at a time when the working relationship between Imperial authorities on Hydraphur is as strained as it is.' He looked curiously from the table to Calpurnia and she belatedly realised the meal had been set out for more than one.

'You're talking about these conflicts between the Ministorum and the Navy,' she said, leaning forward and trying to identify the least risky-looking dish.

'Well, the Ministorum and this hot-blooded campaign by the Eparch to get control over the Naval investitures is the current flashpoint, but it's turned the whole role of the Adeptus on Hydraphur into a sore point again. Hydraphur looks like an Imperial world like any other when you're on it, but don't let that fool you. It's a Navy system, and the Navy have never been happy with having the primary planet denied to them. It's been that way since the Age of Apostasy, of course. The mark that Bucharis and his cohorts left on this whole segmentum was profound. Here, the Administratum's decree of partition was an attempt to create a civilian counterweight to Navy authority in the system and balance them out against one another.'

'The way that the Imperial Guard isn't allowed to have its own fleet or the way Guilliman divided up the Astartes,' put in Calpurnia, picking up a slice of white fruit and chewing on it cautiously. It was eye-squintingly tart.

'Well, the same principle, yes,' said Dvorov, reaching for the caffeine pot on its little spirit-burner in the centre of the table. 'The planet was where the non-Navy presence had always been, what there was of it – a dedicated Ecclesiarchy shrine, an Adepta Sororitas convent, a way station for Navigators, that kind of thing. Even a lot of what the Navy did here wasn't military. Farms to supply the better class of provisions for the officers, estates for the better officer dynasties. Naval parlance still refers to families who lost their planetside holdings as "the Evicted lines", apparently, the same way the prouder Naval families call the Monocrat and the new planetary nobility "transplants". But they found all sorts

of ways to delay and appeal the decree. The Navy had holdings on Hydraphur right up until Lord Admiral Invisticone
was assassinated about two hundred years ago. After he was
dead the Inquisition took over the fortress he had occupied
in the other hemisphere and since then the planet Hydraphur has been the pocket of non-Naval authority that it was
meant to be.'

'Has it worked?' It had taken Calpurnia a moment to shift
gears from talking about the assassinations to the history of
Hydraphur, but she was becoming interested despite herself.
Dvorov finished pouring his caffeine into an odd little cup,
a flattened brass ball with a cavity the size of a shot glass
drilled into it, and reached for another kind of syrup to stir
into it.

'Not really,' he said. 'I've always been pleased by the idea
of the Imperium as a glacier. Powerful, rigid, grinding its way
forward beyond anyone's ability to stop. But when you consider our society in the large it's often more like just water.
Hard to restrain and always wanting to find its own level and
its own way around things.'

'Not sure I follow, sir.' She braced herself and took another
bite of the fruit.

'Well, there has certainly been a growth of parallel power
on Hydraphur, as intended. Civilian shipping increased,
there's a far greater Adeptus presence, the Navigators and the
Scholastia Psykana have a much bigger permanent base at
the Blind Tower, and the Cathedral has become quite an
important centre of power in its own right, the junction of a
whole series of pilgrimage routes from the northern sectors
through to Gathalamor and points south. The trouble is that
it hasn't provided the counterbalance to the Navy that it was
intended to. All it did was give the Navy the excuse to insist
on even tighter control of the rest of the system. They covered the other worlds and all the major orbital paths in both
ecliptics with fortifications and shipyards – as is their right,
of course, their perfect right, but the terms of the partition
allowed them to run all that territory with even more autonomy than before. And then of course there's all the
loopholes through the decree that I was talking about, the
intermarriages and treaties and the guilds. Anyone with

holdings or interests on the planet isn't allowed to exercise any authority off it, and the mercantile cartels want people in the civil community on Hydraphur they can trade with...'

'The syndicates?' Calpurnia put in as Dvorov took a sip of caffeine. He nodded and poured a second shot for her.

'You'll find this in your briefing dossiers when you have time. Each syndicate is nominally sponsored by interests outside the system under Administratum charters. That provides the access to civilian shipping that the Navy doesn't have, the access to commerce and travel off-planet that the on-planet aristocrats are forbidden, and the navigational privileges and letters of passage that only the Navy can provide and the other two need. That combination made the syndicates an institution within two hundred years of the decree of partition taking effect.'

'To the point where syndicate relationships seem to be as entrenched as family ones. Nobody introduces themselves as Lord Kalfus of the Medell syndicate, it's Kalfus-Medell from the first.'

'Exactly so, although you'll find it's only really a custom on the Hydraphur end of the arrangement. To the outsystem cartels the syndicate relationship isn't so all-defining, and for the Naval families getting too close to the whole thing is a little gauche. And of course even as the syndicates constantly manoeuvre for position among themselves – the opportunities for activity around Hydraphur are wider than the partition meant them to be but they are still finite – the families are also sparring all the time for the leading positions within the syndicate.

'Which makes it interesting that you should ask,' he added as he scooped fruit mash onto a wedge of crispbread, 'about the rules on defending oneself from assassination attempts. There actually are some pretty elaborate traditions about how the parties in those kinds of wars behave, depending on whether it's inter- or intra-syndicate, the relative statures of the parties and so on. How far those traditions are honoured once they stop being convenient is another matter, of course.' Dvorov noticed the piece of fruit in Calpurnia's hand and pointed her to a tureen of stewed berries. 'You should actually start off with those.'

'I hope I'm not supposed to be following these rules myself,' she said, picking up one of the little enamelled bowls from next to the tureen. 'The Adeptus Arbites answer to the Emperor and the Law, or we should. Are we supposed to tie ourselves down to some idiotic noble code? Well, then again, this is Hydraphur.'

It must have been the tiredness talking. She had time for a moment of shocked disbelief at her tone and words before she put down the bowl of berries and turned to him.

'Sir, my apologies for that outburst. I was careless of who I was–' but Dvorov was already smiling and waving her to silence.

'Don't apologise, Shira,' he told her when he'd finished his mouthful. 'This isn't your old post. We're conferring here as two senior officers of the Adeptus, not in some barrack-room bawl-out where you stand at attention and stare at the wall while I shout at you.' He nodded at the bowl on the table. 'You need to eat that while it's warm. Use one of those little ladles from the stack there.'

Letting herself breathe a little easier, Calpurnia picked up a ladle and tasted from her bowl. The berries were faintly tart, slightly reminiscent of the fruit, but stewed in some musky-sweet spice that made her want to sneeze.

'Actually, though, this talk of you adjusting to your new position and me shouting at you does seem to bring us back to why I called you up here.'

'Not to take me from a day of flaying myself alive over the interrogations?'

'Partly. But there's something I do think I need to say to you, and I prefer to make these sorts of points in person.' He caught Calpurnia's look. 'Eat your berries, Shira, I'm not about to strip your ranks or put you on charges. You haven't failed in your duty. In fact, I suppose I want to talk to you about the opposite problem.'

'The opposite? Doing too much of my duty? I've acknowledged that I've tried to stretch myself a little far, perhaps.'

'I'm bothered by a particular aspect of that which came to the fore at the Aquila Gate and in that counter-ambush you led down-city. Shira, the Imperium has a noble and cherished tradition of leading from the front. As you walked through

the antechambers out there you would have passed the likenesses of any number of men and women from our own
order whose statues honour exactly that. It's not as though I
disapprove on principle. Nevertheless, I have to wonder: if all
this effort was expended to set up a trap designed to culmi-
nate in your death, was it perhaps a little unwise to then rush
into the trap and offer them exactly what they wanted?'

'You believe I should have retreated from the ambush?'
Dvorov waved the question away.

'I'm not in the business of second-guessing every decision
my subordinates make. I'm not going to drag out a map and
make you justify every single step you took. I'm not even
going to try and tell you that it's always going to be a bad
thing that you lead your troops. You're making sure that you
don't send the people under your command into a situation
without demonstrating that you are prepared to face that situation yourself, isn't that right?' Calpurnia nodded and ate
another ladleful of the distasteful berries – she had been
about to say exactly the same thing herself.

'I won't claim to know every thought that passes through
your head,' Dvorov went on, 'but I can take some guesses. You
are very aware of the newness of your rank and position. And
you are also aware that you are on a new world in a new section of the galaxy in which very little is familiar to you. It's only
natural that you want to conduct yourself impeccably, and that
to you means never flinching from danger and standing shoulder to shoulder with the members of your command.'

'Most of the time I haven't even known the names of my
command,' she said half to herself, but Dvorov caught it.

'So, it's a difficult situation for you and one you're dealing
with well. Really. And I'm not going to try and put a leash
onto you and I'm not going to try to take away your freedom
to exercise the abilities that brought you to my attention in
the first place. But I don't think it will be any great impedi-
ment, at least not once you get used to it, to tell you that
until the assassination cases are better unravelled you will
restrain yourself. Risk is part of the work of the Arbites, combat is part of the work of an Arbitrator, but nevertheless you
will not fling yourself into the teeth of whatever fresh attacks
are sent your way.'

'You're saying, sir, that I should send another Arbitrator out into the line of fire while I keep myself safe.' She controlled her voice, but she was knotting with anger inside. Comments about her recklessness didn't feel any better coming from her own superior than they had from Zhow.

'I'm saying that while that may be distasteful to you–'

'*Distasteful.*'

'–you are up against an enemy who wants you dead, and our business is to deny that enemy, not hand him his objective on a platter. You may consider that an order, if that's what it takes.'

'I understand, arbitor majore.' Calpurnia took another mouthful of the now-cold berries and made herself swallow it.

'If you're done with those, now's the time to eat that daggerfruit.' Dvorov had switched directions again. Calpurnia picked up the first morsel she had tried and bit into it again. Its flavour was muted a little by the residual perfume from the berries, and she found it cleansed palate.

'Good. Now, pick a syrup for your caffeine – I recommend the Hercus, that's the pale yellow one in the corner there – and tell me what you've been able to find out about the attacks on you down in the city this morning.'

She blinked, poured, and drank – the syrup gave the caffeine a smoky, malted taste that she cautiously decided that she liked – and then began to talk, starting with their departure from Cross-Four and finishing with her overseeing the prisoners' parade. Dvorov listened in silence, cutting small slivers off a half-melon and chewing them thoughtfully as he looked out over the hive.

'Why not a bigger convoy initially?' he asked after he had had a few moments to digest her story on top of the melon.

'To confuse anyone who was monitoring the departure ramps at the fortress. Three Rhinos is the size of one of the routine night-shift patrols. This was before we knew that they'd be able to home in on our actual route.'

'And you selected the scaffold... but no, scratch that, I said I wouldn't micromanage you and I meant it. Do you see a direct link between the sabotage at the Aquila Gate, the flight of the *Aurum Sanctus* and the attacks on you?'

'It's looking tenuous, and we may find it wasn't there to begin with. It would be flattering to believe that someone made incredibly elaborate arrangements to catch me in the dray explosion at the Aquila Gate, but I think it was simple sabotage. The containers were of a sort of perfumed lamp-oil on their way to a storage house in the Pilgrims Quarter. It was either for the Procession of the Further Saints or the big lantern-light congregation tomorrow night.'

'So I understand. There have been some developments there, too, I understand?' Dvorov handed her a silver needle like the one he'd been eating from earlier and nodded towards the pastries.

'The rigged oil containers seem to be linked less to the *Sanctus* than to foul play in the warehouse where they were stored. I haven't had time to go over the verispex report in detail, I only got it when I got back to the Wall this morning. But the freight-house is full, completely packed, with supplies of more oil. None of it has been bomb-trapped the way the first lot was, but the verispex turned up several seals that they say show some tampering. Barck is continuing to work on it.' Dvorov gave her a quizzical look. 'Lead Verispex Barck, sir. The leader of the forensic team at the Aquila Gate. She's taken charge of the freight-house investigation too.'

'Ah. Thank you. I don't normally work at the team-leader level. Move onto the melon if you're done with the pastries.'

The melon was watery and weak-flavoured, but it chased the richness of the pastries out of her mouth in a pleasant fashion. She finished two slices and her caffeine. The strange little drinking-ball seemed to be heavier and she realised fatigue was catching up with her again. She breathed deeply a few times and looked out over the morning-lit fortress-teeth of the Wall and the smog layer that was already settling over the city below it. She was familiar with the first signs of the grey exhaustion that crept up on her during long, tense operations – it wasn't too bad once you knew the signs and could brace yourself for them.

She proved herself a liar straight away by realising she had missed what Dvorov had just said.

'I'm sorry sir?'

'I said you need to remember the order that you ate in just then. This combination of foods is associated with the sacred feasts of the Vigil, and they'll be served at the prayer breakfast you're due to attend with me tomorrow morning.'

'Will there be time for that?' It was the first thing that had come to her mind.

'I believe so. Let's review the threads of the case to date, Shira. You have a verispex team straightening out what happened at the Aquila Gate. The investigation of the *Aurum Sanctus*, after the interception carried out by yourself and Ryo, seems close to disqualifying it from suspicion. An organised attempt on your life last night was foiled and the perpetrators are in custody. The original assassin is dead, and although he is proving hard to trace we now have the aid of the Imperial Inquisition in tracking him down, do we not?'

Calpurnia realised she had not given a thought to Zhow since they had parted ways at Cross-Four. 'The inquisitor declined to meet with me on his own return, but he did condescend to let me know that he wants to be the sole chaser of your invisible friend's trail. We are to suspend our own operations on the matter unless and until he requests and authorises us.' Dvorov arched an eyebrow as he raised the brass drinking-ball to his lips. 'The patrols around the Adeptus Quarter have been reporting that he's been there for the last three hours with that savant of his, pacing back and forth on the laneways leading up to the Kathisma and getting into a lot of quiet arguments.'

'So we do have people with him?'

'No,' Dvorov said cheerfully. 'I told you, we've been warned off. But the patrol teams in that area happen to have team leaders a little more senior than the usual proctors and lead arbitors, and who happen to feel it part of their duties to send reports up through certain direct lines of communication to their arbitor majore.'

'I see.' It made sense. 'You have eyes on him the same way the Eparch has had one of his staff appointed to watch us. Lord Kalfus-Medell tried the same kind of thing. Just another part of the way things are here, then?'

'Part of the way things are everywhere, I think you'll find. I'll admit I'm mildly surprised you've never encountered this sort of thing before. You had a garrison command at Ephaeda, didn't you?' Calpurnia sighed.

'I'd like to think that things were different there. Perhaps I'm just not the sort of person to have much to do with them.'

'That sounds more like it to me. Well, you're here to learn, as are we all.' Dvorov drained his caffeine. 'Have you given any thought to a staff of your own?'

'No. There hasn't been time. I remember Zhow talking about custom-fitting a Rhino. Was that the kind of thing he was talking about?'

'Among other things. I'd strongly advise it. You're an arbitor senioris now, Shira. You want to requisition a carrier from the hangars, get the best one out, pick your choice of items from the armoury to go into it for your use and your staff's, select people you need for your operations from day to day. Arbites, Judges, Chasteners, Garrison preachers, Tech-Adepts. Once again, I can't believe that this is the first time you've run across the idea of a commander forming their own staff.'

'I'm familiar with the idea, sir, just short on the time. A standard-pattern carrier and whoever is assigned to me will suffice for the moment.'

'As you wish. What of the lead arbitor who's been accompanying you since the initial attack? Adjutant material?'

'Bannon?' She considered him. 'No. The reason he wound up being my offsider for the investigation is that he was heading my escort squad at the start of it all. He sort of got attached to me by default. He's obedient enough, but he's not up to the work. I won't keep him in that position.'

'Hm,' Dvorov said. 'The Vigil of Balronas begins in two days as the final lead up to the mass. Are you prepared for the problems that religious restrictions will cause for your operations?'

'I will be,' said Calpurnia. She was getting used to Dvorov's sudden changes of tack – she had thought they were to test her, but it seemed to be genuinely how he thought. 'I've been focused on the Arbites side of the operation but if we can get hold of the Reverend Baragry to continue advising me on what I can and can't do–'

'That will be an interesting exercise. How did you manage to sideline him when you took off for the *Sanctus*?'

'How? He had appointed himself the confessor of one of the prisoners who gave us the ship's name in the first place. We left him with the prisoner and, uh, never really told him that we were lifting off to join *Judgement's Clarion*.'

'I do believe, Shira, that you have rather more cunning about you than you give yourself credit for. Although the side effect was that Baragry was utterly livid that he had been left behind. My adjutants had a blistering audience with the man himself and I got two formal letters of reproof from the Eparch's chambers. I'll have to show them to you sometime. Did I mention Nestor spent the time you were in space putting rather a lot of his energy into hosing things down?'

'I'll apologise when I see him next, sir.' Dvorov waved her words away.

'It's his specialty,' he said. 'Anyway, my point was that I think we're going to have to resign ourselves to the fact that you're going to face your first holy season on Hydraphur with a little less instruction than we were counting on. Can you keep the order of the courses here in mind?'

'Berries, daggerfruit, pastry and syrup, caffeine and different syrup, melon.'

'Good. There are certain nuances that, well, never mind, you know what you need to do. This meal is eaten at dawn at the start of the Vigil and on the first day of the Sanguinala. It's supposed to be unique to the occasion, by the way, so don't try ordering it at other times. My stewards were scandalised when I told them to prepare it for today, even after I told them it was for your religious instruction. Which is something that I'm not sure we can expect much help in from Reverend Baragry.'

'I agreed as much with Arbitor Leandro,' said Calpurnia. 'Well, advice on how we can carry out our operations is one thing we probably can depend on Baragry for. I'm getting more confident that I can winnow out the political interference from the genuine direction. If I can keep getting bare-bones guidance like this from yourself and the other Arbites, just enough to avoid actually disgracing myself, then I think I can scrape by for this year. I'll settle for being someone who does her duty over someone who has impeccable table manners.'

'Well spoken. Well then, arbitor senioris. With your delegations in hand, what do you plan to do now?' Calpurnia chuckled.

'I need to rest and get back some energy, sir, and I also need to burn off some tension. I was going to say that I plan to work out how I can do both in one day, but I think I just thought of a way.'

SHE COULDN'T GET a clear look at what had shot at her, but the glimpse of movement was enough to judge its direction and speed and reflexes took over. Her shotgun was locked into the shield's gunport and the gun-grip bucked as the shield juddered against her shoulder and thigh. Her eye had been true: the gun-platform dropped to the floor with a clank as its clamps released their hold on the railing.

She spun back in the other direction straight away, ready to pump out more shots, but there was no movement in the brief flick of the torch clipped to the top of her shield. Four long paces and she was at the end of the alleyway, scowling upward: there were several ways an Arbitrator was trained to scale a wall, and all of them were damned awkward if you were on your own, but there was nothing for it. She disengaged the shotgun and flipped it into the scabbard at her back, then slung her shield so that it sat over the angle between the walls.

One hand on the wall and one on the shield grips, she swung her feet up, hung for a moment growling with effort – she was in worse shape than she had realised – then slid and dropped into the space beyond, already swinging the shield back onto her arm and turning to face the shape rumbling out of the darkness.

It was roughly humanoid, an automaton torso built onto a randomly-lurching ring of motorised castors. Chains and control cables snaked from its head up into darkness. One heavy arm finished in a snub gunsnout and the other in a thick piston: two shots from the gun rang on her shield before a blow from the piston knocked the shield-edge back into her face and bounced her off the wall.

There was no time to redraw the shotgun, let alone to lock
it back into the gunport so she could fire it one-handed with
the shield to steady it. Although the thing was too fast for
her to dodge out of its path she was able to quickstep to one
side and let the next piston-blow propel her out of the
machine's way. She had to bound backwards to soak up the
momentum and leave it to faith that there was nothing waiting behind her while she drew her stubber: the reassuring
feel of the lock-glove clicking together around its grips was
instantaneous and it took a second for her to plant one foot
behind her to fire. Her aim was perfect: the round boomed
through an armour-seam under the automaton's arm, and
after a moment it slumped over as whoever was directing it
decided it was out of the fray.

She took a moment to catch her breath and pan the lamp
around, then moved forward again. Half a dozen cautious
paces. She had just holstered her pistol and was reaching
over her shoulder for the shotgun when a rack of searchlights came stabbing down on her. Reflexively she ducked
and skittered to one side, pulling the shotgun the rest of the
way out and getting ready to shuck her shield – the gunport
was good for point-blank shots and suppression fire, but
now she was going to need two hands to aim. Even with her
helmet visor darkening to counter the lights, she was still
blinking from the change in illumination when the floor
began to move.

It took her a moment to register the clatter of gears and
winches and faint shouts from the machine-crews on the engineering level below, but now she felt the floor vibrating and
tilting, tipping her in the direction of the lights as the wall she
had pressed her back to slid downward and out of sight.

Change of plan. As the floor steepened she grabbed her
pistol again, letting the slope carry her down, body braced
behind her shield to let her sock the slab of armour into anything in front of her. The lights still bore down, keeping
everything beyond arm's reach in shadow so she knelt,
braced herself against the slope and chanced two shots over
the top of the shield at the searchlights.

She missed, but there was no chance to re-aim. More clatter came from beyond the retracted wall and she could see

lights bobbing down there, red and green, passing before and behind one another as though they were being carried by members of a mob. She fired a shot, then another. The bruising recoil hammered through the glove and up into her shoulder, but the shots told: four red lights went out as each round punched through two of the milling shapes beyond the ramp.

With a grind the floor tilted steeper and she had to scuttle across it like a frantic black-shelled crab, a crab that was desperately trying to stow its sidearm and scrabble for its power-maul. She jumped off the ramp a second before it would have tipped her away completely and careened into the crude shapes beyond, hulking humanoids dangling from chains with arms stretched in front of them and green and red lamps for faces. Four lay motionless on the ground: the chain-clamps had released them when their operators saw they had taken a hit.

Calpurnia swivelled away as the first hulk tried to snap its arms shut on her and into another whose face-lamp was red: she slammed the lower edge of the shield into where its knees would have been, and as it swayed and bobbed she finally got her maul free and drove it upward. Sparks flew and the target dropped from its chain as the red light snuffed out. More servo-arms grabbed at her from behind and another red light glared over her shoulder but she had her equilibrium back now, flipping the maul around and driving the tip backward. The target that had grabbed her crashed to the floor and she turned, danced around a green-lit shape and into the thick of them.

She was aware of how harshly she was breathing and of the way that the shield was starting to weigh on her arm. She brought it close in to her body to minimise the strain but that caused problems too as she slashed at the targets and their reaching arms: it was harder to use the shield as a weapon, to slam it against bodies or smother attacks, and it made a blind spot on that side of her. The hulks could not be knocked off balance with a shield-slam the way a human would – they simply swung away on their chains and back at her. She tried to compensate by always moving away from her shield-arm, circling to her right and redoubling her efforts with her maul, but now that arm was tiring too and her feet stumbled on the hulks she had already dropped. The targets pressed closer even as their numbers thinned.

Eventually she hit a green one, downed it with a wild stroke of the maul that was supposed to knock a red target away from her shield. The error klaxon broke her rhythm and it didn't take long for the shield to be grabbed by two sets of rubber-covered arms. She had to release it, and although she got her maul and pistol switched between her hands in a deft cross-move and began to use both, within minutes she was hemmed in, weighed down by her own exhaustion and a target hulk that had fallen onto her. A pair of arms clamped around her brutally tight and the smell of scorched rubber from the targets she had hit mingled with the smell of her sweat for the twenty seconds it took for the buzzer to go.

WHEN SHE LOOKED from the debriefing platform the little pit where she had been finished off had extruded walls and become a gun-tower. Calpurnia stood on the transparent slab of the platform behind the bank of controllers, watching the emplacement raining high-speed paint rounds on a gaggle of Arbitrators who were trying to work their way forward through a graveyard of simulated Rhino wrecks to fire grenades into the mechanism. They hadn't got very far.

'Fresh inductees?' she asked a controller, who was watching through one of the tower's slaved ocular spirits and working stops and levers to aim its guns.

'Oh, and it shows, doesn't it, ma'am?' he replied with a chuckle as another rattling spray of pellets raised shouts of alarm and pain below them. From around them in the dimness came more noises: the bang of firearms and the doublecrack-screech of bolters, the crack-sizzle of power weapons, sirens, voices, and the ceaseless rumble of the heavy chains, pistons, belts and cables under the floor and over their heads that operated it all. Walls and floors moved, attacks were sprung by automata, servitors or practice hulks lowered on chains, areas filled with smoke or were showered with water, light, artificial hail, blasts of sand or disorienting noise.

Calpurnia was exhausted again, aching and her hair hanging in strings, but it was a good kind of exhaustion. It had been far too long since she had trained in a Klavier Maze, and she realised this was the most relaxed she had felt since she first touched down on Hydraphur. The meal with Dvorov, several more hours of sleep and a turn through the Maze had done exactly the kind of good she had hoped it would.

'Perhaps the debriefing of youngsters meeting their paint-spitting nemesis below could include a review of your own most laudable performance, my arbitor senioris.' Nestor Leandro's rich voice rolled over them as he stepped onto the platform, the finery of his Judge's uniform glinting in the lamps.

'Not my best, Arbitor Leandro.' He was holding the print-out from the session she had just completed and she had to reach up to point to the lists of hit percentages and target ratios. 'I was sloppy and impetuous,' she said, 'you can see it in the logs for minutes eight, twelve and seventeen to twenty-three, and I've allowed my condition to decline inexcusably during the voyage here. But thank you for your kind words.'

'Not at all. Are the Maze configurations in the Segmentum Ultima garrisons similar to ours?'

'I can only speak for the systems I served in,' said Calpurnia, scooping up her kit before they headed for the exit, 'but yes, by and large. There's more of an emphasis on mobility and reflexes – this maze makes a lot more use of the judgement and target-selection drills, which we used the firing ranges for.'

'Just so.' They had emerged into a tiled hallway, the passage that linked the ablutories with the main entrances to the Maze a level below, the whole training complex cut deep into bedrock halfway down the Wall. The air was damp from the shower blocks at the top of the corridor, and Leandro's judicial cloak looked over-lush and out of place amid the Arbitrator and Chastener uniforms.

'Searching for an appropriately poised and witty segue into the news I have for you, Arbitor Calpurnia, I find myself at a loss for one and must perforce present you with developments bluntly, before we reach the ablutories and respect

for the modesty of a fellow commander compels me to with-
draw.'

I love the way developments always seem to come when
I'm doing other things, she thought. Well at least I didn't
snap at him out loud this time. What she said aloud was, 'I
appreciate your coming down here to brief me in person.'

'Not at all. Well, to be brief.' He cleared his throat. 'The
dray full of lamp-oil came from the Tell-Kerligan shipping
house, a minor freight broker out past the foot of the
Telepine Way. Tell-Kerligan specialises as a dealer in religious
artefacts and supplies and the export of a consignment of
icons and specially-crafted bindings of religious texts bound
for private missions and colleges along the Segmentum border, which had formed the *Sanctus's* official pretext for
breaking orbit and heading out of the system, passed
through their holdings. The house's ties to the *Sanctus*
extended little further than supplying part of its cargo,
although a position brokering artwork purchases and transport connections to the Ecclesiarchy was a part of the
Kerligan syndicate's activities that the Tell family had been
manoeuvring to get into for some time and this represented
something of a breakthrough for them.'

'Doesn't the *Sanctus* operate under a direct Ecclesiarchal
charter?'

'Such charters,' Leandro answered, rather awkwardly dodging a knot of hurrying Arbites, 'leave a gap between the
bonded church storage houses around the hive and loading
aboard proprietary Ecclesiarchal ships, a gap within which a
number of specialist transporters and orbital-lift operators
with close ties to the Eparch's chambers exist quite prosper-
ously.'

'I see.'

'A team of detectives has joined the cordoning taskforce,'
he went on, 'and they have been making all manner of
requests for lexmechanics and savant staff and access to the
data mills in the Wall. The most telling progress, I must however inform you, has been that of a colleague with whom
you are familiar – Lead Verispex Barck and her team, who
took on the task of examining the shipping houses as an
extension of the work you set her in the aftermath of the

Aquila Gate. They were initially looking for evidence of machining work, signs that the sabotage that came so close to engulfing you was conducted on the premises. But the sabotage that has occupied them was not mechanical, Arbitor Calpurnia. It was chemical.'

They had reached the ablutory door. The steam and splashes coming through the doorway rather spoiled the drama of Leandro's conclusion, although people were backing up on either side of the doors to give the two commanders space.

'What do you mean by that, Arbitor Leandro?' she asked when she realised he expected it of her.

'Lamp-oil. The warehouse was massively stocked, stocked to the ceiling, with lamp-oil. Consecrated and scented lamp-oil, to be exact, prepared specifically to be burned in the ceremonial lanterns used during this holy period, but in greater quantities than anyone could possibly expect to use. And every cask that the Verispex had been able to tap and test prior to their report back to us had been tainted. Poison, my arbitor. Carefully mixed and deliberately placed. Poison.'

Thirteenth Day of Septista

Five days to the Mass of Saint Balronas.
Feast of the Rhetores. Vigil's Eve.
The Quiet Congregation.

TODAY IS THE *last day before the Vigil of Saint Balronas begins and Ecclesiarchal strictures conduct come into force throughout the Bosporian Hive and its surrounds. This should be a day of contemplation and fortification. The Feast of the Rhetores begins an hour after sunup and although it is permissible to use the feast to prepare for the fasting ahead, gluttonous conduct is a mark of spiritual weakness that must be reported to a preacher or confessor. When a particular feast is declared done by its host the remaining food should be removed immediately.*

Between the end of the Feast and the Quiet Congregation is a time for individual prayer in the home, although spiritual strengthening may be sought from the Ecclesiarchy if urgently needed. Time should be allowed for ensuring that dress is clean and orderly, that lanterns are trimmed and filled with the scented oil supplied by the Ministorum. Dress should be sober and respectable; official garments or uniforms are permitted providing that their brighter colours are dulled with a coat or shawl. Speech should be kept to an absolute minimum while moving to the High Mesé and maintained until the bell is rung. Lights should be extinguished in buildings where there will be no one to extinguish them at the sound of the bell.

This day is a day of particular significance for the Imperial Navy and no communication, social or otherwise, should be attempted with Navy personnel on this day. To do so, or to for example invite a Naval officer at another time to a function that falls on this day, will be taken as a personal slight.

CHAPTER EIGHT

POISON. THE THOUGHT was still weighing on her mind the next day through the prayer breakfast that celebrated the Feast of the Rhetores. The poison in the lamp-oil.

The prayer breakfast was hosted by the Prefect of the Hydraphur Monetariat, a rail-thin woman with nervous, skittering eyes. The service was conducted in the Monetariat Chapel, a side-gallery off the main counting-hall so narrow that the aisle could barely accommodate even one at a time and the pews were no bigger than chairs. The incenses for ceremonies on Hydraphur were sickly and over-perfumed, and smelling them set Calpurnia to brooding on the poisoned oil again so that she kept losing her place among the odd, singsong rhythms of the otherwise familiar Imperial prayers. Outside she could hear the droning of the savants processing their financial algorithms, murmuring the numbers and trigger-phrases that would feed each piece of data through the complex formulae hypnotically implanted into them. As a counterpoint to the sacred liturgies they were saying it struck her as rather impious.

The breakfast itself was more comfortable. They ate on an arboretum balcony that circled the Monetariat tower five floors up, enclosed by a glittering curtain of jewelled armourglass that turned the yellow daylight into an odd, watery rainbow. 'Best not to mention we had this same meal yesterday,' Dvorov had said. 'No harm in no one knowing we broke religious protocol a little.' Calpurnia, who knew herself to be a very bad liar, had not been sure about that, but the subject had not come up.

She had remembered the order to eat in, though, and avoiding any obvious gaffes seemed to be enough – the other Adeptus seemed put off by her Arbitrator uniform and spoke to Dvorov instead. She didn't mind: it gave her the freedom to wander over to the glass wall and look out through one of the clear spots, through the sloping forest of towers, to where the Cathedral spiked up from the hive's summit. Beyond the hulking base of the building were the shrine and statue-lined avenues and pilgrims' barracks of the Sacred Quarter, the steep south-west slopes of the Augustaeum that the conspirators in her cells had tried to fill with poison.

The nature of the conspiracy hadn't become properly clear to Calpurnia until she had found a moment the previous night to reread her dossier on the religious stations of the sacred Vigil. (And if, she thought bitterly, the Eparch had seen fit to send her the tutor she had been promised instead of an agent and informant, she would not have needed to piece it together on her own.) It had struck her as odd that such extravagant quantities of fuel for such an old-fashioned kind of lantern had been the subject of so much attention, but now she understood. During the Vigil the lights of the hive and of the city – all across the planet and throughout the swarm of ships and stations that made up the Hydraphur system – were dimmed or extinguished, the nights left dark to commemorate the spiritual darkness of the Plague of Unbelief.

The seaports and spaceports, the docks and military bases would keep their lights, and the Arbites city patrols and the Adepta Sororitas watch in the Augustaeum itself would light their way through the streets. But for most in the Hydraphur system the nights of the Vigil could only have their darkness broken by tiny candles or the low glow of the little brass hand-lanterns, burning the sacred oil made only for the Vigil nights, oil that burned low, warm and with the bitter scent of mourning incense.

The dray had just been the start. Not even very much of the oil it had carried had been tainted. But the Tell-Kerligan warehouse was vast, and nearly all its space was filled with great drums of the poisoned oil. Throne alone, but if that stuff had actually been distributed and burned…

That thought kept her so preoccupied that she spent nearly half an hour at the glass curtain, staring out at the Cathedral compound and the ridge of the High Mesé with its obelisk teeth, brooding about the last few days and wondering every so often why it irritated her so much that the districts of the Augustaeum were still called quarters even though there were more than four of them.

For the past couple of days she had resented the time she would have to take away from the investigation to attend the breakfast, but as she finished eating, made her excuses and slipped away she found herself glad of it. It had done for her mind what the turn through the Klavier Maze had done for her body: grounded her, taken her out of near-total immersion in the investigation and cleared away the cobwebs.

But the break was over. It was time to visit the cells again.

PART OF EVERY young arbitor's career included duty as a penal guard, and Calpurnia had done her share. She had spent an eighteen-month round trip on a transport carrying penal legionnaires from Drade to suicide battalions mustering on the border with the xenos tau, and had finished her tour at Don-Croix as a section leader aboard one of the Arbites picket-ships that kept guard over the hellish in-system prison worlds. Her commendations and her scrupulous reputation had even earned her a six-month stint on the infamous deep-space prison known as Cage Twenty-Twenty, where the most toxic of heretics were quarantined for interrogation or ritual chastisement before their execution.

Even so, she had never seen a system quite like Hydra-phur's. Not the physical prisons – she doubted that there would be anything on the planetary camps much different to the bunker-compounds on Don-Croix's inner worlds, and the Cage had been state of the spaceborne art. What fascinated her was the Grey Prison.

The Penitential Calculus was its proper name. Hydraphur held its prisoners in a long chain of camps strung across the planet's face, on two giant space stations that stood out from the Ring in heavily-guarded pockets of space, and aboard an endless circuit of shuttles and runner-ships that kept them all linked in carefully patternless migrations. Governing that system was the Calculus, a code, a maze, a cat's cradle of encryptions, double-blinds and randomisations. A cipher for a prisoner here, for a cell or a penal ship there, sentences and transfer times and locations all swimming deep in a lightless sea of false data and ever-shifting code-keys. Even had the Grand Provost Marshal stirred from his palace on Earth to demand the whereabouts of the least of the prisoners held in Hydraphur, he would have had to wait until the name had been passed through the calculus and a coded report brought back out to know whether the subject was a prisoner in Hydraphur at all. She had never encountered anything like it in her career, but the reason for it was obvious: in a system like this, one of the best ways to keep prisoners safe from interference was to make sure that not even the prisoners themselves could ever be entirely sure where they were or where they were about to be moved to.

The role of Master of the Calculus had been gifted to one Arbitor Consul Narranze as a hereditary office twelve hundred years before, and since then generations of Narranzei had carried the rank and title, spending their lives in the lowest chambers of an oubliette beneath the Wall's lowest catacombs. With them were the finest logisters the Adeptus Mechanicus could craft and three families of savants and lexmechanics whose children were indentured to the Calculus at birth. The codes and formulae had grown so intricate with the passing of time that now each generation of savants began their training and mind-conditioning almost from the moment they could talk and count, and the officers who took food and messages into the oubliette were hereditary positions too, oathbound and guarded in turn.

Awaiting judgement were the draymen, the staff of the Tell-Kerligan shipping house and the survivors of the botched streetcrawler ambush. Those who didn't wind up in gibbets would be taken into the maze of penitentiaries. But before their identities vanished into the matrices of the Grey Prison from where it would take months to extract them, Calpurnia wanted to see them.

The Chasteners and interrogators had already spent a day and a night on them, and had told her that they had extracted what they believed was a full account, with as much duress as each accused seemed able to physically stand. It was no less than Calpurnia had expected, and she didn't care. She still wanted to see them for herself. Maybe it was still the unreconstructed street-tramping Arbitrator in her, but she wanted them in her memory as a pair of eyes she had looked into rather than as a name on a data-slate display. It gave her a sense of rightness, that things were moving back onto a correct keel, and she sat and read the interrogation transcripts from the previous day as the Chasteners prepared the room.

The Chasteners' Tower had any number of chambers, depending on what environment the interrogators thought would best break their prisoner. For those who had been someone of substance, used to deference and personal space, there were tiny cubicles where an interrogator could loom over them, blotting out the light and swallowing all the available room. For commoners, used to the crowds and claustrophobia of the city-sprawl, there were chambers the size of ballrooms where the soaring spaces would press down on the cowering prisoner more heavily than the visored gaze of the Arbites or the questions boomed over a voxcaster.

Calpurnia was using no such extremes. A room of moderate size sufficed, walls of plain stone and a single bright electrolumen in a grille in the ceiling. They set up a dais for her, with a high-backed judgement seat and a thick stone lectern it took three bull-shouldered Chasteners to lift and position. There were rows of lights on a series of girders and rails overhead, but only the ones behind her were on.

Calpurnia had attended any number of these kinds of interrogations, but this would be the first time she had ever presided over one. She had time to feel a few brief twinges of nerves, which paradoxically were made worse by the quiet obedience that the burly Chasteners gave her, before she ground the doubts under a mental heel and nodded for the first prisoner to be brought in.

'Galpen Tell-Kerligan. Outlaw, condemned in the eyes of the Adeptus Arbites and sentenced by our hand!' boomed Lead Chastener Zimny, and a slender man with his scalp-locks roughly shorn away was marched into the centre of the room and anchored to the ring. His wrists were anchored low, but a shock-maul jabbed into his back when he tried to sit, so that he peered up into the lights from a painful hunching crouch. From the expression on his face, Calpurnia knew the careful tableau they had set up was perfect.

'I am innocent!' His voice was shrill and broken. 'I am wronged! I am a pious man! I will swear it! Only bring me a holy aquila and I will swear–*uhnk*...' The guard behind him jabbed him again, for silence.

'A pious man?' Calpurnia glanced at the papers on the lectern. 'You have confessed to presiding over a house of business which was used to store poison, meant to infect the rites of the Vigil and kill those observing it. You made an attempt on my own life that caused many other lives to be lost. Make no mistake, I came here only to see for myself what sort of blaspheming murderer we were sentencing.'

'No!' His tone was agonised. 'My piety was used against me!'

Calpurnia glanced over at Zimny and stage-whispered 'What's he talking about now?' The transcript was on the paper in front of her, but she wanted Galpen to hear her and keep scrambling to clear his good name.

'I took secret instructions, I confess to that, I've already told you!' he cried out, not disappointing her. 'I received a letter from the Ministorum, the curia of the Eparch! I could not refuse! I am a pious man!'

'A cleric with the Eparch's office wanted you to poison the Vigil-goers?' she asked dryly. 'Oh, certainly, we'll purge the whole Cathedral on your say-so.'

'No, no! The oil, I didn't know about the oil I don't even know about this poison!'

'He's contradicting himself,' declared Calpurnia. 'I think we're done.'

'No! You have to hear me! I'm not what you think!' Galpen was crying. 'I only wanted to restore my family in the eyes of the Emperor. I wanted to earn back the favour we had! I did no wrong, I am pious!'

'Perhaps not,' Calpurnia told Zimny, who of course had not moved. 'Let him tell me what he needs to,' and for ten minutes Galpen Tell-Kerligan talked.

The Tell-Kerligan family handled shipping from the Sacred Quarter up to orbit, true enough, but these days only texts and religious art. Time was that the family done more than that, contracting with the old Eparch for all manner of duties. They had outfitted Ecclesiarchal preachers and missionaries, accommodated important pilgrims, been people of standing. Then that had all been lost in ructions in the Ministorum, a feud among the clergy, the collapse of something called the Order of the Taper in which Tell-Kerligan fortunes had been bound. The family had fallen – not quite into oblivion, but low enough for the Galpen to feel the sting when he looked at their histories and heirlooms.

'So it was your separation from the Ecclesiarchy that made you attractive,' Calpurnia mused. 'The Eparch wanted some senior men of the Adeptus Ministorum to be able to move out of the system without Navy knowledge. There's an Ecclesiarchal penance ship in orbit to carry them out of the system, but the carriers who could bear these people up to the Ring are all known and watched. And so who better to use than a family with access to orbital lifters, a record of ties to the Ministorum, and who are desperate to re-earn favour with the Church?'

Galpen blanched at the word *use* and said nothing more – something in Calpurnia's tone had stalled him. She made a gesture for him to be removed, real this time, not a ploy to make him babble. His wrist-irons were unclipped from the ring and onto his ankle-irons and he was taken away in that same stooped shuffle. There was only a moment between the door in the right wall slamming behind Galpen and the door on the left clanking open for the next prisoner.

'Hlinden Fochs. Outlaw, condemned in the eyes of the Adeptus Arbites and sentenced by our hand!'

Hlinden Fochs was a heavy woman whose deep-set eyes glittered in the lights. She stayed silent as she was brought in and manacled. Fochs had thick fingers, callused from dray-ropes, and the brands and electoos of a minor guild official across her cheeks and shoulders.

Silence. And in her eyes, that deep, far glitter.

'Was there a reason for me to sit here looking at this woman?' Calpurnia asked Zimny. 'Who is she, exactly?'

'One of the chief conspirators, madam arbitor senioris,' he told her. 'Fochs was the draymistress in charge of moving the poisoned oil into the shipping-house.' A junior arbitor arranged the papers on the lectern to bring Fochs's interrogation transcripts to the top. The expression on the other woman's face had not changed.

'The interesting thing about this, Arbitor Zimny, is that this criminal outcast was indeed undone by an attempt on my life, but did not actually make one herself.' Was that a twitch in Fochs's face? Calpurnia leaned forward and put her elbows on her knees, staring into those shadowed eyes.

'The poisoned oil was not aimed at me. Anyone cunning enough to set up the poison and the bomb was not going to then use such a sloppy, hit and miss technique as that exploding dray. My death would have been an added cause for rejoicing, I'm sure, but no, that wasn't the object. For a while I thought it was all about snarling traffic down the Telepine Way, causing the greatest possible disruption during a sensitive time, but that wasn't it either.'

Fochs wasn't rising to it. She didn't want to gloat and she didn't want to rave.

'The object was the storage bays cut into the Cathedral foundations at the edge of the Artisans Quarter, wasn't it, Fochs?' Calpurnia asked her. 'That was where those shipments of oil were headed, to the Cathedral's own storehouses to be given out to those who will be attending the lamplight services. By the time that last dray drove up to the Aquila Gate the stocks were topped up, and the doors were due to be thrown open to the first of the faithful the following dawn. There was one last shipment to be added to make sure the stocks were adequate. I don't know yet whether that shipment was genuine or if you, Fochs, manipulated it for your sabotage. I will know soon.'

Fochs's face was a mask, unmoving.

'The flight of the *Aurum Sanctus* was spectacularly badly timed. It meant enough confusion and secrecy in Tell-Kerligan's shipping houses that you were able to poison nearly every drum of lamp-oil. I will know the details of how you did that, too. It went off beautifully. Isn't it a pity that the nerve of your people broke? To break Imperial law is to break faith with the Emperor, Fochs, and both are signs of degeneracy. A mind that can do so is by definition flawed, invariably creating flawed thinking and flawed behaviour, which are symptoms of the essential inferiority of a human being who can set themselves against their Emperor. Criminals err. And when they err, we have them. Is that not the truth, Lead Chastener Zimny?'

'Praise the Emperor! The Emperor's word is the Law, and the Arbites are the voice by which that word is spoken!' Zimny's voice filled the chamber. Fochs did not twitch a muscle.

'This, I suppose, is what you need to leave this chamber knowing. You chose weak, flawed men to crew the dray. They saw my worthy Arbites at the Aquila Gate. They didn't know about the general decree of vigilance, and they weren't prepared for an Arbites checkpoint. They panicked. That bomb was supposed to go off in the Cathedral stores to incinerate their oil stockpiles, wasn't it? Supposed to wreck them and make it look like some kind of accident so that the Cathedral procurators would be too frantic to properly check the replacement shipments that the Tell-Kerligan so-fortunately had to hand and would pass out poisoned oil to hundreds, thousands of loyal worshippers. And Tell-Kerligan would have been the guilty party and would have humiliated the Ministorum even more by their association. They would have had to protect the secret of the *Aurum Sanctus's* passengers, or at least try to. Do you know that one of the dray crew, the first one we broke, was so ignorant he even thought that the *Sanctus* was what we were after? He must have overheard something in the warehouses while he was about your sordid little business.'

Somewhere in the tower, someone wailed – the far-off, anaemic sound came down air-ducts and through vent grilles high in one wall. No one in the chamber acknowledged it.

'I thought I was dealing with some grand and subtle attempt on my life only to find out that what really caused the explosion at the Gate that night was just a pair of criminal weaklings who took fright, blew their cargo and ran for it at the first sight of an Arbites line. Were you as disappointed as I? Had you hoped that you would all hold out a little longer before your flawed, criminal natures caught up with you?'

No answer. Calpurnia wondered if Fochs had been damaged somehow in the cells. She frowned on head wounds during interrogations – they affected the reliability of testimonies.

'The other thing that it will be useful to know, Fochs, is that we are going to find the rest of this little ring you were part of down in the slums. This, what was it?' She glanced at the papers on the lectern. 'Society of the Fifty-Eighth Passage. After we have finished the Ecclesiarchal interrogators will go to work. The Adeptus Ministorum has little patience for assaults on its sacred ceremonies, and when they asked to share jurisdiction over this matter with the Adeptus Arbites we were not minded to say no. We dealt with you as the Law demands we deal with criminals, but they will deal with you as faith demands they deal with heretics. This society of yours has days to live at best.' She glanced indifferently at the papers and tilted her head. 'That's all.' And that was when Fochs spoke, in a dusty croak that took a moment and a cough to be recognisable as a voice.

'Worship of the Emperor is a blessing, the Church of the Emperor is a curse. The Emperor is in all things, His truth suffers no human to carry it but only the blessed Others, and the Society of the Fifty-Eighth Passage will see the dead shell of the false church brought low so that–' When the power-maul found her kidneys Fochs clacked her jaw shut and convulsed silently while the Chasteners dragged her away.

'She lived literally in the shadow of a great Cathedral and all the inspiration it offers, and look at how she poisoned herself,' Calpurnia remarked to Zimny.

'Do you require a moment to compose yourself, arbitor senioris?' he asked, stepping up to the seat, but she shook her head and waved him away.

'Cullos Sclay. Outlaw, condemned in the eyes of the Adeptus Arbites and sentenced by our hand!'

Another arrogant one, thought Calpurnia as the prisoner, gawky, pale-eyed and stubble-cheeked, was dragged in and manacled. His eyes went to Calpurnia, fixed on her face and stayed there, although her expression would be lost in shadows from where he stood.

'Bring the lights onto me,' she murmured to Zimny, and two more lamps blazed on. Calpurnia fought not to blink as they bathed her in light from the front, and when she adjusted to the illumination she saw that Sclay's insolent expression had not changed in the slightest. She reached up and touched the scar-lines over her eye.

'Remember me?' He did not reply. 'I am the arbitor you were sent to kill. The female arbitor with the scarred face you were told to murder. You and your fellow criminals killed the wrong woman, and that made you afraid. I saw it in your faces when I watched you go into the cells.'

'Part of me fears pain and fears for my life. Part of every man does. But I have no fear for my soul.' His eyes stayed calmly on Calpurnia.

'Your record is a good one. You were a lay chemicae practitioner, a mixer of paints. That was what you were doing on the works crew, was it not? You were there to help the painters on a mural of the...' she glanced over at the lectern.

'The mural of the Thesean Martyrs,' Sclay told her. 'Brave men and women of the Imperial Navy who would not bow the knee before the Apostate. I will claim them as my patron intercessors when I stand before the Ecclesiarchal judges.'

'Patron intercessors? You're certainly a different matter from the wretched pieces of work I've just seen. It seems to me, Sclay, that you're bound for the Calculus and eventually an execution yard, but there's also a standing treaty with the Navy to supply convicts for their work crews. Using your skills to prepare the city for a holy ritual is my idea of noble toil. But the Imperium might yet get some useful service out of you before you die.'

'Should I accomplish nothing more before I go to my grave, I have accomplished enough. I stood ready to fight you. I would have fought you.'

Fochs had been hard to crack, betraying nothing despite Calpurnia's gibes at her competence. Tell-Kerligan had been easy, convinced of his innocence and frantic to protest when she loudly assumed his criminality. She had not quite expected this.

'That's right,' she said, 'you weren't on the gantry. You were rounded up a street away, weren't you? You weren't actually party to the murders.'

'You cannot say the same, woman.' There were shocked gasps around her at the words and the guards drove their mauls into his back. He thrashed against his manacles, moaning, but Calpurnia waved the Chasteners away. They all sat in silence as Sclay jittered on the floor and rode out the spasms until his eyes were open and his breathing regular. His eyes wove their way up to hers again.

'None of this came out in your initial interrogation, Sclay. Were you saving it up for when you met me face to face?' He nodded, weakly. 'Well,' Calpurnia went on, 'I shall hear your accusations.' Gasps again, and once more she gestured for silence. 'And all of you can listen. "To stand upon the bedrock of the Law is our great duty." Zimny, finish the quotation.'

'"To presume to stand above it is our worst heresy,"' Zimny replied. 'But arbitor senioris, to allow *this* to accuse you with his words!'

'You heard me,' Calpurnia told him coldly. 'And you and every arbitor in this room can take instruction now in the fact that we are loyal and humble before the Law, and we do not arrogantly hide from accusations. Well, Sclay? You have the chance here to speak accusation against an arbitor senioris before a chamber full of Arbites. This is not a common occurrence, sir, so I'd advise you make the best of it.'

The expectant silence from the other Arbites was almost palpable. Somewhere on the other end of that maze of air ducts, that anonymous prisoner wailed again.

'Because of you, two innocent men have died.'

'I do not recoil from the fact,' Calpurnia said. '"To be just, our law must be cruel." No arbitor will resile from what is necessary for the rule of Law. When I stand before the Emperor the souls that I have sent ahead will be there and I will face them with a clear conscience. So, these men died at the Aquila Gate?'

For the first time Sclay's eyes flickered with doubt.

'Where the Arbites burned people who had knowledge of their crimes?'

'The place,' Calpurnia corrected him, 'where innocent servants of the Emperor paid the price for the criminality of a pack of murderous blasphemers called the Society of the Fifty-Eighth Passage.'

'No,' said Sclay. 'They did not die there. They were murdered in their beds in our barrack-camp in the plaza beneath Bialtes' Obelisk. You know the one, arbitor.'

'No, Sclay, in point of fact I do not. Zimny?'

It took a moment of whispering with a subordinate before he turned to her.

'A square at the outskirts of the hive proper, ma'am, downslope from the Kathisma Gate. A lot of temporary barrack-camps there for the crews who were working through the night. Those have all been broken up since the attacks.'

'And so you hide the evidence of your crime,' said Sclay, 'as you tried to hide it by murdering the men and women that Robika and Janand worked with.'

'Did I? *You* attacked *me*, and with a moderately sophisticated and well-armed multiple ambush at that. That was a murder attempt by me on you?'

'We knew you were travelling through our city, and we determined to avenge ourselves on you.' Some of the fire was coming back into Sclay's voice. 'Those who came to us who had lost dear ones to your murders, they gave us weapons. We were told that there were people trying to wreck the sacred Vigil of Balronas with murder and sabotage and that we ourselves might be targets, and that a scarfaced arbitor-woman from another world, who came here full of contempt for our ways, would be behind them. And sure enough, within hours of the news reaching us, Robika and

Janand, our overseer and our paymaster, were both murdered.'

'How?'

'Burned. Good men, burned like vermin, although they were innocent and faithful. A fuel-bomb into the camp-hutch they were sleeping in. Then others came with weapons and said that they knew when the woman who had caused all of this would be passing within striking distance, and we took our roadworking engines and we came out to stop you and make you pay.'

'Who told you all this, exactly?' she asked him. 'And how did they persuade you to take up arms against an officer of the Law whom you are bound to obey?'

'An Adeptus who hides sin behind an Imperial seal is no Adeptus. I remember my lessons. Did not mighty Dolan himself declare, "I will steal from the plate of decadence to feed the mouths of the powerless"?'

'That was Thor, not Dolan,' Calpurnia corrected him. 'And since you're about to go back to your cell I'll suggest that you think on matters such as the cheapness of your faith and the readiness with which you twisted it. The explosion at the Gate was sabotage, and your attack on me follows one by a mutant witch-assassin just days ago. I refute and reject your accusations, Sclay. Had you reported what happened to you, you might have done the Imperium a service. By embracing half-baked lies you have caused more undeserving deaths than you sought to avenge and weakened what you thought you were protecting. You are the criminal, Sclay, and you will die for it.'

His eyes were still on her, even over his shoulder as he was marched out, but she could not read the expression in them. Maybe he would think on her words and repent, or maybe not. It was, she decided, not her problem any more.

AUDIENCE-ROOMS AND Rhinos. For Calpurnia, the whole of Hydraphur was coming to be defined by audience rooms and Rhinos.

She stood now in the second antechamber past the Cathedral doors. On her first visit she and Leandro had passed through these chambers too quickly to look around, but now she was trying to get a sense for its shape and layout. The outer building, she knew now, was much larger than the great space of the Cathedral itself. Between them was a great honeycomb of chambers and offices from which the affairs of the Eparch and the Ministorum were run, mazes of cloisters and rooms that filled the walls and met above the Cathedral's vaulted ceiling to fill storey after storey in the spire as it climbed to the sky.

She had ridden up in a convoy, a mechanised echo of the guards she and Leandro had brought on their first visit; this time it was a rumbling square of gleaming black APCs, Rhinos to front and rear and the ominous Repressor tanks on the flanks, the flamers in their cupolas ready to sweep away any sign of attack. Calpurnia had still sat in the cab and brooded on all the ways the convoy could still be stopped and destroyed if someone were determined enough. Apparently, no one had been, and now the tanks sat at the foot of the carved ramp, guarded by their crews and inside a semicircle of black-armoured Arbites and white-armoured Sororitas which cut the ramp off from the crowds on the High Mesé.

Those crowds were not the genteel aristocrats that she had passed among five days ago. Now, with the religious fervour of the Vigil taking hold, all the streets around the Cathedral were full of hessian-wrapped postulants, wild hair streaked with ash, shouting prayers and entreaties. The Cathedral acted as a magnet for the most intense of them, and Arbitrator squads had been forced to create an aisle for the carriers and then form a perimeter behind them, the devout beyond them howling in frustration at being pushed away from the Cathedral, the odd one managing to lunge over the top of their shield-wall, trying to touch the shining white armour of the Sororitas for luck, or holiness, or forgiveness.

Calpurnia turned her back on the noise of it, and looked back up at the wall. She was surrounded by mosaics that flooded dazzling colour up the walls. Ceremonial thrones were set into high niches with no apparent way up or down – Calpurnia guessed there were hidden entrances so that curates could be in their seats, arrayed and staring down at whoever was there to beg a favour, without the indignity of steps or ladders.

Ceilings on Hydraphur were sharp-vaulted, not the flat surfaces that Adeptus buildings in the Ultima Segmentum favoured. That meant that the artists had to lay out their works in different ways, with certain consequences for theme and composition. She was craned back looking at the mosaic above her when Dvorov's convoy pulled up outside, and they were admiring the frieze of the Passion of Dolan together when Leandro arrived to complete the delegation. There must have been spy-eyes in the room, because the instant the three of them were standing together the doors on the far side of the antechamber opened and Baragry marched through, Lord Hallyan Kalfus-Medell a pace or two behind him. The five of them stood in a little knot in the centre of the chamber and talked in low tones that made the great space seem conspiratorial, despite the warm afternoon light sluicing down the light-wells.

Calpurnia felt odd, briefing them all in what felt like such a public place, but as briefly as she could, she took them through it: what she knew of the Ecclesiarchy's plan to smuggle emissaries out to the other diocesan centres aboard the *Aurum Sanctus* (Hallyan flared his nostrils and twitch-glanced around him, Baragry simply regarded her expressionlessly); the role of Tell-Kerligan in that smuggling and the disarray it had caused the Tell-Kerligan operations; the way that this disarray had given a cell of heretic saboteurs calling themselves the Society of the Fifty-Eighth Passage an open pass to set up a bomb to incinerate the Cathedral's oil so that the poisoned replacement stocks would be rushed into circulation ('Just what is this Fifty-Eighth Passage, any-way?' Hallyan demanded. 'Who knows? Dvorov told him, 'Secret societies on Hydraphur favour obscure names. It probably only means anything to the conspirators them-selves. I'm sure it'll come out in interrogation.'); how the dray-crew's panic at the Aquila Gate had crippled the scheme; and how there were still two fatal blank spots in this whole pattern.

'The connection to the gunman who shot at you that day in the Adeptus Quarter,' said Baragry thoughtfully, 'and the connection to the ambushing forces that mobilised against you as you came back from your landing.'

'The efforts to cover the tracks in each case were quite sophisticated,' Calpurnia said. 'The first assassin had considerable work performed on him to make him untraceable in the event of capture or death. The ambush crews had misinformation fed to them through their supervisors, who were in turn murdered in such a way as to seemingly confirm the lies while making sure that the crews had no way of knowing who was behind them. There is a deftness there which doesn't fit with the Fifty-Eighth Passage operations.'

'It seems to to me,' declared Hallyan, staring at her. 'The infiltration of the Tell-Kerligan house strikes me as skilled work.'

'One was a sabotage attempt aimed at the Ecclesiarchy,' said Dvorov, 'and the other two assassination attempts against an Adeptus Arbites commander. They are different enough that we believe them unconnected.'

'We will confirm it of course, Lord Hallyan,' Calpurnia put in. 'I've given orders for detective and verispex resources to be redoubled to trace the people who incited this. We will know who they are soon enough.'

'Just so,' agreed Hallyan after a pause, and still stood looking at Calpurnia.

'Sunset is not waiting for us,' said Baragry, just as she was starting to feel uncomfortable. 'On to the second reason for your visit, Arbites. This way.'

The more she moved through it, the more comforted Calpurnia was by the Cathedral. In some ways it little resembled the plain Arbites fortresses: the walls bore hundreds of years' worth of inlays, carvings, murals, niches for urns and icons of priests and Sororitas gone by. But as they left the anteroom and began to move through the cloisters she found the formal and purposeful air made her feel at home.

She only had a brief glimpse of the main Cathedral itself, through the great double doors that stood open after three more anterooms. They stepped up to the doors to bow to the altars and pay their respects before they began their climb up through the Cathedral, and that was enough for it to awe her. There was no fussy crowding with pews or sidechapels – the Cathedral was a single vast space whose roof soared away above a crisscross of yellow beams redirected down through giant mirrored light-wells. Two rows of columns, thicker than a Rhino carrier was long, marched down its length, separating the expanse of polished flagstone floor into three aisles each big enough for an Arbites division to march down; concentric rings of steps rose up around the base of each column like an amphitheatre turned inside out. The stone saints and primarchs lining the walls were so tall that Calpurnia would have needed a grapnel and rope even to scramble up onto their feet.

At the far end of the space, beneath a great rendering of the Emperor in gold leaf on the far wall, were the Cathedral's four altars, rearing up just as Galimet had described them. Each was atop a ziggurat bigger than some chapels she had been in: the Altars Dolanite, Sanguinal and Thorian side by side, and the Altar Imperial rising above them from behind. Above each altar hung a marble angel, suspended silently in a gravity column, head bowed and hands folded in prayer. She bowed to each of them and murmured an old Low Gothic blessing from Ultramar, then stepped backwards from the doors and turned away.

They were hours working their way up through the building, as outside the afternoon began to shade to the thick Hydraphur dusk. The tour was part courtesy, part consultation: neither Church nor Arbites could afford to take chances with the security of the Vigil now, and Calpurnia and Dvorov were intent on making sure that the two organisations would be working perfectly in tandem. With Baragry and Hallyan in attendance they prowled through level after level of the giant building in the company of a succession of Adepta Sororitas guides.

The Order of the Sacred Rose garrisoned every part of the Cathedral, and at the corner and end of every corridor a white-armoured Sister stood in a guard niche like a statue, bathed in soft white light and with bolter presented. Calpurnia and Dvorov were escorted down wide echoing cloisters and through mazes of tiny passages they had to move through in single file, past great walls of stained glass or tiny vision slits in the thick ramparts. Calpurnia took a mini-slate from her belt and scratched one name after another into it, fighting to ram faces into her memory for when she met

them again. From each they took an account of the garrison
and security set out for that section of the Cathedral, and a
list of requirements for the Arbites who would complement
the garrison for the mass. When they went out onto the terraces Calpurnia kept peering down at the Mesé, the lines of
Arbites and Sisters and the crowds of worshippers getting
smaller and more blurred as they moved further up the
Cathedral's spire, and out at the light-spangled slopes of the
Bosporian Hive dropping away beneath them in the deepening orange-black twilight. The Sisters on the terraces stood
guard on circles of armourglass over great spotlights which
threw up columns of blue-white radiance, making them
shine like stars in the gathering gloom. The white and scarlet pennons on the hafts of their ceremonial banner-staves
fluttered and snapped in the evening breeze.

Finally, after climbing more floors than Calpurnia could
keep track of, they followed a narrow zigzag corridor onto a
balcony with a single chained-off stairway. Up here the wind
was chilly and the height dizzying: Calpurnia turned her
back on the drop with a grimace. She had not grown up
around heights – there were few tall buildings on Iax.

Their Sororitas escort, Sister Iustina, was handing out little
half-loops of wire with murmured blessings. Calpurnia
stared at hers, and at the intricate little globes on the ends,
until she saw the others looping theirs around their heads
and followed suit. There was a brief, disturbing moment as
the beads writhed and fitted themselves to her ears; the
sounds around her grew tinny but no less distinct.

'A tech-arcanum provided by our companions in the
Adeptus Mechanicus,' Leandro told her as Sister Iustina
unchained the stairway and motioned for them to follow.
'Certain sounds are filtered and certain ones permitted. You
will see why in a moment.' And with that they emerged from
the stair to the highest platform in the Cathedral's spire.

They stood in a great gallery, two hundred metres long and
lined with giant open arches that framed the fiery Hydraphur sunset. From here Calpurnia could see out over the top
of even the Monocrat's palace, and the dusting of lights
spreading away over the plain beyond it. Behind her when
she turned were the silent ranks of the mountains, spreading

away in a wedge and disappearing as night slipped forward over them. The height had suddenly ceased to bother her; she felt almost weightless.

'My Arbites.' Hallyan Kalfus-Medell's voice pulled her back to earth, and she turned to face him. He was a black shape against a fire-opal sky in the western arch. His guard-servitor must have been waiting for him here, and it made a monstrous, looming blot beside him.

'Our timing was perfect, and your presence here, my Arbitor Calpurnia, is an honour and a delight. This is something I had greatly hoped to show you, the kind of introduction to the magnificence of my homeworld that I felt you deserved. It is a delight to be in your presence here.' His voice was gentler than she had heard it before, and he took Calpurnia's elbow to walk her to the arch behind them – she stiffened at the familiarity but saw Dvorov give a quick let-it-go shake of the head in the corner of her vision. She suffered herself to be led to the eastern end of the gallery and the arch facing back over the Mesé; there were no tiers against this side of the spire and the drop to the ground was almost sheer. It was getting on for full night now and the plaza, brightly lit, was a distant haze of colour. Calpurnia realised that it was more than just the mobs that had been around the gate on her arrival. The whole Mesé was packed shoulder to shoulder. It looked as though half the population of the Augustaeum had been flooding in while they had been touring the Cathedral.

She felt another touch on her arm, but it was not Hallyan this time. Sister Iustina checked that her ear-beads were secure and stepped away. She consulted a timepiece on the back of her gauntlet and made a gesture and Calpurnia, seeing the others all drop their mouths open, followed suit. Hallyan said another brief word to his servitor in that chattering code-cant and then pursed his open lips as though blowing a smoke-ring.

The beads cut out most of the sound and so Calpurnia felt the toll of the bell mainly as a physical shock. It was like a weighted punching bag swinging in and hitting her from every angle at once, vibrating her diaphragm as if she had just coughed and setting her carapace armour thrumming and buzzing on her body. It took all her reflexes not to stumble forward a step and all her self-control not to whirl and shout once she saw that the rest of the party had not taken alarm.

And below her, the lights of the hive went out.

For a moment the only illumination was the faint and dimming lights of the hab-city complexes far out on the plain, and then light started creeping back into the jungle of towers and steeples on the slopes below them. Subdued, modest floods began to shine from the palace and the walls of the Cathedral, the Sororitas lit up by their spotlights as if the side of the Cathedral had been strung with diamonds.

A moment later, the citizens' lanterns began to light in the square. At first just a sprinkle, points here and there, but the light grew until the plaza shone like a carpet of fireflies, then like a river breaking its banks as more lanterns were lit in the darkened streets of the Kathisma and more all the way down every road and alley in the hive. In the silence as the single ring of the bell died away, the glittering web was magical, hypnotic.

'Do you see, Arbitor Calpurnia, why I am so concerned for you? Look out over this hive, look at the throngs below us. Imagine what it will be like when the bells ring at the start of the festival of the Sanguinala! Picture what it will be like,:the crowds casting the mourning cloaks from over their scarlet festive garb, the red banners unfurling from all the steeples and towers, crimson petals filling the air.' He was almost whispering.

'This mass will be a thing of beauty, my arbitor. I have worked so hard, so long to make such a holy time one that will be remembered and retold down the years. Whoever would harm you, or any of the great Adeptus or myself or even the lowliest servant of the mass, would defile what the Eparch of Hydraphur honoured me with the task of making. I want you to understand that.'

'I think, my Lord Kalfus-Medell, that I do.'

They stood and watched the lights in silence for a time.

Fourteenth Day of Septista.

Four days to the Mass of Saint Balronas.
First day of the Vigil of Balronas. Commemoration
of Girza the Demi-Sainted (Adepta Sororitas).

As of this day all travel by vehicle in the Augustaeum is prohib-
ited, as it is in the lower city unless on Adeptus business. These
laws will be enforced by Arbites and Sororitas, to whom any
breaches of these laws must be reported. A religious curfew
descends at nightfall and no citizen should be outside their homes
unless on religious business. Travel to and from religious services
should be as part of an Ecclesiarchal procession, of which there
will be dozens for each shrine and chapel in constant motion
throughout the night. The only illumination permitted in the
home are candles of the size specified by the Ecclesiarchy or the
scented lamp that was lit for the Quiet Congregation. Householders should admit officers of the Ecclesiarchy or Ministorum who
may by law enter any house at any time during this period to
police this edict and pronounce a blessing on the house if all is
well.

CHAPTER NINE

BOTH ECLIPTICS OF the Hydraphur system swarmed with Navy fortifications, from the Ring itself, through the necklaces of orbital fortresses that every world in the system wore, the free-stations surfing the shifting gravitic tides between the ecliptics, the lumbering battlegroups of the Squadron Hydraphur prowling the system like panthers in a cage, the tiny sentinel stations and free-floating hardpoints tucked into the curling asteroid belts, the clouds of deadfall torpedoes in the system fringes, and the bunkers and citadels spread across every world and cut into the crust of every moon. But the bulk of the Navy's second-line facilities, the fief-planets it controlled, its forges and shipworks, the Navigator stations and telepathica matrices, the four giant Naval academies and the luxurious spaceborne estates of the officer-aristocrats, were concentrated in the Gyre Marmarea, the larger ecliptic that tilted towards the borders of the Segmentum Obscuras.

At 09.57 on the fourteenth day of Septista, while Shira Calpurnia was sifting through incident reports trying to find links with the attempts on her life, an authorisation code was mistransmitted to *Aventis Sapphire 7*, a dromon runner carrying half a household's worth of dignitaries from the League of Blackships station in the Gyre Marmarea in for the Vigil. When the ship's astropaths and logisters tried to authenticate their respective halves of the code with the Naval patrols above the Ring, it registered as correct for the first pass and the dromon was cleared to close. Halfway through its approach the code transmissions, despite the layers of security and elaborate fault-tolerance procedures, abruptly began to clash and contradict and the runner arced gracefully into the path of *Highcaster*, a cargo barge accelerating away from the Ring towards an outbound Navy cruiser.

The dromoni were designed to double as system defence boats in an emergency, and the ship had enough agility to turn and glance off the barge and enough structural toughness not to break up immediately. Its starboard side a mass of furrows, bleeding oxygen from its decks and plasma from its drives, the dromon spiralled slowly away as klaxons screamed through the Ring and tugs and emergency boats scrambled through the launching-gates. The barge was less lucky, knocked directly toward the Ring with its back broken by the impact. The roared commands of the Gunnery Control commander for the fortress batteries to wait bought it enough time for about a third of the crew to reach saviour capsules, but the rest, or as many of them as had survived the collision, were incinerated with the ship when the Ring gunners decided they had no more time.

Within fifteen minutes of *Highcaster's* final death throes, the Transmechanics and Astropaths had been dragged from their communications cupolas. Twenty minutes after that the Commander of the Watch was shouting questions at them in his own chambers in one of the Ring's command domes. Over the next half-hour that dome was besieged by the Navy, directors of the line to which *Highcaster* had belonged, furious Adeptus Astropathica envoys demanding to know how their esteemed brethren could have been subjected to this, and rather more discreet representations from the Monocrat's palace.

Two hours after the collision the postmortems of the failsafe systems were coming in. The good news was that whatever problem had caused the collision had been localised, and the failsafes had contained it. The downside of it was that it was starting to point to something darker. Sabotage.

A formal envoy from the offices of the Master of Orbits arrived at the three-hour mark. He walked into the command dome at almost the same moment as two members of the Naval Adjudicature, there with a team of Naval Security invigilators to make their own formal report. One of the first things they found, after demanding to see those involved, was that the astropath who had first broadcast the hails between *Aventis Sapphire 7* and the Ring had committed suicide with a slap-syringe that he had picked loose from the lining of his robe. Talk of sabotage intensified.

At 14.04, just over four hours since the first of the wrong codes had flown into the minds of the *Aventis's* astropaths, Shira Calpurnia took ship at the Arbites Cross-Seven fortress and was carried up to board the Ring yet another time. By the time she stepped through the docking hatch, paranoia was thick enough to be wrung out of the air by the double-fistful. And the entire transmission and astropath crew were in the custody of the Navy.

'THEY'RE WHAT?' CALPURNIA snapped, fighting the urge to step forward and slam a fist down on the desk.

'In the custody of the Navy,' said Hadre Gutamo, Commander of the Watch for the twenty-eighth segment of the Hydraphur Ring. Standing behind the great slab of polished wood in the tiny office in the heart of his chambers, surrounded by rich tapestries and framed Imperial honour scrolls, Gutamo had the bearing of one determined to bravely wear pain and disgrace: formal and straight-backed as though on ceremonial parade, but still somehow giving the impression of sagging, as though his body had gone limp and was only being held up by a harness and wires. One eye was green, the other yellow-orange and surrounded by scars – Calpurnia took it for a tissue graft of some kind – and both mismatched eyes looked dully at his hands, folded in front of his chest. A tiny quaver of misery in his voice and the smallest twitching of his waxed moustache belied his apparent composure.

'I see. This is the boundary area between planetary – that is, full Adeptus – jurisdiction and Naval jurisdiction in open space, is that right?' From what she had heard on her way up Calpurnia had already guessed that the people involved in the mistransmission had been spirited off-station, but she had reined her anger in until she had the word of their commander to go on. Now that she had confirmation her temper was starting to creak for release.

'Yes. The Master of Orbits reports to both the Monocrat and Adeptus and to the in-system Naval Command.'

'And you report to the Master of Orbits.'

'Yes.'

'And did you ascertain from him, or did he tell you, that this may well be related to a string of sabotage and assassination attempts in the heart of the Bosporian Hive down on Hydraphur, aimed at the Vigil of Saint Balronas itself, and that maybe you should bloody well have allowed the Adeptus Arbites access to these people?'

He swallowed. 'The chain of communication that caused the… incident… the crash, it actually began with a Naval station in far-perimeter orbit. The Inner Charisian Gate, under Gate-Captain Sambin de Jauncey. Captain de Jauncey made immediate petition for all guilty parties to be handed over to him so that they could face a court martial along with members of his own crew under Naval protocol.' Gutamo looked up as he finished talking and flinched. 'Green as Macragge glacier-ice', was how one of Calpurnia's brothers had described her eyes when she was angry. His gaze returned to his gloved hands. One of them had developed a slight tic to match the one in his moustache.

'Who will handle the court martial, Commander Gutamo?' Calpurnia's voice was quieter, but the edge had not gone from it.

'There are a number of eligible authorities under the protocols of Naval law.' Gutamo's voice had quietened too. 'The exact strengths of each claim on the trying of this case would need to be weighed in light of the relevant judgements and precedents. It would probably require some consideration by specialist savants and archivists, since the majority of cases would date back to pre-Apostasy–'

'I am sure that such input will be most terribly helpful,' Calpurnia told him, 'but I invite you, commander, to take a guess. I don't doubt that the Arbites will want to carefully examine the role of *every* member of the Ring crews in this incident and I would certainly hope that our working relationship here is going to get off to the best possible start. I hope that nothing in your own co-operation has the effect of prejudicing that examination against your colleagues here.'

Gutamo registered the not-very-veiled threat with the air of a drowning man who has felt it start to rain. He gave a long blink and then lifted his eyes slowly back to Calpurnia's face. She had looked into a great many condemned eyes, but still the weight in Gutamo's bi-coloured gaze almost made her step back.

'From what I have seen in the communiqués from the gate,' he said, 'Captain de Jauncey proposes to chair the hearings himself and make all sentences immediate. There was talk of summary executions, and those may already have been carried out. That is all I can reveal to you, Arbitor Senioris Calpurnia, without endangering myself further with the risk of inaccuracy. As it stands my family will be provided for after I pay the penalty for what happened on my watch. If I make things worse for myself they may not be. I trust you understand.'

She did understand, but she pushed it aside as irrelevant – suddenly she was itching to get to the Inner Charisian Gate before the trail of the saboteurs, whoever they were, was closed off. She gave the briefest of formal Arbitrator salutes, which Gutamo returned with the curved-hand salute of the Battlefleet Pacificus, then jerked her head for Bannon to follow.

'Are we not arresting the commander?' he whispered as they double-timed back out through Gutamo's chambers under the eyes of the dome staff. She waited to reply to him until they were well on their way back to their cutter, tramping loudly through corridors of tarnished, raw-looking iron whose walls were run through with heavy girders and studded with great rivet-heads twice the size of Calpurnia's fist.

As they came to each new corridor or stairwell she saw little knots of station crew break up with alacrity and hurry away, not wanting to linger in the sight of a senior Arbitrator so soon after such a terrible crime.

'Gutamo isn't going anywhere. He understands his duty and I believe he'll do it. And we're close enough to Hydra-phur that he's arrestable if he should be found wanting. But doesn't it worry you that the inner gate, that's what you call that ring of way-fortresses just outside maximum orbit, isn't it, the inner gates? Right. The inner gate which might be implicated is the nucleus of the squadron that gave that run-ner its clearance, and within hours the station commander has arrested every *other* implicated crewmember, to a spot where he'll be able to kick them out of an airlock with a bolt round through the back of the head without anyone else being able to interrogate them or gainsay any report he pro-vides? Nothing about that bothers you?'

'Perhaps we should be co-operating with the Navy author-ities in the trial, maybe? Maybe we can send them an envoy...'

'Fine if this de Jauncey is simply being enthusiastic,' Calpurnia replied, striding down an already-moving lift-stair, 'and utterly useless if he's doing what my unpleasant Arbitrator's mind is suspecting him of doing. What plan of action did we log before we took off from Cross-Seven? I think I left it to you to word, didn't I?'

'Uh, um. We instructed that we would, um, be conducting immediate questioning of the Commander of the Watch, then conducting what action we thought was necessary aboard the Ring while we awaited a fuller task force of Judges and judicial savants to begin negotiating the overlap of legal jurisdictions.' Bannon's voice firmed as he gradually recalled what he had written.

'Right. Good. I'm countermanding that as of now. No,' she added, catching his expression, 'you didn't do anything wrong, you did just what I needed you to do. It's just that "what action we think is necessary" has just become a little more urgent.'

'We're going out to this station now, without waiting for the taskforce?'

'I know about picking taskforces. It will be hours before they're ready to lift, and I need to be at this station now. Throne alone knows what de Jauncey will be able to get away with if he's hiding something.'

'The jurisdictional issues…'

'In orbit over Don-Croix,' Calpurnia told him coldly as she half-vaulted down a steep grillework staircase to the dock levels, 'we conducted a full boarding action of a Navy cruiser when we had reason to believe that there was a xenos infestation being protected by the crew. Don't try and tell me that there has ever lived or breathed a single Navy officer who is outside the reach of the Law. What did they make you chant on the parade ground every morning of your induction, Bannon?'

'We determine the guilty. We decide the punishment.'

'Damned right we do. And I'm pleased to hear there are some things that are the same the whole galaxy over. Anyway, we seemed to inadvertently generate some goodwill from the Navy when we stopped the *Sanctus*, so maybe that will help when we show up and push our way on board.' *I'm talking like Dvorov*, she thought ruefully, then barked at Bannon again. 'Go ahead of us and order our cutter to prepare for cast-off. Have the pilot lay in a course for the gate and order the Ring controllers to clear a path for us, on my authority. This is a level four delegation. *Run!*' He shot away from her as though scalded.

For a moment she was alone at the top of the docking-well, and stopped to catch her breath. She realised she didn't even know how much of a trip out to the gate she was in for. Maybe she could requisition a dromon of her own… but no. She'd send a transmission to the gate as soon as they launched and not risk getting bogged down in haggling with the commander if there were no ship readily available. If only the *Judgement's Clarion* had still been stationed at the Ring, but the little carrier had been called from the *Aurum Sanctus* interception to a suppression operation at the edge of the Gyre Aurucon and would not be back at Hydraphur for weeks.

For a moment Calpurnia wished she could be as confident as she had sounded to Bannon, then told herself she was being pessimistic. She was Adeptus Arbites and she had the goodwill of the Navy; that much she knew. And the attack on the Ring was an attack on them both. As she started down the steps, listening to the rumble of launch preparations starting to shiver the walls, she told herself this wouldn't be hard.

'DON'T GO THINKING you'll be allowed to stay here,' snarled the voice on the Charisian Gate's vox-channel as grapples clanged against the hull outside. 'We are docking you on sufferance. Your craft will be refuelled and its anima rested, and then you will be on your way, under armed escort until you reach the Ring. The Gate-Captain issued specific instructions to that effect.' Startled out of any immediate reply, Calpurnia steadied herself in her crash-couch as the cutter was jerked gracelessly toward the Inner Charisian Gate's docks. The crackling voice coming from the grille was a rude bucket of icewater over her earlier optimism. Suddenly she felt stiff and awkward in the couch, and as if on cue the knot of scar tissue in the front of her right hip seemed to tense and stiffen.

In the systems Calpurnia had served in on the south-eastern fringe, the fortresses that rode vital positions in the system's ecliptic were known as points; in Hydraphur they were known as gates. They rode the gravity well at points where the heaviest traffic tended to pass, where it was easiest to slingshot from one Gyre to the other, or to skirt around the largest gas giants or past the dense asteroid belts that looped and twisted through the system. That made the stations gates in more than name – nearly every ship that wanted to pass into the system by a safe and stable route would at some point have to pass through space that a gate station controlled.

The Inner Charisian Gate was one of the smaller ones, not a self-contained fortress but part of an array of platforms and stations that stood out from orbit to form a second, dispersed Ring of guns and attack-craft bays. Small it might be by the standards of the giants further out, but it still filled the cockpit window when Calpurnia slipped forward to watch their approach. It wove and tilted in front of them as their pilot threaded them through the stacked minefields and the fire-lanes of the outrigger turrets. The half-glimpsed silhouettes of the dormant mines and the hungry turret gunports were in their own way a powerful sign of entering a new domain. Soon the gate had spread to fill every corner of the port, a fat pitted egg of an asteroid, glittering with windows, ringed with void-shield spines and docking gantries and with great tiered steeples of reinforced adamantium jutting above and below it.

She had left orders at the Ring to inform the gate's astropaths of their arrival, and the hails and counter-hails had been smooth if curt as they closed in. It was not until the approach controller's sudden bark at her from the vox-grille that her feelings about the visit suddenly turned bad. She looked back over the team in the cutter: Bannon, and two Arbites she had collared from Cross-Seven when she realised she should probably have an escort. The cutter juddered and rang as it was pulled taut against the station's docking arm and Calpurnia thought about all the empty space between her and the nearest Arbites reinforcements.

There was nothing for it but to square her shoulders, chill her gaze down to the appropriate authoritative stare, straighten her rank insignia and climb up the ladderwell. To someone outside the station it would look as if the cutter had been seized by a long metal fin stretching out from the station and clamping to its back; from the inside that hollow 'fin' was a high oubliette where the top of the cutter's hull formed the floor. Calpurnia stood on that hull now, boots planted on the frosted metal, and stared upwards.

The docking level was an assault on the senses. The metal around her was as bitterly cold as the hull beneath her, and she could watch her breath pluming up from her lips and the dew turning to rime on the walls and the catwalks, and on the giant chains that had snaked out from the dock mouth and clamped onto the cutter's hull. Squinting past the arclights above her Calpurnia could make out giant cylinders that she took to be the capstan array. The noise of the machinery was like a hammer.

Their pilots had remained in the cockpit, and it was only Bannon and her two-arbitor impromptu escort who joined her in the oubliette. Calpurnia smiled inwardly as they huffed and stamped at the cold air slapping their skin: they were all used to Hydraphur climates, while the chill reminded her pleasantly of the ocean cliffs on Talassar and her one visit – half a pilgrimage – to the poles of Macragge. Then she muttered at them to stop it and collect themselves. She had no doubt they were being watched, and they had to comport themselves properly.

Thinking that in turn made her realise how long she had been standing there. She tilted her head back and called out. 'I am Shira Calpurnia, Arbitor Senioris of the Adeptus Arbites. I wish to make a formal greeting to an officer of this installation so that I can be about my business here. I am being kept waiting.'

Her voice was clear and powerful, ringing up and over the rumble and clank of machinery. And either her tone had made the reception jump or they had been just about to start anyway, because a moment later they could see a grillework carriage come rattling down one hoarfrosted wall. It descended evenly until it was two or three times head height, then ground down a gear and lowered the rest of the way with aching slowness. Lights over the top of its door clanked on and glared at them, and Calpurnia had to take her helmet from Bannon and don it; once behind the polarising lenses she was able to get a good look at the group in the carriage.

They were not a welcoming sight. In the middle of the carriage, taking up much of the room despite the bunched, controlled posture common to constant space-travellers, was a Naval petty officer whose knee-length green uniform coat was adorned with the crimson slashes of decorations for shipboard-combat actions. His sabre and a heavy Naval pistol were hung at his sides and the right half of his jaw was augmetic steel that glittered in the lights. He was flanked by two ratings, faceless in heavy rubberised work-ponchos and hoods, carrying heavy-duty chainblades on the ends of bulky fighting shafts, blades to cut through wrecked bulkheads, tangled cables or enemy flesh with equal ease. A Naval Security trooper in a uniform that was almost a mirror of the Arbitrators' rounded out the party, flamer held ready with the igniter jet lit. The intended effect – and the snub it implied – was obvious. Calpurnia gritted her teeth. She was an arbitor senioris, the fourth highest-ranking enforcer of Imperial Law in this damned system, and she was not going to be scared out of acting like it.

She strode forward to the carriage doors and glared at the petty officer through the bars until they ground open.

'My escorts and I are here to carry out arrests over sabotage and deaths at the Hydraphur Ring. Kindly escort us on board the station. Gate-Captain de Jauncey should have been alerted to our arrival and will be expecting us.'

'If you're here, madam, then you know that the people behind that act have already been arrested. Arrested and brought here. You have nothing more to worry about. We will even do the executions for you.'

The man's speech was odd, the synthetic lip on the artificial part of his jaw not quite able to do its part in forming words. His expression was not quite a sneer.

'The guilty parties that you took it on yourselves to arrest are wanted by more than just the Navy,' she told him. 'They are implicated in…' she paused for a moment, long enough to wonder if *implicated* was too strong a word to be truthful, and then to decide that she was not going to justify herself to a junior officer. '…in planetary matters which I will discuss with the gate-captain. If you are not he, then kindly make the arrangements for my admission.'

'You are not a Navy officer. Beyond the Hydraphur Ring, the system is a Naval fief, world, moon and space alike.' His expression had turned sulky, and Calpurnia liked that. It vindicated her: he didn't have the authority to order her off the station, no matter how much he wished and acted otherwise. Keeping her dignity in mind, she simply stared at him as he started to shift uncomfortably in the freezing air, and motioned her escorts into the carriage when he grudgingly stepped aside. With the other Arbites between her and the Navy party she looked out through the bars at nothing in particular until the cage had rattled its way to the top of the oubliette and they were able to step through the series of airlocks into the gate itself.

In spite of their reception, Calpurnia found herself relaxing as they passed through the station. Physically it seemed as exotic to her as much of Hydraphur, with that taper-arched shape to its doors and the passages looking more like a succession of vaulted chambers than plain corridors. But like the Cathedral cloisters or the operational levels of the Wall, this was a *working* place, not a place existing for the sake of its own grandeur. It was full of emerald-uniformed officers, enlisted ranks in coarse grey-green hurrying under the bellows of their superiors, indentured station-hands with their grafted-shut mouths and facial brands. Once or twice she caught glimpses of other adeptus, too, Mechanicus magi on some errand for the system-arcana of the station or astropaths in hoods or psi-dampening metal head-cages, shuffling along in lines with their heads down. There simply wasn't the space on a station to set aside space for ceremonial disuse, and the gate had the comforting bedlam of a place at work.

As they made their way out of the central rock into the steeple and the walls around them changed from stone to steel, the crowds changed too. Here there were more officers, and the enlisted hands had better uniforms and more pride in their gait. These were not the mass-pressganged labour of the lower levels, who would toil until they were crushed in machinery or cooked or electrocuted in system malfunctions and replaced as a matter of routine. These were the skilled crew, the ones who directed the workings of the engines or the aim of the defences, who monitored the dronings of the astropaths or the crackling void-shield generators.

Calpurnia had thought they were being taken to the bridge, but their grudging host instead took them to a double shuttered door flanked by two more ship's security troopers, holding fat-barrelled hellguns on the corridor. He nodded to them and shoved the doors open, motioned the Arbites gracelessly through, and swung the doors shut without another word.

They were in an orrery. The spherical chamber was big enough that the gallery they had stepped into was several metres above the floor, or at least above the lowest pole of the sphere. The walls were painted a midnight blue, and the sun that hung in the middle was a globular lantern of burnt-orange smoked glass. Hanging in formation around it were intersecting silver hoops for Hydraphur's twin ecliptics, metal orbs for the planets and moons gliding along them with a faint hissing sound. The dust clouds were gauzy nets of wire towed between little semicircles of silver; asteroid belts were strings of crystal beads. She stared in frank admiration of its understated elegance as much as the complexity of design.

Gate-Captain Sambin de Jauncey leaned against the railing, his back to them. He was a slender man, not tall but seeming so from his haughty posture. His hair was silky-black and short, his skin dusky, his movements cat-graceful and his eyes, when he turned to face them, cat-alert. He wore no ceremonial sabre, just a slender dagger on a braided gold cord around his neck. The high collar of his uniform bore a richly embroidered emblem that Calpurnia supposed was a family crest.

'You are trying my patience, madam arbitor,' he began without preamble, 'which was not abundant today to begin with. So tell me, what can I do to get you out of my station and on your way?'

'I am here to pursue the perpetrators of sabotage at the Ring which destroyed two ships, cost many lives, endangered many more.' Calpurnia had thought that his snubbing tone was coming and kept her own voice cold and level. 'Those people were aboard the Ring but were removed from it into Naval custody, apparently on your orders, and brought here. There have been similarly callous and destructive sabotage actions on Hydraphur itself, and I propose that the same agency might be behind both. By co-operating we can remove a criminal threat to the Arbites, the Navy, the sacred Vigil on Hydraphur, and an enemy of the Imperium and its people.'

'You're certainly ambitious, but not very attentive. You haven't answered my question.' He had taken a step toward her, dark eyes blazing, and Calpurnia realised de Jauncey was not just being rude. He was furious. 'My question, and I will repeat it for you, is this: what must I do to have you out of my way?'

'Your question, gate-captain, was "what can I do, pray tell me, to get you out of my station and on your way as soon as possible?" Your memory is in about the same state that you allege my attentiveness to be, apparently. And as for an answer, what you can do is accommodate myself and my escorts on the station until my additional Arbites personnel arrive. Then you can join me in interrogating the prisoners, who are most certainly guilty under Imperial law and therefore must answer to the Imperium's premier lawgivers. To show goodwill I am prepared to allow you to co-prosecute once the interrogations and the verispex evidence-gathering is done. Then you can allow whatever sentences and punishments are called for to proceed, participating where you need to, and after that, gate-captain, you will be free of me.'

'Not acceptable.' He turned away and leaned over the railing again. A silver ball representing one of the outermost worlds whispered by an arm's length from his face, twirling a pair of gemstone moons around it. 'This is a military system, Arbitrator, and until we were forced off it by politics Hydraphur was a military world. The attack was on space shipping, which is a matter of Naval prerogative. To subject myself to the orders of a planetary authority, to surrender authority over prisoners being held on my station under my orders… I wonder if you fully understand what you ask. What you dare ask.'

'My title, Gate-Captain de Jauncey, is Arbitor. Arbitor senioris. You may address me as arbitor senioris or Arbitor Calpurnia, as you wish.'

'If the best you can manage by way of a riposte is to correct me on some point of formal address–'

'I can also correct you on a point of formal *law*. We are the Adeptus Arbites. The vessel by which the Emperor's laws have travelled down the ages. We light and keep the beacon of the Emperor's Law so that all in His Imperium can guide their lives by it, and we see to it that those who turn away from that beacon and cause themselves and others to stumble are made to pay. We determine the guilty, we decide the punishment. I have witnessed judgements of officers of the Navy and of the Imperial Guard and of planetary and system governors. I have twice helped to pass sentence on men and women of both those organizations, some of them more highly ranked than you, gate-captain. If you wish me out of the way, then I suppose the way is to have me murdered before the ship full of Arbites arrives on-station, and then to have some way of making sure that those Arbites then don't get suspicious enough to declare you renegade and exact the appropriate punishment on you as well as on whatever wretches you have in your brig.'

De Jauncey was gripping the railing he leant on. He was wearing soft gloves that hid his hands, but she could tell from his posture that under the quilted green silk his knuckles would be white.

'Or,' she went on, 'you could join with me in doing what we are both, my gate-captain, supposed to be spending our lives doing. Combating threats to the Imperium and to its people. Is it really so hard to see what we have in common here?'

'How much do we have in common, do you think? How much do I have in common with some woman who marches onto my own station, the station of which I am the duly appointed captain, to demand that I jump to her tune? Every last one of the crew of this gate would walk out of the airlocks if I ordered it, because a captain, on his ship, and this gate station is my ship, *Arbitor*, embodies final authority.'

'If you do not feel you're answerable to the Arbites, de Jauncey, then fine. You can argue the exact points of law with the savants and locutors when they arrive on my heels. We can all meet back in this chamber and explain your position to you. If you still want to resist the will of the law then, well, I think I mentioned that you won't be the first renegade Naval officer I've helped to take down.'

He swung around again, fists knuckle-cracking tight and eyes alight.

'That was a threat, *Arbitor* Calpurnia. You threatened me. You came onto my gate and you stood there and you *threatened* me.'

'Yes, gate-captain, that is exactly what I did. I'm fed up with dancing around and mouthing fancy words to get the co-operation I should expect by rights. I have the authority and the justification to threaten you and I am using it.'

'You will regret this,' de Jauncey said. He was breathing hard. 'The *Crusader Ascendant* is due to dock at this gate within six hours. I refer, for your information, to the flagship of Commodore Hayl Omenti, commander of the Fourth Hydraphur Squadron and Warden of the Inner Gates. Do not doubt that he will have something to say about the way some,' he made a dismissive gesture, 'some little Arbitrix came scuttling aboard in a planetary-orbit cutter to try to subvert a gate-captain's authority.'

'There's a pleasing symmetry to that, gate-captain, because although I can't quote a fancy name at you, a ship full of Judges is on its way likewise. So, then. You will give me and my fellow Arbites suitable accommodation. When my colleagues arrive then we will sit down with yourself and whoever from the commodore's staff is interested and we will make clear exactly how much authority you have in this matter. And when that is done we will proceed with the trials and the sentences.' She took a step to the door. 'Have someone show us to our quarters, please. Now.'

THEY WERE GIVEN quarters of a single stateroom and ablutory, that would have been snug for one and was full with four. Calpurnia made a point of talking for a little while to each of the two Arbites she had brought from Cross-Seven: Gomry, a sleek-muscled, almond-eyed young man from Hydraphur's island archipelagos, and Syldati, a woman whose hair and skin were as white as her eyes and lips were dark, with an odd accent that she said came from the DiMattina system two sectors to rimward. Both were relatively junior and feeling as uncomfortable as Bannon with being suddenly trapped in such a spat between their own commander and the Navy. Calpurnia kept talking on and off, as much to relax herself as them, and the uncomfortable silences gradually mellowed to companionable silences as they sat side by side, stripping weapons and kit and trading the occasional anecdote and joke.

Calpurnia wasn't sure how much time had passed before the change of watch was sounded. They all jumped as the horns went off through the corridors outside; it was a harsh, ear-filling sound with an oddly layered quality as horns in passages further away joined in the chorus. The hall outside filled with hammering boots and shouting voices for nearly half an hour before the racket of the changeover died down. She was starting to wonder about organising sleeping shifts when they all jumped again at a bang on the door. It was a station-hand, shifting with discomfort at the unfamiliar duty. Behind him, the corridor was in shadow – the lights, already muted as a nod to the Vigil, had been dimmed further for the night cycle.

'Ma'am, Gate-Captain de Jauncey instructs you to be advised that the dromon runner *Lumen Geodess* has entered the outer reaches of our defences and should dock within the hour. *Crusader Ascendant* has hailed us and will soon be inbound also.'

Calpurnia nodded, snapped her fingers for him to stay for a moment and beckoned to Bannon and Syldati.

'Escort my two staff to whichever docking point the *Geodess* will be using, please. You two, report to the leader of the Arbites taskforce when it arrives. Give him a quick report on what's happened here to date – you were both with me the whole time. Then escort them here. You have a Level Two delegation, reporting to the taskforce leader until you rejoin me.'

The crewman looked nervous enough at that to reassure the two Arbites, who traded glances, donned helmets and stamped away at his heels, in heavy and confident step. Gomry looked after them, and then quizzically at Calpurnia.

'We wait here,' she told him, 'in case there's a new message from the gate-captain. And because I'm fed up with doing every last bit of bolting about myself. I'm going to stay up here, catch my breath and stretch my legs. Lucky you, Gomry, you get to stay here and stretch your legs too.'

The constant traffic and noise of the day shifts was gone, and the cool dimness of the passageway outside their room seemed spacious and tranquil in the quiet. Calpurnia sauntered a short way from the door, breathing deeply. She had no idea whether or not it was just her fancy, but the air seemed cooler. She risked a stretch, standing on tiptoe and tilting her head back, started to run through the list of things she had to go over with the taskforce, then gave up. There would be time to–

There was a soft sound behind her and then a pair of arms clamped brutally tight around her, level with her biceps, pinning her own arms to her body and lifting her onto tip-toe. Heavy arms, a strong and confident grip.

'Got you now, haven't we?' leered a voice in her ear, and a tickle of alcohol fumes curled around to find her nostrils. The voice was husky, male, young, muffled. She was spun around to face back toward the door to her room, spilling light out into the passage; three more men stood there, in Navy uniform breeches and loose shirts with identity pins taken off, dark wraps of cloth muffling their faces, heavy truncheons in their hands. What she could see of their skin looked flushed. Whoever was holding her didn't seem to be the only one to have braced his courage with a bottle.

Gomry stepped through the doorway a moment later, hel-metless and unprepared. His eyes widened and his instincts betrayed him: his first reaction was not to spring back into the room to grab a firearm, but to say 'Unhand the arbitor sen-' Then a vicious truncheon swing cracked into his fore-head and he pitched soundlessly back into the stateroom.

'You're going to pay for that,' Calpurnia said over her shoulder to whoever held her. 'Up until a moment ago I could have written this off as some kind of stunt by overzeal-ous cadets, but now we've got an arbitor who's going to need a medicae bed or a funeral. Don't think I'm not going to per-sonally end you for this. All of you. And I'll end de Jauncey, too, if I so much as suspect he's behind it.'

'Full of bragging, aren't you, you meddling little bitch.' The stink of alcohol again, but her captor was managing to keep his voice down to a hiss. 'Think you can come where you're not wanted? Think you can just push your way in here and order us about and disgrace us? We've got a nice idea for a little present for your friends to find. We're going to send a little message about little bitches who push their little noses into places they have no right to be.' His companions were sniggering, and the one who had felled Gomry was slapping his truncheon into his gloved palm.

Calpurnia was taking things in. They were drunk, but probably not enough for her to count on them being slowed or blurred. They were bigger than her, more powerful. Their truncheons were solid bludgeons, either wood or plastic, she couldn't tell, but reliant on their weight and not powered like her maul. The adrenaline they were getting from their own daring was carrying them along. They were badly positioned, taking too long to gloat, not taking her weapons off her.

She was yanked toward the stateroom again. Once they got her in there her chances would be radically worse. Experimentally, she shifted her weight. The hug was still strong, but the man wasn't trying to control her balance or her centre. Ah-ha.

She shifted her hips to the right. Her shoulders didn't move, and the man gripping her had his sense for her movements dulled by his height and inferior balance and by the armour around her chest and shoulders. She pushed the hilt of her maul forward, pivoting it and levering the tip up behind her. He grunted in annoyance, then the grunt turned to a soundless whoop of agony as she thumbed the maul into life. The arms around her vanished, and she ducked away as the man who had held her doubled up so quickly his feet left the deck and he crashed down in a foetal curl.

His three associates were stunned and motionless in their own turn and Calpurnia moved to cut the numbers while she could, taking two quick, graceful steps forward and sideways, angling so that when she drove the maul forward into the second attacker's gut in a textbook fencer's lunge the power discharge sent him retching and cannoning back into the man behind him.

Tangled together, the two of them crashed into the passage wall and Calpurnia turned in time to duck and slip her head to one side to dodge a stroke that would have split her skull. Instinct stopped her counterattacking straight away, and she avoided the backslash that whipped by in front of her nose, but after that the other man had leaned into his strokes too much and given away his balance, so she had a moment's opening to step in and crack his knee with her boot. Then she was inside the third truncheon swing, positioned to catch the man's arm on her shoulder, sock her hip into and under his and let his own swing twist him off his feet. His broken knee folded and he landed awkwardly, yelling in pain and shock and trying to drag her over with him.

She stamped hard on his face and kicked him harder in the ribs and head, then turned and hunched and caught the blow from behind her on her shoulder armour. The man who'd managed to get out from under his half-conscious companion got a double-handed grip on his truncheon for a swing to take off her head.

Calpurnia, who had still felt the impact and was grateful beyond words she had kept her carapace on, didn't give him the chance. Now humming and spitting with power, her maul didn't need a big swing to do damage and she feinted low with it then swatted his hands when he tried to block. She had upped the setting a notch and the crack of power blew the truncheon out of the man's hands and took off the tips off six of his fingers. He yowled and staggered back and Calpurnia, in no mood to be merciful, tilted her shoulder in and made a sharp downward chop that shattered his collarbone and left a scorched, ruined weal from his shoulder to his belly. The maul bucked in her hand as it hit and the man crashed backward, slid along the wall and down it to jitter on the floor.

She slammed the maul back into its clip and ran to Gomry. His eyes were rolled back, his pulse fluttering, and the bruise across his forehead cruel and dark. Calpurnia snarled to herself and would have spat at the prone forms out in the passageway, but there was no point in wasting the energy. She listened to his pulse, talked to him, helped his breathing when she had to, harangued him, ordered him not to die, and she was still hunched over him, doggedly keeping him as alive as she could, when Naval Security arrived.

Fifteenth Day of Septista

Three days to the Mass of Saint Balronas.
Second day of the Vigil of Balronas. Procession of the
Thesean Martyrs. Commemoration of Cartigan and of
Lucullus Traph.

BY THIS DAY *all food remaining from the feast on Vigil's Eve should have been consumed. Any that does remain by sunrise must be cast away, ideally burned in the braziers before the nearest chapel after being blessed by the preacher there. If the food is burned at a home shrine a reading by the head of the household of the* Fourth Ophelian Psalm *or the first ten verses of* Thor's Epistle to the Dannites *is appropriate. It is also acceptable to place the food on the tithing-step at a street pulpit.*

Those attending the Procession of the Thesean Martyrs should fast from sunrise until after the caskets have passed them on the third and final of their circuits around the Cathedral. While the caskets are carried past it is traditional to reflect upon one's conduct before one's masters and the Emperor over the past year. Traditional clothing for this day should be a dark headband or kerchief around the forehead for males, and the same or a dark veil for females. Particularly devoted citizens may wish to wear a blindfold or strap over the eyes during religious observances.

By the end of the day citizens should have decided on the fast they will make to prepare themselves for the remainder of the Vigil. The beginning of the fast at sunset at latest is to be greatly encouraged as a pious practice. During the early hours of the fast,

221

thoughts should be turned to one's sins and misdeeds and the need for repentance and redemption – the keeping of a vigil without sleep until the Services of the Quills is considered a mark of devotion at this time.

CHAPTER TEN

'IT WOULD NOT,' Calpurnia remarked aloud, 'have occurred to me to provide you with medical care. Any of you. I can think of at least one man who had – who has – far better claim on the gate's medical resources than any of you.'

She was standing at one end of the twin-level central concourse of the Inner Charisian Gate, ignoring the curious or sullenly hostile looks of the station crew around her. Stairways curled up on either side of her to the tribunal chamber on one side and the Astropathica suite on the other, and on either side of each stairway was a set of heavy plastic stocks bolted to a plate in the floor.

Leftmost was Station Cadet Gintis, the second assailant to go down in the fight the night before. Like all of them, he had been anchored into the stocks in full uniform from which the rank and identity pins had been ripped. He seemed to be the weak link: the youngest, the least criminal, and now the most frightened and miserable. Across the stairway from him was Senior Cadet Bourdieu, the last one she had taken down. He was slumped badly, his ruined hands swathed in white gauze; the marshals had improvised a metal frame to stop him collapsing and choking himself, since Calpurnia had damaged his torso badly enough to stop him holding himself up.

By the right stairwell was Junior Ensign Cicourel, whose knee she had broken. Her subsequent kicks had broken his nose, cheekbone and two ribs but not, apparently, his insolent spirit: the stare he gave her as he propped himself on his good leg and snuffled through the dressings on his mashed nose was hateful.

'If you have any scrap of honour in you,' Calpurnia told that hot gaze, 'if you are actually capable of building yourself up to worthiness of the uniform that has been taken from you, then you will have the ability to learn from this.'

She walked to the fourth man, Ensign Talgaard. He was the one who had grabbed her, the ringleader, the one who had let his drink go to his head and spawn fantasies about putting the little planet-crawling arbitor-woman in her place and amending the insult done to his captain.

'I don't doubt that your gate-captain wouldn't mind seeing me under a gauze sheet in his station's medicae, a breath away from parting with my life like Arbitor Gomry. But when you four took it into your heads to act, what did he do? What side did he take? Look at where you are now. Your gate-captain took the side of the Law.'

'You… don't understand… insult… honour… must…' It was Talgaard talking. How much of the choked quality of his voice was from the pain of his injury and how much was the constriction of the stock on his throat she wasn't sure. But his words and the curl of his lip were enough to convince her that she was going to be wasting her time standing here and trying to talk him around. Some people were just determined to resist correction.

She walked past him and up the stairs to the doors of the hearing chamber. She would probably have been able to stay inside and listen in, even participate, as Commodore Omenti's staff and the Arbites haggled and argued, but good form dictated that she absent herself while her case was discussed.

The commodore and the Arbites had arrived on the station almost simultaneously. Nestor Leandro had taken charge of the Arbites delegation once he heard Calpurnia had gone on to the Inner Charisian Gate, and the commodore himself had come aboard once he had heard that an arbitor senioris had been assaulted by a gang of junior officers.

By the time they met in de Jauncey's chambers Gomry was lying in a coma in the station medicae, attended by four Navy physicians. Calpurnia had eventually accepted a meal, and slept a little on a spare cot, but Gomry was still comatose when she was woken by a runner-boy from de Jauncey's offices. She took her time, returning to her little cabin, washing and getting herself in order before she set out for the gate-captain's office.

Commodore Omenti, shaven-headed, droop-moustached and with skin as dusky as de Jauncey's, had been the picture of cool politeness, pouring punchy black caffeine laced with brandy into little brass globes like the ones Dvorov used. De Jauncey had remained silent throughout, Leandro had been unusually reserved, for him, which meant that he talked only a little more than the others in the room put together. Omenti made sympathetic conversation about the sabotage attempts at Bosporian Hive and Calpurnia's ordeal, as he put it, aboard the Inner Charisian Gate. Something seemed to have come of the attack on her after all: the fact that de Jauncey's own junior officers had assaulted a visiting dignitary had tripped up his complaints and Leandro was using all his diplomatic finesse to press the point with the commodore while the gate-captain was still wrong-footed.

Calpurnia was much more at ease with Omenti's manner, firm but conciliatory. Although she didn't care for the way his eyes kept dropping to her hip and the line of her thigh in the black Arbitrator bodyglove, she was starting to feel cautiously optimistic about co-operation from de Jauncey and access to the prisoners.

Cautious optimism, she would think later, was the bane of her life.

'FINE TIMING, MA'AM' said the Navy attendant who opened the door as she reached the top of the stairwell. 'The commodore and the arbitor senioris wish you to be present. The other arbitor senioris, that is, ma'am,' he added diplomatically.

The tribunal chamber seemed startlingly plain, an affair of simple benches and a horseshoe-shaped table. Leandro and Omenti sat on the far side of the table's curve, far enough apart to acknowledge their differences but close enough to make it a discussion, not a confrontation. By Omenti's shoulder stood a thick-waisted man in the sinister black uniform of the Imperial Commissariat, whose ruddy face and neck seemed to bulge out of his stiff collar as though extruded from it, like paste from a tube.

Apart from the commissar, each side's retinue of legal savants and clerks had withdrawn to the corners of the room.

De Jauncey entered through a side door, his black eyes suspicious. Neither Leandro nor Omenti rose, each simply motioned his respective colleague to join him. The commissar stared at Calpurnia, then de Jauncey, his expression unreadable.

'Straight to the issue, then,' Omenti began. His voice was soft and his diction well-educated, but for all that he looked like the kind of man who would never speak below a roar. 'The matter at hand is the overlap and conflict, or at least the question of it, between the Adeptus Arbites and the Imperial Battlefleet Pacificus in the matter of arresting and prosecuting those responsible for what seems to have been a deliberate act of sabotage against our brethren-in-service of the League of Blackships.'

'The question which, in our preliminary and contingent opinion, will resolve carriage of the issue is at whom the attacks, for such we consider them to be, were set.' Leandro took up the thread. 'Such an act of aggression is one that both our orders, and indeed any servant of the God-Emperor, would delight in seeing balanced out with the commensurate acts of judgement. However, discussion of the precedents and accords from several hundred years of interaction between our organisations – scarcely enough to do justice to the full complexity of the subject, but which must needs suffice at this moment – the approach that has commended itself to our attention is that the offices of the good commodore and the estimable Gate-Captain Sambin de Jauncey shall be entrusted with tracking any offence specifically directed at the venerable League of Blackships, while the work done by the respected Arbitor Senioris Calpurnia in the pursuit of the saboteurs who have set themselves against the completion of the Vigil and Mass of Saint Balronas should, in the event that this work is found to bring us to the matter of the attack at the Ring, continue.'

De Jauncey was scowling, Omenti had an eyebrow cocked, the commissar remained expressionless. There was a moment of silence.

'You're saying, sir,' burst out de Jauncey, 'that these people are going to remain on my station, interrogating prisoners I have already given orders on?'

'He's saying that if that attack was directed at the Blackship brass and happened over Hydraphur by coincidence then it's all yours, de Jauncey, and the Arbites back off.' The commissar's voice was a flat rasp that spoke of some kind of augmetic repair to his throat. 'If it's another one of these attempts to ruin the mass which happened to be directed at the Blackships by coincidence, then it's the Arbites' and you give them whatever help they need.'

'And how do we establish that? Don't you think I would have reported anything I learned in my own hearings here? I am a law-abiding and Emperor-fearing man, regardless of what this, this woman might have told you.'

'Your behaviour gives the lie to that, gate-captain. Such a man would show a little more respect to the Emperor's Adeptus than you have shown me.'

'Enough, de Jauncey.' Omenti cut him off. 'Arbitor Calpurnia will be conducting her own interrogations along with Arbites specialists that I gather Arbitor Leandro has brought with him from Hyraphur. The Arbites have more knowledge of the early stages of this conspiracy and they will know more about what questions to ask. There's no question that that's their field more than ours.'

De Jauncey drew himself up.

'Commodore Omenti, I respectfully but formally protest. These Arbites assert that we are all on the same side of a struggle against criminals and the Emperor's enemies, but

were that true they would take the word of an officer of the
Imperial Navy and depart forthwith. I have given them my
formal and solemn word as an officer that justice has been
done–' (Calpurnia, who remembered no such undertaking,
caught Leandro's eye and gave a tiny shake of her head; he
gave a similarly tiny nod of acknowledgement) '–and the
sabotage that destroyed the *Aventis Sapphire 7* has been pun-
ished. To imply otherwise is not only a subversion of my
authority, it is a slight upon my honour. Perhaps the Arbites'
concept of such may differ from our own, sir, but this
demands nothing less than redress for me.'

'Redress?' asked the commodore. 'You seem determined to
make trouble for me, de Jauncey, but if you're going to say
what I think you're going to say then let's hear it so we can
get on with things.'

'Aye, sir. My honour has been slighted by Arbitor Senioris
Shira Calpurnia of the Adeptus Arbites. She has rejected my
word as an officer and by her words and actions has clearly
implied a suspicion of me in these lamentable events. The
expectation that I will co-operate in this outrage only com-
pounds the insult, and on behalf of myself and the family de
Jauncey I demand redress.'

'I see.' Omenti turned to Calpurnia. 'You probably followed that, Arbitor Calpurnia, but in any case I am required
to inform you that Gate-Captain Sambin de Jauncey of the
Hydraphur Squadron of the Imperial Battlefleet Pacificus has
claimed insult from you and demands redress. According to
traditions within this fleet on matters of honour between
officers, he may stipulate that redress as a precondition for
any future association with you.'

'You're talking about a duel, I take it?' she asked him.
Omenti nodded; de Jauncey's expression was triumphant.
'Does this tradition between Battlefleet Pacificus officers
extend to members of the Adeptus outside the Navy, then?'

'Honour duels between rival Adeptus orders do have
precedent once certain formal preconditions have been met,'
Leandro began. 'Two recent examples are the dispute
between Kjin Bassonel of the Administratum and Curate
Varengo of the Adeptus Ministorum, who exchanged insults
over an interpretation of tithing decrees in 942.M41, and–'

'I am sure Arbitor Leandro is correct in his citing of precedents of the planetary Adeptus,' Omenti cut in smoothly. 'My apologies, Arbitor Leandro, I intend no disrespect,' and Leandro inclined his head graciously, 'but precedent is not an issue. Not only tradition, but formal decree that it is not in my power to overrule, prohibits honour duels between a Navy officer and any person outside the Navy. No formal honour duel can be held, and no redress can be supplied.'

Omenti clearly was going to say something more, but de Jauncey straightened, clicked his heels and snapped off a salute, his smile like a white torch. The commissar leaned over Omenti's shoulder and murmured something.

'Calpurnia and de Jauncey will absent themselves for a moment's deliberation,' declared Omenti, and the gate-captain sauntered out of the double doors after Calpurnia rather than away through his private entrance.

'So do you genuinely feel I've insulted you, de Jauncey, or do you just think you've found a way to avoid having to co-operate?' Calpurnia's voice was as cold as the gate-captain's smile was warm, and although she knew that the question could open up the whole honour issue all over again she was too angry to be diplomatic.

'What I feel is that I have found a way to rid myself and my station full of brave and loyal warriors of an insolent menace to our authority, our integrity and our ability to continue performing our duty of watching over the gates of the Hydra-phur System and over all those in this system who depend on us keeping that watch. Satisfied?'

'Do you think that I'm going to let you exploit some loophole in tradition so that you never have to co-operate with me over some trumped-up insult?'

'Trumped up?'

'You told the commodore that you had given me your word as an officer that justice had been done. You have not done any such thing.'

'He will believe me over–'

'And you accused me of accusing *you* of being implicated in the sabotage attacks, de Jauncey, and I *know* I never did that.'

His expression grew uncertain.

'You clearly, I mean, the whole way you came onto my station with these accusations–'

'What accusations were those? I came onto your station with the intention of interrogating prisoners you had arrested on the Ring and brought straight here.' She remembered her words to Bannon about her suspicions over that action and knew she was uncomfortably close to lying. 'Show me where I slighted your honour by making an unfounded accusation against you.' That, she was slightly more at ease with. It had scored, too. De Jauncey simply stood and stared at her.

'Well, gate-captain, what's one insult more on top of all you claim from me already? I had no reason to think you were involved in anything before I came here, beyond an arbitor's normal, free-floating suspicion.' She cursed the truthfulness that had made her add that last, and bulled on regardless. 'I do now. I think you have something to hide, and it's making you nervous and you're overdoing the efforts to get us off the station. That makes me as suspicious as hell, de Jauncey.'

'Suspect all you like. You will think twice before you lock horns with the Pacificus Fleet again. You should be glad I am the man I am – were I of a level with so many of you planet-crawlers, I might give those men another crack at you.'

She was readying a reply to that when the doors swung open for two black-clad figures: Leandro, cloak in place and judicial headdress under one arm, beamed at her from beside the commissar.

'Gate-Captain de Jauncey, Arbitor Calpurnia, I can announce that only the barest discussion has proved necessary for a solution to our impasse. It was a small matter to bring the particulars of the issue – the concepts, rather than the facts – to the scrutiny of legal resources on both sides of the debate. It pleases me as much as it must surely please the both of you–' his eye twinkled '–that we have found that on any interpretation that we can muster the judgement deriving from the prosecution of war crime allegations against certain elements of the followers of the renegade Fleet-Admiral Krayle in the century previous to our own supports a way forward.'

'*War crimes*?' For once Calpurnia found herself in agreement with de Jauncey, whose tone was incredulous. 'Are you seriously alleging war crimes now?'

'Calm down, de Jauncey, nothing of the kind,' snapped the commissar.

'I stand corrected and admonished by the good Commissar Modjeska's bluntness,' said Leandro with a bow. 'The news I have for you is not, I reassure the gate-captain, news of charges or prosecutions. The news is that there is not the deadlock we thought there was. The precedents in question are to do with the mechanisms of Imperial justice within an organisationally self-contained body such as a Segmentum Battlefleet, and the role of the Fleet Commissariat.'

'What he's saying,' put in Modjeska, 'is that Commodore Omenti has ruled that law allows for a proxy in cases where an honour duel is not resolvable in any other way, including where it involves a disputant from outside the fleet.' De Jauncey's eyes widened, and Calpurnia could understand why Leandro had been smiling. 'The challenged party in this case is not able to participate in the duel, which means she's precluded from nominating a Naval proxy, but precedent says that a member of the Fleet Commissariat provides the proxy in a case like this. Accordingly, gate-captain, your duel for redress will be with me as a proxy for Arbitor Senioris Calpurnia. Commodore Omenti has volunteered the use of the duelling-floor on board the *Crusader Ascendant* as acceptable neutral ground, and will preside over the engagement. As presiding officer he has set the time of the duel at an hour into the third watch, two hours after the conclusion of the service to the Thesean Martyrs.' He saluted de Jauncey. 'Thank you, gate-captain, I shall see you on the duelling floor.'

And with that he spun on his heel and marched back through the doors in a swirl of black storm-coat, back ram-straight and boots clanging on the deck. Leandro and Calpurnia both turned calm, level gazes on de Jauncey, but he too had spun and marched away, through a throng of station crew who suddenly were busily about errands that had, by remarkable coincidence, required them all to be standing within earshot of the stairs until a moment ago.

'The dromon I came here in is a semi-dedicated Arbites one, Shira,' Leandro told her as they stood under the silent stares of the four young men in the stocks. 'I ordered your escorts onto it for a little rest and some food – shall we step that way to treat ourselves to the same? Perhaps even something a little unusual and rich. Despite the austerity that is supposed to accompany this time of year I can't help feeling that we perhaps deserve some self-awarded latitude.'

'More of that brandy-laced caffeine? I noticed you enjoyed that a great deal.'

'Ah, perhaps no intoxicants, but yesterday I managed to acquire two pitchers of syrups from the Shequa Archipelago, each suitable for a slightly different caffeine brew. I confess to being indulgent enough to have brought them with me.'

'I think it would be wasted on me, Nestor. I have a very uneducated palate by Hydraphur standards.'

'The syrups are something of a trademark of Hydraphur cuisine,' said Leandro. 'Not always so, of course. There was an extended period which seems to have ended about the time of Ecclesiarch Thor, where particular brews were allowed to crystallise and served as powders or resins. That resulted in certain cooking techniques becoming favoured, but the change to syrup-based seasoning can be traced back to the migration in from the Colonna Sector's outlying worlds which saw the introduction of – am I holding forth again?' Calpurnia smiled.

'A little. And I have business elsewhere on this station. But one of these days, Arbitor Leandro, I'm going to manage to find an aspect of Hydraphur about which you actually can't launch into a seminar on the spot.'

'A challenge to which many aspire but none have vanquished,' said Leandro happily. 'Well then. We are not invited to the devotions in the Navy chapels and so shall be conducting a short service to the Thesean Martyrs aboard the *Geodess* in honour of the day. I would encourage you to come aboard for that, my arbitor, if you possibly can – I worry that the rush of events has seen you falling behind in your religious duties. But if circumstances do not permit, I shall set eyes on you again at the *Crusader Ascendant's* duelling-floor.'

They saluted one another, and Calpurnia couldn't resist a last satisfied glance at the men in the stocks before she marched away to the medicae chambers.

THE GALLERY CONTAINED wooden pews so steep and narrow that the head of the person in one row would be practically wedged between the knees of the person behind them, and the heads of the top row would brush the low ceiling. There was a deep drop from the railing in front of the foremost pew; after a metre of empty space there was the *Crusader Ascendant's* duelling floor, a strip of pitted plastic, soft and rough to give traction to boots, four metres wide and stretching about ten from one little doorway to the other. It was bathed in deep yellow spotlights that Calpurnia presumed were there to reproduce Hydraphur daylight; on the other side of the strip she could see the glint of braid and medals as an identical gallery filled with officers.

On her way over Calpurnia had been too preoccupied to be nervous. She had a little experience with duels in Ultramar, where such wasteful infighting was considered contemptible, and Arbites internal laws on duelling were iron-hard. But she knew about the reverence that ceremonial duelling was held in elsewhere and knew this was an earnest event, even without de Jauncey's co-operation at stake, and she was fretting that she would make some gaffe that would disgrace Modjeska or damage the conduct of the duel. All she had been able to get from her hosts so far was that Modjeska was to be given 'the forward advantage', whatever that was, and that the two men would be using lethal weapons despite the duel officially being to first blood or to yielding. She looked around now ready to zero in on the actions of those around her and make sure she conformed.

She needn't have worried. The first thing that had hit her when the door had opened was a wave of chatter, pungent cigar smoke and the clink of glasses. The rows of officers were all deep in jocular conversation at the tops of their voices, twisting about to call up and down the gallery to one another, passing little silver platters of sweetmeats, tobacco and snuff back and forth and pouring decanted liqueurs whose scents alone made Calpurnia's head spin. She had to push her way to Leandro through a crowd of green uniforms all bent on cheerfully ignoring her, but she decided as she sat down that it was better than the hostility she had been bracing herself for.

'And how is your wounded one?' Leandro asked her.

'His name is Arbitor Gomry, and he's better than he was, which is not saying much. He's deeply unconscious, but the station medicae are good at their jobs.'

'One might be forgiven for placing a certain amount of faith in the ability of medics aboard a military station to handle combat injuries.'

'Just so. Well, the next step is trying to get him strong enough to travel. If they do a good job of it, and there's an apothecarion aboard your dromon–'

'There is such.'

'Good, well, we might be taking him back to Bosporian with us. It would be good for him to come around in the Wall, among friends. If Modjeska wins, I wonder if we can push for those four bastards to be–' Leandro motioned her to cut the sentence short and tipped his head back at the crowd of officers who had all but filled the pews behind them.

Gate-Captain de Jauncey had emerged at one end of the duelling floor and was standing with two others Calpurnia took to be seconds, talking quietly and sipping from a brass drinking-ball. The gate-captain was stripped of his long uniform coat and wearing a close-fitting white vest that emphasised his slender build. He made no sign that he registered any of the rowdy mobs of officers on either side, and the reaction was mutual: if anything the clink of utensils and the cigar-smoke had thickened. The general conversation seemed to have turned to elaborate puns about the duellists and other fleet personalities. Calpurnia guessed that they would still be meaningless to her even if she knew the system – she was aware that she didn't have much of a sense of humour, and that she tended to vaguely distrust people who did. She supposed that pointed to some kind of terrible character flaw, but she had never got around to worrying about it.

The lights over the two sets of spectator pews dimmed as though they were at a play. Calpurnia saw that de Jauncey's seconds had retreated back through their door and the gate-captain himself now held a weapon. A moment later the far door slid back, Modjeska strode through it and the duel began.

Calpurnia expected elaborate pre-duel formalities after all the talk of tradition and custom, but there was not even a salute. Modjeska simply marched up to de Jauncey and began swinging in short, brutal arcs. Stripped to boots, breeches and singlet like his opponent, he carried a single-edged hacking-blade, part falchion and part hatchet, the blade flared and weighted at the head to allow vicious, limb-severing strokes. His other hand held a weighted baton, meant more as a parrying device and shield than as a weapon by the way he used it.

De Jauncey was fending him off with something longer, a ludicrous-looking weapon that put Calpurnia in mind of a double-handed axe with a bizarre tuft of hair like that on a comic tumbler in a circus. It wasn't until she had watched them trade lunges for at least a minute that it clicked home from a long-ago weapons seminar: it was a shipboard weapon, the whippy bristles on the end needle-tipped fibres that drew a charge from a power pack in the counterweight at the far end of the shaft. It was a weapon for boarding action when quarters were too close for firearms or flamers, designed either to swing and cut into the enemy or to be thrust forward so that at least one or two of the bristles would find their way through a weak point in the heavy rein-forced suits and hoods that ship-to-ship boarders wore for protection. Watching de Jauncey use it that way now, skil-fully keeping the bundle of spear-sharp quills between him and each attempt of Modjeska's to close, Calpurnia realised that it must be charged now. Either or both of these men could easily be carried away to the hospice or morgue at the end of it.

The duel was a deft contrast of techniques: de Jauncey's elegant, dancing poses, the thrusting jabs his weapon as quick as a lizard's tongue, and Modjeska's aggressive, brutal style that concealed a cunning offence behind a veneer of crude aggression. De Jauncey's technique was classic aristo-cratic fencing, emphasising poise, skill and finesse, and

Modjeska's was the classic Commissariat style, designed to make a political point as much as win a fight: an assertion of the commissar's savage authority to impose Imperial discipline by whatever means necessary.

De Jauncey had given ground. He had been a third of the way out onto the floor when Modjeska had entered, but now another step backward would see him barking his heels on the door behind him. He needed space, and made it with a complex pattern of lunges and swipes that forced Modjeska to give ground to his right, swatting the electrified quills away with the baton in his left hand. It must be ceramite or plastic, Calpurnia thought, watching sparks spit between the quills but nothing come down the baton to the commissar's arm. Then de Jauncey spun the haft around and sidestepped cat-quick to his own right, trying to shuffle around Modjeska and away from the door. He almost made it, but he had to correct himself to keep away from the drop off the edge of the duelling floor and Modjeska, who had obviously seen the move coming, used the moment of distraction to wind up and whacked the haft of the long axe with a backhand hit that crushed de Jauncey's knuckles and almost shuddered the weapon out of his hands.

His mouth twisting in agony, de Jauncey frantically backpedalled as Modjeska kept the turn of his body going and aimed a forehand slash at de Jauncey's other arm. Sliding his grip down the haft the gate-captain tried to create some distance with long, whooping swings of the axe-head that needed less of a fine grip, but Modjeska had the timing to press in just a little further behind each swing, forcing de Jauncey back if he wanted to control the space he needed for the big strokes. Finally he gave up and tried to drive the Commissar back with a series of deep, low lunges that forced Modjeska to give ground or bend down to block and expose his head.

There was complete silence in the chamber now, except for the scuff of the duellists' boots and the sound of their breathing. Both men were shedding sweat: de Jauncey's smooth dark skin gleamed while Modjeska's, rough and coated with coarse red hair all down his shoulders and arms, trickled and dripped.

De Jauncey's nerves betrayed him yet again. He had become carried away with his low lunges and was trying the same thing, over and over again, not registering that Modjeska's defence against each one was growing more and more assured and that the commissar's footwork was getting shorter, tensing him for a return sally. The officers had realised it too, and Calpurnia heard a murmur of 'Mistake there' from somewhere.

A moment later Modjeska moved. De Jauncey was telegraphing badly: a certain placement of the feet, a small backward swing. Modjeska watched him as he placed his feet, swung his weapon backward, then moved forward in a step-pivot that spun past the bundle of quills. He was suddenly on de Jauncey's blind side, behind his shoulder, and as the other man frantically tried to reel in his lunge and take control of the space between them the head of Modjeska's cleaver bit into the bicep of his good arm and a second later the baton cracked into his head. De Jauncey staggered and drooped, Modjeska swatted the axe-head down with the back of his cleaver and stamped it out of the gate-captain's hands, then grabbed de Jauncey by the arm before he could topple off the side of the duelling floor and dragged him into its centre.

They held still in a tableau for a long moment, the slender officer sprawled on the floor and the heavy commissar standing over him, boot on his chest, and then de Jauncey tremblingly raised a hand. The doors clanked back and attendants came flooding out onto the floor and, as Calpurnia and Leandro saluted Commissar Modjeska and began to make their way to the door, the officers of the Battlefleet Pacificus rose to their feet to applaud.

DE JAUNCEY CO-OPERATED. He had to. The duel had been the last shot in his locker, as Calpurnia inelegantly put it to Leandro as they had crossed along the slender, vibrating and frankly alarming docking bridge. At least it had gravity, which was more than the link to the *Geodess*. Leandro accompanied her back to the station medicae, but Calpurnia suspected it was more to do with putting off the passage through the shifts in gravity and orientation. Leandro, it turned out, hated the sensation even more than she did.

'He'll submit to being questioned?' Calpurnia asked as they made their way to the Charisian Gate's upper medicae bay.

'He will. I think I managed to achieve sufficient rapport with the commodore and to consider myself informed, and I can inform you that Omenti has strengthened his views on the matter. You may have noticed that the most respected commodore has a different attitude on co-operation with the Arbites than does a certain gate-captain under his command. Said gate-captain is considered to have brought quite enough disrepute to his battlefleet, never mind unfavourable attention from an order of the Adeptus who, as you have apparently pointed out to the gate-captain, is capable of exacting perfectly legitimate penalties from the Navy should it see the need.

'He has proved himself unable to control his station to the point where a member of that same order of the Adeptus was forced to fend off a vicious attack from no less than four of his subordinates. And now a matter of honour for which he insisted redress has instead brought him low–'

'He lost the duel, Omenti has told him he's out of options and to tell us what he knows.'

'Ah, my Arbitor Senioris Calpurnia, your words cut to the heart of the matter with the swiftness of Macharius's own sword.'

'Did Macharius use a sword?'

'I believe he is shown with one in most of the historical illuminations in my library. In all candour I had taken the matter on faith from those.'

'My father kept an excellent collection of military histories. I used them to teach my brothers to read and orate. I had the impression he leaned more toward firearms and some kind of power weapon.'

'The sword I have seen him illustrated with may well have been a power weapon. I shall have to inspect the colour plates again. After all, we are far closer to the areas of Macharius's actual conquests than Macragge.'

'The books I read when I was younger were sourced from this Segmentum, though, Nestor.'

They bickered amiably enough in the medicae outrooms, while the doctors came and went around them. They were still disagreeing over the issue when the report came that Gomry was drifting between coma and dazed, disconnected waking – Calpurnia refused to leave without looking in on him but he was unconscious again.

'It must have been a terrible strike,' said Leandro softly as they came away.

'It was,' said Calpurnia, 'and he was struck down because of me.' She was very quiet during the walk to de Jauncey's chambers.

The gate-captain had already begun talking by the time they got there. Pale and tired, he sat in a padded chair by a half-metre-thick window of armour-glass that looked out over a cluster of lance muzzles and the dim shapes of two docked dromoni.

Commissar Modjeska was sitting in a chair opposite him. A second commissar, younger and thinner and with a certain resemblance to de Jauncey himself, nodded to the Arbites when he was introduced as Gate-Commissar Chalce. Halfway across the room was a a clerk perched on a stool with braided leads trailing from his skull augmetics to a data-slate perched on his knee, and another green-coated officer whose aquila-and-balance badges marked her as part of the Naval judiciary. She introduced herself simply as Lieu-tenant Rybell, and went back to staring at de Jauncey. The whole scene looked casual enough – with de Jauncey's arm-sling and dressings and the attentiveness of the others an observer might have thought they were well-wishers there to pay respects to the injured captain. But the fact that it was a questioning session became apparent soon enough.

'Lyze-Haggan,' the gate-captain said, and Leandro was instantly galvanised.

'What did you say?'

'The House of Lyze-Haggan. I have told the commissar what I know about the setting-up of the sabotage. I had no hand in it myself. My… my wrongdoing was in not lifting a hand to stop it when I knew it was being planned. I thought it would form a strike against Kalfus-Medell. The Kalfus fam-ily and the de Jauncey…'

'I am aware of and understand your history,' said Leandro. Calpurnia made a sour face that only Rybell picked up, and the other woman looked at her curiously.

'Then I will not dwell on it,' de Jauncey was continuing, 'except to say that the hereditary postings of commands in the Gyre Aurucon, the same ones that have brought us into conflict with the family Kalfus, have also given us reason to monitor movements and dealings of members of the Adeptus Astropathica. What goes on between those folk when they congregate at the Blind Tower is anyone's guess, but because they must spend time around the officer corps when at their posts it is not hard for us to track them.'

He was getting into his stride, now, and Calpurnia fought down the urge to thump the cut on his arm to remind him that this wasn't a mess-hall anecdote. But she knew enough about interrogating not to interrupt a man who was picking up momentum. This interrogation was what she was starting to think of as a 'Hydraphur special', all kid gloves and etiquette.

'The Haggan syndicate is now influential on a great deal of the inner-system civilian routes. The Lyze family, I understand, Arbitor Leandro, is senior within the syndicate, wealthy but boorish and barely considered among the gentry.' Leandro made a noncommittal nod. 'But over the last two years they have been everywhere on the Ring and as guests aboard as many Naval stations as will have them visit. Since they became of interest to the family de Jauncey we have had the opportunity of watching them build diplomatic ties to half a dozen leading astropath cabals.'

'A fact which didn't seem to concern any of you unduly,' put in Modjeska. He had shifted so that de Jauncey had to look back and forth between himself, Calpurnia and Leandro, a basic questioner's tactic.

'The purpose of the exercise was to outflank Medell interests in the civilian docks, which would chiefly have disadvantaged the family Kalfus.'

'You're saying that your feud with Kalfus meant it was expedient for you to sit by and watch these people get their hooks into who knows how many astropaths,' finished Calpurnia, unable to quite hide the contempt in her tone.

'Astropaths are not infants, bald and bulbous though they are,' replied de Jauncey. 'They were capable of understanding the Lyze-Haggan motives perfectly well on their own. As far as I was aware the Adeptus Astropathica enjoyed formal, excellent and honest relations with Lyze-Haggan.'

'Excellent and honest?' Modjeska sounded like he was grinding his teeth. 'Does that extend to–'

'To sabotaging transmissions to engineer a collision?' The gate-captain's eyes were steady and solemn. 'No, sir, it does not. The infiltration they effected to create that disaster was deep enough that it slipped beneath the net that any of my family's agents were able to track.' De Jauncey put a slight emphasis on *my family*, and Calpurnia had to grudgingly concede the point: it should not have been up to the private efforts of a single Naval family to uncover a plot like this. 'My family have held commands in the Imperial Navy for more generations than I can remember. The thought of countenancing such an act as took place on the Ring is repellent to me. I will confess that I was motivated in my behaviour toward the Arbites by the desire to preserve my own name, but do not doubt that I wanted punishment for the guilty ones as much as they do. That was my reason for exerting my authority to have them brought off the Ring, no other.'

'And what were you able to find out from those people you had brought here, de Jauncey?' Calpurnia asked him. 'Did you interrogate them when they arrived?'

'I stood and watched them when they were brought off the dromon I had sent,' he replied, and it must have sounded ridiculous even to him because he immediately shifted onto the defensive. 'Your own rather abrupt arrival was hot in their wake, if you will recall, Arbitor Calpurnia, and once I had word that you were inbound I felt I had certain other matters to attend to. I had to simply muse on what I had learned from seeing them marched up the docking bridge.' His defensiveness had sharpened, and Calpurnia had to remind herself that he was only co-operating at all because he had been beaten into it by the commissar.

'And what were you able to conclude from these observations?' Leandro asked him in a gentler voice. The change of tone worked, as it almost always did.

De Jauncey turned toward Leandro and spoke more quickly.

'I recognised several of the astropaths brought on board. I believe that is where this all originates, with the astropaths themselves, not the tech-adepts or transmechanics. My officers reported that several attempted suicide on route to the station and one has successfully killed himself since his arrival here. Their behaviour is odd – yes, I know, but even for astropaths it's odd – bodily twitches, facial tics, false starts at conversation directed at thin air. I had my own astropathic representatives watch them over a pict-link and they recognised the signs immediately. They demanded the opportunity to re-enter their trances and send a message to the Blind Tower immediately.'

Both Arbites and both commissars were leaning forward intently.

'They told me that these are the symptoms of a psyker-trick,' de Jauncey went on, 'a mind-command bored so deep into the brain the victim himself may not know of it. These can be built subtly by an experienced psyker to make the catspaw almost impossible to detect, or they can be hammered into an otherwise untouched mind full-force. Such a command will echo inside the mind and soon burn out the one it has been forced into, but until that happens it will be irresistible.'

Psykers. Calpurnia saw the image for a moment, clear behind her eyes: wreaths of smoke, panicking, screaming crowds, and a tottering, collapsing shape that seemed to fade into existence out of the air…

'To drive a command into a mind as strengthened as an astropath's takes a powerful will,' de Jauncey went on, 'such as is not found among the lower orders of the Adeptus. I did not interrogate any prisoners, Arbitor Calpurnia, but I had my astropaths give me an idea of the ranking that such a feat would need and then compared that to transmission logs and movement notifications such as are my right to access as a gate-captain.'

His jaw lifted a little at that. 'I may not be an agent of the Arbites, but I found a name. Would you like to know who, and where he is?'

Calpurnia stayed silent, allowing him his face-saving little moment of pride.

'Master Astropath Yannod Dwerr was the leader of the Astropathica cell for that segment of the Ring. All three of my own senior astropaths confirm that Dwerr is easily powerful enough to force an embedded command into a strong mind, a command such as to engineer a collision and commit suicide afterwards. They have told me that reports they have received from their brethren aboard the Ring seem to point to Dwerr spending time alone this morning with the poor wretch who sent the tainted transmissions. My astropaths also confirm, although reluctantly, that Dwerr is also involved in some kind of internecine intrigue against members of the League of Blackships. And according to my transmechanic and logister savants, Master Astropath Yannod Dwerr was recorded as leaving his post in the Ring three hours before the collision, on his way down to Hydraphur. His destination was listed as the outskirts of the Bosporian Hive. The Lyze-Haggan family citadel.

'There, now, Arbites.' De Jauncey looked at Calpurnia again and all the arrogant fire was back in his voice. 'I trust my assistance to you has been worth all your trouble?'

Sixteenth Day of Septista

Two days to the Mass of Saint Balronas.
Third day of the Vigil of Balronas. The Service of the Quills.
The Dedication of the Scourges.

THREE HOURS FROM *midnight priests and deacons will travel through the streets calling to the pious to make their confessions ready. This is the time to light the lamp from the Quiet Congregation, and by its light all members of each household or barracks write out the matters of which they wish to unburden themselves and atone for during the Vigil. These must use parchment of the type decreed by the Ministorum and perfumed with the required incenses, and be sealed with plas-wax tablets given out by the priests.*

The clergy who travel out to spread the call to begin writing carry this paper and wax but the shame of being unprepared and having to request it of them should not be taken lightly. It is appropriate for scribes and clerks to assist the illiterate, but this must only be permitted where that person has taken oaths before their preacher and bears the corresponding seal. During the Service and afterwards, reading one's list of misdeeds should prompt thoughts on repentance and redemption. The Creed of the Gyrae *is an appropriate communal reading for the evening once all the confessions have been written.*

Confessions must be recorded by dawn, and then sealed to the outside of the home or to a pulpit or shrine. From dawn, citizens should walk the streets with eyes on the confessions and thoughts on guilt and salvation. The clergy will continue to process through the streets and any who wish may follow them or join them in prayer.

One hour from sundown, all citizens should present themselves at a chapel with the blades for their scourges for the following day. These must be blessed and ritually sharpened by a member of the Ministorum or Sororitas. Children too young for scourging should assist in sharpening their parents' blades as a way of preparing them for the age when they will participate. Those who have not begun to fast must do so after their blades have been blessed.

A downcast demeanour and quiet voice are essential for this day, especially when travelling outside the home. Plain cloth or sackcloth garments are appropriate for this day and all until the Mass itself.

CHAPTER ELEVEN

RUSHING TO INTERCEPT the *Sanctus*, rushing to investigate the Astropathic sabotage, now rushing to chase Dwerr down to Hydraphur. Calpurnia suspected that for the rest of her career she was going to associate the groaning halls and curling black ironwork of the Hydraphur Ring with desperate haste.

They came bulleting back from the Inner Charisian Gate with the engines on the *Geodess* open to the fullest, unable to converse for the noise over the voxcasters. The magos overseeing the plasma core had declared this was an ill-omened time for high-speed, high-output engine settings and his congregation of tech-priests were broadcasting their chants through the entire ship in an effort to keep its anima appeased against the strain. The buzz and rustle of machine-hymns wove in and out of the plainsong of the organic adepts in a blend of sound Calpurnia found disturbing.

They had been careful to keep all their astropathic communications as routine as possible, but it was not possible to disguise the the code-red overrides that had yanked normal traffic out of their way. If there were still astropaths in the

Ring implanted with Dwerr's deep-buried commands, commands they themselves would not know they carried, they
could not be allowed to know something was amiss.

Once they were aboard their lander things became easier.
Calpurnia was bent over a tight-beam vox-station, shouting
to make herself heard over the engines and the wind-friction
scraping the hull, ordering patrols to change course,
storming-teams to mobilise, Chasteners to ready weapons
and cells. Her orders went to the Wall, then to the precinct
fortresses out in the sprawl, and gradually the net was
thrown around the great family citadel of Lyze-Haggan.

By the time they were in the lower atmosphere she was
starting to get collated updates from the precinct controllers.
Exhaustion was dogging her heels as always and having to
concentrate over the noise was giving her a headache, but
even when she had the reports repeated they made no sense.
Two patrol teams barricading the streets to the citadel had
come under vicious attack from its walls, but then the attacks
halted as suddenly as they started and Lyze family militia
came filing out to surrender. On another approach storm-
teams had heard gunfire and rushed to break in one of the
fortress doors, to find them unlocked and the barricades
beyond them already wrecked by explosive charges. Some
kind of autogyro had tried to take off from a landing-shelf
halfway up the citadel's northern wall only to be shot down
by a stream of rocket-grenades from the very shelf it had
taken off from, and it had then steered itself around and
rammed its own launching-pad rather than crash.

After forty-five minutes of this Calpurnia gave up, crumpled the notes she had been trying to make in one
gauntleted fist, and started to run pre-battle checks and
blessings on her weapons instead. Whatever insanity was
unfolding down there, she knew where she stood with a
maul and a stub-gun.

At first approach, the Lyze fortress looked daunting. It
stood far from Bosporian, at the shore of the polluted
lagoons that ended the sprawl's northern and eastern march.
Three thick towers, gnarled with external skyways, overhangs
and habitation-shelves big enough to hold houses, reared up
over the fifty- and sixty-storey minnows around them, and

the elevated bridges between them had become thicker and heavier until now the three spires simply formed the corner-posts of a great triangular hulk whose curtain-walls left a bizarre fifty-metre gap down to the ground.

The Lyze household guard had commanding positions, good weaponry and, at least at first, determination. Arbitrator weapons tended to be for crowd suppression and storm actions rather than the building-levelling artillery of the Imperial Guard, and so the cordon had retreated from the walls, particularly when precinct records showed that at last inspection there had been two layers of minefields under the gap and deadfall grenades built into the walls' undersides. The commanders dug in and waited for the siege weapons.

But that was before madness took hold. By the time the lander carrying Calpurnia and Leandro went bellowing over-head some of the erstwhile defenders had thrown open doors and remote-detonated some of their minefields to allow the Arbites in. Suspicious at first, then frantic to grab the opportunity, Arbitrators by the tank-load surged to the doors, and by the time the lander had managed to set down nearby the lower floors were breached a dozen times over.

The fighting was quick, vicious and fragmentary. Arbites found themselves here battling mobs of household staff swinging pieces of furniture and table-knives, there pinned down in firefights with skilled and tenacious Lyze militia gunnery teams, elsewhere in bewildering three or four-way skirmishes, fought at a flat sprint through the fortress between the Arbites and rival gangs of householders.

By the time Calpurnia and her escorts walked through the wrecked doors into the south-eastern tower, the descriptions coming over her vox-torc most often were 'insane', 'demented', 'brainless', and 'bizarre', mixed in with Hydra-phur expletives that she didn't recognise and didn't want to. By then occupation of the lower levels was uncontested, leaving level after level strewn with smashed furniture and the slumped forms of householders, dead or too injured to move, shoved gracelessly aside for the Arbites mop-up teams. The battles with the invading Arbites had been around the kitchens, plant rooms and workshops. Calpurnia was starting to think that was because the Arbitrator forces had taken it for granted that those would be the objectives and sought them out early, drawing the fighting there. The worst of the internecine violence seemed to have broken out in the dormitories and mess-halls, and only migrated outwards as the violence had spread.

She was on the eighteenth floor when the word came that the storm-teams were in action, and ground her teeth with the urge to be up there shoulder to shoulder with them. She thought of Arbitor Gomry, comatose on a Naval medicae bed because of four men she had let sneak up on her, placed his face side by side in her mind with Dvorov telling her she was not to rush blindly into traps. It occurred to her that her determination not to back away from difficult duty was misaimed: courage to put herself in harm's way was something she had never lacked, but remaining behind the lines while others fought under her orders was turning out to be cruelly hard.

She stopped, blinked, and turned back toward a knot of corpses at the entrance to a freight-lift. Bannon and Syldati, who had nearly run into the back of her, hefted their shotguns and looked around; two Arbites engineers who were working to excise the fused locks on the lift doors under the eye of a proctor doubled their speed on the assumption that she had stopped to look at them.

'Look at those bodies.' She pointed. On the other side of the corpse-pile the proctor barked at his charges to keep working.

'That one. And the woman, there. And that white-haired man with the boning-knife.' All three had the front of their thin tunics soaked with blood, and Calpurnia traced the outline of one of the blood-smears. It was oddly regular in shape, oddly clean in the centre, oddly similar to the other two. She hooked the tip of her weapon into the old man's shirt and yanked it downward, breaking the button-snaps, and the other two peered over her shoulders. The man's chest had been cut, lightly as if with a small belt-knife or a kitchen tool, in a crude outline of an aquila. It looked as if the thin material of his clothes had been deliberately pressed against his body for the blood to soak through and create the same image on his shirt.

'Either of you remember odd-shaped bloodstains on any of the other bodies? Or on any of the ones who've surrendered?'

'I hadn't registered it as a pattern, ma'am,' Syldati said. 'Shall I speak with the command post and try to verify how widespread those marks are?'

'Good thinking, arbitor. Let's keep moving.' They set off again, Syldati muttering into her torc. Calpurnia noticed Bannon fidgeting sheepishly at not having thought of it first.

In the central tower, where mechanised screw-stairs clanked and ground between the floors, the Arbites had set up a staging-post: a first-aid apothecarion, a mustering point, caches of ammunition and fresh supplies of the articulated manacle-trains that would lock captured prisoners into long lines for herding away.

Surrounded by black armour, the tramp of boots and battle-smells – gunsmoke and the ozone of discharged power-mauls – Calpurnia felt in her element, at home again. She watched dispassionately as two prisoner-trains were goaded out of the stairs, stumbling a little as the metal steps moved under their feet. Both at first glance were a random gaggle of Lyze householders, until she looked more closely and saw that the second column all had bloodstains covering the fronts of their clothes. On most the stain had smudged out and was unrecognisable, but when she ordered an Arbitrator to tear the cloth loose the aquila outlines cut into the skin were clear.

'We had to separate them, ma'am,' one of the handlers told her. 'Even after we had them chained up they were still trying to get at each other. I don't know what's got into these people but they're just feral up there.'

'How far does the fighting extend?' she asked him, eyeing the rows of prisoners. She could catch occasional flickers between them still – a poisonous glance or a spit in the direction of the other line.

'How far? If I understand you, ma'am, then it seems to be through the whole citadel. I don't think we've yet found properly organised resistance that hasn't been broken up by this fighting. The Emperor has been provident, ma'am, and set them against one another.'

'I actually think you may not be too far off,' said Calpurnia half to herself, with another look at the cuts in the nearest prisoner's flesh. 'Alright, so what have they been saying? To you and to each other?'

'Saying?' He looked puzzled for a moment. 'I can't say I've been paying all that much attention, ma'am. Was there anything in particular that we should have been listening for?'

'No way to tell now, is there?' Calpurnia asked a little more sharply than she had intended. She weighed up staying here to question some of the prisoners, but odds were it would take too long to try and break them here. She called Bannon and Syldati to her; suddenly she had an idea of where in the building to head.

THE SCREW-STAIRS finished at the fifty-fifth level with another foyer, almost indistinguishable from the one she had left but for fewer prisoners and injuries, more combat teams and ammunition carriers, and an arbitor with the red badge of a lay tech-adept who had overridden part of the citadel's vox-system. Calpurnia took the speaker-wand from him a little tentatively. On the one hand, she had been raised to believe that the Machine God of the Adeptus Mechanicus tech-priests was at most a subordinate, and more probably just one aspect of the divine Emperor, so that the rituals of a duly ordained member of the Emperor's Adeptus ought to subjugate the system. But she couldn't quite shake off the dark superstitions about renegade machine-spirits that she had heard whispers of on Hazhim and at Machiun – what if the forces that ran the communicators had retained some blasphemous loyalty to the Lyze? How could she trust them with her voice?

The mechanic seemed to have had the same thoughts, because he began a new check of the system with a device of his own, examining the tuning-dials and murmuring abjurations as the transmission shifted. After a minute the vox-officer at the command post responded; a moment after that she was talking to Leandro at the command post outside, through the hisses and cracks of the resentful transmitter.

'The prisoners here?' He seemed a little surprised by her question. 'Lacking the knowledge of my own eyes, I will hazard a guess that they are behaving as prisoners do, remaining in their chains and awaiting sentence, since I have heard no alarms to the contrary. My time has been occupied chiefly with monitoring the fighting through the citadel and briefing the commanders on the interest of the Arbites command in this matter, a courtesy the initial haste of our landing did not permit us.'

'Very well. How is the fighting going? I'm at – you there, where is this? – the upper mech-stair foyer on the forty-fifth level just off the second core.'

She had to wait for a minute for Leandro to answer, through a bark of static and then the distant sound of voices and the distinctive clinks and buzzes of an Arbites command holo-tank updating its display.

'You are below and behind the fighting,' he told her when he came back to the link, curt and businesslike now. 'The third core from level eighty and above is where most of our combat and shock teams are mustering, and the advance teams report great crowding and more violence from about the eighty-fifth level on. Levels ninety and upwards of the third core are wilderness to us as things stand now.'

'Is that all? No other major activity?'

'Not at present, although the room-to-room scouring has not yet begun. Two detachments of cyber-mastiff handlers are on route to facilitate hunting out any pockets but they won't be here for another half hour or so, as they estimate it.'

She leaned away from the console and shot another look at the prisoner trains. Something she hadn't noticed before: the prisoners without the aquila cut into them, who from their more battered condition had put up more of a fight against the Arbites, all still bore Lyze family crests on shoulders or chests, some on headbands, some as belt-buckles. The ones with the aquila cuts did not – but she could see rips where the crests had obviously been torn off. She spoke into the wand again.

'Where is the main chapel in the citadel?'

More hissing, more chatter and clinks and beeps and what sounded like data-slates being docked and read.

'Arbitor Calpurnia? Are you there?' Leandro's voice came through a sudden buzzing on the line.

'I'm here. The chapel?'

'Is at the highest-but-two of the levels on the core that you are in. There is a thoroughfare up to each of its side gates, along the top of the hundred and eighteenth floor of each of the wings. A screw-stair will take you to within ten floors of it, and a spiral ramp, some kind of ceremonial concourse, runs to the main chapel gates. There has been next to no fighting in that area… wait–' there were faint voices behind him '–and the combat teams met no resistance in that part of the building. The urgency of the fighting below and beyond them in the far wing drew them away. Has the chapel itself been swept?' That was directed to someone away from the pickup. Then, back to her: 'No. There has been some lamentable oversight regarding the securing of the chapel itself.'

'We'll look into that later,' she told him. 'In the meantime, please have the operational command relay orders to all combat teams in that area of the tower. All routes up to the Chapel are to be held and watched. How many shock-teams are nearby?'

Another pause, more voices. Another sharp *hiss-crack-rattle* made her eyes want to water.

'None,' Leandro's voice came back. 'They have all moved into the northernmost wing to begin breaking the stairwell barricades around the ninety-second levels. There are two squads that had to stop to allow reloads and fresh grenades to reach them and should be about ten minutes' travel from the major stairwell. Shall I hail them?'

'If you would, thank you, arbitor senioris. Have them at the foot of the ramp you mentioned, with as many combat teams as can be comfortably spared. Leave–' She was about to start specifying numbers and deployment patterns to cordon the chapel before she caught herself. Leandro at the command post had the maps, and the Arbites already in the upper floors had the direct knowledge. 'Leave it to the Aedile commanding that section to determine who is needed where. Pass on a Level Four delegation, please, Arbitor Leandro, until my arrival.'

* * *

HONOURING AND PRESERVING the family name, yes, remembering and paying respect to family achievements, yes, dedicating libraries and galleries to the works and memories of respected forebears, yes. Calpurnia could understand all these things because she was from a family that prided itself on its service to Ultramar and the Imperium and saw nothing wrong with teaching its traditions to younger generations. Once or twice she had even dared imagine her own likeness, in paint or marble, in the upper of the hearth-house on Iax, and then, typically for her, had fretted at length over whether such dreaming was conceited and unworthy or whether it was part of a desire to perform commendable service and therefore noble and justified.

The ramp to the chapel gates was a useful reminder, she decided, of what happened when such thoughts decayed into self-aggrandisement. The approach to a sacred place should inspire faith and devotion, or warn of the consequences of failure before the God-Emperor, but here the great space on the inside of the spiral ramp was full of the busts and masks of great members of the Lyze family, hanging from the dome high above on gilded chains, and the outer wall sported tastelessly lush murals in silver-leaf, blue and green velvet and opal, religious only as an afterthought. Lyze-Haggan on pilgrimage to Dimmamar, Chiros and Ophelia, Lyze-Haggan presenting rich gifts to the Ecclesiarchy who were always shown with expressions of rhapsodic joy at such beneficence, wealthy Lyze-Haggan helping fund regiments of Imperial Guard or arm Missionaria Galaxia crusades, who were then shown standing on heaps of dead heretics or aliens directing adoring looks back at their patrons.

There would be time for a ritual scouring of this place later, but Calpurnia's first urge was to have a flamer or a few blasts of shot ruin this walk of vanity just to make a point before she found someone had beaten her to it. The fine trappings of the ramp had been ritually scarred, the faces of Lyze grandees scorched or ripped with blades. The higher they marched, the worse the damage became. Calpurnia's suspicions about what was behind all this were firming with every pace.

She came to the head of the ramp with two shock-squads
walking behind her and three combat-squads behind them.
Up here the inlays on the walls were shot through with gold
and threads of tiny diamonds, and the sculpted likenesses
hanging in the central well were crusted with sapphire. The
high-peaked doors of the chapel showed the Golden Throne
attended by angels carrying shields and scrolls, all decorated
with the Lyze family crest, now crudely defaced. To Calpurnia
the Emperor sitting on that Throne seemed to be scowling,
but she thought that probably hadn't been the sculptor's
intention. Two more combat squads were spread across the
ramp to block the doors at its top, in a basic double-rank
shield-wall. A thickset Arbitrator with the wreath-and-pistol
of an arbitor aedile on her carapace saluted Calpurnia as the
rest of the Arbites drew up behind the line.

'We've checked the doors as much as we can without alert-
ing whoever's inside, ma'am; we made no other move
pending your authority. They're unlocked and unsecured as
far as we can tell. There has been no sign of resistance, but
we now believe that there are numbers of people within the
Chapel.'

'Your reasoning?"

'We can hear singing, ma'am. Er, prayers and catechisms
and suchlike.'

'Any that you recognise?' Calpurnia asked. The other
woman thought for a moment.

'Some from the *Sancta Adeptorum*,' she said, 'mostly the
second book. Some common hymns, common on Hydraphur anyway, ma'am, excusing your presence. And a couple
of old militant psalms I haven't heard since my schooling.'
Her tone was a little baffled, and Calpurnia could tell these
weren't the questions she had been expecting. No matter. It
was time to gamble on her instinct about what had happened here, on what she was sure now was a winning hand.
She drew her pistol and took a place in the second rank
behind the shock-squads, took a moment to give a few terse
orders and make sure they were understood, then ordered
the doors shoved open.

And oh, it was nice to be right. The chapel was a little
amphitheatre, a semicircle of softly-padded gilded seats,

enough for maybe fifty at a time, looking in and down on an altar adorned with what had once been the Lyze coat of arms. That had been smashed and scorched and now a gold devotional aquila had been propped up in its place. As Calpurnia looked around she could see that the act had been repeated all around the walls and over each set of side-doors. The replacement aquilae were often little more than silhouettes scraped on with ash or burned on with a hand flamer at low setting. The lowest parts of the walls, from eye to floor level, were covered in crude handwritten sheets plastered hastily to the walls.

Before the altar, the foremost and richest seats had been broken up for pyres, and smoke filled the space of the chapel and stung Calpurnia's eyes as she moved in. Beneath it was the smell of flamer gases and the thicker, greasier stink of burning meat. And around the pyres were the congregation.

Not more than thirty strong, they were ragged, deliberately ragged, their clothes and skins torn. They held shards from the broken Lyze crests and were using them to bruise and gouge their own flesh in time to the chants and hymns. They barely registered the Arbites filling the aisle-tunnel and pouring out into the open area before the altar, not stopping their singing and if anything only redoubling it if they happened to catch a glimpse of an arbitor out of the corner of an eye.

Calpurnia cautiously moved through the crowd, ducking this way and that to avoid swaying bodies and swinging limbs. Differences in the penitents began to become clear: they were of all ages, both sexes. All were ragged, but the clothes of some of them had been of far richer fabric and cut than others. Some had combat wounds, powder and lasburns, as well as those they had inflicted themselves.

Silent, her pistol back in its holster, she made her way through the half-circle to look at the pyres, both now burning strongly, each just big enough for its flames to engulf one body. On one, an obese form whose skin and clothes had been scorched away but whose rich jewellery was still visible through the flames as it cooked into the flesh underneath. On the other, likewise half consumed, a spindly figure with the high cranium of an Astropath and the glint of metal plugs and neurocerebral augmetics still visible through its blackened flesh. The reek of cooked fat was intense.

The singing died away as the figures before the pyres made a gesture. Two women, both hard of eye and regal of bearing, had been leading the singing in clear, powerful, trained voices. They regarded Calpurnia now amid the crackle of flames and the intermittent metallic sounds of the self-punishment of the congregation. Both wore holy aquilae around their necks, and the fleur-de-lys insignia of the Adepta Sororitas. These were not the power-armoured Sisters Militant of the Order of the Sacred Rose who guarded the Cathedral; rather, they wore the elaborate gowns, cloaks and veils of the Order of the Sacred Coin, one of the Orders Famulous, appointed by the Ecclesiarchy as teachers, chatelaines and spiritual overseers to the great families of the Imperium across the galaxy. Calpurnia nodded, and when the Sisters took that as a greeting they both made deep, formal kneeling curtseys to her and the confused Arbites behind her. Calpurnia responded to that in turn with a parade-ground-sharp Adeptus salute. Oh yes, it was nice to be right.

THEIR NAMES WERE Sister Mimetas and Sister Superior Gallans, and while the congregation took up its hymns again they briefed Calpurnia in quiet voices out by the chapel doors. She had been half-expecting another little ritualised speech like the ones aboard the *Sanctus*, but the two Sororitas gave her a quick, thorough summary that, Calpurnia decided, one of her own staff could have been proud of.

The Haggan syndicate, they told her, had attracted the suspicious eye of the Sororitas a hundred and fifty years before when the Inquisition found cause to purge one of its families' holdings towards Hydraphur's southern pole. And within the Haggan syndicate, the ruthlessness and declining piety of the Lyze had prompted quiet but increasingly urgent efforts by the Order of the Sacred Coin to contain it as two generations of Sisters Famulous found that efforts to inculcate Imperial faith and ideals were less and less successful. Gallans and her own mentor had begun their own subtle manoeuvres twenty years before. They had diligently worked to counter the expansion of the Lyze power-base into space by nurturing relationships with planetary families with impeccable religious records, and quietly redirecting as much of Lyze's economic efforts as they could into ventures that involved contact with Ministorum officials. When the Lyze had begun actively courting astropaths as allies and contacts the suspicious Sisters, in careful collaboration with their counterparts elsewhere in the city, had begun to lay a fifth column, arranging marriages of lower-level retainers with devout deacons and ex-missionaries who moved into the Lyze fortress and began to inoculate the population of the citadel with loyalty to the Golden Throne and the Holy Emperor above its masters' loyalty to themselves and their coffers.

They had recieved word from the Cathedral to be careful as soon as word of a well-resourced assassination attempt against a senior arbitor had flown around the hive. They had kept their eyes open as much as they could, but despite the sudden flurry of Lyze activity around the orbital docks they could find nothing that firmly pointed to the attempts on Calpurnia's life or the deaths at the Aquila Gate.

That had changed with the sabotage at the Ring. Word had come back to them quickly that Yannod Dwerr had been the Master Astropath in charge of that segment, and hot on the heels of that Dwerr himself had arrived in secrecy in the Lyze household. Sister Superior Gallans had politely asked paterdomus Therion Lyze whether she should report Dwerr's visit to the Administratum and the Adeptus Arbites, as was the requirement on Hydraphur, and was told that that had already been seen to by Therion's own staff despite Gallans' own informers telling her to the contrary. At the same time word reached Mimetas that the family was preparing some kind of secret bolthole for Dwerr. That was when Gallans had begun overseeing discreet thefts from the House armouries to her own chambers, and the Sisters had used the schedule of religious observations dictated by the Vigil to assemble and arm their own partisans, ready for their signal.

When Arbites APCs had appeared on the avenues outside, that signal had been given as the voice of Therion Lyze was broadcast through the citadel exhorting family retainers to stand against the forces of a corrupt law (Calpurnia blanched when Gallans repeated the words) with their lives while the unjustly-wronged Lyze family made good their escape. Then the Sisters' own loyalists began deserting their posts, sabotaging the attempts to resist the Arbites, collecting weapons from the chapel and receiving the aquila symbol cut into their chests (and Sister Mimetas held up the little finger-knife she had used to make each mark), as a sign of their blessing and as a mark by which the loyalists could recognise one another.

The Lyze retainers had been stunned by the sudden attacks from within their own ranks, but the family militia had maintained the discipline to recover from their dismay and launch a furious internal scouring of their own. Confusion over exactly who had betrayed them and why slowed them down enough for the two Sisters to personally intercept Therion Lyze and Yannod Dwerr as they fled from an autogyro bay that two of the Sisters' partisans had martyred themselves to sabotage. The battered and terrified pair had been quickly dragged to the chapel.

'We had planned a short rite of excommunication and certain ritual chastisements, perhaps confessions given the significance of the day,' the Sister Superior said, 'but the psyker began to lash out with his mind and three of my congregation were given up to the Emperor before we had to perform the execution impromptu.' She had tilted her head to biers set in the Chapel wall where three bodies lay under pale mourning cloths. Spots of dark red had soaked through where the psychic violence that had killed them had brought blood from their eyes and mouths. So Therion and Dwerr had been shot through the face and thrown onto the pyres.

'And so matters are brought to rights in the sight of the immortal Emperor and his Adeptus,' finished Gallans, and Calpurnia followed them in the sign of the aquila.

'You have acted with bravery and resolution, Sisters, and I present the salutes and the respect of the Adeptus Arbites.' They both bowed slightly. 'Although,' Calpurnia went on, 'perhaps our respective orders of Adeptus should confer on matters such as this in the future so that we can act in greater unison on this kind of threat. Had the Arbites known what was happening in this building we could come to your aid and those two criminals could have died under a full sentence of Court.'

'We felt that the pronouncement of a duly-ordained member of the Adeptus Ministorum was sufficient,' Gallans replied a little stiffly, 'and we can cite the condemned ones' breaches of Ecclesiarchal law if we have to.'

'I intended no offence, Sister Superior, simply to fulfil my own duties to my own order', Calpurnia said, trying not to sound hasty about her rejoinder. But she was unable to stop herself. 'I was accompanied here by Arbitor Senioris Nestor Leandro, whose knowledge of the nuances of legal scripture and dogma will be more refined than my own. I am an Arbitrator by training, not a Judge. Arbitor Leandro will be able to supplement your own executions by confirming your sentencing retroactively so that Dwerr and Lyze will stand condemned by the *Lex Imperia* as well as the decree of the Church. An outcome we can agree is desirable, can we not?'

Their agreement was still chilly, and Calpurnia allowed herself a moment to think, well excuse me for trying to do my duty as she left the chapel in the care of the squad leaders and left to oversee the last of the Lyze citadel's scouring. Her anger, though, was partly at herself – listening to the accounts of the two Sisters of their activities in the Lyze-Haggan had given her an idea that she was suddenly kicking herself for not having thought of before.

ONCE THE WORD went out about the loyalties of those with the aquila design cut into them, the cleansing of the citadel went faster. She must be getting the hang of delegation, Calpurnia decided: after trailing behind a leapfrogging formation of shock-squads and manacle-toting Arbitrator mop-up teams and watching the speed and skill with which they worked their way through the citadel she decided she was satisfied, let the commanders get on with their work and made her way back down through the citadel to where Leandro was waiting. She found him standing at the foot of the metal fold-down steps to the extended-chassis Legatus-pattern command Rhino with its forest of transmitter vanes, looking benignly out at the crowded, chaotic Arbites encampment that the Lyze main gates had become.

'We have been listening to the directions you have been voxing over the citadel's systems, my arbitor senioris, now that our own adepts have managed to tame it.' Leandro had donned a surcoat of heavy ballistic cloth over his judge's robes as a precaution, although the last shooting at the main gates had been hours ago now. 'The taking of this place seems to have been the model of thorough method and efficient execution. And what I have been able to understand of your messages to the command post from this citadel's chapel lead me to believe that you have good things to impart to those of us who must lurk behind the line of battle?'

'A few things,' she told him, 'some of which can wait until we're back at the Wall. I think we've closed the matter of the wrecking of those two ships, with the help of the Adepta Sororitas, but from what they have told me, and their inside knowledge of what's been happening with the Lyze family seems good, Lyze had nothing to do with the attacks on me.'

'A regrettable lack of involvement, then,' Leandro said as he watched the first of the aquila-marked prisoners submitting to fingermark scans, eye-readings and stinging blood-samples. 'Not that I would wish the enmity of anyone on you, my arbitor, I merely regret that this whole chain of events seems to have brought us no closer to the essential problem of an assassination directed at yourself.'

'Now as to that, I think we may well have a very useful little avenue of inquiry opened up to us. When we have a moment in a slightly less hectic setting—' they shuffled back against the Command Post hull as a file of Arbitrators double-timed past leading clinking, hissing cyber-mastiffs '—I'll fill you in. It will involve some diplomacy with the Adeptus Ministorum, or at least the Adepta Sororitas.'

'I see. Well, the Sacred Rose Preceptory is attached to the Cathedral and therefore to the chamber of the Eparch, but although the initial approach should by protocol be made to the Eparch it is Canoness Preceptor Theoctista who will then make the decision. She has the autonomy to do that, you see.'

'I trust your skills, Nestor. I don't think that co-operation will be an issue.'

'Good. I believe we will need the help of the Ecclesiarchy in any event, in the matter of–'

'Oh, Throne alone, how did those two get here?'

Walking towards them through the milling formations of Arbites and crowds of prisoners and rumbling APCs were Lord Hallyan Kalfus-Medell and Inquisitor Stefanos Zhow.

'IT'S NOT THAT I don't enjoy your company, my lord,' Calpurnia said, 'but I have to question the wisdom of coming from the Bosporian to here in this.' They were sitting in the lord's litter, a slender carriage on a gravitic cushion a metre above the ground, with a driver at the front and a shelf-seat for Hallyan's giant guard at the back. The body of the litter was enclosed by a silver-blue ribcage that arched up from the chassis underneath them to support rich blue velvet curtains and chains of tiny blue-tinted lanterns, and which now at a gesture of Hallyan's created a shimmering privacy field that blanked them out from anyone outside. Hallyan had instructed his driver to begin a slow circuit inside the perimeter that the Arbites had created before the citadel, and Calpurnia could feel the slight rocking of the seat beneath her cushion as the team of elegant, stilt-legged servitors tugged the carriage into motion.

Zhow was not with them. He had pushed past Calpurnia and Leandro, spoken to one of the marshals in the command Rhino, then disappeared into the citadel. His staff were apparently on their way, probably to examine whatever the pyre had left of Yannod Dwerr. Calpurnia didn't care. Let the inquisitor ignore her and chase his own ideas if he so insisted, she was sure that Dwerr had nothing to do with the psyker-gunman or the roadwork ambushes.

Privacy-screened the litter might have been, but armoured and shielded it was not. Calpurnia felt naked sitting in it.

'We are starting to understand the scale of resources the enemy is mobilising against us,' she went on, 'and in future I would ask that you bear that in mind. If the objective is damage to the Vigil then you are leaving yourself horrifyingly open to attack. A privacy veil is no protection. What if our enemy simply decided to detonate an incendor round over the litter?'

Hallyan, who had been about to say something when Calpurnia had started talking, was now simply watching her through hooded eyes. When she finished he gave a stiff, jerky bow of the head.

'Well-chosen words and excellent caution, my arbitor, although in my defence, for an opponent as distinguished as that behind the attempts on your good person, well, had I been the target as well as yourself do you not think that I would have seen something directed at me? I have been all over the Augustaeum over the past few days overseeing the Vigil, and nothing has come against me. Nothing.'

HIS VOICE HAD been getting harsher and harsher but Hallyan caught himself and softened his expression. 'My... apologies, Arbitor Calpurnia. Two things, perhaps, made me forget myself to a degree. I have observed the Arbites being deployed throughout the upper hive with a commendable degree of caution – I have met and conferred with Arbitor Nakayama and his senior adjutants and your stringent security. Now that the Adepta Sororitas are supplementing them and guarding the sacred places of the hive according to their own duties the guard is doubled.'

The litter tilted as it made a sharp turn, back the way they had come. Calpurnia couldn't quite understand why Hallyan hadn't just left the thing standing if all he wanted was the privacy shield.

'You should also remember that we are in the last stages of the Vigil,' Hallyan was continuing, 'a time when the people of this hive are enjoined from purposeless or distracting tasks. An Ecclesiarchal curfew is in place as well as your judicial one, and there are bans on dining and drinking-houses, gaming, theatrical entertainments, any manner of public association other than certain religious processions. You stood by my side, Arbitor Calpurnia, and watched the hive's lights extinguished in the signal act that began the Vigil proper. Any activity launching another assassination attempt now would be too obvious and out of place and your Arbites and the Cathedral's own garrisons of Sisters are too alert to allow such an act to get far.'

'Arbites are Arbites the Imperium over,' replied Calpurnia, returning his gaze, 'and I would and do trust their vigilance with my life. But these are exceptional times, and I believe my advice stands.'

Hallyan made as though to look out of the litter's doorway, although there was nothing to see except the shifting, depthless greys of the privacy field. Looking at it made Calpurnia's skin creep: she could understand the aristocracy's liking for such things but it made her feel furtive and underhand. Besides, she hated the idea of not being able to see what the other Arbites were doing and what might be happening. Her fingertips traced the scars on her brow.

'You said two things, my respected Kalfus of Medell,' said Leandro, and Hallyan replied with the air of one who had been patiently waiting to be asked.

'The second matter, my Arbites, was one which I believed could not be allowed to grow stale once I thought upon your mission to the esteemed Tudela.' He tugged a slender braid of blue-white silk, and a floor panel rose on rods to become a table. On it Hallyan placed a silken bundle bound in cords of aquamarine velvet.

'It is now well known in good circles that you are trying to ascertain the source of the weapons used in the attack on the noble Calpurnia.' Hallyan's voice was more animated now – Calpurnia was still fairly sure she had offended him at first, but he seemed to have ridden over it. 'I fell to discussing a certain unfortunate war of assassins between families among the Medell and certain nobility of... well, the details, my Arbites, would only be tedious. But consider this.' He untied a cord and unrolled the bundle, and for the second time Calpurnia found herself staring at dull metal parts on a rich cloth bed. Augmetic plates with a certain pattern of flesh-clips and filaments, half of a phylacterial headband radiating slender perception spines. And a long-barrelled assassin's pistol with a swept-back grip.

It took a few moments for the details to sink in, but when they did suddenly the feeling of potential that she had experienced at the start of the Tudela audience flooded back.

Leandro was already turning one of the parts over in his hands. They were not identical, certainly not identical, but the similarities...

'I have never had much of a military sensibility,' Hallyan was saying. 'But I do recall being shown these items in the Kalfus trophy halls and told we had kept them for curiosity value. I gather, my Arbites, that my family's counter-assassins were never able to track their creators conclusively. When I heard that the trail of your assassin's weapons was of importance to your investigation, naturally I thought that I could provide you with something of value.'

'What specifically was their origin?' Calpurnia had picked up a grip-and-feed system that seemed very similar to the one that they had showed the Tudela smiths. Leandro was holding the stripped-down pistol frame and peering at the housing. Hallyan was shaking his head.

'These weapons were seized from certain retainers of my opponents' households, their creator never traced for certain. There are traditions in this kind of matter of which you, my Arbitor Calpurnia, would not be aware, but there are established practices in this kind of conflict...'

'No there aren't.' Hallyan's smile slipped a notch at Calpurnia's words. 'I may be new to Hydraphur, Lord Hallyan,' she told him, 'but I already know enough to know better than that. And I know aristocratic politics, too.'

'Really.' The noble's voice was flat.

'Really,' said Calpurnia. 'The streetfighters on Drade-73 had their traditions, too, when I was an Arbitrator there. "Trenchman's Honour", they called it. You never struck an opponent who couldn't see the blow coming, you never drew a blade against bare hands, there were a dozen other rules. And it never stopped any of them from lunging at your back with a bottle-fragment or ganging up five to one if they thought no one was looking. So pardon my cynicism, Lord Hallyan, but I don't believe with the kinds of things at stake in a place like this, people play their feuds out as courtly chess-games except when it suits their exact purposes to do so. If you were about to tell me that Kalfus-Medell deliberately never went looking for who was providing these weapons, I have to wonder if it's simply that no one admitted they'd done it.'

Hallyan's face was expressionless and paler than usual. Calpurnia met his gaze until Leandro interrupted them in his smoothest, richest tones.

'Why, my admired companions, shall we not wait until we have more to go on, until more light has been shed on the path immediately in front of us, before we dispute how sure our footing is? My Lord Kalfus of Medell, I trust you brought these pieces to place at our disposal?' Hallyan's eyes narrowed, but he could hardly do anything other than agree. 'Why then our own Verispex have tremendous skills to bring to bear and I am sure if they share an origin with the instruments of assassination that Calpurnia's abominable assailant bore that this will be known to us very quickly. Why we have not only the resources of the Adeptus Arbites but no doubt those of the redoubtable Inquisitor Zhow.'

'We may even take them back to Tudela,' took up Calpurnia, 'there will be measures of design and workmanship that I want to go over. And detectives will come to you, sir, to discuss the conflict in which you came by them.'

'Pardon me, my arbitor, but I must be clear.' Hallyan was pointedly addressing only Leandro. 'You are going to confirm that these were crafted for a noble family?'

'That,' Calpurnia said, 'and we can use your accounts to piece together which families issued their agents with weapons like these and see about tying them in to anything we can draw a bead on about the initial attack. Not to mention adding a little extra surveillance to those families' representatives in the Bosporian Hive.' She smacked her gauntleted hands together. The agenda struck her as impossibly ambitious even as she spoke it, but that feeling of potential, of a breakthrough almost in her grip, bore her on. 'I'd appreciate a list from you, Hallyan, of what you consider to be the central possibilities. I'd like to start drawing up cordons and search teams, even if we won't be able to mobilise until tomorrow morning. Hah, having everyone go about by lantern-light certainly adds to the atmosphere of the Vigil, but it will complicate our movements just a little.'

Hallyan's jaw had dropped.

'I cannot permit this! I am the presiding envoy, appointed as Master of the Vigil by the Eparch of Hydraphur himself! Do you have any idea of the consequences for the Vigil if this, if you…' He shut his eyes for a moment, collected himself and then fixed Calpurnia with a pale-blue glare.

'It would befit you to learn at least a little of how things are done here, rather than in the gutters of Drade. Despite what you may think of us, the Vigil of Saint Balronas is no idle conceit. The edict of restrictions on the hive is very real, and there are similar restraints on every other city on this world. No one may go about trade. Affairs other than bare necessities and devotional duties may not be conducted out of doors. Not only that but the Vigil demands devotions and worship! Look at the streets around you, from here all the way to the Bosporian Hive and the Augustaeum itself! Look at the confessional screeds sealed to the walls, and at the devout of the Emperor preparing for the scourging of the Passion Redemptor! Need I remind you also that these are equally binding on the Adeptus, however much you might like to think yourself above piety? If you have no respect for my own rank, are you still so ready to antagonise the supreme Ecclesiarchal ruler of this subsector?'

'Your command of religious detail is admirable, Lord Hallyan,' put in Leandro as Calpurnia forced her fists to uncurl. 'So I won't need to quote the Vigil of 198.M41 when an overloaded venting station in the lower Bosporian threatened a major fire and toxin leak and the laws of the Vigil prevented the Mechanicus crews from working to repair it. I'm sure you'll know that the then Eparch granted indulgence and absolution to the magos-engineers who took charge of the operation and the Canoness Preceptor of the Sacred Rose who skipped the Mass and spent the day by the station. You should know that the arbitor major and I are making the case to the Eparch in a letter today that such a potent assassination attempt implies a potentially equal threat and circumstance. Arbitor Calpurnia will be at the Cathedral tomorrow to swear an oath and be given a seal of absolution so that she and her staff can continue to do the Emperor's work during the strictest period of the Vigil.'

'And make no mistake, sir, the Emperor's work is what I am about.' Calpurnia hadn't known about any absolution, but she grabbed Leandro's point and ran with it. 'Did you have any other questions?'

Hallyan grudgingly lowered his eyes and kept them lowered while Calpurnia tucked his bundle under her arm, then gave a flick of his hand. The privacy field faded into a sudden rush of sound, and the two Arbites climbed wordlessly out of the litter and walked away to the command post. Calpurnia did not turn and look back until she heard the clink of the servitors' long augmetic legs on the paving and turned to watch the litter being towed away. Either those servitors had a hell of a turn of speed once they hit their stride, Calpurnia thought, or it had some other engine – it would have had to have taken a day to cross the city at the pace they were going.

Hallyan had engaged the privacy veil again and the litter's silver ribcage was filled with grey. On the back the servitor still sat, its massive shoulders rounded and its head bowed. Calpurnia pointed at it as the litter glided away and said 'Ah-hah,' and Leandro gave her a questioning look.

'That servitor,' she said, 'that enormous bodyguard construct. Did you see it? It was in some kind of cradle on the back of the litter. That means it has to have a more sophisticated trigger than those phrases he uses. I knew it had to.'

'Interest compels me to be so rude as to ask you to explain your reasoning.'

'I've yet to see Hallyan without that monster tagging along somewhere. It's obviously something he'd rely on heavily for defence if he's attacked. And yet he had the privacy field between him and it – there was no way to activate the thing verbally. There had to be a more advanced signal that he could activate through the field. I didn't think anyone would be impractical enough to set up a guard that sophisticated with just a spoken command pattern.'

'Ah, well, an accurate observation so far as it goes. That would indeed be considered the logical, practical way to set about it.' Calpurnia's expression soured.

'Don't tell me, I can guess. This is another one of those damned local-knowledge things, isn't it? Wonderful. Tripped over my own feet again. What have I missed out on this time?'

'Ah, now, be easier on yourself, Arbitor Calpurnia. Hydraphur's idiosyncrasies make it a tougher place than most to settle into.'

'I used to think I was up to tough jobs.' She was still scowling. 'Alright, so what did I miss?'

'Just an aristocrat custom, such as is found all over the sector and I have no doubt further afield still, in different forms. The custom of setting about a task, whatever it may be, in an inefficient way as a matter of deliberate choice, the intention being to present and emphasise the symbolism of that inefficiency.'

'I understand,' said Calpurnia as they threaded their way between two Arbitrator squads marching from the command post to the citadel doors. 'You rub everyone's noses in the fact that you're too privileged to have to worry about being practical. You're right, it happens everywhere. The deep-space foundry masters at Hazhim used to wear loose robes that were impossible to work in if you were weightless. That was how they advertised that they were above menial work.'

'Exactly so.' Leandro tipped his head in the direction in which Hallyan's litter had disappeared, beyond the outer lines of Arbites and through the crowds shuffling along the paper-lined streets. 'And now you have observed the self-same principle in operation on Hydraphur. Much of the supposed honour and gentility of the armed conflicts in amongst the aristocracy here is a façade, as you have accurately perceived. What really counts is that certain factions – and I might nominate Kalfus-Medell as an instructive example – grow so powerful that their best weapon is the sheer terror of what they can do in retaliation, what you might consider a reverse show of force. The carefully calculated message is: "My power and position is such that the mighty servitor you see before you is programmed with a clumsy verbal activation code… and still I walk in safety that you can only envy." The true cream of the elites won't even put in autoreactor commands, you know. One could walk up and punch them in the teeth and the guard would stand there and watch you until they actually told it to kill you. We might presume that to be the configuration behind Lord Hallyan's guard too. You'll see versions of that gesture around as you deal with the local elites some more.'

Calpurnia sighed, stared up at the bulk of the Lyze citadel for a moment and then followed him the last few steps to the command post.

'Does any of this bother you?' she asked as they walked up metal steps.

'Bother me? That foolishness with the servitor commands?' Leandro tilted one black-cloaked shoulder in an elegant shrug. 'I think it's pointless, as I see you do. And I could discourse for a week and a day about matters of historical law dealing with the rights and obligations and expectations that a Judge might have of a citizen at any given rank regarding that citizen's use of force of arms. There are enough conflicting judgements and precedents and decrees for an army of counsel-savants to weigh and debate on, and every shipment of new volumes of the *Book of Law* from Terra adds more of them. Where were we?'

'You were talking about that foolishness with the servitor commands,' Calpurnia said, suppressing a grin.

'It's what they do,' Leandro said simply. 'They behave in a way that suits them, and we perform our Emperor-given duty to the best of our ability and in due service to the Adeptus and the Law. What else, really, is there?'

They walked into the command post and the hatch shut behind them.

Seventeenth Day of Septista

Mass's Eve. Fourth day of the Vigil of Balronas.
The Service of the Taper. The Passion Redemptor.
Commemoration of Master Reynard
and of Saint Chye Balronas.

ALL CITIZENS MUST *be in the streets an hour after dawn, although
ideally the practice of walking the street with the priestly processions throughout the night is to be encouraged. On the hour mark
the clergy in the streets will give the order and each citizen should
put the confession they previously sealed onto their home to the
torch. Priests, deacons and the heads of households or masters of
barracks will lead the prayer once the confessions are alight. Members of the Emperor's flock must remember that their souls should
be unburdened of sin as their confessions are burned away, and
the small blades blessed the previous day should already be bun-
dled on the end of the scourge lanyard ready for the prayer to end.
The scourging should bring on collapse by the time the confessions
are burned away, and those too physically or morally weak to
achieve such a state in time may plead assistance from members
of the clergy who will be patrolling for this purpose.*

*Citizens should attempt to return to their homes as soon as they
are able; all doors and shutters should already be closed. During
the night no lights should be lit at all. Now the cleansed soul may
mourn for the weakness and fall of Hydraphur all those years ago,
and for the good souls who perished beneath the rule of the Apostate and the unbeliever.*

CHAPTER TWELVE

CALPURNIA HAD MANAGED to get her first good rest in over a week, sleeping for eleven hours and waking with the heavy stiffness that exhausted, motionless sleep brings. But the rest had reawakened an appetite placated mostly with morsels grabbed on the run, and the fact that now she had time for a proper meal she was bound by the fasting edicts of the Vigil was an irony she was in no mood for. She felt stretched and snappish as she polished her rank and honour pins and cleaned her weapons to prepare for another trip to the Cathedral.

Leandro had not been bluffing about Ministorum absolution, or if he had he had turned bluff into action. Today Calpurnia and a small handpicked team would be granted indulgence to work unimpeded by the edicts of the Vigil, able to ride in a vehicle, speak with impunity, enter houses, fight. And now she had a whole new line of investigation to launch. Ultramar being a fief of the Adeptus Astartes, her own family had never experienced much of the attention of the Sisters Famulous, but the conversation with the two Sisters at the Lyze citadel and Hallyan's evidence that nobility was behind the first attempt on her had her twitching with excitement. Between them they pointed to a rich vein of information that she had simply not thought to tap. She had been gratified when Leandro had agreed with the approach.

Zhow was another matter. After an hour of futile vox-hails at the Lyze citadel she had given up and set off through streets full of crowds silently studying the fluttering confession-scrolls that covered every wall or trotting behind the priests' palanquins, yelling pleas for benediction and tearing at hair and clothes.

Then the report came that Zhow had marched into the command post and ordered every single arbitor off the site, then stationed Inquisitorial militia at every entrance, each team holding up elaborately-worded interdiction scrolls nailed to staves and ready to shoot to kill at anyone who tried to enter the fortress. Finally he had visited the nearest precinct houses and had servitors carry away every data-slate, pict-capture and note-sheet on the raid. The Lyze fortress and the recent activities of the late Yannod Dwerr were now under the direct aegis of the Inquisition. While Calpurnia accepted that this was as it should be, on behalf of all the Arbites she was also starting to feel taken advantage of. As a final, winning touch the message chit told her that Zhow's staff had mentioned formal warnings and reprimands to be served on all four of the Arbites commanders for not notifying Zhow of the assault in advance.

She was no better off with Baragry, who was indifferent to the details of the assault but had sent messages disapproving that Calpurnia had not been part of the Passion Redemptor. The Arbites were not under obligation to take part in the great self-scourging that had filled the streets that morning, but Calpurnia got the impression that she was supposed to have done something mildly symbolic for the occasion. She knew she was lagging in the observances she was supposed to be making – she hadn't even made sure of the fit of the ceremonial uniform she would wear to the Sanguinala, which was supposed to have been done days ago – but she covered her irritation with herself with irritation with Baragry, whose dedication to his supposed role as her instructor seemed rather selective.

What had stuck in her mind was the last thing that Syldati had said to her before she had returned to her own precinct house, an hour after the news that Arbitor Gomry had died in the Inner Charisian Gate's medicae ward. Syldati had hovered after her dismissal until Calpurnia had asked her what she wanted.

'I just wanted to say, with your permission, ma'am, that, well, we won't forget what you did up there.'

'Did? I don't follow.'

'What you did for Gomry, ma'am. You stayed with him in the medicae, wouldn't leave him.'

'Of course not. He was under my command.'

'There are commanders here who wouldn't have, ma'am. What you did… it's all over the barracks. We won't forget it.' And she had saluted and retreated, leaving Calpurnia puzzled but vaguely pleased.

To Rhinos and audience chambers, Calpurnia added another thing that was defining her picture of Hydraphur: smoke. The coloured and scented smokes of that terrible masquerade in the Adeptus plaza, the still, sickly haze that had filled the Aquila Gate, the reek from the charnel-pyres in the Lyze chapel. Every time she thought back over the past two weeks her memories were always shrouded in it.

And now here she was again, marching through smoke. That morning the people of the Augustaeum, and of the rest of the hive and of the city beneath it, and throughout Hydraphur, had leaped and cried and wept and thrashed their backs with clumps of sliver-blades as the great flapping sheets of parchment coating every building had caught and burned, burned slowly as they were treated to do, burning away each penitent's account of their sins while the pain of the scourging burned the sins themselves from their souls.

Now the flames were long dead, only echoes in the grey haze in the still air, the flakes of paper-ash that scurried about their feet like strange snow, and the scraps of paper and dribbles of melted plas-wax that still stuck to the scorched building walls. They would remain, someone had said to her, until the first rains of the wet season sluiced them away in a month's time.

There was human detritus left in the streets too: sprawled and moaning, their backs bloody messes, men and women who had thrown their whole hearts into penance and were too weak to rise. Calpurnia had not been sure of how to react until she had seen the ghostly forms of Sisters Hospitaller moving through the streets, directing bearers to carry the stricken ones away. The only other people they saw were squads of Arbites or Sororitas, moving with slow dignity through their watches, the black-armoured Arbites looking for lawless acts, the white-armoured Sisters for blasphemous deeds, the two orders nodding to each other as they criss-crossed in jointly planned patrol routes. There were no voices, no engines.

Calpurnia marched at the head of her score-strong forma-tion, uneasy in the empty, eerie streets, looking around her at the shuttered buildings and remembering her own words to Hallyan about caution, telegraphing movements, persis-tent assassins, bullets and bombs. She almost cursed the planet whose tangle of rules and customs made it so damned hard to follow her own advice, then cut the thought off. The laws had been made by the Ecclesiarchy, just as much a part of the holy Adeptus as she was, not some puffed-up planetary aristocrat. And besides, she told herself as they marched down the length of the Mesé to the Cathe-dral ramp, the Adeptus Arbites do not hide. And neither does Calpurnia. The great spire towering over the end of the Mesé made her feel humbled, uplifted, braver.

Some citizens had enough strength left to crawl and stag-ger to the Cathedral ramp and more than a hundred lay there, running their hands over the ramp carvings or sprawled on their bloodied backs looking up at the spire, protesting feebly as the Hospitallers carried them away. As the Arbites came marching up the Mesé two Sisters detached themselves from the door guard and led the way down a street that narrowed to a high-walled alley around the side of the Cathedral, leading to the fortified quarters of the Hydra-phur Preceptory of the Order of the Sacred Rose.

The Preceptory was nothing like the ornate Mechanicus chapel or the imposing maze of the Cathedral proper, and more like the barracks in the Wall, bare and functional. But the ritual quickly brought her visit to Sanja to mind: it was quick, it was strange, it was certainly not what she had expected. White-gowned Sororitas met them as soon as they had entered the gates, their badges of office and eye-prints coolly and thoroughly checked while armoured Sisters Militant took their weapons. From there they were shepherded deeper into the building, where Calpurnia was smoothly separated from the others and steered down a long, echoing hall and down a narrow flight of steps which ended, rather against her expectations, in a garden.

'Welcome.' Canoness Preceptor Theoctista's hair was as white as her habit and hood, her skin lined and coppery, her voice soft. 'Kneel, please.'

Kneeling in the clipped grass with her eyes down, Calpurnia felt the Canoness's hand on the crown of her head. She put her own right hand on her armoured chest and repeated the lines of the oath as they were recited above her.

'I am Shira Calpurnia Lucina of the Adeptus Arbites, and I take this oath in devotion and duty to the God-Emperor of Earth. I beg His absolution for my actions and will, and I swear that this absolution shall be a weapon in my hands for the service of the almighty Emperor and no other. This is my oath in devotion and duty.'

'Rise.'

She stood, and the Canoness leaned forward and pressed home her badge of absolution. A traditional Ecclesiarchy seal, crimson plas-wax with fluttering streamers of white silk covered in illuminated High Gothic script.

'When the Vigil is completed you will return here and I will take the seal back. All of you must display those at all times until then. The Sororitas know to aid and obey you if you bear that seal and to… sanction you if you do not.'

'Reverend Canoness, my other staff, the ones who came here with me…'

'Their oaths and absolutions are under way elsewhere. Do not concern yourself, their blessings will bear a different seal but carry no less authority. You were separated at my instruction. There is a matter I must discuss with you.'

The Canoness rose slowly, leaning on a cane of pale wood. Two novices, their faces invisible beneath white veils, spirited away her seat and the little lectern that held her signet and the heated pot of plas-wax. Calpurnia wondered if one of them was Rogue Trader Kvan's granddaughter.

The little garden was circular, totally enclosed in a round stone shaft that opened out to the sky two storeys up, laid out in concentric arcs of lawn and path. The order's heraldic white roses grew in simple stone-rimmed beds, shaded a delicate yellow by the sunlight. In the very centre of the garden, another heraldic piece: a statue of the order's device, a gauntleted hand holding a rose aloft, done in the same bare stone as the garden walls. They began a slow circuit of it.

'You are in pursuit of assassins, powerful and unknown, with the unclean and the mutant in their fold.'

'The psyker gunman, yes.' Calpurnia noticed that at the word *psyker* the canoness touched the white-gold aquila at her throat. 'We may have destroyed the one who sent him at me, though, Lady Canoness. We now believe that an astropath psyker–' that touch again '–led some kind of cabal against other Adeptus members, members of the League of Blackships, myself–'

'No certainty, just belief?'

'Just belief, Lady Canoness,' said Calpurnia, wondering if *just belief* was an incongruous expression to hear from a Canoness Preceptor.

'Hm,' the other woman said, and they made half a lap of the sculpture. Eventually Theoctista spoke again.

'During your pursuit of those who are attacking you, you have been dealing with one Hallyan of the family Kalfus and the syndicate house of Medell.'

'Yes.'

'You should know that at some time during the night Sister Arlani Leyka of the Sacred Coin, assigned by the Order Famulous as chatelaine to the household of Lord Hallyan, was murdered.'

They walked a few more paces in silence. To Calpurnia the air she was breathing suddenly seemed icy cold.

'Sister Leyka contacted me by a sealed message late yesterday,' said the Canoness. 'She told me she needed to confer with me, and that only a face to face audience in one of our sealed chambers would be sufficient. She said that she would provide me with more information then. I felt you should be advised.'

Calpurnia's mind was whirling. A strike at her, a strike at Hallyan. Or Hallyan's household. One dead, and the canoness had said, 'murdered' so it couldn't be a large-scale raid, not a pitched battle. She would have heard if that had happened, wouldn't she? Did this mean a shift in strategy by Dwerr's allies, or something different? Another strike by the Society of the Fifty-Eighth Passage? It would certainly fit with their desire to wreck the Vigil.

'Arbitor?' Theoctista's eyes were on her own; Calpurnia realised she had been silent for several moments.

'I'm sorry, Reverend Canoness. I was trying to factor this into our own investigations. Clearly it's related. We're going to have to find out how. Depending on some final tests on some weaponry that Hallyan made available to us, we think we can narrow it down to a selection of noble families on Hydraphur. That was why I wanted to start putting requests out to all the Sisters Famulous, but if this is connected things become uncertain again and we…' She collected herself. 'My apologies again, my thoughts are skittering a little. The last few days have not been... restful.'

'Collect yourself, then, arbitor,' the canoness told her crisply. 'I shall pray for the Emperor's hand to guide you.' Calpurnia took a deep breath.

'I should see for myself the message that Sister Leyka sent you yesterday. The body, too. I may be able to–'

'Out of the question. The affairs of the Sororitas, the orders Famulous in particular, are a sacred trust.' Theoctista's voice was so quiet that Calpurnia had almost wanted to lean in to listen to her, but the simple authority in it made her feel she should be standing to attention at the same time. Somewhere in the building a gong rang, and as it faded a high, clear voice sang a call to afternoon prayers from the cloisters above the garden. 'Remain here or come to pray with us, arbitor,' the Canoness told her, 'and I will give you what assistance I can when I return.'

Canoness Theoctista turned away, her two novices reappearing to attend her. As Calpurnia watched their stately walk to the stairway arch she finally became consciously aware of a sound that had been pushing through the last notes of the prayer-call, an odd, gritty sound from above and behind her. At first she could see no other movement in the garden, then the sculpture rocked on its plinth and that sound came again, not from the base but from the tip, and rock chips spat from the carved hand and flower. And then, finally, the stone cracked to fragments and fell away and the buzzing black mass the statue had held poured down towards them.

NOT A SINGLE mass, Calpurnia realised. It was a swarm, a swarm of fat metallic-black insects, now writhing down the statue like grubs, rushing like ants, hopping like ponderous crickets. They made a buzzing that began as a cicada-chirrup and deepened to the sound of a chainsword grinding into rock.

At the base of the statue the swarm puddled in place for a moment, and Calpurnia could hear an odd and almost mechanical clicking as the little black shapes bounced and crawled over each other. Then, as she began to cautiously back away, they began to wriggle forward, tracking her steps across the grass.

Calpurnia was motionless for a moment, then grabbed a small stone from one of the rose-beds and skated it into the swarm. There was a slight sizzling sound as it passed through the cloud and fell to the grass on the other side. The swarm seemed to follow it back and down, as though it were a piece of cloth that had become snagged around the stone, and for a moment Calpurnia could clearly see the grubs crawling over it were leaving scored trails in the stone. Then they flowed forward again.

'Get the Canoness to safety!' she shouted over her shoulder, but the novices were way ahead of her: she looked around to see a flash of white cloth disappearing up the steps. She thought about following them for a moment, then pushed the idea away. She didn't know what she was going to be able to do to this thing, but she wasn't going to leave it here unwatched.

The little insects advanced on her, grinding and chattering. Calpurnia danced two steps to the side, expecting it to move to head her off, but instead it accelerated to where she had been standing and then curled around. Looking back over its path she saw that the swarm had turned the grass into stripped, pulped wreckage in its wake. Somehow she wasn't surprised. The creatures had sped up slightly too, and... yes, the swarm was definitely growing. It was broader, denser than when it had first poured down the side of the statue. Calpurnia had an idea of where the mass from the stripped grass and earth had gone, but how could anything reproduce that quickly? Fear gnawed at her belly and she stamped on it, crushed it, tried to think.

Her back was against a row of roses and she shoved her way back through them, thorns squeaking against her carapace. A moment later the swarm reached them and for a split-second Calpurnia could see the trunks of the rose bushes fray and evaporate under hundreds of grinder-jaws before the bushes toppled over and into the swarm. It increased its speed another notch and traced her steps.

Again she pushed fleeing out of her mind. It was tracking her, she couldn't draw it into the cloisters where it might go after the Canoness, an innocent novice, Emperor knew who. The alarm must be raised by now, someone would be back before this whole garden was ankle-deep in scuttering, chirruping black shapes.

She misstepped and had to correct her balance, and a lunging vanguard of the swarm made it to her foot before she could pull away. Calpurnia hopped backwards and up onto a stone bench and kicked the instep of her foot into the bench and into the back of her other boot, praying for the sound of crunching shell. The rest of them piled around the bench legs and fat armoured bodies began to climb over each other to reach her. There was a faint sensation as of a fingernail lightly scraping the top of her boot, and she could feel a similar vibration coming up through the stone of the bench as the things ate away its supports. A frantic shake of her foot dislodged the grubs that had crawled onto it, but each had left a part of itself, a head that kept drilling and champing at her armoured instep. Calpurnia fought off panic, gave it a moment more until she was sure they were as tightly packed around the base of the bench as they were going to get. Then she squatted, pistoned her legs out and dived over the pile of insects to roll to her feet on the grass.

Her foot thrummed, and the instep of her boot was crumpling – she could feel it about to give. She needed time to unbuckle it, get the boot off, but the swarm had pulled the bench down into itself and the chewing ant-grubs were starting to sway in the air as though they were sniffing for her. Calpurnia's blood chilled as she watched the pile fold over on itself to follow where she had arced through the air. Now the black of the carapaces shot through with streaks of grey and silver and she thought she could see different shapes of creature – worms, grubs, ants, flies – as they came after her again, close to running speed now. She crashed through another row of roses as one end of the swarm found her trail.

The material of her boot parted and jaws began to pinch and bite at the fabric underneath. Her skin crawled at the thought of them on her skin, but she couldn't stop moving to take the boot off. She tried to think. They were blind, they had to be, they didn't see her movements but followed her trail. (The skin on her foot began to itch and sting). They had trouble getting up into the air. Could she use that? Could they climb? She eyed the garden walls: rough, but not rough enough for footholds, and the things had chewed away the base of a stone bench. (The itching on her foot was becoming a burning, and in another moment the swarm would widen enough to start encircling her. She had to *move*).

'Why are you still here?' a voice snapped from across the garden and Calpurnia tried to limp-run back on an angle to the tall, power-armoured Sister standing at the base of the steps.

'Needed to contain them, watch them,' she yelled back. 'They're tracking me somehow. Don't let any contact you! I may be contaminated!'

The Sister regarded her for a moment, then raised a bolt pistol and fired a careful shot into the middle of the swarm. The bolt disappeared into the black and they both heard the *bamm* as it detonated just under the topsoil. The creatures roiled as the explosion flung up dirt. The Sister grunted, fired three more quick shots. The swarm ignored her, condensed and closed on Calpurnia.

'It's too thick, I can't blast a path for you.' The swarm was sending a column straight toward her injured foot. The Sister raised the pistol carefully, this time at Calpurnia's head. Calpurnia realised what her intention was and swallowed, closed her eyes and began to stumble through the prayer she had been taught as a child, taught in case she ever needed the Emperor's Grace to put her out of...

The bolt shell yowled overhead and slammed into the wall behind her. The Sister snapped again:

'Open your eyes, woman, I've shot you a handhold but it's only going to buy us a moment.'

The pain in her foot was searing now but she spun, ran two paces and jumped to hook the edge of the little crater in the wall with her fingertips. The swarm washed up against the base of it underneath her feet, and Calpurnia planted her toes against the stone and braced herself, wondering how long she could hold on.

Behind her, the Sister's voice said 'Here, hand it to me. *That's* better' and then the crawling mass under her turned to yellow-white as the whoosh of a flamer and a thick, scorched-metal smell drenched the air.

'ARBITOR! ARBITOR CALPURNIA!'

The top of the garden steps was surrounded by Arbites and Sisters, the Sisters were grim-faced and hefting weapons and the Arbites peering down to try to see her. The tall Sister had grabbed her foot and jammed the hot flamer nozzle against it, scorching the little metal ticks under her skin into immobility before handing a combat knife to Calpurnia to dig them out. They came out easily, but now Calpurnia was hobbling on that foot and the instep was weeping blood through the cauterised skin. She stood swaying for a moment in the babble of voices, then tried to answer them.

'No, I don't know what they were. Sister, were they familiar to you? I said I don't know. You saw them, some kind of predatory creation, self-reproducing. Alive? No, I don't think so, Because look at what got into my flesh. Here. That's metal. Those things were *built*. Some kind of killing device.

They moved faster the longer they were… out, or there, or whatever. They tracked me, but ignored the Sister. No, I don't know why.' She shook her head. 'Wait, stop, all of you.'

She looked around at their faces.

'Let me tell you what we're going to do next. Canoness Theoctista, you tell me you cannot reveal details of Sister Leyka's message to you. Save it, Bannon,' she waved his question away, 'I'll explain later. Can you confirm for me, canoness, that it was something to do with the Vigil?'

Theoctista's eyes widened. 'I have said nothing to that effect.'

'No, but Sister Leyka was of the Order of the Sacred Coin, an Order Famulous. You're of the Order of the Sacred Rose, an Order Militant. I know Sororitas order structures are rigid enough that Leyka wouldn't have come to you instead of her own Canoness without an extraordinary reason. And the extraordinary thing your Sisters are involved with at the moment is policing the Vigil and standing guard over the Mass. Well?' The other woman gave a grudging nod.

'There were things that she said had come into her possession. Some information, something that I think she wanted to show me. She wanted my guidance about how it affected the Mass. I was surprised – Sister Leyka was not one of my own charges but I had heard of her as intelligent and resourceful. I decided that if something had forced her to depart proper practice I should find out what it was.'

'But you never did.'

'No. The next I heard from that household was when one Master Nomikros, Lord Kalfus-Medell's major-domo, visited to tell me of her death. He seemed to be aware that she had planned to see me that afternoon. I saw him not long before I received you, Arbitor Calpurnia. He sat before me in the same garden, he insisted on it being a tranquil place because the news grieved him so.' She waved a hand at the smouldering mess below them. 'And he did seem grieved. He brought in a cushion from his lord's litter and insisted on sitting in the garden with it. He kept wringing it in his hands. It bespoke a certain lack of composure, I thought.'

'Thank you, canoness. Bannon, the rest of you, we have our dispensations, our target is the Kalfus household. She looked down at her foot. 'I won't try and walk there. One of you can get a message to the Justice Gate and requisition a Rhino, no, wait, we're the ones with dispensation to drive. A team of you, then.' She scowled, trying to focus past the pain in her foot and come up with a plan.

'One moment, arbitor.' The tall, dark-haired Sister who had saved Calpurnia's life in the garden stepped forward. 'As to that, with the canoness's permission, I may have a better idea.'

THE SORORITAS RHINO's interior was a copy of the Arbites transports Calpurnia had ridden in for nearly twenty years, but different too. It felt weirdly spacious with no lockers, racks of stub guns, mauls, grenade and net launchers, grapplehawks, shotguns, shields, no riot gear stowed around the walls and ceiling. But it had been designed with power armour in mind: narrow benches, friction-taped to stop armoured bodies sliding on the metal, the seat-backs studded with couplings for armour connections. Those had made the benches unbearable, and Calpurnia had soon given up on them and wedged herself into a standing position by the transport's rear ramp-door. The wrong size and shape for seats designed for broad armoured shoulders, the other Arbites were all squirming and jolting as they slewed around corners, sped up and slowed down at intersections: the crew were coupled into the controls and drove faster and more brutally than any Arbites crew could.

Peering through the vision slit at her shoulder Calpurnia could see a second Rhino following them in perfect formation. The Order of the Sacred Rose had its own particular freedoms during the Vigil, and Theoctista had not hesitated to order her Sisters out to take Calpurnia straight to the Kalfus mansion.

Five Sororitas sat on the far benches, heads down and engrossed in their work of praying over each shell as they loaded it into bolter clips. At the front of the compartment sat the dark-haired Sister from the garden, who had introduced herself as Celestian Superior Aurean Romille. Romille had already loaded her silver-filigreed bolter and latched a sarissa to its top, a short heavy power-spike with a razor tip.

That tip was now scabbarded and braced against the floor as Romille sat with her forehead resting on the stock, eyes closed. She had a round, pale face and a nose almost as long and sharp as Hallyan's, and Calpurnia was reminded disrespectfully of the auspex dishes arrayed by the landing pad at Cross-Four.

The notes of the Rhinos' engines changed as they swooped down a terrace-drive, with a cliff-face on their left and a hundred-metre drop to the next street on their right. Calpurnia braced herself as the Rhino slewed through ninety degrees and the ramp ground down and open. They came out of the tank quickly and quietly and Calpurnia led them through the Kalfus gates without another word, limping on the wounded foot in its chewed boot but her face expressionless.

The Kalfus household blocked the end of the drive like a rockfall across a mountain road. It was not the spire or palace that Calpurnia had been expecting, certainly nothing like the raw might of the Lyze citadel, but a clump of ungainly grey-brown boxes and domes spilling down a kilometre or two of hive-slope sheer enough to be almost another cliff-face. The heavy steel shutters that sealed the compound off from the roadway were slid back into the cliff. Seeing them, Calpurnia turned to Bannon and Romille.

'The gates are open. There may have been more trouble. Be wary.'

'That's local law, ma'am,' Bannon corrected her, and Romille nodded.

'It's part of the Vigil,' she said. 'The Master of the Vigil represents all the faithful of the system and must never place barriers before them. It dates back to…'

'Thank you, Sister Celestian, I get it.' Calpurnia limped through the gates and boots crunched on gravel behind her as the Arbites and Sisters fell in behind. Romille strode forward to catch up.

'I was going to say, though, that I agree with your warning. A Sister is dead and that law about no shut gates has been exploited before.' She had matched actions to words and charged her sarissa: the speartip was surrounded with a hazy blue power field, and Calpurnia thumbed her own maul into life so its energies cracked and spat.

'Ready for anything, arbitor?'

'Halfway hoping for it, Sister. I'm in a killing mood. I'm so sick of trotting up and down the hive as someone's moving target, running after shadows when I'm not jumping at them. Every lead we've found has just withered away and disappeared up itself and I'm no closer to knowing who wants me dead than I was ten days ago. Guilliman's ghost, I just want something I can shoot!'

'Raised voices in public are not fitting during the Vigil, arbitor. Sorry.' Calpurnia was trying to think of a retort as they reached the steps of the house itself and marched up them to the open doors and the figure in deep blue.

Calpurnia had picked up enough Hydraphur manners to know that navy-blue was the traditional colour of senior members of an aristocrat's household, not of the nobility itself, but the man's robes were of fine cloth and cut, rather finer than the harshness of the Vigil's laws was supposed to allow. She took a guess.

'Major-domo Nomikros?' He blinked and nodded. 'I am Arbitor Senioris Shira Calpurnia of the Adeptus Arbites. This is Sister Celestian Aurean Romille of the Order of the Sacred Rose. We travel with members of our respective orders and commands. Good of you to meet us in person.'

'I... well, it was by chance, arbitor, in all candour, since much of the household went to the public shrine at the Ascension Arch to mourn the terrible passing, the, well...'

'The murder.'

'The *murder* of the dear Sister Leyka. She and I prayed together only the previous evening, madam, and she spoke of the terrible events of recent days and the magnificent way in which the Arbites had risen to the occasion. And then this!'

'She was on her way to the Preceptory, then?'

'Did you not know of this, arbitor? She took no one with her but a maid I had assigned her myself, but the servant told me that the attack had come as she passed along the Second Imperial Way, below the Savants' Hall.'

'She got about a third of the way, then,' said Romille. 'But on one of the smaller, more winding streets.' Calpurnia felt her expression harden.

'We had patrols on every corner. Someone should have flagged us down.'

'The laws–'

'I know about the laws! No vox-link contact, direct speech in hushed voices only when in public. I knew about them when I vetted plans to rework the policing of the whole damned Augustaeum when we thought we weren't going to catch the assassins in time. Every patrol was instructed to keep visual contact with at least one other so that we could transmit information without breaking the Vigil. Someone should have flagged us down.' She collected herself. 'But alright. We're here now. Nomikros, I take it Sister Leyka had her own chambers here in the household? Good, we'll start there. Show us, please.'

The major-domo drew himself up.

'By no means! Have your senses deserted you, arbitor? Does the sacred Vigil mean nothing to you? Must you rifle even the household of the Master himself and disturb the serenity of the Vigil with less than a day until the very Mass itself? Lord Hallyan will hear of this!'

'The sooner the better, then. Where is he?'

'He… if you wish to speak with him you will need to await his return from the shrine. My lord is a pious man, arbitor, and has led the household in the mourning of Sister Leyka's terrible death. Although I think that he will be rather more interested in taking your conduct up with your superiors. I trust you have a formal delegation from the lord marshal to behave in this way?'

Calpurnia pointed to the seal at her chest and tilted her head at Romille.

'I have all the authority I need, Nomikros, and yet again I find myself tiring of talking to an upstart local who doesn't know his place.' And she shoved past the man and marched through into the house's atrium, the others with her.

The place did not look palatial from the outside, but inside it lived up to its owner's station. They were in a vaulted space of green-veined marble, lit by soft free-floating suspensor lamps and threaded through with intricate lattices of vines, treated to grow along invisible patterns of micro-wires. The splash of water came from fountains out beyond

the vine-curtains that made up the aisle into the house's centre courtyard-hall, and now a quartet of servitors at the far
wall registered their arrival and began a light melody on
harps and tap-bells. Over the melody came the sound of
booted feet not their own: a half-dozen Kalfus retainers in
glossy dark-blue tunics had appeared out of the greenery.
They wore no uniforms, but their bearing was familiar –
Calpurnia recognised household guards when she saw them.
Each had a hand resting casually near a pocket or on a belt-
clip, and she had no doubt that their weapons would be as
expensive as the rest of the setting.

'This is utterly impermissible!' Nomikros was spluttering
behind her. 'What next, will you want to cancel the holy
Mass itself? Rifle the reliquaries of the Cathedral?'
Responding to his tone, the servitors changed to a faster,
harsher tune, full of minor keys and percussion, until
Nomikros waved them furiously to silence. 'You impose
grievously upon the Lord Hallyan's authority and good
nature!'

The muscles of the lower chest and upper stomach are
important to the breathing. On its lower settings the Arbites
power-maul, when tapped lightly against the solar plexus,
will carry just enough charge through a layer or two of clothing to painfully convulse those muscles for several seconds.
Nomikros doubled over and staggered back, whooping for
breath, and Calpurnia kept her maul raised as she turned
and stared down the closest of the household guards. All of
them now had pistols out and pointing, and she could hear
quick movements behind her as her party took firing positions.

'I am done playing games, believe me. If you all are as
loyal to your master as I would expect, consider how much
harder it will go for him if the Arbites and Sororitas had to
fight their way into his house while attempting to safeguard
the Vigil he himself presided over.' There was silence for a
moment, then the weapons cautiously started to lower.
Calpurnia motioned behind her for her own side to follow
suit. 'At ease,' she told them, 'there are still people in the
household of Hallyan Kalfus-Medell who know where their
duty is.'

The point was lost on Nomikros, who was on all fours in front of her drooling and retching for breath. She walked around him and pointed at a guard.

'You. Show me to Sister Leyka's rooms. Appoint someone else to show Lead Arbitor Culann to the rooms of the maid who accompanied her.' She pointed to the two squad leaders in her escort, Bannon and a young man from the Justice Gate command. 'Culann, your particular objective is anything that Sister Leyka had with her on the trip that the maid brought back after the murder. This is a Level Two delegation. Sister Celestian, you might want to send some of your own with him.'

Her judgement had been good: by the easy, low-key way he murmured orders the man she had picked was the ranking officer in the guards. The Sister's chambers and the maid's were next to one another in a long terrace that jutted out of the slope of the main building like an upside-down shark fin, and the two parties ended up walking down the long halls of the household together. Nomikros had stayed in the atrium, sitting on the floor and groaning softly. The doors to the two chambers led off an arboretum whose stained-glass walls made kaleidoscope palettes of the Sisters' white armour: Calpurnia whirled at the double-crack of a bolter behind her but it was one of the sisters shooting the locks out of the maid's door.

Her own grim-faced guard had unlocked the door to the Sister's chambers and Romille insisted on entering first with an intricate Ecclesiarchy amulet in her hand.

'What did you touch?' asked Calpurnia when the Sister opened the door a minute later. Romille didn't answer but motioned them inside.

SISTER LEYKA HAD had three rooms assigned to her, and she had kept each of them spare and eye-wateringly neat. The walls were covered in charts and lists, some obviously of Kalfus family genealogy and holdings and others that Calpurnia didn't begin to understand. A rack of books and slates by the hard little futon was obviously religious, topped with two incense holders and a silver aquila on a stand, but the other rooms were crammed with filing stacks and slate-holders and the desk held reams of notes and memos in the Sister's neat, rather impersonal hand. Calpurnia sighed.

'We should have brought another Sister Famulous or two and some Arbites detectives with us.'

'We've got a place to start,' Romille replied. 'In answer to your question, arbitor, this is the only thing I touched, because you wouldn't have found it otherwise. You haven't been trained in our concealment protocols.' Romille held out a small document case, then stood at Calpurnia's shoulder while she opened it, glaring at the Kalfus house guard until he retreated out into the arboretum again.

Through the archway to Leyka's bedchamber there was the thump of furniture being moved. There turned out to be nothing under the bed, but there were still the private religious books in the bedside shrine and a quiet but vehement argument broke out between Bannon and Sister Rea Mankela about whether it was proper to go through the dead woman's lectionary.

After several minutes they agreed to take the matter back into the study and let the Sister Celestian and the arbitor senioris argue it out, but by that time the point was moot: Shira Calpurnia was hunched saucer-eyed over Sister Leyka's journal and Aurean Romille was outside rounding up her Sisters and shouting at them to get reinforcements and block off every exit from the Kalfus household that they could find.

THE NOTEBOOKS WERE plain vellum, with a neat aquila and 'Nomine Imperator' handwritten at the top of each page. She had skimmed the summary of attempts within the Medell to wrest the position of Master of the Vigil off the Kalfus family, and then attempts within the Kalfus to seize it from Hallyan. Leyka had simply commented that Hallyan had moved to keep his prize with 'far in excess of even his usual ruthlessness', a dry statement with implications that chilled her increasingly the more she read. Leyka had documented his obsessive drive for perfection in the performance of every rite and function, and her own role in helping his initial efforts, and added her commentary on his growing paranoia too.

> *No one within the family may now move to block him, for*
> *it has reached the stage where the fortunes of all the Medell*
> *are bound up in what Hallyan will accomplish and they are*
> *committed to his support lest they share the disgrace should*
> *anything go wrong. But H. knows full well that other inter-*
> *ests will work to undercut him, disrupt and disgrace him by*
> *bringing the Vigil undone. He fears the Haggan, particu-*
> *larly the Lyze-Haggan, and certain Naval dynasties who*
> *will be attending the hive for the mass, but also…*

More names, but ones that meant nothing to Calpurnia.
She flipped ahead.

> *A new commander in the Arbites has come into the system*
> *and there was an attempt on her life today. I have been able*
> *to find little more so far, but I will record that H. was tense*
> *and moody throughout the morning as he is when there are*
> *risks or threats in the making, and when he heard news of*
> *the attempt he went into a rage and locked himself away. I*
> *have sent word of this to the preceptory but no reply yet.*

But the first message Hallyan had received had told him
that she was still alive. He had said so himself.
She skipped ahead again.

> *H. has ordered a consignment from his personal weapons*
> *gallery in secrecy – the couriers were instructed not to*
> *reveal this to me but the pilot was one who had often peti-*
> *tioned me to hear confessions of unholy thoughts and I was*
> *able to use this to get the intelligence from him. The casket*
> *was locked but he said that he knew it to contain weaponry,*
> *something that H's own grandfather in the Kalfus had used*
> *in an internal war two generations ago. I believe it is this*
> *that H. has prepared to take with him when he goes to*
> *meet the Arbites. He is well pleased with the harsh mea-*
> *sures they have taken to keep the hive and the Augustaeum*
> *quiet but there is something in their actions that has dis-*
> *turbed him. He will not confide in me and I must be*
> *careful to conceal my knowledge and suspicions.*

The weapon parts. The components Hallyan had told her
came from an enemy. No. They were his own family's, his
own grandfather's. His own.

Another page.

> *H. no longer has what I now know to be gun parts. The*
> *Arbites must have them. He returned in a rage but the*
> *household guards are armed and the locks will not respond*
> *to me. H. must plan crimes spiritual as much as temporal*
> *if he wishes to keep them from me and from the Sisterhood.*
> *Whether he has watched me in ways I have not known*
> *about or whether I am betrayed to him I do not know, but*
> *I believe he knows he must move against me. He has used*
> *the laws of the Vigil as a pretext to shut off vox-traffic and*
> *the guards are watching my movements. He brought a*
> *cushion out of the litter and spoke to Nomikros about it,*
> *something to do with the new Arbites commander but I*
> *could not get close enough to hear what they said.*

The last entry.

> *Nomikros is planning to take the cushion to the Chapter*
> *House. He has talked to one of the House armourers about*
> *some kind of scent-sign. Emperor protect me, by their words*
> *this vicious House has managed to extend its reach into our*
> *own sacred cloisters, there was talk of some trap for the*
> *arbitor to be triggered there. I do not know what it will be.*
> *H. has donated servitors, weapons and artworks as tithes to*
> *all the Orders, perhaps it is in one of those.*
>
> *I cannot delay. I must reach the Chapter House before*
> *Nomikros. The Canoness of the Sacred Rose knows I am on*
> *my way to meet her. Nori will accompany me, and I go in*
> *haste and armed. Nomine Imperator.*

The exchanges outside the chamber were growing more
and more heated. Nomikros must have got his breath back;
she could hear him shouting that a message had been sent
to his lord. Calpurnia saw Bannon peering around the door
and spoke to him, quiet and deadly earnest.

'Go and talk to Sister Romille, then commandeer one of
the Rhinos we came in and drive like hell for the Justice
Gate. Bring back a full suppression detail equipped for a
massed prisoner drive. If they move on foot and come
straight here they should be within the laws of the Vigil, but
order it how you need to so they can get here without any
Ministorum problems. Get Romille and Culann to finish

locking down the house as best they can. Order the household guards to co-operate. Execute any who resist. You and Culann both have Level Four delegations.'

Bannon hurried out and Sister Mankela followed him. Alone in the chamber, Calpurnia took deep, careful breaths and stared at the journals again.

She said the name out loud, the name of the man who had sent them against her. The psyker with his ghost-trick and pistol, the ambush crews blinded by lies, the hidden devouring-machines.

'Hallyan. Kalfus. Medell.'

CHAPTER THIRTEEN
Eighteenth Day of Septista
The Mass of Saint Balronas. The Sanguinala.

ON THE MORNING of the Mass of Saint Balronas, three of the four most senior Adeptus Arbites of Hydraphur met at the Justice Gate an hour before dawn. Shira Calpurnia had been up for an hour and a half, too nervy and distracted to sleep. She knew that Dvorov, Leandro and any number of other senior Arbites were groomed by valets from the moment they awoke but she had resisted the practice until today, when her ceremonial clothing arrived with two attendants and she dressed in it while they fussed about her. Now she wore her formal dress uniform duplicated in brilliant scarlet, the insignia and braid in bright cloth-of-gold instead of silver-grey on black.

Calpurnia kept getting taken by surprise by the flashes of colour when she moved – she couldn't remember the last time she had worn something so extravagant. They had given her clothes to wear over it, too, for the last few hours of the Vigil: a sober grey skirted tunic that fell to her ankles and a cloak with a hood of mud-brown hessian. Almost as an afterthought she had fastened Theoctista's absolution seal at her throat beneath the cloak-pin. She walked out of the gate into the pre-dawn dimness of the unlit Augustaeum, Leandro walking ahead at the lead of a procession of Judges and a dozen armed Arbitrators and Dvorov beside her.

'You're still nervous, Arbitor Calpurnia.'

'Shows, does it? I know we're walking because walking to the mass is Ministorum law, but I received absolution from that law and I'm sure you could have too, sir. We could have ridden out in one of our own Rhinos or talked Romille into ferrying us again, kept a guard up, checked on some of the patrols on the way.'

'The street presence is doing fine, Shira. There are plenty of excellent squad commanders making sure no one can repeat what happened to Sister Leyka.' Dvorov gestured to the black-armoured Arbitrators standing in long lines down the centre of every street, facing alternately left and right, shot-guns ready.

They passed through the Avenue of the Defenders and met up with more Adeptus, likewise walking, likewise cloaked and shrouded. By the time they had passed the Arch of the Scarii and passed up the Titheman's Way they had joined a modest stream of other mass-goers coming up from the Kathisma Gate, and the growing crowd was swallowed by the flow of people from the Nobles Quarter so that they finally entered the High Mesé in a great, slow-moving tide of dark-dressed figures that filled the avenue from side to side, all walking with heads down and in silence. Occasionally one would glance up at the Cathedral towering overhead and Calpurnia would catch a flash of crimson under their mourning robes. To her, the walk was almost dreamlike in its silence and stateliness. The rich fabric of her new uniform felt oddly soft and heavy on her skin, and it seemed strange that she would not wear this again for a full year.

A twinge from the still-tender wounds on her foot brought her back to earth, and she grimaced and tried to walk more carefully. Pain she could deal with – it was part of the ritual of this occasion, after all – but she didn't like the idea of being slowed if anything happened. In the formal robes and regalia of a Judge, with his mourning cloak over it to boot, Dvorov was having to take care with his step too. The man-tles worn during the morning had to be treated with care:

the pins that held them were designed to break so that they could be cast off at the moment the Sanguinala was rung in at noon, but to have them come away before that and stand there in scarlet festive dress would be a deep disgrace.

'It still chafes at you,' he told her after a moment, 'I can tell.'

'The new boot? No, it fits fine.' It came out thin and flat. She had never been good at jokes. She stepped in closer to him and dropped her voice a notch. 'Having to be here while Nakayama and Zhow are on the other side of the planet sacking the Kalfus-Medell holdings? In honesty, sir, it does. Two assassinations were aimed at me. Hallyan's slimy mock-solicitous speeches about my safety were directed at me. His attempts to order us around and his sanctimony about keeping the Vigil sacrosanct were pointed at me. So yes, I'd like to be over there. I feel I *should* be over there. I want to turn his rock over and drag him out into the light in front of all the other members of his so-fine family and his damned syndicate and sit them all around him in chains as Leyka's notebook is read out at his execution. I've been running back and forth playing shadow-games ever since I arrived, and I wanted to get some proper Arbites work under my belt.'

'You'll get your chance, Shira. Nakayama's good at his job and he has a taskforce of almost a thousand and a Level Five delegation. Zhow is backing him up with the Inquisitorial seal and his own staff and militia. The Kalfus family were broken as of the moment you found Leyka's notes, their allies have deserted them, there's no way they can keep hiding him even assuming they want to for much longer. They're coming to the point where cutting their losses and handing him over will be by far the easiest course. We'll find where Hallyan has disappeared to.'

'It's…' Calpurnia sighed as she tried to find the words. 'It's just the feeling of being so out of place. Like I'm an adult in a world of children playing incomprehensible games, except it's with each other's lives. They bury themselves in these twisting little intrigues and lavish so much on themselves and their Emperor and their Imperium just disappears from their memory. I think it's ironic. I'm from Ultramar, a world that isn't even governed by the Administratum, and here I

am on a planet renowned as one of the greatest fortresses in
defence of the Imperium and I'm the one talking about due
deference to the Adeptus and these puffed-up skankwits
around me are the ones convinced that they're somehow
born outside and above it.'

'A Hydraphurn might quote a local saying about rank having its privileges.'

'And the privilege of rank is service. That's what they teach
us at home, and I used to think they taught the same everywhere. If you serve well you are rewarded with rank and the
privilege of being allowed to perform greater services. By the
manner of that service you show that those privileges were
not wasted on you.'

She looked at Dvorov sidelong – he was smiling under his
cowl.

'Tell me you sympathise with me at least a little way, sir. I
took you for someone who saw through all the blueblood
crap.'

'Be at ease, Shira. I was smiling at another irony that I
don't think you've picked up on.'

'Oh?'

'I know a reasonable amount about you, Shira Calpurnia.
I selected you and oversaw your appointment myself, it
could hardly be otherwise. The same quirk of the immaterium – the Shodama current, I think it's called – that
brought you to this Segmentum so quickly allows message
traffic to come the same way, of course, and it is customary
to share dispatches among Arbites of a certain rank. Your
background has certainly not escaped my attention. The
Calpurnii are not well known here, but then we are almost
on the other side of the galaxy to your home. But yours is a
remarkable family, prominent in the governance of Ultramar
ever since records have been kept and part of every elite one
cares to define – mercantile, scholastic, military. And outside
Ultramar, once I started looking, I found illustrious
Calpurnii in every arm of the Adeptus. Imperial Guard commanders, officers in the Battlefleet Ultima, Arbites like
yourself, servants of the Ministorum and Sororitas, high
posts in the Administratum, one with a Rogue Trader charter. I even consulted rosters of the Adeptus Astartes, and

there's a Scaero Calpurnius serving in the Ultramarines' Second Company…'

'My great-great-grand-uncle.'

'…and a Phaedrus Calpurnius is listed in the roll of dead for the First Company during the First Tyrannic War.'

'From a cousin's side of the family. Not a direct relation.'

'Nevertheless, there you have the irony. I was smiling at the way you were talking about the nobility and the aristocracy, walking beside me there with a pedigree that probably half the nobles in the Augustaeum would give an eyeball for. But you really don't think of yourself as high-born, do you? You see your lineage as a responsibility to live up to, not a mark of superiority. It says a lot about you, my arbitor. That's why I was smiling.'

Calpurnia walked on beside him, trying to favour her good foot and not knowing what to say. Around them the crowd was thickening even further as more joined them from the Alabaster Well and the Avenue of the Saints, and along the iron roadways from the Forge Gate. As the press became close the two Arbites gave conversation away and Calpurnia's imagination put a knife in every hand and a pistol under every cloak. She silently gave thanks for the absolution seal at her neck that allowed her to keep her own weapon.

She had read that in most years the walls of the Cathedral before the Mass were surrounded by supplicants and penitents in a rapture that bordered on frenzy, packed fifty or more deep, howling out the Emperor's name and begging visions and divine blessings. This year the Arbites were taking no chances and they had been cleared away, the ramp and that whole end of the Mesé empty and sealed off until the dignitaries had all processed into the Cathedral. From around her Calpurnia heard one or two murmurs about how quiet the morning was before she and Dvorov moved up the ramp, through the doors and into the darkness beyond.

THE CENSER SMOKE was bitter and almost chemical, crafted to recall the stink of flamers. Skeletal mock-angelic servitors glided overhead on suspensors, trailing ragged scrolls of dark scripture and transmitting grief-stricken groans over their voxcasters. The Cathedral was in dimness, the columns and the vast statues disappearing into high shadow. The choir, massed like an army in lofts to either side of the altar steps and over the doors, sang a low, discordant chant of lament and despair. The angel-statues hanging over the altars were swathed in black sackcloth.

Calpurnia had gone over it in her mind over and over again. She wanted to be sure she had left nothing out, but every time she tried to convince herself of it she could not. Hallyan had not been at the chapel. He had left as the rest of his household prayed for Leyka's soul, telling the retainers at the doors that he was going back to the house to speak with the arbitor. And then he had vanished, simply walked down one of the paths from the Gate and, as far as anyone could tell, just dissipated into air.

The congregation had assembled on the flagstoned floor, herded by Ministorum attendants into four thick masses with three empty aisles running through them. Now down each aisle came a shuffling procession of black-robed deacons with the tattered banners of all the Houses, the Navy ships, the guilds and regiments and orders that had bowed the knee to Bucharis. The first had already reached the steps of the little ziggurat on which the main altar stood, the end of the processions were still lost in the shadows behind them. The Chief Commandant of the Hydraphur Naval Commissariat stood on the steps below the Altar Sanguinal, reading each disgraced name from a scroll as its banner arrived in the growing press before him.

There had been odd sightings from Arbites patrols all over the Augustaeum, reports from different streets of him heading in conflicting directions, but when the orders had gone out to bring the man in… nothing. Romille's Rhino was the only vehicle to have driven the streets all day; the Gate watches monitoring the exits from the Augustaeum to the rest of the hive reported that Hallyan had not tried to exit it. The Arbites at the airpads and landing-crosses out in the city-sprawl reported no launches of aircraft, not even attempts. How had he managed to flee?

A high, fast song sprang up from the choir, sharp and urgent soprano notes, fierce words, pain and sacrifice, penance and contrition. Fires sprang up around the walls as Sororitas guards lit sacred braziers, and in the flame-lit Cathedral Canoness Casia of the Order of the Lexicon walked to the base of the Altar Dolanite and began to read from the *Dialogues of the Confessor.*

Calpurnia was at floor level, toward the front of the congregation among the more prestigious worshippers, but she could imagine how the rows of braziers would look to those in the high tiers behind them. She thought again of standing with Hallyan atop the Cathedral's spire, of watching the lights go out and the soft ghost-lanterns of the Vigil light up the square below. She remembered his descriptions and those she had read of what the square was like at the moment when the crowd at the Cathedral doors threw off its mourning robes, remembered him talking about the care he had taken over that pivotal moment of the festivities. A pity he couldn't see them.

And it was so simple she wondered how she could ever have missed it.

Shira Calpurnia stepped from her place and edged her way out of the line of Arbites. Dvorov and Leandro stared after her but did not interfere as she backed into a clear space, gave a salute in the direction of the altar for safety's sake, then walked as fast as dignity permitted toward the back of the Cathedral and the passages to the vestry chambers. A bow-wave of scandalised sound spread out from her path, almost too low to hear over her footsteps: no one dared talk aloud, so the susurrus was made of intakes of breath, muttered questions and exclamations, the rustle of cloth as heads hurriedly turned back to watch the ceremonies at the altars. Two deacons stepped out from one of the tiered column bases to block her way, but glanced at one another and stood aside when she pointed to the seal at her throat.

A drumbeat, and the braziers went out. Calpurnia clamped her lips together to keep in a curse and sidled out of the aisle she stood in, right into a clump of startled Navy officers. Through the darkness, each under a single lamp carried by one of the gliding angel-skeletons, came three processions, at their heads priests robed in black, with leering masks representing the traitors of the Apostasy: Bucharis,

Sehalla and Gasto. A column of Sisters Repentia followed each priest, keening and raking their nails across their crudely-shaven heads and emaciated faces. Calpurnia shifted from foot to foot until they had passed a respectful distance, then began walking again. She was sure she could feel the gaze of the people around her on her shoulders like a weight. She reached the vestry chambers at the same time as the processions reached the Altar Thorian, and the booming dirge of the choir followed her through the doorway.

Her entrance very nearly got her spitted on two honour-blades until the Sisters at the door saw the seal and put up their weapons. Beyond, a shocked senior pontifex in dazzling white and cloth-of-gold stared at her over the mask of Dolan he had been about to put on to lead out the next procession. Calpurnia ransacked her memory for the name of the people they had placed in charge of security for this area.

'I need to speak to Sister Superior Zafiri and Proctor Essker.' The pontifex was still staring bug-eyed at her as a deacon hurried her through the vestry and into the marshalling rooms beyond it.

'Arbitor senioris!' Essker looked as shocked as the pontifex had, spinning away from the far window and snapping to attention so fast Calpurnia half-expected him to wrench something in his spine. Fed up of the constricting layer of cloth, Calpurnia snapped the pins and the cloak and tunic dropped away as they were designed to do. The junior arbitor gulped.

'Ma'am, you shouldn't go about in Sanguinala dress before–'

'Don't stand on ceremony, Essker, we haven't the time. Where is Sister Romille stationed? Celestian Superior Aurean Romille. And I think Lead Arbitor Bannon is outside, get him in here too.'

'I don't know. Uh, I'll find out.' Essker was collecting himself.

'Do that and get me whatever squad is on duty as floaters at the moment. Have someone get me the security journals for the Cathedral garrisons, too, both ours and the Sisters'. But first show me where you've got the equipment dump, I want a carapace to put on over this.'

She was glad they had decided to keep an equipment stash, and gladder that there was a body-carapace there that fit her. By the time she had clipped it on Romille, Essker, Bannon and half a dozen Arbites were standing and watching her. She supposed she looked a little odd in the scuffed black battle-armour over the gorgeous red and gold of her uniform.

'I'm giving you the benefit of the doubt, madam arbitor, because I have some respect for you,' said Romille coldly as Calpurnia reattached her holster. 'Walking out of an Ecclesiarchal ceremony, let alone the Mass of Saint Balronas, is not something my order or anyone in that Cathedral takes lightly, however they do things where you came from.'

'I am fully aware of what I just did, Sister. In a moment I'm going to show you my reasons.' She took the log-slates without looking at whoever handed them to her and began going through the information in them with quick, careful taps of a forefinger. If I'm wrong about this, she thought, then I am utterly and undoubtedly–

But she wasn't. She cut off a triumphant smile before it could show and held the slate up for the Sister to see. It took a moment for Romille to take in what she was pointing to, another moment to understand it and snick off the safety on her bolter. After a moment more her face split in a grin.

'What,' she asked Calpurnia, 'are we waiting for?'

'ARE THESE DELAYS wise? I want to get up there and see if your hunch is right.' They had stopped again for Calpurnia to pass contingency instructions to the sentries in the cloisters. It was the fifth such stop as they worked their way up through the building: they had gone almost high enough now to be level with the ceiling of the Cathedral space itself. Two floors ago they had passed a window that looked out into the central chamber where the mass was being held: the swathing was gone from the marble angels and they blazed in white searchlights as the Chief Confessor Militant led the congregation in the Second Psalm of the Martyrs.

'The bells will ring in fifty-three minutes,' Calpurnia said, checking her timepiece. 'I'm positive we'll have at least that long to get into position and I want to make the most of the time. But if it makes you any happier…' She reset her timer into a reverse countdown. 'Does that match yours? Can you pinpoint to the minute when the end of the mass is rung?'

'To the microsecond. It's written into the laws of the mass itself.'

'Silly of me.'

Romille simply grunted, checked Calpurnia's timer countdown again and led them on.

They picked up two more Arbites from one of the balcony details; Romille had commandeered three more Sisters. Calpurnia was pausing them at each level, methodically making sure that each area knew what was going on, listening as Romille gave out orders to the Sororitas and collecting Arbites from their liaison checkpoints. Romille had eight white-armoured Sisters behind her now, and the impromptu Arbitrator squad following Calpurnia and Bannon was a dozen strong. She was being careful to leave a good guard presence behind, and she was being careful to have the passages between each level sealed behind them as they climbed. Flight back down through the Cathedral was going to be impossible. Not that it would come to that, she corrected herself grimly. Not at all.

Another five-second lift ride. The forty-second level, ecclesiastical libraries, bare teaching rooms and devotories. Two edgy Arbites in the lift foyer and another twenty Sisters moving around the floor. The two women gave their orders and moved on and upward. By the sixtieth level they had fifteen people apiece and Calpurnia began spacing them back along the corridors, fearing that things would get too unwieldy if there were trouble. By the ninety-eighth level there were twenty-two minutes to go, Romille was grinding her teeth and Calpurnia had started to bark her orders and eye her timer. At the moment that she stepped out of the little corridor to the foot of the bell-colonnade steps and gestured for the squads to assemble, her countdown read exactly fifteen minutes.

AT THIRTEEN MINUTES and forty seconds to go, Hallyan's servitor came down the stairs from the bell-chamber with the fluid, silent speed of a closing shark. Its crusher-claw arced in like a wrecking ball and Proctor Essker flew up and out past her, dead from the hit even before he cleared the balcony railing and began to fall. The flesh-machine used the momentum of the swing to turn and drive its other arm forward and rammed a bundle of high-velocity drillspikes through Sister Iustina's chestplate. The drill teeth buzzed against the ceramite as the fat little pintle-stubbers on its shoulders whined and tracked and spat bullets out of barrels no longer than Calpurnia's little finger. It seemed to be squealing, but Calpurnia realised it was coming from her vox-torc. Something was jamming their transmission band.

Romille shouted a battle-blessing and the crackling sarissa-spear on her bolter slid effortlessly through the thing's armour plate; she might have been bayoneting air. It was a perfect killing stroke, neatly through where the heart should have been, but the servitor slammed Iustina's body into Romille's with a swipe of its arm and she went sprawling, her weapon clattering on the stone. By that time Calpurnia had her pistol out and was placing careful shots, trying for the base of the neck where the helmet visor stopped, her shots tearing gouges out of the thing's shoulders. The servitor lunged and crushed an arbitor into two with its claw. The arbitor and Sister behind him got off two shots apiece before the drillspikes in the thing's right arm retracted, a triple-chainblade array extended and sheared them both in two in a terrifying double stroke. The gold visor was spattered with red, its blankness more frightening than a living, snarling face would have been.

Calpurnia shifted targets now, backing away and firing at the thing's hips and legs as Bannon stepped up beside her and pumped scatter rounds into its face to try and blind it. Her shots tore into its knees, but it barely slowed as it twisted about and put a bullet from each shoulder-stubber through an Arbitrator's face. Bolt-shells from two Sisters blew red craters into its side before it dropped one with another headshot and the other with a drill-lunge, then smashed a third with the claw. Romille was on all fours, shaking her head and trying to stagger to her feet until it knocked her flying into the wall at the other end of the balcony hard enough to crack the stone where she hit – she collapsed and lay still. Bannon ducked away, trying to place another shot into the thing's side between its armour plates, but the drillspikes were too quick. They skewered Bannon's chest and hoisted him high, then retracted to drop him onto the chainblades. A swipe of the arm sent the wrecked corpse tumbling wetly back down the stairs.

Calpurnia, the only one left now, wove her maul in front of her before the crusher-claw plucked it out of her grasp quicker than she could follow and snapped it. She spun to flee and get some room to reload her pistol when the claw hit her on a downward angle that shattered her left shoulder and arm like porcelain and drove her to her knees. She had time to watch the gun drop from her hands before her vision washed red and she shrieked. No second blow came and she tried to half-stand, to look around for a weapon, until a second, lighter hit buffeted her against the wall and a third sent her sprawling back towards the final set of stairs. For a moment she lay there, retching and gasping at the raving storm of agony that was eating her left side whole, before somewhere underneath it she realised what was expected of her. White with pain and staggering on her feet, Shira Calpurnia climbed the stairs to the gallery beneath the Cathedral bell, to meet for the last time in her life with Lord Hallyan Kalfus-Medell.

HALLYAN STOOD WITH his back half to her at the north-eastern end of the gallery, looking out over the Mesé as they had done on Vigil's Eve. He wore drab mourning-grey as she had been doing, although she could see scarlet at his collar and ankles where the mourning robe did not quite reach. Hallyan was dressed for the mass. Calpurnia tottered to a stop and her left leg gave out; at the sound of her toppling to one knee Hallyan spoke.

'You thought I wouldn't know.'

'Wouldn't know what?' Her own voice sounded thin and stretched to her ears.

'Wouldn't know, you little sow, that you were coming up here after me. I have eyes and ears keener than yours, you know.' He turned and gestured at the servitor as it padded up beside him. The damage it had suffered in the fight appeared not to have slowed it at all. 'A step ahead of you, little Shira. A step ahead of you every single time. A step... Little Shira-bitch.'

For a moment she was back in the dark passageway on board the Inner Charisian Gate. She found herself sniffing for the smell of alcohol on Ensign Talgaard's breath.

No. Mustn't lose touch... mustn't lose track... She tried to regain her feet and couldn't. Hallyan's posture was haughty, his clothes neat, but his eyes...

She made herself gasp out words.

'You didn't get ahead of Sister Leyka, did you, Hallyan? You barely managed to catch up with her before she could let anyone know what you were doing.'

'She... questioned me. The same as you are doing. *She* tried to judge *me*. She tried to judge me. I am... you know who I am. And you people, you are... you think that I should... *justify*...' His hand twitched, and again, and even through the fog Calpurnia realised what iron will it was taking for him to keep himself composed. His eyes were ragged with near-madness. 'The words don't matter. Anger, anger is done with and you wouldn't have what it takes to understand me.'

Hallyan's gaze wandered again and Calpurnia took the moment, lunging and getting her left leg under her and taking a step towards him. He caught the movement and spat a code-phrase; the servitor took a step forward and raised the drillspike arm until she stepped back again. *Emperor help me, Emperor help me.* 'Never understand,' he said as though he had not been interrupted. 'The rest of them will all talk about how terrible I am, and my family will tell that peasant oaf Nakayama that I acted alone, that I was a rogue, their undoing with mine ...' he tailed off and seemed to shake for a moment.

Her arm and shoulder sang, and colour swung in and out of her world, but behind it her thoughts were becoming weirdly clear.

'That's... that's why you showed us those gun parts,' she said. 'I wondered why you gave us something that would lead the search closer to you. But that wasn't how you

thought, was it? You didn't realise that we–' she heaved a
breath and it was like breathing hot metal '–felt the same
way about the nobility as you do. You pointed us to it being
a noble family at the root of all this so that I would remember my station and call off the investigation rather than
harass my betters.' She made herself stand straight, although
she could not stop herself swaying as her shattered bones
yowled. 'For whatever it's worth now, that was never even
close to working.'

She had been wondering if that would provoke him; it did
not, and suddenly another thought sailed by on the hazy
swells of agony. She couldn't provoke him, not yet. She had
to bide her time.

'It didn't work, no. You clung on like hive-mud. Hah! You
are hive-mud. Mud. Mud and disease!' He spat on her, on
her broken shoulder. She looked muzzily down to see his
spittle mingling with her blood. 'No doubt you're so terribly
proud that you eluded a device that cost me any amount of
time and resources to secrete?'

'The swarm in the garden.' She blinked sluggishly as
another connection slid in. 'The litter-cushion. It was…'

'Nomikros took the cushion you had sat on in my litter to
get a pheromone trace of you into the garden for the nest of
machines to pick up. A tech-arcanum that is beyond our production now, you know. One of the few left in the whole
sector, the only one my family had at its disposal, do you
understand that? Of course not. What can you understand?
You can't even understand *obedience*.' His hands were twisting in the cloth of his robe. Hallyan was starting to come
apart. 'I had originally placed that swarm with the intention
of using it for something considerably more important than
you, you wretch. I had wasted my prize wyrd-shooter on you
as it was.'

Her eyelids felt heavy. Shock. She was going into shock.
She couldn't. She couldn't go into shock she couldn't she
couldn't. Her thoughts raced around in a bewildering rat-
maze of agony. *Holy Emperor, beloved Protector, by Your light do
I walk unafraid in the bleak places…* She cradled her broken
left arm in her right, gritted her teeth and jogged it. She
mewed and hissed with the pain, but the dazed feeling

ebbed. Hallyan hadn't noticed. She looked at the servitor, took a step forward. She remembered what Leandro had said. Oh, Emperor grant him right, Emperor...

Keep him talking.

'You didn't start anything more against me until you realised we were going to specifically come after you. We spent days on a lockdown of the Augustaeum, the whole hive, but you didn't care.' She took another step forward. Her lips felt numb and her words sounded sludgy to her ears. 'But I think I know why. It was never us at all. It was your rivals. The Lyze-Haggan, the people in your own house and syndicate, the aristocracy. I know enough to understand what they had to gain by disrupting the festival while you were appointed to preside over it. If they could disgrace you they could undo you.'

He was staring at her. She wanted to drop her eyes to the timer but she forced herself to hold his gaze.

'That's what started it all. The assassination of the fourth most senior arbites officer in the system would... give all the Adeptus the jitters. Stir us up. Killing some other local noble wouldn't. I was newly-arrived and from far away, easy target. And my death would have forced the Arbites to lock down the whole place so tightly that none of your rivals would have had room to try anything, and you'd be safe because who would ever have thought that you would undermine your own Vigil like that?'

'And it worked. You did exactly what I wanted. You did lock the hive down, there were no plots able to take hold against me. And step back, please, arbitor, before I instruct my guard again. It will place a shot between your eyes if I tell it to.'

Fighting off despair, she shuffled back a pace, gasping. Blood was flowing steadily out of her arm and the floor seemed to be rolling softly under her.

'So you got what you wanted, Hallyan. You got the Arbites dancing to your tune, you get to stand on top of the Cathedral and watch them ring in the Sanguinala.' She cursed herself for using the word, hurried on before he could pick up on it. 'You never dreamed, though, that we'd keep following you, that my fellow Arbites would be so... loyal to

me. You don't realise people think like that, do you…
Hallyan? Except for the trifling matter of underestimating…
the Emperor's Arbites, you have come through this…
remarkably well.' She managed a glimpse of her timer.

'Underestimating.' Hallyan's hands were balled into fists
in his robe. 'I am an idealist. I thought I lived on a world
where people behave as they should, where a little gutter-
trash such as you had respect enough to leave those born her
betters alone. You're smiling!'

She was. She wondered if she was delirious. Her left eye
seemed to only see blurred reds and greys. 'You remind me of
something the lord marshal said. No matter.' Hallyan took a
deep breath, and she looked at the timer again. *Not long, not
long. Emperor please, oh holy Guilliman lend me your strength…*

'But I am a man of will and a man of my word. I swore I
would see you dead and that I would see the Vigil end and
the Sanguinala begin. I swore it.'

'And I realised it.' Calpurnia could hear her voice getting
stronger. *Not long now, not long. Keep him talking.* 'Down there
on the Cathedral floor. There was no way you would allow
anything to get between you and your triumph, you had to
be here to see the end of your Vigil with your own eyes. Once
I knew that the security logs for the Cathedral entrances confirmed it. You never fled after we took your house. You cut a
zigzag path through the hive so that your movements would
be hard to predict, got here before word of your crimes did,
strolled by the guards and hid. Do I have it right? You're as
brave and ruthless as your reputation told me. You might
have made a good arbitor if someone had taken you in
hand.'

That scored, and Hallyan had to squeeze his eyes shut for
a moment. She noticed that his mantle was speckled with
dried blood, blood that was not his own. He caught her
looking.

'What? You think I liked having to do this? You think I
liked sitting in a rathole somewhere in this place looking at
that scrawny old man's corpse all night? I should not have
had to… someone like me… someone in my, my station…
Even after I killed him his eyes mocked me and he wouldn't
listen.'

That was where he had hidden. He had murdered one of the anchorites in their meditation-cells somewhere in the Cathedral spire and he had sat in the cell all night with the corpse and his silent servitor. Talking to the corpse. Throne of Earth, the man was coming apart at the seams. She wondered how long this side of him had been bottled away as he smiled and made polite words and bred his plots, the pressure eating him alive. She should have stopped him, should have seen–

Calpurnia groaned in pain and dropped her eyes; her timer display blurred in her vision and she came close to panic again. She squeezed her eyes shut and made them focus. Hallyan cackled.

'Unlike you, I need not sully my own hands with the labour. I will kill you. It will be this weapon beside me but my command and therefore I will be killing you myself. Another concept that only my kind can understand. But I will not kill you yet, woman, I will make you see that square light up with–' He stopped dead. He had seen her staring at the timer on her wrist, and he snarled. 'What are you doing, bitch, what have you cooked up? Very well, to hell with you. I'll kill you now and die happy when the mass is done.' He turned to his servitor, pointed at her, and spoke the words that would send it lunging to end her life.

Calpurnia's countdown hit zero.

She had barely heard the whoop of air behind them as the hammer flew into motion, but now the toll of the Cathedral bell slammed into them as though the bell itself had been hammered down onto their backs. Calpurnia felt the sound drive into the sides of her skull, was sure she felt it buzzing in her splintered bones. The noise was monstrous, the noise was the whole world.

She had seen Hallyan's mouth move, knew he had spoken the trigger phrase. And it was swallowed, buried, beaten down by the god-voice of the Cathedral bell.

She forced herself to move, felt herself lurch forward and struggled to not pitch onto her face. As she ran forward, shouting noiselessly at the pain as she dropped her left arm to free her right, she was sure that any moment the servitor would leap at her, but even Hallyan's second call was barely more than texture against the fading ring of the bell. He spun goggle-eyed to face her and Calpurnia drove the edge of her knuckles forward and upward, crushed his voicebox and left him staggering against the parapet choking for breath.

She could have killed him there with a single good shove. He was stunned, gurgling and could not have resisted. She thought about it for a long moment.

No. There was only one right way.

She left Hallyan wheezing and choking against the side of the arch and walked unsteadily back down the stairs. Her pistol was where it had fallen in the litter of bodies. She picked it up and wondered dimly how she was going to load it, managed to fumble it open somehow. She worked the loader in, groaning as the pain seemed to send stealthy wires across her body, down into her legs, up into her head. The snick of the lock-glove helped her focus as she gripped the gun and stood up again. She walked back up, gun-arm heavy and hanging as limp as her ruined one. Her head wanted to sag, her body wanted to faint. *No. Must be done right.*

Hallyan was still up against the little parapet over the Mesé. He was leaning on his servitor, staring imploringly into its visor and making pleading gurgles to it. It stood impassively, staring into the distance ahead of it, ignoring his clawing hands on its arm, waiting for its command. Hallyan's mourning-cloth had come away and the red of his mass silks mingled with the blood from his servitor's wounds, and the blood of Arbitrators and Sisters that slicked its weapons. She saw his ears were bleeding and realised hers must be too. Her hearing was full of hiss and din, she could only hear her steps as faint, gravelly sounds and her voice, when she addressed him, barely registered at all.

'Lord Hallyan Kalfus-Medell of Hydraphur. With the evidence of my eyes and the proof in my hand I condemn you as is my right as arbitor senioris of the Adeptus Arbites, in service to the law of the God-Emperor of Earth. I condemn you for murder and for unholy conspiracy against the God-Emperor of humankind. Blessed be the God-Emperor, in His name do I carry out sentence.'

Hallyan looked at her, paralysed and seeming to only barely understand, as she took careful aim and shot him once between the eyes.

The bell had rung at the moment the dawning sun cleared the horizon, and down on the Mesé and in all the streets of the Augustaeum and the Bosporian Hive and its great surrounding city and in every place across Hydraphur the crowds had shed their mourning robes and were leaping and shouting in their scarlet festive clothes: the Vigil was over, the Sanguinala had begun. Red pennants had unfurled from every tower and red streamers spilled from every window; bright red pyrotechnic showers brightened the already rich dawn light.

Calpurnia watched as Lord Hallyan's body, its head gone above the bottom lip, tumbled off the gallery and away, turning end over end, disappearing from view in air thick with confetti, fireworks, shouts and exultant hymns. She reeled and lurched a step backward, then another. It dimly seemed to her that this wasn't right, that there had been a party on already. She knew this next part: there was a party and then someone she couldn't see would shoot at her and then she would meet nobles and fly into space and be chased in a garden. She shouldn't have to do all that again...

It caught up with her, finally, and Calpurnia crumpled slowly to the floor of the gallery as her mind slid down into the dark.

EPILOGUE

JUST AFTER NOON on the twenty-fourth day of Septista Shira
Calpurnia, in dress uniform and a dusty-black funeral mantle, waited by the outer doors of the Cathedral of the
Emperor Ascendant. The other mourners were gone into the
bright day outside. In the middle distance across the Cathedral floor she could see men and women in the
yellow-brown gowns of penitents, citizens who had been
carried away and committed some minor infraction at the
Sanguinala feasts for which they were now atoning. They
bustled about the column steps and the altars, sweeping and
polishing and fanning away the funeral incense. Calpurnia
knew that the air needed to be sweet for a procession that
afternoon, but she still wished she hadn't seen this. There
was an impersonality about it that saddened her.

The Eparch Baszle had performed the funeral rites himself at the Altar Thorian. The noble families had sent
representatives to the service because none of them had
dared not to, and none of them had looked happy about
such a distinguished ritual for what they thought such
lowly functionaries. The Cardinal had filled his eulogy with

317

references to the greatest nobility in humility and duty, heroic deaths and true worthiness, and Calpurnia didn't imagine the assembled upper crust had taken that gracefully either. The only person to approach her after the service had been Inquisitor Zhow, who had presented his condolences and congratulated her stiffly but apparently sincerely on her 'victory'. She had accepted both graciously, and Zhow had stalked away with no more ado. Calpurnia had heard no more about the reprimands he had threatened after the Lyze-Haggan assault, and she suspected he was going to let it slide.

There was a discreet cough from behind her. Baragry was standing there in a simple black and red clerical gown, proffering a black linen scroll. Unrolling it awkwardly in one hand – the arm shattered by the servitor's claw had been rebuilt on grafted bone but it was still strapped to her body while it healed – she looked at the neat column of names in white ink, the names the Eparch had read from this scroll during the funeral, the dead Arbites and Sisters from the fight below the bell chamber. Arbitor Essker, Sister Iustina, more. Bannon's name was second from the bottom and she closed her eyes and bowed her head for a moment when she came to it.

'The Eparch sends you his personal blessings, my lady arbitor,' said Baragry as she rerolled the scroll and tucked it into her belt, 'and he hopes that he may meet with you in audience soon. But he is curious – and I will say that I am also – about the roll of names. We happily make you a gift of it, but what will be its use?'

'The prayer book I was given at my induction instructs us to reflect upon service and sacrifice, Reverend Baragry. I will place this on the shrine in my chambers and read these names along with my scriptures. I can think of few better scriptures than the names of the men and women who died alongside me because that was their Emperor-given duty.'

Baragry nodded, understanding straight away, and blessed her with the sign of the aquila. Calpurnia returned it as best she could and walked out of the Cathedral. She had dismissed her guard when the service had ended and now walked alone down the ramp, studying the carvings under her feet. She had decided she was going to learn the stories of all the Segmentum Pacificus saints they depicted. Maybe Leandro or one of the precinct chaplains could teach them to her. There was a clean cool breeze coming in from the mountains – wet season on the way, people were saying – that lapped around the Cathedral spires and tousled her hair, and for the first time in three days the micro membrane repairs to her eardrums seemed to be itching a little less as they healed.

She stowed the scroll in her belt and rested her other hand on the hilt of her maul. Her new maul, presented by Dvorov from his own armoury to replace the one the servitor had crushed, the one that she had first been given at Machiun. That had been a classic Ultima pattern maul, short and heavy, unadorned, best for choppy strokes. The new one was a Hydraphur style, longer, lighter and slenderer, with a spiked handguard that made it impossible to perform the grip-reverse manoeuvres she had been trained in. Her old maul had been blunt and powerful, effective as a truncheon even without the power field, able to break bones with choppy strokes; the new one carried less weight of its own and needed greater finesse, almost a fencing technique, lightly jabbing with the tip and letting the power field do the rest. She supposed she would get used to it.

Her Rhino waited out beyond the ramp, engine idling, ready to carry her away down the Mesé and back to the wall. She could see her guard around it, one at each corner, and caught herself wondering which one was Bannon before she pushed the thought away and kept walking.

There was a knot of subdued colours at the foot of the slope, a pack of funeral-goers who had stopped to talk before they went on their way. They noticed her, and the conversation fell silent. Arbitor and citizens regarded one another for a moment, then the group parted uncertainly to let her through.

She knew they would never forgive her. She knew as well as they that Hallyan Kalfus-Medell had died an excommunicate criminal, officially unmourned. And she knew as well as they that it didn't matter – she was a crude outworlder and he had been one of their own.

One of the last to move aside was a young girl in purple-black with an odd dark mask – not a mask at all, Calpurnia realised, but a catastrophic bruise, a ridge of swollen black flesh across the bridge of her nose, fading to deep yellow on her cheeks and forehead where it had begun to heal. It was several seconds before Calpurnia realised who it was.

'Lady Keta,' she said, and tipped up her new maul in a token salute. The girl flinched, and Calpurnia looked into her watery grey eyes.

She wondered if she could ever explain it to the girl. She doubted it. She could even see herself through their eyes, all cruel smile and weapon flourished in their faces, the new bully revelling in their submission, the new power who had destroyed her enemy and was setting herself up in his place. That was how their minds worked.

One day, she promised herself, she would sit down with Keta, or Athian Tymon-Per, or whichever of them she thought she could persuade to listen, and try to make them see. She would read them the maxims she had learned on Ultramar, get out her old children's primers if she had to. She would talk to them about her duty, about Law and honour. That the Law could be cold and the Law could be cruel but the Law was their guard and guide and peacekeeper and protector. She would try to talk to them about doing what was right.

All of this passed through her mind in a long, silent moment there before the Cathedral. But right at this moment she had work to do. Silent, eyes streaming, the other woman stepped aside and Shira Calpurnia, Arbitor Senioris of Hydraphur, walked proudly past her and away to where her Arbites were waiting.